INCENDIARY

Scot Froelich

This is a work of fiction. Names, characters, places, and incidents are products of the author's imagination or are used fictitiously and are not to be construed as real. Any resemblance to actual events, organizations, or persons, living or dead, is purely coincidental.

Second paperback edition: June 2020

For information, please visit: http://www.scotfroelich.com/

Incendiary

ISBN-13: 978-1-7347232-2-9

Cover design by Mary Weber-Moore
Edited by Megan Murphy
Back cover photo by Heidi Garrido, http://www.hmphotomn.com

For my mum

Chapter One

Isaac Truesdell was a young man, nearly thirty in looks. He'd been doing the job, at least according to his resume, for ten years. This was the job of protecting invaluable items. For many years, he had built a reputation as the only man who could keep objects in transit from being stolen. Burglars frequently elected the night something was being moved to steal it, as it was a simpler time to create confusion. This meant that the night of transit was most critical for an item's safety. Isaac's regular contract was to work for this one night only. In his ten years as a specialist, Isaac had never allowed anything to be stolen. Ever.

He insisted on working alone. His reputation was enigmatic enough, but this was where the intrigue heightened. How one man could protect all the entrances to an entire building was a mystery to even the most astute security experts, but his record stood for itself. No one had ever stolen from him. He was a confident, strong young man whose success was eclipsed only by his ability to calm his clients. They would interview him for the job, frightfully concerned about the safety of their possessions, and by the end find themselves fully assured nothing bad would ever happen.

Isaac made it a habit never to ask what he was protecting. This ambivalence caused him to be labeled as something of a mercenary in the security industry. He'd been hired by millionaires, gangsters, foreign heads of state, and lawyers. The only line item that changed was the price, never his commitment to the job. The less money the client had, the less he charged, which Isaac felt was a fair and equitable way of doing business.

He was afraid of no one, and, according to his resume, had never harmed anyone. While there had definitely been attempts to steal from him there had never been any evidence that he and the burglars came in contact with one another. His methods of doing business were a complete mystery, never the results.

Now, despite the resume lines that indicated Isaac had been working for a mere ten years, there was something in his eyes that suggested there was more to the story. However, when Frederick Casperson hired Isaac to protect his most prized possession the night before its transfer to another facility, he didn't ask Isaac what it was. He merely gave Isaac the cursory interview and hired him on the spot. Frederick trusted Isaac implicitly.

The guardian's policy not to ask the nature of the object he was to protect was helpful for Frederick since he had no intention of sharing. Isaac didn't even ask what security system the building used. His process was to work alone, just him and the night. Frederick knew his choice was correct when he brought Isaac to the location, a late nineteenth century storefront in the middle of a town square. The locks were shabby and the large panes of glass at the front of the store were simple and leaded, nothing that couldn't be entered easily. Regardless, Isaac didn't flinch. He smiled humbly and said, "This'll do just fine."

Frederick and the guardian parted that night on good terms. Frederick thanked Isaac for taking the job and, as he left, informed the guardian he would have visitors. Isaac asked who they were, so he could let them in. Frederick indicated they were his daughter and grandson and that they lived upstairs. There would be no need to let anyone in. Accordingly, Isaac assured Frederick the door would remain shut all night.

With Frederick gone, Isaac could begin his contractual obligation. He sat on the floor in the middle of the shop and focused his breathing. With only a moment's effort, his magic began to work. The shabby locks transformed, becoming impenetrable iron seals enveloping the full circumference of the doors, and the glass of the windows became reinforced transparent steel. A warm glow rested on the shop, generating light from every object within, each item sending a nearly audible chord to all the others. Heat rose from the floor and Isaac began to float among the ambience. He was in concert with every object in the building, acutely aware of its location, harmonic frequency, and ability to communicate both tangible and intangible energies to him at any given moment. He placed his feet softly on the floor and opened his eyes. It would be impossible for any human to enter.

Isaac began to walk around the shop, visually surveying the intricacies of the objects. There were common trinkets of all kinds. Glass ornaments, weapons, looking glasses, tools, dolls, books… the list went on. Frederick appeared to be a junk collector, but Isaac's connection to his world allowed the guardian to perceive each of the objects as something more than the usual fare; he was able to grasp an emotional understanding of the history behind each of the items in addition to the physical impressions of use and ownership.

There was a knife that had belonged to a lumberjack nearly one hundred years before. As Isaac handled it, he could feel the man's pain over leaving his family to work in the lumber-rich regions of the Northwest. Through bizarre happenstance, the knife found its way into the pocket of the man's undertaker, who shortly thereafter traveled back to Maryland, was shot over an unpaid debt, and dropped the object into the street. It was picked up by a newsboy who carried it for a number of days until he came across a crying woman and her daughter. They purchased a paper from the boy and, when asked about their unfortunate emotional state, explained to him about the death of their loved one. The boy recognized the man's initials as those etched into the handle of the knife he'd been carrying in his pocket. With some reluctance, he removed the object from his pocket and returned it to its bequeathed owners. As luck would have it – and Isaac chuckled a bit at the sequence of events – the woman and her daughter had purchased a rather sizeable life insurance policy on their husband and father and, upon claiming it, re-gifted the knife to the insurance salesman who had just cut them a check.

The story of the knife went on from there, but there were so many objects' histories to digest that Isaac didn't have time to study them all. Instead, he decided to breathe in the history as a whole and sort out the details later. Some of the objects whose history he most looked forward to analyzing were the China plates belonging to an old Russian immigrant, a hand-scrawled 400-year-old biblical text produced by a voiceless monk in the Alps, and a plain looking cast-iron spoon that, by all indications had been used by Pope Pius II. These weren't the histories scrawled under the objects on their shelves but rather the histories Isaac felt from being in their presence. His connection to the world around him was unparalleled and was the secret to his unmatched success as a protector of all things material.

He moved undisturbed among Frederick's possessions for nearly three hours until approximately 11:30 p.m., at which time he heard a sound akin to light footsteps on the stairs. In addition to his unique connection to inanimate objects, Isaac was also capable of sensing a person's whereabouts without a second thought. However, his spine tingled when the stranger's presence didn't reveal itself until they had moved. Frederick had told Isaac that his daughter and grandson lived upstairs, so Isaac cautiously chalked the incident up to an oversight. Considering his age, he felt that he was entitled to such a slight imperfection within his craft.

She descended the stairs something like an angel; Isaac scarcely perceived the movement of her feet on the warm oak treads as she approached. Her face glowed as though she were one of the objects Isaac had illuminated. Confident that his craft was perceptible only to him, Isaac felt no need to relax his charms on the shop. The young woman on the stairs, however, gazed about herself as though she could see every bit of it. Like a child waking to the lights and smells of a glowing tree and hot cider on Christmas, she barely acknowledged Isaac's presence until she spoke. "I'm glad you're here, Mr. Truesdell."

"You can call me Isaac." He smiled, plying his comforting trade on the girl as he had her father. Yet as Isaac assessed the young woman, he felt something amiss, as she appeared far too young to be Frederick's daughter. Her father was eighty or possibly older, whereas she was no more than twenty or twenty-five.

"Well Isaac, my father has made a wise choice for his day of rest." The woman nodded as she finally made eye contact with the guardian.

Isaac was of average height, pale skinned, with black hair and an unassuming wardrobe. He currently sported a hip-length black coat, a white, collared shirt, jeans – as crisp as they come – and black leather shoes. She was adorned in nothing but a white robe that seemed to glow along with her hair and face; another seeming chink in Isaac's craft. But seeing as how he'd never encountered another person who was welcome in his protectorate, he felt that maybe she belonged that way.

Frederick's daughter finished assessing the guardian and

addressed him directly. "As I said, I'm glad you're here."

Isaac smiled a genuine but crooked smile, and in an almost sheepish tone replied, "I'm glad to be here. This is a magnificent shop. Your father should be proud of his collection. I'd want to protect it, too."

The woman had returned to gazing about the shop in measured awe as she answered quickly, "It's garbage mostly. This isn't what you're here to protect, Isaac."

Slightly taken aback, he asked, "It's not?"

"No," she said. "There is a box upstairs. You're not to touch it, but make no mistake, that is your job tonight. That box must not leave this building."

Isaac was stunned by her forwardness and her certain control over the situation. Without wanting to be rude, he entertained her need for such control and asked, "What does the box look like?"

She turned back to him again with a wry smile on her face. "Mr. Truesdell, something tells me that you of all people will know exactly what that box looks like if you see it. There's no need to go into details now."

Having no other way to respond, he said, "It's Isaac."

"Thank you for being here, Isaac. But I want you to know that you won't be alone tonight," she uttered mysteriously as she began to ascend the stairs.

Isaac smiled and retorted, "Of course not. I've got you... I'm sorry, I didn't catch your name."

The woman stopped on the seventh stair. "Calypso. My name is Calypso."

Isaac replied, "That's a beautiful name."

"My father was an aficionado of rare art. But Isaac, I'm not the person I'm referring to. There will be others."

"Others?" he asked.

"Yes, others." She breathed deeply, though no discernable amount of air moved around her. "My son, and quite possibly a young woman may disturb your watch tonight."

Isaac nodded, and in an assuring tone explained, "I promise you, Calypso, that in all my years as a protector, no woman has ever distracted me from my duties."

A broad, calculated smile stretched across her lips as she responded, "It's not the young woman I'm worried about."

Isaac had no response, so Calypso continued her ascent up the staircase. As she neared the top, she turned gently and looked down at the strange man staring up at her. With a sardonic tone she said, "Although it appears, by your estimation, I've just done the impossible."

Indeed, Calypso was a woman, and she had distracted the venerable guardian. He looked around at his domain, noticing that some objects had dropped out of his magical perception. Instead of panicking as a young man might have, he instead took a couple deep breaths and re-engaged himself with his surroundings. She watched this process with utter fascination but ducked out of sight before he could turn back to her. She was gone. Isaac was once again alone.

In her absence, he decided to refocus his charms and properly commune with the shop. He returned to breathing in the objects around him. There were hundreds of years of histories within his grasp. As he breathed, eyes shut, lines creased his face then disappeared, as though he aged with the objects only to return to a youthful state. The room warmed with the flow of energy and the locks and windows strengthened with every breath until he was awakened from his task by a gentle wrapping at the window in the front door. Without releasing any of his craft, he opened his eyes to see a beautiful young woman huddled in the exterior entryway of the building. Her face lurked mere inches away from his impenetrable fortress, like glass itself reflecting the light within. A simple blue dress peaked out from under a slim, white cashmere coat, both noticeably stained with the crimson mark of human blood.

Isaac approached the door but did not open it. "Are you okay?"

She looked up at him. For the second time in a short period, he became distracted. A pair of shock-green eyes peered up at him from within elegantly marked lashes and eyebrows. Her petite nose, burgundy lips, high cheekbones, and rigid jawline framed a freckled face trimmed by unnaturally white teeth. Her hair was quite dark, nearly as black as his, but with the slightest trace of chestnut brown highlighting her visage. Any question he may have had about how she came to be there was erased under the distraction of her presence. Still, his youthful exterior gave way to his gruff, wise interior, and he repeated, "Are you okay?"

"I'm hurt," she replied and revealed her hand, cut nearly to the bone by a knife or other jagged chunk of metal or glass. "Do you have any antiseptic?"

"I don't know. I'm just the night watchman. That's a lot of blood, though. I'll call an ambulance."

As he turned to find his phone, she yelled through the now nearly-soundproof glass, "Wait! I don't need an ambulance. I just need some antiseptic and a bandage; then I'll be on my way."

Isaac looked at her with compassion and found her returning the expression. In her eyes, he seemed to find an understanding of the loneliness that he endured. In truth, Isaac was lonely. His craft and occupation didn't allow for much interaction. He was afraid of rejection from mortals and knew of no other such wizards or witches with whom he could commune. He was, in the strictest terms, alone. In this young woman's eyes, Isaac found all the compassion he'd ever desired in another living being.

He inched closer to the door as her face cried for the connection he too desired. Nearly against his will, he reached for the doorknob. But just as his hand approached the cold, brass-embossed shell of the shop's iron doorknob, her face changed ever so slightly. Her lips, which had only just a moment ago welcomed him with love and tenderness, now elicited a nearly imperceptible smirk. He stopped millimeters from the doorknob and withdrew his hand. Isaac blinked and shook off the emotion that had overwhelmed him. She stood and looked at him with abject sadness, as if to ask, "Why have you left me out here?"

Isaac stumbled back against the table that separated the entryway from the rest of the shop and looked back upon her with a clear head. "I'll call you an ambulance," he said and turned to grab the phone.

She gave up her trickery and stood straight in the doorway. "Oh, will you?"

"Yes," he said and grabbed the shop's phone from its perch on the counter.

She raised her hands to the heavens and began her art. The clouds overhead began to gather, and lightning circled within them. Isaac slowly returned the phone to the cradle and strode carefully to the front of the shop.

"You will not stop me tonight. I've waited too long for this to have you challenge me, Isaac. I will destroy you and your black art to get what I came for."

Shock overcame Isaac. He couldn't understand how she knew his name, or what she meant, or how she knew of *his* art. In all the years Isaac had been applying his craft, he had never encountered another soul who knew of his connection to the natural world.

Until that night, he believed himself alone. Between the mysterious woman through the glass and the enigmatic presence of Frederick's daughter, he was thrown into turmoil regarding the nature of the world he felt he so strongly understood.

While Isaac's focus was thrown into disarray by his immense confusion, the locks and windows he expertly reinforced began to rattle in their casings. He watched as the young woman called the wind to her command, pushing exponentially against his authority. The wind pounded against the glass.

Unfocused and shaken, Isaac clenched his fists and closed his eyes. A few moments of breathing later, the storefront renewed its impenetrable shield and the witch's tempest was repelled. She lowered her arms to approach the front of the shop again. His mouth locked in a state of awe, he met her at the door. "So, you do exist. All my life, I thought I was alone."

"You're a fool," she replied confidently.

Isaac couldn't disagree with her assertion. He analyzed the work that she'd done and the energy she was radiating. There was something fractured about what he saw. Curious to know what he was up against, he asked, "Is that all you've got?"

"No. But I'm testing to see how much *you've* got," she retorted.

Her response shook him to his core. A job needed to be done, and he felt it was time to flex his mystical strength. Isaac closed his eyes. She peered curiously through the windows to see what he was doing but couldn't discern the specifics of his intent. Then, without warning, the clouds dispersed and the wind she'd been commanding reared and tossed her fifty feet through the air, causing her to land on the cobblestone walk surrounding the fountain in the town square. Indignant, she rose from her graceless landing and glared back at Isaac – outmatched. With nothing to say she simply huffed and disappeared into thin air. Isaac grinned and uttered to himself,

"Now *that* was impressive." He exhaled to regulate his beating heart and doubly reinforce the shop.

While he had no idea where she'd gone, he no longer sensed her presence. The whole sequence of events was bizarre and unsettling, but nothing could be done about it at the moment, so Isaac turned his focus back to the items in Frederick's shop.

Once he was in touch, a strange-looking tea set presented itself to him as the former possession of a fifteenth-century earl of English descent. Upon further concentration, however, its history reached farther back to reveal its original proprietorship to that of a fourteenth-century glass smith in northern Germany. The collection, along with its owner, traversed the sea to the British Isles upon the assassination of the smith's cruel landowner.

A hand-turned wooden bowl next revealed itself to Isaac, having previously belonged to a late nineteenth-century politician who'd fought in the American Civil War. It was on this item that Isaac stopped and paid special attention, not because the object was of any particularly impressive lineage, but rather because Isaac saw an image of himself in the bowl's history. His otherwise impenetrable exterior tweaked for just a moment as he hesitated on the bowl. Why would he see himself in the history of one of the store's objects?

A look of comfort graced his face as he recalled the fine maple, the complex knotting, and the crude oils he'd used to make the bowl. This was Isaac's trade before he became a guardian. He'd made the bowl and sold it to the politician's wife four days before the man's birthday. Isaac recalled the trouble he'd had with the pedal-powered, spring-pole lathe he'd used to make the bowl and how proud he was that it had turned out so well. It was while perfecting this ability that he discovered his uncanny connection to the natural world. Isaac's understanding of the natural world was what had allowed him to control his form and features. It was what allowed him to remain physically unchanged for nearly 120 years. Isaac was, indeed, a powerful sorcerer.

However, he had had no training. All of Isaac's understanding of sorcery came from his unparalleled ability to tap into the energy of things around him. He had remained permanently in control of his surroundings until this night. All at once, everything had changed for him. He began to take stock of his 150-year existence and the things that had changed both in the world and in him over that time. In light of his distinctly attentive existence, he wondered how he had lived that long and never once encountered another person who shared his grasp of the energy between all things. No matter age and experience, it was a revelation that would have shaken even the world-weariest of souls.

Isaac took comfort in the bowl, something both distant and familiar, and breathed deeply into the room around him. Just as he was beginning to have a sense about the nature of the daughter Calypso, who had visited him earlier, a patter of small feet traversed the staircase above him. Again, he was unnerved by his inability to anticipate this presence, but considering all that had happened that night, it was no longer a surprise.

As he opened his eyes, a young boy peered around the corner of the railing at the bottom of the staircase, wide-eyed, and joyously exclaimed, "You're Isaac?!"

"I am," Isaac responded as he smoothly rose to his feet. "And what's your name?"

"My name is Ezekiel," the young boy said shyly, adding, "My grandfather hired you to protect my mommy."

Isaac's head involuntarily cocked at the new information. For one thing, that was not at all part of the contract. Furthermore, he wondered why Frederick had not shared the same cursory – and seemingly important – information with him as he clearly had with his daughter and grandson. Most people would have regarded this information with a sense of annoyance. Isaac, on the other hand, merely approached it as an adjustment to his duties and another detail in the bizarre landscape of the night. He asked the boy, "Well, Ezekiel, your mom said I was here to keep something from being taken. Was she referring to herself or was she referring to an object?"

Suddenly confused, Ezekiel averted his eyes and shuffled his feet. "Yes? I don't know. Grandpa Freddy said you were here to protect mommy."

"That's no problem, Ezekiel. I'll protect her. But you... shouldn't you be in bed?" Isaac asked.

A perplexed look washed over Ezekiel's face as he looked at the guardian. "You're silly."

Laughing self-effacingly, Isaac replied, "Yes, I guess I am."

Suddenly, Ezekiel exclaimed, "I wanna go outside and play!"

"Wait!" Isaac shouted and started after the boy.

Since Isaac had only ever dealt with keeping objects from being *taken*, he'd never bothered to work up a spell to keep objects from willfully removing themselves from a space. Accordingly, there were no charms to keep Ezekiel from opening the door and letting himself out. Isaac cursed himself as a fool, knowing all the while it was useless to waste the energy. Before he could stop the boy, Ezekiel grabbed the doorknob and rushed from the confines of the shop into the chilled night air.

As Isaac reached the door, a blinding light erupted from beyond it and a rush of wind pushed the door toward him, slamming the corner of it into his forehead and nearly knocking him unconscious.

When Isaac fell to the ground behind the door, Ezekiel

stopped in his tracks and looked back at the shop. He saw the matching panes of glass and center door alight with a powerful white and yellow glow. A shimmer rushed from its midst through the door and past Isaac, pushing its way up the stairs. Ezekiel instantly realized his folly and the danger presented by the entry of the spirit into the building and ran back to follow it.

Reeling, Isaac picked himself up off the floor, grabbed Ezekiel as the boy came back in, slammed the door shut – its magical locks instantly resealing themselves – and bolted up the stairs to follow the spirit that had rushed past them. He began to turn left but Ezekiel corrected him, pointing at a door to their right. Isaac stopped briefly to calm himself and assess the door. It was bedecked with ancient oak carvings and a meticulously formed bronze doorknob. From under the door emanated a soft glow and the sound of weeping. Isaac grabbed the doorknob and tried to turn it, but it was sealed. He then closed his eyes and placed his hands on the door. Ezekiel watched in simultaneous remorse and fascination as the door began to warm with light and sound. The knob slowly turned and the door opened.

Within, Isaac discovered Calypso kneeling on the floor, pleading to the young woman who was now holding a strange, multi-material box. Ezekiel ran to his mother's side and began begging forgiveness, tears running down his face. She made no comment but held him tight and stroked his hair.

The young woman was holding the box with as much intense affection as Calypso was holding her son. A light from within the box shone on the sorceress' face, refracting through the tears that now trickled down her cheeks. An eternity had passed in that room since Isaac had been hit in the head downstairs. Exactly what had occurred was somewhat beyond his grasp. His senses about the girl's intentions were mixed and faulty. Regardless of his desire to learn more, Isaac had a job to do. The guardian raised his hand to summon the box from her clutches, but she in turn raised hers, saying, "Stop. I won't take it." For the first time since Isaac and Ezekiel entered the room, she looked up at him, the tears dripping from her soft, pale cheeks onto the floor. "I know you'll take it from me," she started, glancing back to the container's mysterious contents. "It's just so beautiful."

Those contents were still masked from Isaac and, in agreement with his contract, he made no effort to see them. Instead, he approached the young woman and physically took the box from her hands, slowly and gently. He closed it, the light from within ceasing. He heard Calypso breathe deeply and turned to her. She smiled gratefully and nodded her approval of his actions. He looked down at the box, ever so slightly tempted, and then back at Calypso. She held out her hands, and without hesitation, he placed the box in her grasp. She inaudibly thanked him, cradling her son in one arm and the box in the other.

The young woman was also looking at Calypso, perhaps for the first time feeling some sense of regret over what she'd done. Isaac looked back at her and she back at him. For a moment, she felt him share an energy with her, as if he were promising some form of connection. Isaac resisted the connection, however, and placed his hand on the side of her face.

"Please don't," she begged softly. The guardian made no comment and closed his eyes to concentrate on his new task. She went to reach for him, but with his other hand he restrained her and breathed hard into his environment. In return, the environment was called to his will. The air, the dust, and all the objects in the building, the building itself became alight with his presence. Calypso and Ezekiel watched in awe and disbelief as Isaac transformed the young woman standing before them into particles of light. They could see her attempt to speak as she dematerialized, but no sound came out. He breathed again, and this time the light he'd created from the young woman was forced out through every vent, crack, and scarcely identifiable opening in the building. She was gone.

This task done, Isaac turned to Calypso. "I know you told me not to touch it. I apologize for…"

She interrupted him, her gratitude palpable. "Please, Isaac. What you did… There are no words… I…"

Isaac understood that what occurred should never have happened. While her gratitude was welcome it was also unnecessary. He smiled sheepishly. "I'll be downstairs if you need me." Then he turned to go back to the shop.

"Thank you," Calypso finally said.

"You're welcome."

"I know I told you not to touch it, but…" she stopped.

"Yes?"

"There are still a few hours left. I wonder if you wouldn't mind holding on to this until the sun rises."

Isaac was honored. Even his hard-as-stone exterior nearly cracked as he asked, "Are you sure?"

"It's clear to me that it's safer with you than anywhere else in the world." She offered it to him and he took it. Isaac nodded and returned to the shop, Calypso and Ezekiel in tow.

In return for her trust, Isaac gave Calypso and her son some of his. He informed them that he was capable of communing with the forces of nature, and that he wasn't the young man he appeared to be. True, his body was genuinely youthful in form but only as a result of the charms he'd used to keep it that way. He then invited them to be part of his craft for the remainder of the night.

Ezekiel asked, "Do we have to sit in a circle and hold hands?"

Isaac smiled, himself unsure of the particulars. "I don't think so, but we can if you like. All I do is close my eyes, concentrate on the air around me, and breathe. Keep breathing, and after a while the air will begin to act as a conduit between you and… the things around you."

"It speaks to you?" Calypso asked.

"Something like that."

Out of habit and social conditioning, Calypso held her son's hand as she closed her eyes and began breathing. Isaac observed for a moment while they attempted his craft. As it became obvious that they were trying too hard and not understanding the method, Isaac chose to take a step for them and act as an intermediary. He closed his eyes and began the process of connecting with the objects in the shop. Then, as the objects completed their connection with him, he transferred the connection to the woman and her son. As the connection grew stronger, Isaac could feel himself growing weak with the effort and strained to maintain it.

While the three were communing within the building, a great wind began to build outside. Isaac knew of the disturbance but knew he need not address it as long as his craft remained firm within the shop. Still, he became more and more aware of the activities beyond the front door. A voice was calling to the heavens and summoning the wind, the rain, the hail, and the lightning. Like bullets, the hail smacked the glass with great force, and the wind rattled every exterior surface of the building. The tempest became a mighty force of nature, thundering against their refuge with every ounce of power that didn't belong to Isaac. Despite all this, the locks, door, and windows were unscathed.

Finally, the sunlight cracked over the horizon, and the storm began to subside. Isaac held on with every last ounce of power he had, his eyes sealed shut and his breath waning. His exhaustion was staved off only by will, which was nearing its end just as a knock came at the door. The guardian opened his weary eyes to see only a light rain falling outside, Calypso and Ezekiel gone, and Frederick standing at the door.

When Frederick saw Isaac within, cradling the box, he smiled a relieved, grateful smile, for he knew the job had been done. Isaac placed the box on the counter, itself sealed with his charms, and strode wearily to the door, opening it for the old man.

Frederick laughed at him, saying, "You look like you've had better nights," and walked past Isaac toward the box.

"I'll be honest with you; it was not what I expected," Isaac said.

"Oh? Tell me about it."

Isaac wasn't sure where or how to begin. Did the old man know about the young woman? Did he know the contents of the box? More importantly, did he know about Isaac's magic?

"Well, there were certainly a few visitors."

"She got in, didn't she?" Frederick asked in a wry, knowing tone.

Isaac knew he'd done the job as asked and felt no need to bare the scorn of failure. "Mr. Casperson, I think you may have withheld some information from me when you offered me this job."

"And you withheld some information from me, too. But, then the information you withheld had no way of harming me. I guess you probably deserved a bit more disclosure than I gave you. I just had to know, you know?" Frederick paused, awaiting a response from Isaac, but there was none. "You see, Isaac, I've heard about you. I know that you aren't quite what you seem. For example, I know you're nowhere as young as you appear to be. I know that you have a connection to a number of the objects in this shop. I know that you work alone because you don't want anyone to know *how* you work. And I know that you do it all…" Frederick paused for emphasis as he reached toward the box, levitating it off the table, leaving it to hover in midair. "…with magic."

Isaac was speechless. His eyes locked onto the box for a moment, then fixed themselves on Frederick, who was casually grinning at the guardian.

Frederick continued. "You are the stuff of legends, Isaac. Even the oldest witches and sorcerers have never known someone to manifest their own control over the world the way you have." He now called the box to him and held it in his hands. "I needed to make a trip last night to the ground where my daughter and grandson's souls will be released."

The guardian suddenly became acutely aware of the box's contents, why Calypso and Ezekiel didn't appear to him as normal human beings, and why Calypso had initially forbid him to touch the box, even though Frederick had mentioned nothing of it.

"My daughter and her son died in a car accident nearly 40 years ago. They loved me and my wife very dearly though and didn't want to leave. I built this box as a home for their souls so they could remain here as long as they liked. It was made from remnants of objects you created over a hundred years ago, Isaac. It was the only type of material I believed could keep them safe." Frederick saw the confusion on Isaac's face, realizing the guardian was blissfully unaware of the darker sides of the magical world he so easily controlled. "You see, there are some witches and demons who collect souls, forcing them to do their bidding until they can earn their freedom. I didn't want that to happen to them."

Frederick paused regretfully. Piecing together the relationship between Frederick's explanation and the box, Isaac continued for him. "But you realized that you were behaving in almost the same way as those witches and demons."

The old man nodded. "And after a while, my wife died and there was only me to protect them. I am so very tired and can't take the thought of being their jailer any more. It's time to let them return to the world as free spirits. You were the only person I could trust with allowing this to happen."

"But you don't even know me," Isaac noted.

"I knew that you made it a policy not to ask what you were protecting, and that you were too powerful to be defeated even without that knowledge. You being here acted as a distraction to the young woman who's been plaguing me." Frederick shook off the thought of the young woman coming in contact with his daughter and grandson and stepped toward Isaac. "I drew a map of the place where Calypso and Ezekiel should be laid to rest. And now, I must ask you to do something that's not in your contract."

Isaac nodded. "I'm happy to take them, Frederick." Frederick then handed the box and map to Isaac and ushered him to his car. The guardian thanked him, saying, "I won't forget you. Or your family."

"I know you won't. Now, get out of here before I start to cry, young man." He laughed as the irony of his last statement set in on both of them.

Isaac placed the box on the passenger seat, put the car in drive, and began to pull away. He watched in the mirror as Frederick re-entered the shop. When the door closed behind the old man, his head bent toward the floor and the room lit up with an auburn haze. A moment later, Frederick's body dissipated and he was gone. Isaac returned his attention to the road, holding one hand on the box all the way.

When he arrived at the spot indicated on the map, he stopped the car and got out. It was an otherwise ordinary grassy plane overlooking the sea, but there was a strong, mystical sensation about the ground beyond the road. There were no telltale grave sites, but every few yards or so, there was a stick angling awkwardly out of the ground. He looked down to the side of the road and saw a collection of similar sticks, untouched by time, the elements, or passersby. Isaac knew instantly what to do. He collected two of the sticks and walked to an open area of grass. Despite how all the other sticks were equidistant, he placed the two within only a foot of each other and aimed them convergently. Next, he put the box on the earth between the two sticks and released the seal he had placed on it.

Taking several steps back from the box, Isaac closed his eyes and summoned the lid from its perch. He then opened his eyes, viewing the endless space within for the first time and allowing himself to become aware of the object's history and contents. Calypso and Ezekiel's spirits rushed past him, around him, and through him as if to thank him. They then returned to the earth through the antennae he had placed for them.

The ceremony complete, Isaac studied the container. He perceived a small piece of the bowl he'd observed only hours earlier that adorned the lid of the box. The sides were cut of the top from a table he'd fashioned from oak and sold to a mill worker who'd just purchased a new home for his young family. The man's child and wife were now interred in this ground as well. The bottom of the box was welded out of a clock mount he'd built for a town square not far from that spot. The lid was perhaps the most fascinating part of the entire box. It was one continuous piece of ash, cut from the front door of a now-demolished house in Delaware. That house was where Isaac was born. All at once, he saw his mother and father, his sisters, and his brother who died of pneumonia as a child.

He reached out and called the box to him, knowing that Frederick had bequeathed the object to him. He placed the lid on top and walked back to his car. Sitting quietly in the driver's seat, he stared out at the hill, for the first time acknowledging its vastness and the thousands of little sticks that marked the souls of those who had communed with the earth. He took it in, breathing the fresh, salt air of the sea, and the love that passed from all the souls within the earth's bosom. Contentment washed over him for the first time and he placed the car in gear. He left knowing he would not see the place again until it was his time to join. He also knew that he was no longer alone in the world, and that gave him strength.

Several days after his experience with Frederick and his family, Isaac had an interview to guard a special exhibit at a private museum the night before its transfer to another location. He took special note in advance that the exhibit was purported to hold the souls of several prominent figures from an ancient sect of Chinese sorcery. The guardian smiled to himself at this knowledge, wondering what might befall his watch as a result.

The young man interviewing him was an arrogant, officious weasel, but Isaac didn't mind. He had come on the recommendation of the museum's wealthy owner, and he knew where his influence was needed. Isaac got the job despite the young man's protestations.

On the night of his contract, Isaac roamed the museum halls in the satisfaction that can only come from better understanding one's place in the world. After several hours of communing with thousands of years of history in the building, he heard a gentle knock at one of the windows. As he approached it, he saw a young woman with her back to the window, apparently crying. When she turned around, he recognized her as the witch from Frederick's storefront.

Isaac smiled at her confidently and said, "So, it's going to be one of *those* nights, eh?"

To which she replied, "Might as well be. I kinda got a thing for ya, fella."

Chapter Two

December 1958

The three drunks and two shoplifters sharing the city lockup's processing cell listened intently for the goings-on in the adjacent room. While they couldn't hear any specific words, the officers clicking away at their desks, typing up their arrest reports, leaked the salacious rumor that the newest arrestee was a young woman. Most of the cops and vagrants in town could count on one hand the number of female lawbreakers the town of Tulsa, Oklahoma, had notched in the last twenty years. The possibility that the incoming female inmate could be larger, smellier, and scarier than any of them did not deter the men from imagining what she might look like.

One of the regulars, affectionately and accurately dubbed Nine Toes, mused, "What if she's a beautiful blonde?! Maybe she'll come in here with a white dress! Hey, Snead!" he called to the officer closest to the processing cell. "You got a fan in the floor any-where? You know, somethin' that might just *accidentally* turn on when the little lady comes in?"

Snead chuckled but stayed trained on his typewriter as he hunted and pecked his way through his arrest report. "Listen, Nine Toes, if you don't keep your trap shut while she's here, I might just make sure your lawyer don't see you 'til after Christmas."

Nine Toes gruffly retorted, "Hey, that's my cousin, Snead! He owes me a favor."

"And I think he knows he don't owe it to you 'til you dry out, so pipe down. We're tryin' to do some work here."

The vagrant waved his arm at the officer dismissively and turned back to his cell mates. "Must'a had a lot o' coffee to drink if you think clickin' away on them keys is work."

His cellmates laughed and applauded the man's antiauthoritarian quip, but each was still far more intent on discovering the identity of the female arrestee they would soon be meeting. Slippers – identified as such because of his uncanny ability to both pass out in department store clothing departments and slip out of the grasps of would-be arresting officers – returned to the subject first. "Now, I bet that there girlie was shopliftin' herself a nice purty dress. You know, somethin' for one o' them… uh, whatcha call-its…"

Another man continued for him. "Sock hops?"

"Sure! Why not?" Slippers continued as the typing officers laughed at the men. "Maybe she was too afraid to ask her parents for money, so she ripped it off herself?"

Yet another man, known simply as Mike, who was dressed in a green jacket, leather boots, ripped jeans, and military-cut hair, exclaimed, "If that broad that walks in here is a lady and you bums disrespect her, I'll put each one of ya through the ringer! You got that?"

The other detained reprobates alternately dialed down their enthusiasm, some turning away from him, some uttering defensive phrases such as, "Gosh Mike, we're just tryin' to have a little fun," and others just putting their heads down and avoiding eye contact whatsoever. Mike was a Korean War vet who had spent a winter encamped in shabby confines in the sometimes brutal cold of the Korean Peninsula. He'd lost a finger on his right hand as a result of it, as well as most of his patience. Mike's reputation as a man not to be toyed with was cemented in September 1956 at a bar called Crazy Jerry's Saloon on the south side of town. A local tough named Travis McAdams had been trying to make time with Mike's best friend's girlfriend. While Mike had nothing quantifiable invested in his friend's relationship, he couldn't stomach men who had no respect for a woman. His own use of the word "broad" aside, he generally held true to his morals.

Mike asked Travis to step outside, as his friend's girlfriend Linda had made it very clear she wasn't interested. Travis chuckled and asked why they should bother to go through the effort – indeed, why not fight right then and there? Mike didn't hesitate in obliging Travis' need for violence and shot a right cross into the man's left jaw. Before Travis could get his bearings, Mike turned him around, slammed his face on the bar, broke the neck off a nearby bottle, and started working the jagged end of it into Travis' right cheek. He did all of this without batting an eye or changing expression or emotion. His heart rate barely even increased. Mike very sternly bent down to Travis' ear and said, "We're through botherin' the lady now, ain't we?" To which Travis quickly submitted and was released.

There were two off-duty police officers in the bar that night who had been friends with Mike back in high school. They casually walked up to him and announced that, albeit reluctantly, they needed to take him into the station for processing. Mike cooperated with the officers' every request, and on the way out of the bar, one of them was heard uttering, "Damn, he's good."

Mike spent a year in prison for assault following the incident, but was promised a nice, warm place to sleep whenever he needed it by his friends on the Tulsa police force. December 21, 1958, was just one of those nights. In an attempt to avoid driving home intoxicated, Mike stumbled to the city jail to dry out. However, it would not be a night Mike or anyone else in the third precinct, would forget. That night would remain cemented in his memory far longer than the night he taught Travis McAdams to listen when a woman said no.

As the other men revealed their simultaneous respect and fear of Mike, he began to feel uncomfortable about the prospect of having a young woman in the jail cell across from them. He wasn't worried about what the other men might say or what he might do, but rather how a woman might be affected by time in jail. It wasn't a place for a woman at all in his estimation. And it certainly wasn't right for her to be incarcerated in close proximity to a collection of professional bums.

After realizing he'd completely shut down the conversation – much to the amusement of the officers overhearing the exchange – he continued it in his own way. "You might be right about bein' afraid to ask for money, Slippers. I swear, more and more kids these days are blabbin' about their parents smackin' 'em around."

"Yeah, ain't that the truth," the men responded in varying forms.

Nine Toes added, "When I was a kid, that's how things were done. And we didn't complain about it. If you screwed up, you got paddled."

"Ain't no parent oughtta be smackin' around a girl, Nine Toes," Mike interrupted.

"Now come on, Mike," the older man defended, "I can't even say how kids oughtta be disciplined? Everyone's got an opinion on that. Fine, don't hit the girls. But these boys nowadays, they're completely outta control, Mike! You gonna disagree with me on that?"

Mike nodded his approval. "Well, I don't think there are many boys out there today couldn't use some good ol' military discipline…" The men acknowledged this with gusto. Mike continued, "But you gotta think for a minute: What makes a girl end up in jail? What could she possibly have been doin'?" He motioned to Slippers. "You think she was stealing a dress." Then Mike turned to Nine Toes, saying, "You think she was playin' in some Billy Wilder film." The men shrugged and laughed. "But I think the girl's probably misguided. She's probably got some troubles. You think any of you guys are catches? You think girls are lined up around the block to deal with the problems you guys got? So, what makes you think we all oughtta be lined up around the block to deal with whatever problems this girl's got?"

The men were now silent.

After a moment of inebriated contemplation, Nine-Toes blurted, "You sure know how to bring a guy down, Mike. Thanks a heap." Mike replied by pulling a pack of Lucky Strike cigarettes from his chest pocket, extracting a smoke, and striking a match. He inhaled deeply and held it for several seconds, finally blowing the plume in Nine Toes' direction. The older man waved the smoke from his face and turned away, unamused with Mike's hijacking of the conversation.

Just as the men had hunkered into their uncomfortable silence, the interrogation room door clanked open, the keys rattling harmonically on the steel frame. A voice from the other side boomed, "Open up cell number two, Snead. The little lady's comin' through."

Snead left his desk and hurried to the cell adjacent to the one the regulars were occupying. There was no solid wall between the two, just a row of bars through which the men would be able to keep permanent visual tabs on the incoming woman.

With the exception of Mike, the regulars burst to their feet and moved to the bars, practically pressing their faces up against them to see the troublemaking woman who would soon be in their presence. Mike instead smiled, puffed on his Lucky Strike and asked, "Now, what makes you boys so sure she's gonna to be somethin' worth lookin' at?"

Rain Barrel, a large drunk prone to profuse sweating, turned to Mike and excitedly exclaimed, "Snead and one of the other cops said she was a *girl*, not a woman. Why would they say a thing like that if she was a big, ugly heifer?"

"Because they never get women in here and probably don't even know what they look like. How do you know she's not a female bigfoot, like them things we been hearin' about in the news?" Mike smirked, antagonizing his cellmates.

Snead shook his head, saying, "I tell you what, Mike, if she is a sasquatch, we're stickin' you in with her for the night." He winked at Mike as he opened the cell next to them.

"We'll see," Mike answered, taking another long drag on his cigarette. Just as he began to exhale it, a large officer in his patrol cap and coat came striding through the door.

In one hand, the officer carried a large set of keys, and in the other, the center few links of a pair of handcuffs uncomfortably clasped around a set of wrists too small to properly be bound by them. The hands passed through the doorway into view first, then a foot wearing a black and white Mary Jane heel. The outer edges of a grey, wool skirt passed through the doorway next, followed by the rest of the girl's body all at once. A long, oversized, black top coat – clearly belonging to the girl's father – clumsily covered a white, collared blouse and a dark blue wool school sweater embroidered with yellow lettering. Her hair was staggeringly dark, save for a few wisps of brown, and her skin was pale and faintly-freckled. Even in winter, an Oklahoma girl rarely looked so ill.

As she was ushered into her cell, Mike slowly rose from his

crook in the corner, the cigarette drooping from his lip. Another officer lagged behind her and took the keys from the first officer as he deposited the girl, uncuffed her, and turned to exit. Snead looked at Mike and in a loud whisper exclaimed, "Put that out!"

Mike did as he was instructed and threw the cigarette on the floor, snuffing it with the toe of his military-issue boot. Along with the rest of the men in the room, his mouth was agape at the young woman. That is, all except the two officers who had escorted her, both of whom quickly finished their business in sealing her cell and hurried out, their heads toward the ground. The men in the cell next to her watched as she examined her space.

The girl rubbed her wrists, massaging her reddened skin, and walked about her cell analyzing its meager contents. There was a bed, neatly made up with brown covers and white sheets, a small collection of books, which had been placed there expressly for her incarceration, and a toilet that was blocked off from the view of the other cell by a hastily contrived divider made from tent poles and canvas. As her eyes rested on the divider, she slumped a bit, exhaling audibly. She then became acutely aware of the five incarcerated men staring at her and turned to them slowly. All except Mike shied away, trying not to be caught staring.

Mike, on the other hand, couldn't take his eyes off her. He was transfixed by everything about her: her gaunt figure, her dirty, bruised legs, her posture – likely the result of many years of girls' school – her stark hair, her translucent skin, and an extraordinary pair of bright green eyes that peeked out from her face as though she were a black-and-white painting only partly colored by its creator. She was something neither Mike nor any of the other men had ever seen. He instantly lamented that she was there in the first place, thinking she'd be better off in the hands of a doctor.

When she finished her turn, her head was still angled toward the earth. The sideways glance Mike received from her struck him cold. It was as if she could see past his skin and his flesh right into his bones. He felt a shiver in his spine as she straightened up and glared at him menacingly. She turned away from him and sat upright on the bed in her cell, staring in a straight line parallel to the bars that separated her from the curious men to her left.

The war veteran rested his shoulder on the bars in front of him and coughed, trying to attract her attention. She replied quickly, "You *have* my attention. There's no need for me to look at you."

Mike timidly looked back at the other men for encouragement. Her voice, while bell-tone clear and beautiful, frightened him with its confidence. She clearly was not from Tulsa, but the uniqueness of her tone veiled any discernable accent. The other men urged him on, and he turned back to her. "Well, I was just, uh… see, me and the boys was wonderin' what you'd done to get put in here?"

"I know you were," she replied flatly.

He looked at the floor and kicked the cigarette butt toward the wall. "Yeah, I guess that was pretty obvious. But, uh… well, so why you in here?"

She pursed her lips and closed her eyes, knowing she would not be left alone. Upon opening her eyes, she responded, "I hate small talk. People always ask each other simple, useless questions, like 'How are you doing?' or 'Isn't it a lovely morning?' or 'How are the kids these days?'" The last one elicited a laugh from the men listening in. "I'm assuming that, among criminals, the impulse to ask about the cause of one's incarceration is similarly banal in nature?" She turned to him, locking his gaze with her eyes. "No?"

Most of the men had no idea what she was actually asking. Mike did though, and replied, "Yeah, somethin' like that."

"I see," the girl replied, nodding. "And what makes you think I did anything?"

Again, Mike sought the encouragement of the other men first, though by this time Snead and the other officer had returned to their hunting and pecking. Proceeding solely on the approval of his fellow vagrants, he said, "I don't know that you did, Miss. That's why I'm askin'."

She turned back to staring at the wall in front of her, calculating her response. A droll smile appeared on her face and she returned her gaze to him, rising to her feet. In a sultry manner, she placed one foot in front of the other and trod the short path from her bed to the bars where Mike stood, saying, "I've been accused of witchcraft. My headmistress stabbed herself in the throat, and they think I had something to do with it."

Mike became aware of the dark red stain blotted on the lower part of her white blouse. He was distracted from it, however, as she held up her hand to request a cigarette, obscuring the view. "May I have one?"

The other men looked at Mike, wondering what he would do. To their surprise, he reached into his pocket and retrieved both the Lucky Strikes and the shabby matchbook he'd picked up at the diner not two blocks from the city jail. He positioned the pack with the opening toward her, and she plucked a cigarette from within, placing it delicately between her patchy, dried lips. He fumbled with the match, botching the light on the first one and barely keeping from fanning out the second. She casually reached up and held his hand still so she could light the thing, refusing to let go of him.

Her thumb was pressed against the tender spot in the middle of the butt of his palm, with her middle finger wrapped around to his protruding carpal bone. While it wouldn't normally have been a very sensitive pressure point, she managed to cause Mike a great deal of pain. His combat experience and his confusion worked together to mask the pain, but an audible wince leaked out anyway.

She dismissively let go, saying "Sorry," and strode back to the center of her cell.

The other men laughed at Mike, wondering how a little girl could have possibly injured a war-hardened military man, but a quick glare silenced them all. He turned back to her, the pain relieving some of the shyness he'd felt previously.

"Now, I can't believe such a... pretty young lady could be responsible for that kind of violence. What gave them the idea you was involved?"

She kept her face obscured from their sight. "Because I was in the room with her when it happened."

Mike asked, "But you didn't stab her, did ya?"

"No."

"But witchcraft? You can't be charged with that, can you? I mean, that law can't o' been on the books for what, 200 years?" Mike prodded.

"I don't know," she replied slowly, a puff of smoke escaping from her lips.

He struggled to know how to continue, finally asking, "So, if there's no such thing as witchcraft, and they can't arrest for it, but the woman did die, then how is it you came to be here?"

She raised the cigarette to her lips one last time, took a long, slow drag and swallowed before uttering, "Because there was a witness."

At that point, Slippers suddenly remembered the story from a paper he'd read a few days earlier. The journalist reported that two different teachers had killed themselves at a nearby parochial school. The second such incident was marked by a young girl bolting from the office exclaiming that the teacher had just plunged a fountain pen into his throat, expelling a great deal of blood onto the girl and his Oxford desk set.

Slippers got up and rushed to Mike. "Hey there, man! I think this girl is from that parochial school where the teachers is knockin' themselves off!"

"You mean St. Agnes?" Mike asked.

"No, the school," Slippers responded.

"St. Agnes is the name of the school, numbskull," Mike scolded, then turned back to the girl. "Is that you, girl? You the one from the news story who saw her teachers off themselves?"

She dropped the smoke on the floor and let it burn. "I suppose so."

The men looked at each other with morbid curiosity. Perhaps this young woman was some sort of an angel of death. Mike didn't see this possibility as completely out of the question when he asked, "So, you didn't just reach over the desk and do 'em in yourself?"

"No."

Mike tried to get at her. "Well, little lady, so you s'pose maybe there's somethin' about you drives people nuts? Maybe you don't have to touch 'em at all."

She turned to them, her eyes aglow and the smoke from the half-puffed cigarette churning up from the floor behind her. "What would you know about it, Mike?"

He reeled in confusion. "Hey, how d'ya know my name?"

"Don't you think you've asked enough questions? And what would you know about it?" she insisted.

"I don't kn—"

"Because this is what this conversation comes down to. You can accuse me of whatever you like. I don't know what happened to those teachers. They didn't like me, I know that. I didn't live up to their standards, or grades, or whatever they chose to nitpick.

Sure, they killed themselves right in front of me, but I didn't touch them. Maybe the school is haunted. Maybe something there doesn't approve of how they punish students." She nodded to the interrogation room. "They'll never know that by sending me to jail, but I'm not concerned about what they'll do to me. And the fact is that it's none of your damn business."

By now she had reached the bars and was holding one in either hand, brandishing her jagged, poorly-kept nails before the terrified men. There was no nail polish to be found as each of the nails had yellowed and cracked as if she'd been digging in the earth. This was surprising, but not inconsistent. Mike took stock of her nails and began to assess the rest of her appearance, noting the scuffs on her shoes, the minor tears in the hem of her skirt, and the rumpled, threadbare nature of the sweater. Acknowledging the bloodstain on her blouse, he asked, "Is that from your headmistress, or is that from you?"

The young woman peered down at her blouse, then back up at Mike, saying, "It's mine." Simultaneously with that admission, the men became aware of a small drip of blood running down the jail-cell bar below her left hand. As it reached the weld joint at the cross piece, it ran out to the edge, then down the side of the cross piece until it lost surface tension and descended to the floor, splattering in every direction as an ever-growing pool. She looked to her hand and removed it from the bar, allowing the puddle that had formed under her hand to flow down the bar and pool with the rest of the blood on the floor. The five men in the adjacent cell looked on, disturbed but consumed with curiosity as she revealed the gash in her hand.

Mike realized that the cause of the wound must have been a large burr on the jail-cell bar itself. He rushed to her aide, examining the bar and exclaiming, "My God! Girl, I think this thing attacked you!" He reached for her hand.

The young woman flinched and barked at him, "Don't touch it!" But it was too late. When he grabbed her hand, some of the blood smeared onto his hand.

Mike recoiled, surprised, and said, "Okay, don't worry. I won't touch it again." He examined the smudge of blood that had transferred to his hand. Snead and the other officer heard the woman's shout and left their desks to investigate.

"What's going on over there?" Snead insisted angrily. "Did he hurt you, Miss?"

But she was in no condition to properly respond. The young woman was more concerned with her wound and the fact that Mike had touched it. "You shouldn't have done that. I can't control it. I can't!" she cried, masking her wound from the two officers, an expression of dread on her face.

Mike was focusing on the blood on his hand, unable to respond. Nine Toes walked to the bars and spoke in Mike's defense. "He didn't do nothin'! He saw she was bleedin' and went to help her. God's honest truth!" The other incarcerated men agreed this was true.

The officers, however, were not satisfied. "Ma'am, what did he do to you? That's an awful lot of blood, there. I think we may have to call the medics."

"No! No more! I couldn't take it!" she said to the officers. Turning to Mike she repeated fervently, "You shouldn't have done that. I didn't mean to… I didn't want to… I can't control it, don't you see?!"

None of the men in the jail that night had any idea what she meant. They watched her carefully as she tried to breathe deeply. Unable to control the impending hyperventilation, she closed her eyes, desperately trying to concentrate. Bending down, she clasped her left hand with her right and faced the back of the cell with blood flowing freely from the bizarre wound. The second officer, Wallace, had had enough. "I'm calling the ambulance, Snead."

Snead nodded his head. "That's a good idea, Wallace, and tell 'em to hurry! She's gonna bleed out at this rate."

The young woman turned to them, pleading, "Please, no! Don't bring any more!"

Mike moved quickly to the cell door. "Snead, let me out, man! I can dress that wound." Snead quickly unlocked the door and let Mike out. "Where's the first aid kit?" Mike asked.

Snead pointed to a cabinet under the window and replied quickly, "It's over there." Mike rushed over to it, opening the doors and tossing aside the other contents within. He retrieved the gauze and bandages and ran back to where Snead was holding the keys. Snead fumbled but finally found the one for the girl's cell. Just as he was placing the key in the lock, he looked down at Mike's hand where the girl's blood had spilled. Smoke was beginning to rise from the stain. Mike noticed it too and dropped the dressings.

"What the hell is goin' on, Snead?" Mike implored, the blood beginning to eat through his flesh, releasing a grotesque smell he remembered from years earlier when a private had been fueling a Jeep. A bullet had ricocheted off the gas cap and ignited the fumes coming from the tank of the Jeep, lighting the private on fire. It was a smell Mike would never forget and didn't want to experience again. Snead stood horrified, mouth agape. Mike shouted at him, "Get me some goddamn water, man! My hand is on fire!"

Snead ran to the sink, grabbed a glass, filled it with water and brought it back to Mike, pouring it on his now horribly deformed and smoking hand. The water helped to subdue the pain and the immediate burning, but the wound on Mike's hand was now immense and the burn reached far beyond the skin, causing muscle tissue to blister and rendered skin cells to drip off the side of the wound. The two men looked at the wound, then up to where the girl had been standing, but she was gone. All at once, the seven men became aware that the girl's cell was empty. Mike and Snead looked back at each other, then in the opposite direction.

There, near the wall across from her cell, without wound and standing perfectly still, was the girl. The profound expression of remorse, however, was still on her face. Mournfully, she said, "I'm so sorry. I told you not to touch it." She began to back away from them. Strangely, she did not walk in the direction of the front door, but rather toward the end of the dead-end hallway. She stopped at the concrete wall beneath an egress window. "Please, I didn't mean for any of this to happen."

In anguish, Mike implored through clenched teeth, "What the hell are you talkin' about?"

She responded coldly, "I have to go now."

A bubbling sound began to emit from the floor behind the men. Flowing from where the girl had been standing in her cell was a puddle of blood spreading twenty feet across the floor, reaching like tentacles toward the men. Before any of them could lift their feet, the puddle ignited, setting the men aflame. Mike, Snead, and Wallace stumbled to the sink and began trying to pour water on each other. Seconds later, the two arresting officers burst into the room with a fire hose and doused the three men at the sink, then turned to the four men in the cell. The remaining vagrants, however, had already lost their battle with the unearthly accelerant. Mike, Snead, and Wallace were badly burned but not beyond the point of consciousness.

One of the arresting officers, a large, oafish man asked, "Where's the girl?" There was no verbal response from Mike or the others, but they managed to point in the direction of the wall with the high window. The two officers looked, but she was gone.

In their report, the two healthy officers indicated that in their haste to put out the flames, the girl must have slipped past them. The three burned men, however, knew that she had made no such attempt. She had managed to escape through a seven-foot-high opening. Nine Toes, Slippers, and the other two men who remained in the cell had been burned beyond recognition. The medical examiner's report detailed that such a quick ignition and burning was likely nearly painless to the victims.

Outside the building, the girl stood on the wooded hill facing her escape window. A blinding glow emanated from within. Tears streamed down her face as she knew she was responsible for the deaths of the men inside. Indeed, she had wished for such an event to occur, but as it began to happen, she knew she didn't truly desire it. The wheels, however, had been put in motion and the spell had been cast. She felt she had allowed her youth, inexperience, and emotions to rule her actions. The result was a horrific scene of violence and death. More power was at her fingertips than she was possibly capable of wielding with any reasonable control, and she realized she needed help.

She hurried through the park toward Riverside Drive, her heels digging clumsily into the moist December earth. Eventually, she removed her Mary Janes and continued barefoot, dodging trees, bushes, and broken glass along the way. She came to a bridge that took her to the other side of the Arkansas River and up to the highway. She tried to walk as casually as possible to avoid detection. After the better part of an hour and more than one instance of ducking into an ally or abandoned lot to avoid a speeding police cruiser, she reached the highway and began traversing the shoulder with her thumb extended. Numerous cars sped past, making minimal effort to acknowledge her at all. Three others slowed to identify the girl, but upon seeing her, sped up and disappeared into the night.

All the while her mind wandered. For a time, she focused on the horrific event that had just taken place; then she involuntarily started to drift into thoughts of her father, her brothers, her young sister, and the school she'd chosen to abandon only six months before graduation. Images of her angry father, clad in his filthy white A-shirt and overalls plagued her most. She had flashbacks of him bursting through the back door with a belt, drunk and looking for the two boys who had accomplished some feat of vandalism or other. When the boys failed to present themselves, he would turn on the girls. She would take her little sister into a closet and position herself in front of the girl to protect her in case the old man found them. On some occasions he did, and she was summarily beaten for protecting her brothers by not giving them up. On other occasions, the girls would spend the night in the closet until their father slept off whatever booze he'd imbibed. Even six months more of that hateful life might have killed her, she thought.

This brought her back to the incident at the police station and the objects and events she believed had caused it. Months earlier, when the school librarian took notice of a bruise on the girl's cheek, she realized she wouldn't be able to mask the events of her home life forever, so she took up a new hobby.

The library at St. Agnes was heavily restricted and limited in its variety, keeping her from learning about the things that interested her. But she'd been told by an acquaintance of a local bookseller who dealt in rare books; the kind of material that would almost assuredly be banned at school. She made the trip one day after her last class.

Upon entering the antique bookstore, a smell filled her nostrils that she'd never experienced before. It was the scent of aging leather bookbinding, combined with something much less tangible. There were no other patrons in the store, yet the old, bespectacled, gray-haired man behind the counter made no attempt to engage her. He angled his head back toward his cataloging and pretended she wasn't even there. She smirked, thinking to herself, *All old men in bookstores look the same. Perhaps it's a uniform for boredom.* Still, she tried to keep her mind open.

There were thousands of books. They came in every shape, size, and color she could imagine. The shelves stretched two levels into the air with rolling ladders on each section. On the top shelves were the rarer books, while the common, pedestrian fare littered the bottom shelves. She removed her book bag and sweater and ascended a ladder in the section marked Religion. Never before had she seen an entire section of spiritual literature dedicated to something other than the King James Bible. As she neared the top, the old man at the counter removed his spectacles from his nose and let them dangle at the ends of their chain. He pointed to the top section and moved toward her, saying, "Now, little girl, you don't want anything to do with *those* books. I think what you're looking for would be down here." He motioned to the collection of biblical texts displayed on the bottom shelves.

Shaking her head, she replied, "No, thank you," and continued poring over the collection, searching for something that might pop out at her as a counterpoint to the thoughts and beliefs she felt had failed her in the past.

"No really, you should come down from there, little lady. Now, I don't want your parents to come running in here next week complaining to me about the smut you've been reading," the man protested.

She laughed at him. "I can assure you, my father doesn't care what I read. He can't read well enough to know anyway."

"Well, your mother would know, and you haven't had to deal with angry mothers like I have. Now please, come down from there!" The old man continued blathering on in ignorance, but the young woman didn't care. Her eyes caught sight of a text she knew would be her pride and joy. Excitedly, she lifted it from its spot on the shelf, blowing a generation of dust off its dried-up pages. The book was clearly not a major publication, as the binding was held together with string and the cover was far too large. It warped and wrapped around the thick stack of pages as if it were a set of lips intent on sealing the contents from the outside world. But it was the smell that truly set it apart. She'd noticed it upon entering the store and it had driven her to the book; an amalgam of tin, earth, leather, and a fourth ingredient she couldn't quite place. It smelled as if it were on fire.

Her delicate, yet weathered fingers pried the cover from the first few pages, caressing the edges all the way. The title was worn off the outside cover and the copyright pages had been removed, quite possibly by the bookseller to keep curious shoppers from hunting down additional copies. No Southerner in their right mind would go around asking their friends and neighbors if they were familiar with a book of those contents.

All of the other books had pretentious titles and claimed to have some secret knowledge no one else had discovered. The young woman was too world-weary to fall for those tricks. When she laid her eyes on the blank binding of that tome, she knew she had discovered what she'd come there to find. Leafing through the first few pages of the book, her assumptions were validated. It was about a group of women on the East Coast many years before who had tried to commune with nature to gain a better understanding of their world. While she had no training in such things, it spoke to her as something she had been vaguely familiar with in her own life.

Between homework sessions, bouts of abuse with her family, and taunts from other students, she would embark on long walks through the Oklahoma countryside. When she found something that interested her, she'd kneel down on the ground and examine it. She held a fascination with objects of all kinds. Holding the objects, she would smell them, breathe in their essence – or so she tried – and imagine where the object had been and the stories of the people who had owned it. Occasionally, she'd stumble upon the bones of a dead animal, or more interesting, a human person. The few times this did occur she didn't bother to inform authorities. After all, the person was dead. What would they do with that information? Instead, she would hang her jacket on a nearby tree and start digging into the earth with her bare hands. There were rocks and sticks nearby that could have served as useful tools for digging, but she didn't want to detach herself in any way from the earthen humanity before her. She would dig a hole with her hands, then reconstruct the skeleton exactly as it had lain before in the new home she'd made for it.

Afterward, she sat beneath the earthly canopy surrounding her and, exhausted, took stock of what had occurred. She felt remorse for the lost soul and worried whether it would make it back to its home. One day, after interring the remains of what she assumed to be a dog, she looked around to see if she had missed anything. While there were no bones remaining, she did spy a small, barkless stick, nearly white in color. Curiously, she picked it up and examined it. She contemplated for a time what the stick might have to do with the dog. Had the dog chased it and been injured? She looked around for other such sticks but could find none. As it was the only unique object to behold, she stuck it into the ground she had just lumped on top of the deceased animal. She shifted her lips back and forth, decided that the stick didn't look right straight up and down, and then turned it just slightly so it angled out of the earthen tomb. She stood, satisfied, and bowed in honor of the dog.

A sensation then overcame her, frightening at first but then resolving itself into a calm. She felt like she had done the right thing and that the animal was now rightly interred. Out of respect for the creature, she put on her coat and walked back in the direction of her home.

That same sensation is what came over her when she picked up the book, while the old man babbled incoherently below. She thumbed through the volume, taking in the illustrations and symbols therein. With no more consideration, she descended the ladder ready to make her purchase.

"Oh, now put that back," the old shopkeeper implored. "Do you have any idea what's in that book? That's for a professor at the college to read, or clergy, or—"

She interrupted him. "Or people who want to have a better understanding of their world?"

"That's a new one," he laughed. "Well, why don't I just put that back up on the shelf for you…" The man tried to take it from her.

She resisted and glared at him, her green eyes glistening in the dryness of the musty bookstore air. "How much?"

"Look, young lady," he argued, becoming impatient. "I don't think you understand. I can't sell that to you."

"There is no age limit on books. You most certainly can sell it to me, and you will. I have money."

He shrugged, furrowing his brow, shaking his head, and retreating behind the counter. "Oh, I don't know. Normally I'd go pretty low for such an obscure and useless volume, but considering the personal risk to me as a result of who's buying it…" He looked at her, then the book, trying to think of a sum that might scare her off. "…four dollars."

Initially, the hair stood up on the back of her neck at the ridiculous price. However, since she'd stolen the money from her father's cash canister, poorly hidden above the liquor cabinet, she couldn't, in good conscience, haggle. After all, the man might just reinitiate his protestations, and she'd heard enough of them. "Fine," she replied, and took a five out of her sweater pocket.

He took it, shook his head, and pressed the tender button on the register. The bell rang and the drawer popped out. He retrieved her change, but she was already putting her sweater back on and beginning to leave the store with the book.

"Don't you want your change?" he called after her.

"Keep it," she jabbed, refusing to turn her head on the way out. She confidently strode from the building, holding her book tightly with both hands.

He huffed indignantly and went back to cataloging the new collection on his counter. "Damn kids."

Another car zoomed past her, her thumb once again ignored by the driver inside. It was a warm first-day-of-winter, but still cold enough that she was beginning to feel the pain in her fingers and lack of circulation in her toes from the shoes she had reaffixed upon reaching the roadside. She pulled the collar up right to her chin and stashed her hands deep in the side pockets, rubbing them on her hips to keep them warm. Again, she drifted into thoughts of the recent past that led her to that night.

Within the first week of owning the book, she'd read it thoroughly three times and was working on it a fourth time. While the book contained no actual instructions or spells for communing with her natural world, she was sure that proper analysis of the text would reveal some secret. She began retreating to the backyard and the woods beyond her family's property in an effort to better concentrate on the activities she felt would give her the experience she was looking for. Unlike most people her age, she was strangely comfortable in the outdoors, believing it was her responsibility to be in tune with what nature had to tell her. She knew such odd fascinations would sound ridiculous to both her family and her classmates, so she kept them to herself. The one exception to her secrecy was her child sister.

While she'd never accomplished any particular trick or spell, she felt sure she was getting in touch with her surrounding environment. She sat cross-legged on the ground, dirtying her school clothes and scuffing her shoes as she so frequently had started to do. Before she could accomplish anything, however, she heard voices in the distance. Initially thinking they were the neighbor boys, she disregarded them and returned to her breathing exercises. After a few moments she was again interrupted, this time hearing her name among the various shouts in the air. Gathering her book and sweater and climbing to her feet, she could see her brothers and father in the distance. Instinctively, the young woman started to move in the opposite direction. Her shoes, however, were clumsy in the soil below her and she trudged along slowly.

The boys caught up to her and took the book from her. She screamed for them to return it, but they shoved her to the ground and began walking back to their father. Her father looked angrily through the book, shaking his head at the myriad images and illustrations. She was correct that he couldn't read, but his boys assured him the book was not of Christian origin. He shouted at her, "Witchcraft? Sorcery?! Are you trying to kill me?!"

She propped herself up on her hands and tried to back slowly away. "No! I'm not trying to kill you."

"You know they burn witches at the stake around here, little girl?! They're liable to burn me along with you if they catch you reading this stuff. Now, we got run out of the East Coast on a rail after your mother's death, and I'll be damned if your little stunt makes me look like a fool here, too."

Her father pulled a lighter out from his breast pocket and held it under the book. She screamed and tried to stop him, grabbing at his hand and knocking the lighter to the ground. He pulled his hand back and swung at her, striking her on the cheek. She fell to the ground, her lip cut and yielding a small trickle of life. Saying nothing in addition, he picked up the lighter and ignited the book. He rotated it as it burned to keep the flames from catching his flesh or shirtsleeve.

She wept over the loss of the book, but dared not intercede again. Once the book was sufficiently destroyed, leaving only a charcoal-encased cover and an unburnt corner of still-bound paper, her father dropped it at her feet. She moved quickly to pile dirt on it and keep the flames from spreading to the newly fallen leaves, then peered up at him. He said nothing and returned to the house, his two seeds in tow.

Once they were out of sight, she plunged her increasingly damaged fingernails into the earth and dug a permanent home for the book's remnants. Angrily, she took a discarded shard of glass and jammed it into the earth where she would normally have placed a stick. She heard a low rumble in the distance and returned to the house. She plodded, emotionally spent, up to the meager room she shared with her sister, who was cowering in the corner behind a pile of clothes. "I'm not going to hurt you, Samantha," the young woman mumbled, rubbing her face with her hands.

"I'm sorry I told them about the book," Samantha guiltily

uttered, a dried tear staining her cheek.

The young woman shook her head. "I shouldn't have told you. Did they hurt you? When they asked you where I was, did they hurt you?" When the little girl looked away, she knew her brothers had punished her sister for trying to keep the secret.

Angrily, she rose from her bed and thundered down the stairs to where her brothers were halfheartedly studying for their school work. Unexpectedly, even to her, she grabbed a glass from in front of the older boy and smashed it over his head, nearly knocking him unconscious. She then tackled the younger boy and tried vainly to swing at him. He blocked her punches and shoved her off more than once. Eventually, their father entered from the other room laughing; he had a cigarette in one hand and he threw her to the floor by her collar with the other.

She climbed to her feet and hesitated, seeing all three men staring at her and laughing. Her entire world began to spin around her. All of the things she'd seen, read, touched, and experienced jumped into her mind at once. She saw the blood in the room: the blood from her glass-cut hand had transferred in sloppy smatterings on her younger brother's face; her older brother's blood flowed freely from an open wound in his head that he chose to ignore; and the blood on her father's hand from where he had patted his older boy on the shoulder and cheek, a light reward for surviving the petite young woman's onslaught.

She saw the blood and wished it would ignite with flame. She closed her eyes, breathed deeply, and screamed from the very depths of her soul. As if the world slowed to a crawl, the waves from her voice spread outward through the room, shattering every last piece of glass in their path. The men tried vainly to cover their ears, the noise deafening. Even smaller wooden objects started to splinter. Her eyes remained shut, all the while oblivious to the destruction unfolding around her.

Finally, as her father was about to swing at her to silence the sound she was emitting, the hand he had cocked to do so burst into flames. He grabbed his hand in pain and watched as his son's faces burst into flame as well. The three men fumbled about the room, screaming in pain as she finally ceased her cry. She opened her eyes to find utter chaos had enveloped the room. Fire was spreading from the men to the curtains, the furniture, and their clothes. They rushed past her to the kitchen. In horror, she ran up toward her room, finding her little sister at the top of the stairs. Without any words, she picked up Samantha and carried her back down the stairs. Smoke was rolling along the ceiling and flames were beginning to consume the walls. The door was hot as she grabbed it. Her hand and its fresh cut burned as she wrenched the knob and pulled the door open. She thrust her sister outside and returned to the house.

Fresh oxygen from the shattered windows fueled the flames and the temperature in the house was unbearable. She fell unconscious from the smoke and lay still on the floor in the entryway. The neighbors heard the noise created by the incident and ran to inspect. Through the smoke billowing from the front door, they barely made out the prone body of the young woman and dashed to rescue her. They pulled her into the drive and yelled for water. The women returned to their home to bring some, and the men tried to find another way in to rescue the other members of the young woman's family. After a short circuit around the house though, they decided the fire was too hot and the risk too high. If the men didn't make it out on their own, they wouldn't make it out at all.

Momentarily regaining consciousness, the young woman sat up and turned to the house with just that thought. Once the structure began to collapse she could pass out and pretend that the past eighteen years had never happened. Just a few more moments. Just a few more... At long last, the roof began to cave in. The support for the chimney also gave way, and the brick tower spun in its base, collapsing the entire center of the house with it. As she had promised herself, she then lay down, scarcely acknowledging her little sister on the way to the ground. She raised her wounded hand to examine it only to find there was no wound at all, let alone a cut or a burn. The information overloaded her waning consciousness and she passed out.

The neighbors took the girls in, but the young woman's troubles at school escalated, and she was accused of the three acts of malice that eventually landed her in the city jail. Recounting the bizarre period that had preceded her walking along the side of the highway, she began to feel more at ease with the events. She'd been put in a horrible spot and did what any girl would. That is provided the girl had the capacity she did for controlling her environment. There were two lingering thoughts of guilt. The first was of the coat she'd stolen from her foster father. The second was of her little sister.

After the event at the police station, she would never be able to see her sister again and worried about how the little girl would be cared for. She was too old to forget the events, but possibly young enough that they wouldn't haunt her as something she would feel responsible for. Their host family had been very welcoming and never addressed the girls as though they should feel ashamed or guilty in any way. While she would have preferred to bring her little sister with her, the young woman had to become comfortable with the fact that the little girl's new family would take care of her.

Her mind was no longer wandering, but was now focusing on

the cold that was beginning to consume her last remaining caloric resources. Hunger and numbness ate away at her. Finally, another car crested the hill behind her. It was past midnight at that point and traffic was very light. She wearily held out her hand, extending the thumb as far as she could in her exhausted state.

Unlike the other cars that had ignored or been wary of her all night, this one seemed to be looking for her. Her heart fluttered momentarily at the thought that it may be a police cruiser, but as the car pulled up she realized it was not. It was a 1954 Ford Victoria, cream with a black roof, and was impressively clean, right down to the pristine whitewalls. As it stopped next to her, she bent down to the open passenger window and looked inside. The driver was a middle-aged man in a charcoal gray suit. He smiled at her, not giving anything away, and asked, "Where you headed, young lady?"

She looked down the road ahead of them and back at the man. "Well, eventually to Massachusetts, but I'll go as far as you can take me."

"We can get ya started. I can take you to St. Louis, and maybe you can connect with some friends or family there."

"That would be swell," she smiled.

He grabbed the handle and popped the door open. "Hop on in then, and we'll get going."

She gathered the long coat and plunged, exhausted, into the oversized passenger seat of the man's car. He shifted it into gear and rolled away from the shoulder. As the car settled in at fifty-five mph, the man retrieved a pack of cigarettes from his coat pocket, along with a lighter. He pulled one out and lit it, exhaling the smoke through the triangle window in the driver's door. The young woman picked up the pack and examined it. "Lucky Strikes, eh?" she asked.

The man handed her the lighter, cautioning, "It's not very ladylike to smoke. Probably not somethin' you oughtta start at your age."

She smiled and after a long, contemplative pause, placed the objects back in his hand. "Oh, I'm not interested in smoking. They're just what my father used to smoke, that's all."

"He not around anymore?" he asked, as he placed the cigarettes and lighter back into his pocket.

She replied, "No, but that's okay."

"I'm damn sorry to hear that," he said, then with little hesitation continued, "My name's Al." He stuck out his right hand to shake.

She shook his hand and comfortably replied, "Rebekah. My name's Rebekah."

Chapter Three

Isaac lifted the chunk of maple onto the bed of the lathe with mild skepticism. He'd made eighteen preliminary cuts to get the piece of wood as close to round as possible before working on it; yet he still worried it might be too hard for the thin walls he planned to turn. What convinced him was simple math. Making any more preliminary cuts would start to reduce the size of the piece and would be a waste of time. Tossing his hands in the air, he opted to affix the piece between centers, locking it to both the headstock spindle and the tailstock. The process took approximately twenty minutes between proper measuring, drilling holes, fighting with the aging lathe, and fussing over the best direction to begin. Knowing he'd eventually have to remove the tailstock mounting, he chose to place the bottom of the bowl at the headstock end.

With the raw material properly affixed, Isaac took a broad, flat chisel from his collection. The tools were kept in a large wooden cabinet he'd built just a year earlier upon opening his own shop. It was a basic armoire with large doors on top that guarded his more sizeable tools: axes, saws, and the like. The bottom half consisted of a series of varying-sized drawers. In the top left drawer, pillowed and blanketed with velvet, were his chisels. He was considered the best woodworker in the Wilmington area at the time, but even he felt his chisels deserved a place of honor among the collection.

Therefore, he allowed himself the joy of making them a rather ostentatious home.

He respectfully closed the drawer and returned to his lathe. One more time, he eyed the mounts on either end of the chunk of maple, positioned his stool before the tool rest, and began the pedal. The rope spanning the spring pole, the screw, and the pedal moved back and forth, spinning the lathe faster until it reached a speed he felt sufficient to begin turning. Slowly, he applied the chisel, the eighteen corners gradually shedding their edges and refining into a smooth circle. For a moment, once the circular shape of the bowl had been nearly achieved, Isaac allowed a brief thought of satisfaction to flit through his head. When he did so, the large chisel caught the tiny fluctuation of a burr and pulled the chisel in a deep, gouging fashion across the face of the newly-circular finish. The force of the gash also caused the lathe to lose momentum, and Isaac had to remove the chisel to allow the bowl to stop turning. From the nearly ten minutes it took him to round the corners of the object, it had returned to just another chunk of wood in only a second.

Now, the woodworker pulled out a second chisel, carefully replacing the first in the drawer, and began manual work on the gouge. He skillfully cleared the area around the gash so the larger chisel wouldn't catch on it once he started the lathe turning again. Once the injury and its nearby material was cleared, he transferred chisels again and returned to rounding the object off. This time, he did not allow his mind to wander, and the piece was clear before he removed the chisel. He stepped carefully away from the instrument, allowing it to finish turning on its own, and put the large chisel back in the drawer, not to be used again for this project.

Removing the handkerchief from around his neck, he wiped sweat from his brow and stepped to his rough work table where he had placed his water glass. He lifted the glass and began drinking as the door to his shop, a large barn door mounted on a rolling track, slid open. The back side of the shop was open to the yard behind his parents' house, as well as the barn where the animals were housed. The front of the shop faced the street and had a hand-carved shingle hanging above the door bearing the family name. Through the door walked Bernard Williams, the city attorney.

Bernard was a jovial man and hadn't brought a case before the county judge in more than six months. True, crime had been low in their relatively small community, but the man simply couldn't bring himself to see someone spend time in jail. A number of his friends who'd fought in the Civil War either survived or died at the Andersonville POW camp, and he feared being seen as the next Henry Wirz for sending someone to prison. Bernard's standard practice was to plea bargain just about any case that came across his desk. Fortunately for his standing among the public who elected him, there had been no violent crimes to prosecute, so he was forgiven this weakness.

To the Truesdell family, Bernard represented nothing of a legal matter, but rather the constant annoyance of moneymaking schemes. He acknowledged the great talent that seemed to run through the family and was constantly trying to negotiate some form of public showing or other. While the rest of Isaac's family saw Bernard as a blight on an otherwise sunny day, Isaac saw him as a simple soul trying to find his own modicum of control in the world. His family gladly relinquished the duties of dealing with Bernard. Isaac laughed a bit to himself but welcomed the approach of a friendly face.

Bernard bellowed from the other end of the shop, "Hello, friend!"

Cordially tipping his glass, Isaac returned the salutation.

"Hello, friend. What news?"

"What news? *What* news!" Bernard hurried across the floor toward the woodworker with papers in hand. "I tell you, young Mr. Truesdell, today I have some wonderful news indeed."

"I see. What have you got there?" Isaac asked, motioning to the papers in Bernard's hand.

Bernard smiled first, trying to hold out on Isaac. But since both of them knew Isaac had far more patience than Bernard, the visitor continued without prompting and Isaac went back to drinking his water. "I have a letter from a Harvey Heatheridge. Now, he is the very proper gentleman from Arlington – that's in Virginia..."

"Thank you," Isaac politely interjected.

Bernard droned on, "He's the proper gentleman from Virginia... Arlington, whom I, upon a weekend holiday to our great nation's Capital just happened to run into. I don't know if you know him, but he's one of the former district attorneys from Virginia. Well, he's in retirement now, but he said he regularly meets with Mr. William Vilas."

Isaac looked crookedly at Bernard. "You mean Secretary of the Interior William Vilas?"

"The same!" Bernard exclaimed. "Now, I showed one of your pieces to Mr. Heatheridge and he was stunned! Just stunned, and he told me that Mr. Vilas is a great appreciator of modern carpentry."

Isaac corrected him quickly. "Woodwork."

"Woodwork. Yes, Woodwork. Well, it turns out that before Mr. Vilas was in the war, he was from Wisconsin, where they have vast forests and a great number of skilled craftsmen. Have you heard of the place?"

"Wisconsin?" Isaac questioned.

"Yes!"

The young woodworker indicated he had heard of Wisconsin.

"Well, despite all of the fine work Mr. Vilas had brought with him from the state of Wisconsin, Mr. Heatheridge felt sure he'd not seen a piece of work in the secretary's collection that could rival yours." Bernard kept nodding his head, trying to incite Isaac to his level of excitement.

Isaac calmly responded, "Is that what's in the letter?"

"Oh! The letter. No, that's not what's in the letter. This is a letter directly from Mr. Vilas inviting you and your family to his home in Washington, and he'd like you to bring some pieces along that he can appraise." With that, Bernard handed Isaac the letter.

Isaac was genuinely surprised at hearing this information, and took the letter from Bernard, hastily opening and reading it. Indeed, the contents were as Bernard had promised. Isaac looked up at Bernard, grabbing his shoulder. "This is real?" Isaac asked excitedly.

Bernard nodded, barely able to contain his enthusiasm for securing Isaac an audience with a powerful public figure. While he was ever aware that his own skills were meager, Bernard never doubted that he could manage to have a hand in the lives of people who indeed were great.

Ever since the day he met the Truesdells, he was sure they would be his ticket to all the fancy balls and galas he'd ever dreamed of. Isaac in particular was a unique and promising man. True, he was nearly thirty and not as young as some of the other gifted bachelors in the county, but his abilities knew no bounds. Isaac was an expert with wood and metal, could tame and ride horses better than anyone he knew, and had a remarkable gentleman's personality to boot. He was, in a word, brilliant.

Now that Bernard had all but secured a commission for the

young man with the Secretary of the Interior, he was barely able to contain himself. "Well?! What do you think. Will you go to Washington to meet with Mr. Vilas?"

Isaac nodded emphatically, unable to contain his joy. "Most certainly!"

"Oh, this is wonderful news! When does the Secretary wish to see you?

"The letter says he'd like me to visit sometime next month. Would you write to him for me and let him know I'll be there in the middle of next month?" Isaac held the letter out to Bernard.

Bernard stared at it, honored that Isaac was trusting him with this task. "Do you mean you'd like me to be your manager in this matter?"

Isaac held back the letter, removing most of the smile from his face. "I would like you to act as my agent for this matter, Bernard. And I would be most honored if you would coordinate the event."

"All that you ask, I will do!"

"And no more," Isaac clarified. Bernard saluted him heartily and took the letter, running off toward the front entrance. "I won't let you down!"

Isaac laughed and watched the man exit. After the door closed behind Bernard, Isaac put his hand over his mouth in disbelief. His excitement burst forth in stifled shouts and yelps as he hurried out the back of the shop toward the house where his mother, Cynthia, was resting on the back porch.

"Is that man gone, Isaac?" she asked, fanning herself and shaking her head in bemused wonderment at Bernard.

Isaac ran up to her and grabbed the sides of her face, kissing her forehead. "Mother, you won't believe what Bernard did for us!"

Surprised, she blurted, "Good heavens! I can't imagine he'd do anything worth all that. Please, sit down, Isaac. You're acting like a child," she laughed, confused but pleased at his jubilation.

"Bernard has secured a meeting with Mr. Vilas, the Secretary of the Interior, for him to view my work. If he's impressed with it, we may get a commission from the government!"

"You can't be serious."

"I read the letter myself. Bernard met with an attorney in Arlington who says Mr. Vilas is a collector. The attorney spoke to the secretary, and he wrote me personally to request the meeting," Isaac explained.

Cynthia Truesdell was a staunchly reserved woman. She never became overtly excited about anything except remaining perfectly calm at all times. Consequently, she had a short patience for people she felt were in any way disingenuous. It was a feeling she'd had about Bernard since the day they met. He had discovered their shop when riding past on his way to court the first week he was in town. After he'd filed the papers he was working on that day, he returned to the shop to introduce himself and peruse the wares within. He was so excited by what he saw, she thought, that he must have been up to something. His being a lawyer also didn't sit well with her, and she maintained a safe distance at all times. Then, he began returning week after week, month after month, trying to find some way or other to invest in the Truesdells' business. They explained to him that they were not interested and that they had a time-honored tradition for doing business. Family rules had to reign over opportunism.

The rest of the family backed Cynthia's play, if for no other reason than Bernard annoyed them as well. Isaac was the sole exception. He had never before entertained any of Bernard's schemes, but he always allowed Bernard to say his piece and was committed to letting him down easy. Cynthia would regularly argue

with Isaac that his politeness was the reason Bernard kept returning. In response, Isaac told her that if it gave the man pleasure and
purpose, who was he to destroy that.

Now, however, Cynthia had a problem before her. The man
whose presence she so disdained had managed to bring a great deal
of opportunity to her family. Most of her being was excited and
grateful for the chance. But the small remaining part was irked that
the opportunity had come from Bernard. Still, not wanting to hurt
Isaac or turn away something that she would regret later, she embraced Isaac's enthusiasm, reaching out and hugging him while
saying, "God makes stubborn folk for a reason, Isaac. You better
do well with that!"

"Bernard's stubbornness is almost assuredly the reason for the
meeting, Mother. I wish you'd give him a little leeway now and
then," Isaac said, finally sitting as his mother had requested.

"Oh, I'm going to have to now, aren't I?" She shook her head
and sat back in her seat, fanning herself for another moment
before asking, "What will you do?"

Isaac sat back in his chair, realizing he hadn't considered that
yet. "I don't know. I suppose I could start with that piece of maple
in there. If I make the walls thin enough, that could certainly sell a
few pieces."

"Doing art for the aristocracy. While lucrative, there's something that feels amiss about that," Cynthia warned.

"I know. Believe me, I know. But won't it be great for the
family?"

"Family?" Cynthia now turned to him with a sarcastic look of
shock on her face. "What family? Your father and I are fine. Your
sisters are fine. Your brother, God rest his soul, is in the arms of
his maker. We have no need of extra commissions here, Isaac.
You're not a young man anymore. When are you going to start

making a family of your own?"

"Not this again…"

"Please, don't misunderstand me. I think this could be an excellent nest egg for you and your family… once you start one. Imagine little Isaac Jr. running off to college at Harvard or Yale instead of laboring away in a shop like his father, or his father's father, or any of the rest of the men in his family." She sighed, seeing that Isaac had all but tuned her out. "Take the job, Isaac. Do us proud, but remember this isn't for us. It's for you."

Isaac shook his head and exhaled into the atmosphere, closing his eyes gently, then reopening them. Without turning to her, he said, "Sometimes I feel like I must be a disappointment to you, Mother. All of the other men my age are married, and have families… I sometimes think Thomas must be disappointed in me as well."

Cynthia became quite serious and pointed her finger at the sky. "Now you just stop right there. We don't know what Thomas would have wanted. That's God's business, not ours. You are your own man, Isaac, and I will not have you moping around worrying about what your brother would have hoped, God rest his soul."

"I know. I'm sorry." They sat in silence for some time, both obviously tracing back memories of Isaac's departed brother. Finally, Isaac added, "Still, he would have been old enough to be a husband and father by now. You don't think he'd be hassling me about it just like you are?"

"Not at all. Brothers can't be half as cruel as mothers can be," she stated drolly and winked at him, then returned to her stern disposition. "But, even I cannot tell you who you are or what you should do, despite the fact that I'm getting older and long for grandchildren. Not to mention you're getting older, too. You won't live forever, you know."

Rolling his eyes, Isaac responded, "I become increasingly aware of that every day." Cynthia smiled and began fanning herself again. Isaac looked at her and asked, "So, do you think I should tell the others?"

She placed her hand on his affectionately, not moving her head. "Why not? As if your family didn't know of your genius already, I'm sure they'll be happy for you getting some recognition for it." She patted his hand and exhaled dramatically. "I'd say I'm losing my little boy, but I don't think you're in danger of going anywhere soon." Isaac again rolled his eyes and walked out into the yard where his sisters were playing.

Cynthia watched as her daughters shared in the excitement of the event, inevitably asking if they could come with him to Washington. She shook her head *No*, but Isaac told them they could anyway. She always knew Isaac was a special case. When he was born, she and her husband Richard were very young. They'd only been married six months when the blessed event occurred, and were very nearly ostracized from the church for it. There had been no asserted effort to have a child, but then, pregnancies typically had their own plans for the world and not the other way around.

Five years after Isaac was born and Richard was settled down with his shop, horses, and small farm, Thomas was born. This time, they were all the more prepared for the child but hadn't anticipated how sickly he would be. The boy struggled on for four years until pneumonia finally overtook him and he passed away. It struck Isaac particularly hard, and he hadn't spoken of having children as a result. His parents had never talked to him about it, but it seemed particularly clear that Isaac did not want to experience that sort of loss again. When his sisters were born, he regarded their youth with great trepidation, treating them as if they were priceless gifts. Richard and Cynthia never had to worry about the safety of their daughters, as they knew Isaac would never allow anything bad to happen to them. He was eleven and fourteen years older than his sisters Jane and Alice respectively.

Jane was at the age where young men were starting to call on her, and Richard appreciated that Isaac did most of the work of culling the herd. Granted, some of those men might return in three more years to court Alice. But by then, Richard hoped to have a well-cultivated list from Isaac to work from, assuming Isaac would be gone by then as well. Their son had become the primary bread-winner of the family, and while Richard appreciated the income, it wasn't needed. Richard believed it was more important that Isaac have a family of his own to settle down with. Isaac refused to discuss it.

It was highly unusual for women to call on men, but since Isaac refused to do the work, some of the local women had opted to take some steps for him. There was Katie, the daughter of the pastor. Despite her frequent visits to the shop – alone – while Isaac worked causing a great fuss among the local gossipmongers, it was her eventual exit that made the scenario infamous. Although her father was humiliated by Katie's rather forward behavior toward Isaac, the pastor allowed it. He regretted it, however, when she spent the entire walk home from the shop one day in tears, fussing over the hem of her dress and eventually tripping and being stranded in the rain. It was amusement for most, but Isaac felt miserably about the whole thing.

Then there was Josephine. She was the family's least favorite of Isaac's suitors, as she had no proper family or name. Her father had died years earlier and she lived with her brother and mother on a meager annuity. This financial situation often caused them to be viewed as the town's charity case. Regardless, Isaac was quite cordial with her and seemed to enjoy her company. She was bookish, shy, and quite beautiful. It was Isaac, rather than his family, that put the stops on any possible relationship however. No one was quite sure why, though speculation ranged from fear of alienating his family to lingering doubts about parenting raised from the loss of his brother. In any case, Josephine secured an education and became a writer, in part with help from Isaac's connection to a local patent clerk. Josephine and the patent clerk eventually married.

And finally, there was Hattie. She was the family's favorite. Hattie grew up as the daughter of a tavern owner; she could sing, play piano, and keep a conversation with anyone. She was also incredibly outgoing and had been quite the tomboy growing up. Despite being a genteel socialite, Hattie was caught one evening singing tunes from the bar top, all the while swinging a mug of ale. It was this last part that Cynthia and Richard feigned disappointment at, yet couldn't help but be amused by when no one else was around. She was, they thought, just the kind of fun-loving, outgoing personality to counter Isaac's contemplative nature.

Hattie had a unique way of dealing with Isaac. She would often drop by on the premise of visiting his family on her way home, taking a turn through the shop and telling Isaac, "I'll see you in my tavern this Friday." To which, Isaac would respond, "No, you won't, but I hope you have a wonderful evening, Hattie." Ever patient, Hattie would bat her eyes and turn to walk away, refusing to look back at him on her way out. "I wasn't asking," she would inform him, and then leave. This never permitted Isaac the opportunity to refute and also required him to make some sort of response at a later date. It was a fairly ingenious way to guarantee interaction. It was well known that Hattie was in the process of securing herself a teaching position where she could remain until Isaac "came to his senses."

In Isaac's mind, he knew he could love her and that she would make him happy, but he always felt there was something missing in his life and that he couldn't move on until he understood it. Time was wasting, and it weighed heavily on him.

The day after Bernard's exciting visit, Isaac found himself in his shop working on the maple bowl he'd been turning. He had made little progress, and realized he now had less than a month to produce both the bowl and two other pieces he could bring with him to Washington. In fact, progress had been going in the wrong direction. Isaac had caught a tear two more times, struggling to find the right chisel to work the abnormally hard piece of wood. For the third time, he pulled out a broad, flat chisel and smoothed the sides of the bowl. His frustration was mounting, and he could feel it seeping into every fiber of his being. Despite his better judgment, he picked up a chisel and started the lathe turning. Once the appropriate speed had been attained, he laid metal to wood, and almost on cue, the chisel tore across the face of the wood, nearly pulling the tool out of Isaac's hand. "No! Damn it!" he shouted and pulled the chisel and himself away.

His instinct was to throw the chisel at the armoire, but he restrained himself. Instead, he grabbed another piece of wood and hurled it at the wall, tools rattling in their mounts as it connected. The wood broke and fell to the floor in two pieces. In spite of his anger, Isaac took a step back to analyze what had just occurred. Was the wood diseased? Did it have a crack in it somewhere already? He picked it up and assessed the damage. There was no disease, no previous crack or break. He had broken it simply by throwing it. The next question he considered was why the wall hadn't been damaged in any way. Isaac had been a woodworker long enough to know that wood doesn't break that easily, and that when it does break, it damages other objects as well. This was the most peculiar incident he'd seen in all his years working in the medium.

Breaking perfectly innocent pieces of wood was all Isaac needed to know he should seek some kind of respite, a way to clear his head. Having never been under this kind of stress before, he had no idea what worked best for him. So, he left the shop, went to the kitchen, grabbed some bread and water, and reentered the shop. His goal was to sequester himself in the shop until he understood what had happened, and what had suddenly made the project so difficult.

Three hours and two more innocent pieces of wood later, Isaac was exhausted, shirtless with his overall straps hanging down at his sides. If he ever succeeded at finishing the bowl, it would be no more than three quarters of the original intended size. He pounded his fist on the table and slumped down onto the floor of the shop. Breathing heavily, he tried to focus on the rafters above.

A knock came at the door. He looked up, realizing it was the front door and that a potential customer could be calling. Isaac clambered to his feet, looking for his shirt. Before he could locate it, the door burst open and Hattie came bounding through, shouting, "I've brought you rhubarb pie—" She only then realized Isaac was half naked. "Oh, my!" she exclaimed as she shielded her eyes with one hand and held out the pie with the other.

Finally, Isaac located his shirt and messily pulled it over his head. "I'm terribly sorry, Hattie! I wasn't expecting anyone. I've been working on this project…"

"I see that. That's okay!" Hattie smirked from under her hand, trying desperately to veil her amusement and seem as shocked and appalled as she could conjure. Indeed, she wasn't offended at all.

Sloppily tucking his shirt into his overalls, he approached and reached for the pie. "You brought me pie?"

"It depends. Are you decent?" she giggled.

Isaac bowed and shook his head, ashamed of himself. "I really am very embarrassed about that. It didn't occur to me that anyone might…"

Lowering her hand and turning quickly to him, she finished his sentence. "…patronize your business? You're a terrible business-man, Isaac Truesdell."

He laughed and sighed, saying, "I must be."

"I know a girl who could teach you a thing or two about running a business, though."

"Oh, do you?" Isaac asked, starting to catch on.

"Mm–hmm. Tonight is Friday night. If you drop by the tavern, I'd be happy to show you how hospitality works. We're quite good at it; business is booming." She locked eyes with him, making him even more embarrassed.

"I'm sorry, I can't. I have a new commission to work on…"

"Oh, no you don't. You owe me for this," she ordered, indicating his prior level of undress.

Isaac smiled and exhaled. "You're probably right. I certainly do owe you. Both for… that, and the pie."

"Good. I'll see you at the tavern tonight at 7:00 o'clock. Don't be late; I'm saving a seat for you." And with that, she placed the pie in his hands, made one last intense overture from her eyes to his, and turned to exit the way she came.

Isaac nodded as she went and held the door open for her. His mother and eldest sister were beating rugs on the front steps, and he watched the ladies greet each other kindly when Hattie passed. There was something about Hattie even Isaac couldn't explain. She had dark hair, tanned, vibrant skin, and green eyes he'd only read about in books. Even as she walked away he could see those intense eyes burned into his mind. She was beautiful, intelligent, and loved Isaac. The resistance, he admitted, was his alone. Finally, as he watched her walk gleefully away, he resolved to address the issue instantly upon return from Washington. Seven o'clock, he thought.

Once Hattie had cleared the hill in front of the house, Isaac ran out the back door and into the house, realizing he had no clean clothes to wear. He dropped the pie on the counter in the kitchen and darted up the stairs to his room. The room consisted of a bed; numerous bookshelves all completely stocked and protruding so much into the space that the room seemed cramped; a buffet-style dresser; and decorations made from intertwined flowers and sticks he'd weaved together over the years. Isaac's room was a transplanted library and spring meadow all in one. The closet, on the other hand, consisted of the only mess in Isaac's life. While he was meticulous about how he treated everything else, he wasn't much for laundry, and his clothes lay strewn on the floor of the closet. He rummaged through the pile looking for his dress pants and shirt, but to no avail.

As he flung garments from one side of his closet to the other, he heard a knock at his doorway and smacked his head into the door jamb of the closet turning to see who it was. Cynthia smirked but tried to restrain herself when she asked, "Are you okay?"

"I'm fine. You frightened me is all," he replied, grasping his head in pain.

"Having trouble finding clothes for tonight?" she asked.

"Yes, I… What do you mean? You knew I was going to the tavern tonight?" Isaac asked. His mother shrugged, indicating she knew. He continued, "*I* didn't know I was going anywhere tonight."

She nodded and sat on his bed, holding clothes in her hand. "I took the liberty of washing your pants and shirt so you'd have something to wear."

"Thank you. I appreciate that."

"You should go out and socialize, Isaac. You spend enough time with your family."

He walked over to her and took the clothes. "Thank you."

Isaac padded reluctantly across the town square, taking special note of the shops in the high-rent district and the types of wares they peddled. He didn't look at their trades with disdain, but rather a touch of envy. Perhaps if he pulled this project off correctly, he could afford a storefront as well and finally get both his business and his family off the ground.

He reached the front of the tavern and stopped to straighten up. Breathing in and out fully, he ran his hands through his hair and checked his coat and shirt to make sure they were aligned properly. It was closer to seven thirty than seven o'clock, but Isaac wasn't particularly concerned about punishment for his tardiness. He was more concerned he'd be taken advantage of for it, but something deep down told him that was probably for the best anyway.

Just as he reached for the door handle, the door flung open and a drunk man and woman burst from the hall, singing along the way. Isaac caught the door and held it open for them, laughing as he stepped inside. He watched them go, then focused his attention on the interior of the tavern. Almost instantly, his eyes were drawn to the piano where Hattie was banging away on the keys, singing loudly – along with the rest of the patrons – a tune he had never heard before. Her foot pounded on the floor and her hands danced gracefully across the keys. Her eyes shown brilliantly in the warm, foggy light of the tavern. Isaac couldn't take his eyes off her. He smiled with contentment at the beautiful woman at the piano, and his heart warmed when her eyes met his, a broad, excited smile forming on her face.

I could spend a lifetime in this moment, Isaac admitted to himself. There were so many thoughts and emotions assailing him in that instant, and all of them strange to him. He felt he could live 1,000 years and never feel this sensation again; it was such a rare palpitation. This must be the fuss everyone's been telling me about, he acknowledged, and started to move toward her.

Just as he did, an old, near-toothless man bumped into him and slung his arm around Isaac. "Don't you know this song, boy?!"

"As a matter of fact, I don't," Isaac grudgingly replied.

"You don't?!" the man barked. "Here, have some ale! That'll help ya learn it!" He forced his mug into Isaac's face. The young man took the mug, drank a swig, coughed, and handed it back to the old man, who laughed heartily. "Not much of a drinker, eh? Let me buy you one, young man."

"That'd be fine," Isaac responded with gratitude as the man guided him over to the bar. Along the way, Isaac took stock of the faces around him and noted how a number of them seemed to be distracted by his entrance to the establishment. He watched as some turned to others and whispered as if the news were that of a highly salacious nature. Granted, he'd never been to the tavern before, but didn't feel this fact was anything particularly sensational to gossip about. Still, he didn't begrudge them their moment of excitement.

Upon reaching the bar, the old man ordered two drinks. The barkeeper poured, taking special note of Isaac. "Well, I'm a might stunned to see you in here this evening, Mr. Truesdell. What brings you out on this lovely Friday night?"

"Well, Hattie…" Isaac then realized the barkeeper was the

owner, James Milford; Hattie's father. Knowing it was somewhat unorthodox for a woman to invite a man to social gatherings, Isaac chose his words carefully. "…uh, well, I came to see Hattie play piano."

"Don't you worry about me, Isaac. I know she invited you. You're both too old for me to be playing protective of her now. All I ask is that you treat her right, that's all," the man said, wiping up spilled beverage from the bar top.

Isaac held his glass tightly and exclaimed, "I assure you, sir, I have only the best of intentions." James smirked and nodded at Isaac, walking to the other end of the bar. Confused, Isaac asked the old man, "What did that mean?"

The old man, however, was staring into Isaac's glass. "He poured you a double… for free! I'm guessing that means he likes you."

"You think?"

"He never gives me extra," the old man said, turning back to the room. Isaac couldn't help but think it was probably because the man seemed to have enough of his own to drink without being given extra. But, seeing as how Isaac had never drank much himself, it was far from his mind to criticize anyone for overdoing it a little.

Isaac turned back to see Hattie at the piano, but she was no longer there. The song had ended and she was gone. He looked around and, when he couldn't find her, decided to move to an empty table in the corner of the tavern. Once he reached it, he realized there was a sign on it that read 'Reserved.' Hattie blocked his way as he started to turn around, saying, "It's reserved for you, sir. I've had a heck of a time keeping the vultures from stealing it, you know?"

"You didn't have to do that," Isaac said.

"No really, I did. This place gets crowded on Friday nights. If I hadn't, you'd have been stuck standing up all night. Why don't you take a seat?" She held her hand out, indicating one side of the table. Isaac graciously accepted and sat down. Hattie sat opposite him and folded her hands together on top of the table. "So, what finally made you decide to come and visit me?"

Isaac blushed and sipped his drink, starting to feel warm with timidity and the few drops of liquor he'd had. Finally, he said, "I just felt it was time I started engaging in something other than my work."

"Well, work is good. You shouldn't feel bad about doing work."

"I don't. No, it is good," Isaac replied.

"But beer is better," she continued, holding her mug up for Isaac to meet with his. Ignorantly, he fumbled for the grasp on his cup and smashed it up against hers, knocking some of the suds and liquid into her face. She laughed, grabbing her apron to dry herself.

Isaac was embarrassed. "I'm so sorry! I didn't mean to do that. Can I help?" he asked, rising from his seat and crossing to her side of the table.

"Not unless you've got a towel in that shirt of yours," she cracked, and went about drying herself off. Isaac awkwardly found his way back to his side of the table and plopped back in the seat. His shoulders slumped and he stuck his face near his drink, shaking his head disappointedly at himself.

"Don't worry about it. It wouldn't be a day of work if I didn't have booze spilled on me at some point."

Isaac's proper upbringing caused him to initially blush at this, but he realized it was likely just an occupational hazard, and an amusing one at that. He looked back at her, catching her eyes as she looked up from her apron. "Well, I'm glad you're not upset."

"Quite the contrary, Isaac. You always seem too uptight and controlled. It's nice to see you out of your element," she replied.

"Really? I imagine it's rather like…" he stumbled, unable to come up with the requisite simile. "…like something paradoxical, I guess."

"Like a fish out of water?" Hattie finished for him.

He nodded and smiled at her. "That would be the thing. I'm not very good at this."

She grinned, her bright green eyes glinting devilishly. "Great! Let's keep it that way." She forced his drink to the table, grabbed his hand, and pulled him to the dance floor just as the music picked up. The piano player was pounding out a rousing tune, now joined by a guitar player and fiddle player. Isaac's eyes nearly popped out of his face as the horror of public dancing confronted him. Hattie dragged him to the middle of the floor where several other couples were already kicking up their heels. "You know how to dance a reel, right?" she asked.

"Heavens, no!" Isaac shouted back at her, the noise in the tavern almost deafening in comparison to the usual aural dissonance produced by his workshop.

"Excellent. Let's get started then. Put your right hand here," she said, placing his right hand on her hip. "Take my right hand up here." She put her hand in the air for him. "And just do your best not to step on my feet!"

Instinctively, Isaac immediately looked down to their feet. "Okay…"

She winced for a moment, adding, "Oh, I forgot. One more thing. Do all that, while keeping your eyes up here." Hattie released his left hand, gently touching the bottom of his chin and pointing at her eyes.

Isaac gulped hard. "No promises."

Predictably, the first dance was a disaster. Not only did Isaac step on her feet, but he nearly knocked one of the other couples over. He apologized profusely and struggled to concentrate on the task at hand. The song mercifully ended, and Isaac tried to walk back to the table. But Hattie grabbed his hand, restrained him, and ordered the band to play another tune, faster. Isaac sighed and rolled his eyes. Hattie assured him, "Alright. This time, forget everything I told you and just try to have fun. Just go with the music." Isaac breathed, looked down at his disobedient feet and nodded reluctantly. "You got it?" she asked.

He breathed deeply and answered, "I'll give it my best."

"Here we go!" the pianist shouted and counted off the next tune. Initially, the second experience was as bad as the first. However, as Isaac reminded himself to breathe and tried not to focus too much on the details, he began to let go. As the moments clicked by, he started to feel the music, and even led for a while, Hattie jubilantly following. By the time the song ended, the pair garnered applause from the rest of the patrons, and they bowed sheepishly before heading back to their seats.

Hattie fell into her chair exclaiming, "That was fantastic! What do you mean you can't dance?"

"I can't," Isaac asserted.

"Something tells me you're fibbing, Mr. Truesdell."

Isaac shook his head inexplicably. "I'm not. That's the first time I've ever done that. You said that's a reel?"

Ignoring his question, she remained dubious about his prior experience. "Well, I am astonished. I've got to get you out dancing more often, sir."

He smiled and took another drink from his glass. She glared playfully at him over the rim of her mug before she took a drink of her own. They sat in silence for a while. Isaac looked around the room at all the sights, sounds, liquor, and life. He tried to catalog it all, attempting to comprehend how it all worked together, everything in harmony resulting in the emotion he was feeling. The sense of community, joy, and warmth all rolled into one was something he'd never experienced in this way. Hattie's presence made it all the more visceral for him. Isaac was new to these emotions, but he wasn't oblivious to them. He knew the thoughts and emotions that rushed through his mind when he looked at her were specific to her and no one else. Just like the thoughts and feelings he experienced from drinking the liquor were isolated to the intake of the liquor alone. It was the combination of the factors weaving a tapestry of feeling and wellness that now absorbed him.

Hattie cocked her head curiously. "You okay, Isaac?"

Without releasing his curious focus on the moment, he replied, "I should have done this ten years ago."

"I was too young for you to dance with ten years ago," she jibed quickly.

He exhaled gratefully. "Then I'm glad I waited." For the first time, he looked confidently into her eyes, forcing her out of her position of authority in their strange duo.

Taken aback, she put her mug back on the table, asking, "Do you mean that?"

He nodded. "Yes, I do."

Suddenly like a shy schoolgirl, Hattie flushed and hid behind her mug, eventually revealing herself by saying, "Why sir, I think you made a girl blush."

Isaac swiftly returned to form. "I'm sorry, should I not have said that."

"Stop apologizing. Just tell me you're happy to be here."

"I *am* happy to be here. I'm more happy that it's you who invited me."

They locked eyes, but this time neither of them broke it off. For the rest of the evening, in between Hattie's duties of serving rounds at the bar, she and Isaac danced, talked, and flirted as if there were no other people in the building. Numerous townsfolk took special note of the infatuated couple, smiling and nudging each other when Hattie and Isaac danced or made eyes at each other. Isaac's mysterious bachelorhood had been a topic of gossip for years, and the patrons at the tavern that night felt they'd been treated to one of the most adorable bits of gossip the town had seen for quite some time.

Hours passed and Isaac found himself leaning against the piano while the man playing banged away. Hattie was finishing her duties cleaning up the bar, and she caught his eye while picking up the last glasses at the table near the door. She said, "You don't have to walk me home, you know. I do this every week."

"No, I'd like to," Isaac admitted, slightly inebriated but not completely drunk. The piano player winked at him and smiled, still playing away.

"I'm not saying I'll turn it down. I just want you to know you don't have to."

"I want to," he assured her.

Hattie put the last of the glasses behind the bar, saving the washing for the next morning. She removed her apron and placed it on the counter. "Alright, Charlie, you can rest for the night. I'm going to close up here."

Charlie, the piano player, finished the measure he was playing, closed the lid to the piano keys and stood up, clapping Isaac on the shoulder. "You're a good, young fella. You keep this lady safe on the way home, okay?"

"Rest assured," Isaac replied. Charlie nodded and moved past him out the door. Hattie crossed the dance floor to Isaac. "Thank you very much for inviting me. I think this is the most fun I've had in…" Suddenly, he couldn't recall anything to compare it to. "Ever."

Hattie laughed a full, sensual laugh, her cheeks flushed and her eyes smoky with anticipation. She no longer looked at the seemingly innocent man in front of her with the same caution with which she had regarded him hours before. He was still a mystery to her, but he wasn't the teetotaling puritan she'd initially taken him for. And Isaac was thinking the exact same thing about himself. He'd discovered things he didn't know were there and was acutely aware that while the evening had been a monumental discovery for him, Hattie was fully aware of who she was. Isaac released his inhibitions and proper mentality, allowing himself a brief moment to look her up and down, returning to her eyes. She did nothing to dissuade him.

Finally, Hattie broke the silence. "Do you like me, Isaac?"

"Oh, certainly… Honestly, I don't know the word for how I feel about you, Hattie. I'm a fool when it comes to women, er… a woman." She giggled at his error, allowing him room to continue. "But I think I'd like to know more about you."

She moved up close to Isaac, the space between them now almost closed. "I'll have to consider that then," she said.

Isaac breathed in and out cautiously, as if the air he was breathing spoke to him. He placed his hand on her waist, closed the remaining gap between them, and smiled. "I wasn't asking." He bent down to her upturned face and kissed her gently on the lips.

Hattie was not the type of woman to pretend to be something she wasn't. Rather than pushing him away in defense of her maidenhood, she reached her hand around the back of his head and pulled him down toward her. Isaac's eyes popped open momentarily in shock at Hattie's enthusiasm. The air that had informed him to do it in the first place hadn't informed him how she might respond. They kissed passionately, nearly falling into the piano until the front door of the tavern opened behind them. Hattie stood up straight and faced the door. Isaac leaned on the top of the piano, attempting to look casual.

Charlie and one of the local stable boys leaned in through the door, clearly having seen some of what just occurred. "Uh… well, we're heading out now. Are you sure you don't want a lift? We're heading in the direction of your father's house, Hattie."

"No, I'm fine. I'll be fine," she assured them, her eyes wandering suspiciously from Isaac to the two men at the door. "Yes, I think… Yes, Isaac will walk me home. Won't you, Isaac?"

Isaac turned from the men to Hattie. "Oh, certainly! Yes. Absolutely, I'll walk you home," he rambled, nearly eliciting an elbow jab from her.

Charlie and the stable boy looked at each other conspiratorially. As he left, Charlie said, "Well, we'll just be off then." The boy on the other hand stayed, as if Isaac and Hattie might continue even with him there. They smiled at the boy who raised his eyebrows in response. Charlie reentered, smashed the boy on his head with his hat, and pulled him along. The door creaked shut, the anticipation of its closing flustering the two remaining inhabitants. The second the door closed, they turned to each other and continued the fall onto the piano they'd begun moments before.

Isaac felt his hands wandering along Hattie's back as they kissed. He surveyed her shape, a slender but strong frame of ribs protected by supple, shapely flesh and loosely bound by a bar maid's attire. As they kissed, he could taste the air emanating from her lungs, and in doing so, could very nearly see her heart beat in his mind. Its pace quickened almost in concert with his own. Hattie's hands were fumbling for the piano and its bench so they didn't fall on the floor. She positioned herself on top of him, grabbing his head with both hands and running them through his hair. His skin was rough, barely shaven, and his hair was coarse and thick.

Suddenly, Isaac felt a pang of inappropriateness and grabbed Hattie's shoulders, holding her away from him. "Wait, wait, wait!"

"What?! What's the matter?" Hattie asked, out of breath.

"Have you ever done this before?" Isaac asked, partly because he hadn't and partly out of fear and hesitation.

"Well no, I haven't. Have you?" She asked.

Isaac shook his head, indicating he hadn't. "Should we be doing this?"

"Shouldn't we be?" she asked, their mutual confusion palpable.

When neither had an answer, they shrugged and picked up where they had left off. The sensation of her skin excited him in ways he'd never imagined, and the energy between them heightened exponentially. He placed his fingers between her ribs, studying her skin and her breathing.

Never for a moment did they restrain each other or feel it was anything to be ashamed of. They were innocent. Only their carnal instincts guided them. A trail of clothing led from the piano to the table: a corset, a shirt, a blouse, a skirt, as well as a petticoat or two, pants, hose, and shoes. She was sitting on top of him, her legs around him as Isaac reached into Hattie's hair and removed her hair clip, their last remaining accessory, and placed it carefully on the chair next to the table.

After a moment of serenity had passed between them, Hattie nodded as if to ask, "Are you with me?" Isaac responded by nodding his head. And with that, she thrust herself forward.

***

They laughed breathlessly afterward, lying next to each other on the table, their sweat-steeped bodies glowing in the early morning lamplight. Hattie lay on her back gazing up at the ceiling, her chest raising and lowering with each breath. Isaac lay on his side next to her, watching her body move.

He asked, "Do you think that's the way it's supposed to be?"

Laughing heartily, she shook her head. "I have no idea! But if it isn't…" She looked at Isaac, then continued, "…I'm interested to learn what *is*." They laughed together, their breath synchronized in the moment they were sharing.

Thoughts raced through Hattie's head. While Isaac examined their base humanity, Hattie analyzed what occurred in a more social sense. True, she didn't have any misgivings about making love to Isaac, but she had just lost her maidenhood and knew there would be implications. Even though she was a generally forward individual, she still had reservations about what they needed to discuss next. In a very serious tone, Hattie slowed her breathing and confessed, "Isaac, I love you."

Isaac blinked, locking the moment in his memory as if it were a photograph. He'd see it over and over in his head for decades afterward. The light from a nearby lamp glistened in Hattie's brilliant green eyes. Her supple, naked body lay supine on the table, one knee bent toward the heavens. Her left hand was draped lazily across her stomach, and tousled, dark-brown hair framed the vulnerable, loving expression on her face. He smiled from deep within his soul. The feeling he'd been missing all those years surfaced at that moment. "And I love you, Hattie." He leaned over, bent his face to hers, and they kissed.

***

After a sufficiently suspicious amount of time passed without returning home, Isaac and Hattie decided it was time to dress and finish closing up the tavern. The walk was warm as midsummer had just passed and the humidity of June was settling in on the Delaware landscape. Hand in hand, they joked along the way, sharing stories of their childhood and more recent stories of local events, with wild suppositions of their future together. This last part continued with no filter or boundaries whatsoever. Their ideals, loves, hopes, and fears were in perfect harmony with one another. By the time they reached Hattie's father's house, Isaac's proposition was all but a foregone conclusion.

"Hattie, I have to go to Washington next month, but when I get back..." he hesitated shyly.

Giddy with anticipation, she crushed his hands in hers. "Yes?"

"I wonder if..." he struggled with how to word it, as he hadn't considered the event ever occurring, let alone that night. "Hattie, I want you to be my wife, and I wonder if you wouldn't be amenable to... well, to having the event after I get back from Washington." She was standing on the first step of her father's porch, waves of excitement emanating from her – and three family members crammed stealthily in the upstairs window. Isaac's expression was pure, innocent, and completely vulnerable.

"Yes!" she shouted, jumping on his torso and wrapping her arms around his head. He held her in his arms and kissed her. Simultaneously, two of the upstairs faces were ushered away from the window. The third remained, gazing on with considerable appreciation for the event.

The two lovers again expressed their love for one another, and Isaac placed her back on the bottom step just as the front door opened. James stepped slowly out, tapping his pipe on the railing before stuffing some tobacco into it. "It's nice out tonight, isn't it?"

"Yes!" Hattie exclaimed, holding Isaac's hand.

Full of trepidation, Isaac's response was somewhat more measured. He replied, "It's a wonderful night, indeed."

"You're a good man for walking my daughter home, Isaac. Thank you." James lit the pipe.

"Well, sir…" Isaac started.

"Call me James, Isaac," James muttered automatically.

Isaac continued. "I'd like your permission to marry your daughter, James."

James locked eyes with Isaac. "That's a bit sudden."

Having anticipated that James might protest, Isaac had prepared an explanation. "Well, sir, I…"

"No, no! It's okay! Just sudden, that's all… Well, of course you can, boy! Welcome to the family." James lumbered down the steps toward Isaac, grasping his hand in a firm handshake and smiling broadly.

Isaac replied excitedly. "Thank you!"

After striking their enthusiastic accord, they parted for the evening and Isaac ran all the way home. He didn't want to lose the feeling he'd had all night and how it had affected his senses. As he neared home, a strange sensation came over him, and he ran right past the house into the shop. Closing the door behind him, he moved to the armoire, grabbed a chisel out of the drawer and sat down at his lathe.

This time, he forced the pedal faster than he'd turned it before, spinning the bowl at speeds he'd never worked with. Gently, he laid the chisel against the maple and began to carve. There was no burr, no tear, no anger, and no fear. As the wood turned on the lathe, he could almost see its inner workings. The piece had been transported from Canada along with some barrels of liquor. The men transporting the liquor had used the piece as a doorstop, and as a step to climb in and out of the wagon. Where this information was coming from, or how Isaac was able to obtain it, he didn't know and explained it away as a logical supposition. Still more information came as he turned, however. The cold, Canadian climate had given the tree numerous winters of hard, slow growth that made the wood much harder than the pieces he was used to working on in Delaware.

He stood up from his stool and kicked it away from him, giving him more leverage and allowing him to push the lathe even faster. The whole room began to glow as he focused on the piece, and the inside of the wood blazed from within. Again, Isaac's logic explained it as an effect of the liquor and the now overwhelming sense of love he felt for Hattie. But, just as that reasoning moved through his mind, the bowl lit up as if a great light were coming from it. Isaac stepped back, frightened, and allowed the lathe to slow down. He felt warmth in his hand, and when he looked down saw the chisel glowing. Instantly, the history of the wooden handle rushed through his brain; the tree, the summers and winters, the logger who had felled it. Then the history of the metal revealed itself to him, from the worker, to the forge, and then back to the molten earth that curdled and bubbled from below, cooling to release a vein of pure iron.

It was the wrong chisel. Despite the seemingly brilliant work he'd just been doing, Isaac knew there was a greater level of detail he could attain. He moved back to the armoire to retrieve the correct chisel, then returned to the lathe. This time, he welcomed the newfound connection to his surroundings with his breathing. He inhaled slowly, taking in the smells, the night sounds, the view of his shop. Then he exhaled and the room glowed, the bowl on the lathe shining like a beacon. He pushed the pedal and started turning the lathe, the rope gliding back and forth as fast as physics would allow, and laid the chisel to the bowl. From within the wood, the light guided his every cut until it was finished.

Isaac allowed the lathe to finish spinning and gazed in wonder at the meticulously brilliant piece of work he had just completed. At that moment, the back door of the shop opened slowly and Cynthia walked through. She said nothing, but walked toward Isaac with a lantern. Strangely, her son was standing in an almost completely dark shop, his shirt on the work bench next to him with the lathe spinning. He turned to her and they caught eyes, hers seeming to ask, "Are you okay?"

Isaac was breathless, heaving with excitement and love, and replied, "Mother, I'm getting married!" In response, she put down the lantern and threw her arms around him. Isaac had found what was missing in his life.

Chapter Four

Billowing, black smoke ascended through the air, a crooked smudge on the Detroit skyline. Firefighters drizzled the last bits of water and chemical retardant on the smoldering ruins of a plastic toy factory on the near west side. All the regular news channels were onsite performing their cursory live shots and interviews, attempting to feed the public hunger for news with guts and gore. While the scene appeared akin to the usual factory fire in which an overnight blaze stemmed from faulty wiring or machinery left on after close, the truth was very different.

This fire involved the head of a toy manufacturing company who'd been missing for a number of days. As firefighters battled the blaze in the early hours of that January morning, they discovered the charred remains of the man police had been searching for. He was sitting on a chair, unmoved by the blaze that consumed him. This was of particular interest to not only the police but the half dozen news crews that clogged the south entrance of the factory parking lot.

Human rights violations, unfair labor practices, and anti-union bid selections had plagued the owner and the city for some time. It was a surprise to precisely no one – save the man's insular and utterly clueless family – that he was both abducted and murdered. The real curiosity surrounding the fire was why the factory had been burned down. If the problem was the man and the culprits were punishing him for his elitist treatment of regular working people, why would they burn down the factory those people worked in? The news crews were frenzied to catch the first clue that would allow them to break the story. For now, though, they would have to settle for a run-of-the-mill factory fire and a dead, charcoaled scrooge.

Eight a.m. rolled around, and the crews began to pack up their gear. Channel 3 representative Sarah Dempsey was helping her camera man load the equipment into the back of their truck when a low-level beat cop approached her. She acknowledged him briefly, then went back to handing equipment to her camera man.

"How ya doing?" she asked him, annoyed at the lack of a story but also not wanting to perturb a possible source. The cop shrugged his shoulders against the cold and looked around to see if anyone else could hear him. Curious, Sarah looked around for a moment as well, then back at the beat cop. "You all right, officer?"

Once he was confident no one else could hear him, he leaned in toward her and said, "Cap says he wants to see you."

"Me?" she asked. The cop nodded and she looked around suspiciously. "Just me?"

"That's what he said, Ms. Dempsey."

She took a measured pause, then removed her glove and stuck out her hand. "Sarah. Call me Sarah, officer…"

He smiled a weak smile at getting attention from a TV personality and took her hand. "Frank. I'm Frank Trumble."

"Well Officer Trumble, you lead the way." The two set off across the parking lot, out of sight of the other news crews and left her camera man behind.

Sarah's annoyance only mildly abated at this personal invitation. She'd had the ear of Captain Long for a number of years until she reported a story about the Internal Affairs department's crackdown on police corruption several months earlier. Since that time, the captain had shied away from her. It was an understandable and predictable response to her story, but she was annoyed nonetheless. Walking across that parking lot she ran her first few phrases in her head over and over again, all the while thinking of how she'd like to smack him for ruining her clout among her on-the-spot competition. If this encounter went well, it could erase months of unreturned phone calls and general cold-shouldering from the Detroit Police Department. On the other hand, a bad encounter could leave her on the outs for the rest of her career.

Sarah and Officer Trumble arrived at a loading dock at the back of the factory, the floor of which ended in a rubberized bumper four feet off the ground. Captain Long, a gruff, silver-haired man in his sixties, and two out-of-place men in trench coats loomed over them. A large cigar protruded from the captain's weathered, yellow teeth and a broad smile stretched across his face as he barked, "How ya doin' Sarah?!"

"I don't see any stairs, Captain." She looked up at him, her eyes squinting into the light flowing through a fresh hole in the roof.

His only reply was, "Nope."

"Ah, I see. You just wanna watch my skirt fly up over my head when I try to climb up?"

"Sure, why not." The smile escaped Long's face as he turned to Trumble, shouting, "Well, Christ's sake, Trumble, get your thumb out of your ass and help the little lady up!"

Officer Trumble jumped into action uttering, "Sorry, sir... ma'am," and rushed to give Sarah a hand. He knelt down, letting her step on his knee and the captain and one of the other men reached out to take her hands.

Sarah took the captain's hand with her left hand and reached up for the other man with her right. As she took the man's hand, she instantly identified something horribly amiss with his appendage. As they pulled her up onto the loading dock, she focused on what she felt, trying hard not to stare at it. There was clearly a missing finger, but it was more than that. The texture of his hand seemed more like a leather football than skin. She glanced up to the man's casually smiling face, letting her eyes drift down to his neck, there spying what she was looking for. He was a burn victim who'd been through his share of trouble. The man appeared to be in his late seventies, but his strong grip and broad frame indicated he was still highly active. Her feet connected with the soot-covered concrete floor of the factory and she nodded at the men. "Thank you, gentlemen."

"Don't mention it," Long hoarsely grumbled as he stuck the cigar back into his mouth.

An uncomfortable silence settled over them. Sarah took stock of the men in front of her. The captain seemed somewhat less cordial than his usual self, though she assumed this was as a result of her story about the Internal Affairs issues. The unnamed old man seemed almost like he wanted something from her. She scanned her surroundings and assessed the third man as well, an unremarkable character in his thirties who was carrying a notepad and pen. The silence was momentarily interrupted by Officer Trumble's failed attempts to scale the loading dock entry. No one laughed, but rather just stared until he finally swung one leg up and crawled up onto the floor on his stomach, eventually rising to his feet. He brushed himself off and smiled sheepishly at Sarah who cordially returned the expression.

Long shook his head and muttered, "All right. Let's get on with this, shall we?" They began walking through the factory.

Sarah nodded. "I'm curious, Captain. To what do I owe this

pleasure."

"No pleasure. Just a corpse. Before we get too far, I need to do some introductions. Sarah, these are Special Agents Brad Gilson and Mike Kirkpatrick from the FBI." The three nodded their pleasantries and shook hands, Sarah once again paying special attention to Mike's deformity. Captain Long continued. "Now, Mike, here has been with the bureau since the Hoover days. He works for their Special Investigations Department."

Sarah nodded to him again. "Nice to meet you, Agent Kirkpatrick. I assume you're here as a result of the abduction?"

Mike shook his head and began to speak, Sarah taking particular note of his weathered, subtle southern accent. "It's just Mike. Actually, no, we let the local branch work out the details on the abduction. Undoubtedly, we'll be working very closely with them, but that's not why I'm here."

Sarah replied, "Okay. So why are you here?"

"Well, Ms. Dempsey, we get calls to all sorts of crimes and events. Brad and I assess the nature of the crime and delegate it to the appropriate department of the bureau. I started doing this particular job back in the late '70s when Hoover was gone and folks started asking lots of questions about where the money was going. This way, instead of three different departments investigating a case, we come in and assign the case to a specific department, allowing them appropriate cross-departmental resources," Mike explained.

"So, you've seen a bit of everything, then?"

Captain Long cut in. "Sorry to interrupt, but now that you folks are headed in the right direction, I'm going back to my coffee. You all right?"

Mike nodded, "We'll be fine, Captain. Thank you."

Long added, "And Sarah, you take care of that man. He asked

for you specifically, okay?"

"Most certainly, Captain." She glared after him as she realized he still had no intention of working with her, but rather was facilitating someone else's request. She turned back to Mike to find him smiling kindly at her, clearly having a good idea of what was going on between her and the captain. She averted her eyes momentarily, then returned them to him asking, "That's a pretty subtle accent you have, Mike. Are you originally from Texas?"

"It's pretty hard to tell after all these years away, but that's not a bad ear. I'm actually from Oklahoma," he responded.

She cocked her head and smiled at him. "I'm originally from Oklahoma. Strange that we should meet up here in Detroit. Small world."

"That it is. Actually, that's part of the reason I wanted to talk to you. Did you know the man over there?" he questioned, pointing to a chair behind her.

She turned to view what he was pointing at and instantly put her hand over her mouth as she gasped. In the chair sat the charred remains of the cruel millionaire she and the other reporters had been following for the better part of a week, or longer depending on their involvement in the investigation surrounding his corrupttion charges. The skin was nearly melted off his bones, the clothes were all but incinerated, and some of his skull was visible through the acutely charred remains of the man's scalp. Initial shock wearing off, her journalist instincts took over and she carefully catalogued the details of the scene. The body was not restrained in any way; the arms rested casually on the chair and the feet lay flat on the floor. There had been no struggle at all, even though the body was so badly burned the only smell emanating from it was that of the charcoal it had become. A very journalist-like question popped into her head. Without taking her eyes off the gruesome scene, she asked, "How do you know it's him?"

Holding up a wallet Mike replied, "Whoever did this left his wallet sitting ten feet from him and managed to keep the fire from burning it. The lab will provide a positive ID by the end of the day. I notice you haven't answered my question though, Ms. Dempsey."

"Please, it's Sarah," she quickly asserted.

"Well, Sarah, do you know this man?"

She turned to the old man. "I'm a reporter. I do criminal investigating. There are plenty of us who at least had a general knowledge of who he was, but I've never met him personally, no."

Mike nodded as if that was the answer he expected and continued. "Don't worry, you're not a suspect, Sarah."

"So, I'm not part of your investigation?" she carefully prodded.

"In a way, you are, but not as a suspect or even a person of interest. Do you have a few minutes for a story, Sarah?" Mike asked.

She pulled her cell phone out of her pocket, the touchpad flashing impatiently with four unread messages. Placing it back in her pocket, she confidently answered, "Absolutely."

Mike began walking, motioning for Brad to remain a distance behind, and they slowly moved away from the body. "While we essentially act as a delegation group for the bureau, there are a number of cases we investigate directly. I am personally invested in this particular type of incident."

"Why's that?" Sarah was becoming more and more curious.

"Well, there are some specific, unique variables at work here. You've probably already noticed that there are no signs of a struggle. Also, there's the wallet, conveniently placed where we couldn't help but find it. It's obviously a murder, and that's a piece of the story you're getting that no one else will. But, there's much more." After a breath, he stopped in his tracks and turned to face her, suddenly very serious. She returned his gaze with rapt attention. "There's no fuel or spark for this fire, Sarah. Hot as it was, the fire department had little trouble putting it out. Not only that, but it started right there, in that chair."

"What, gasoline? Kerosene?" she queried.

"As I said, there was no fuel at all. We have a location for the source of the fire, but no identifiable source."

"How is that possible?"

Mike smiled and shrugged his shoulders. "I wish I could tell you. Unfortunately, that's something you'll never be able to report."

"Why not?" she asked indignantly.

"Isn't it obvious? There won't be any follow up to that information and you'd lose credibility as a journalist reporting a ghost story like that. Do you really want to go on the air with that?" Mike replied.

Sarah looked around trying to gauge her response, but could come up with nothing clever. "Then why did you tell me about it?"

"Because I think you have a direct connection to the person who did it."

She put her hands in her pockets defensively and responded, "How the hell would I know anyone responsible for something like this?"

"I didn't say you knew them, Sarah."

"Special Agent Kirkpatrick..." she started.

"Call me Mike."

She continued, "Can we cut the crap, Mike?"

"I like your style, Sarah. Your mother was an orphan, was she not?" Mike prodded.

"This is cutting through the crap?"

"I've already given you a pretty big scoop on this story.

Indulge me for a moment, eh?"

She assessed the situation for a moment before doing so. "Yes, she was."

"And you're from Oklahoma?"

"Yeah. I was born in Norman, Oklahoma; June 21, 1974. But that's all information you already have, I'm sure." He merely raised an eyebrow, begging her to continue. "Fine. My mother was orphaned when her father and brothers were burned up in a fire, and her sister disappeared a few months later. She was raised by the neighbor family, the Dempseys."

"And did you ever hear about the fire at the jailhouse about the time your aunt disappeared?" Mike questioned.

Sarah paused, recognizing the familiar direction of the story. "I have."

"And you're aware that your estranged aunt is said to have been at that fire, yes?"

"I'm aware of a sketchy police report as well as a story about her having been kidnapped and showing up in Boston shortly thereafter. She had nothing to do with that fire."

"Are you sure of that?"

Sarah stepped back. "Where do you get off? You bring me in here, give me information on a story I can't possibly report, and start making accusations about a family member I've never met? Exactly why am I here again?"

"Sarah…"

"It's Ms. Dempsey, Mike."

"I know this may seem a little bizarre, but I'm not falsely accusing anyone. I'm telling you what happened. Your aunt was in the jail that night of the fire in 1958," he asserted, removing his hand from his pocket and holding up the mangled piece of flesh. "I know because I was there. I looked into her eyes and watched her start it, and I've been lookin' for her ever since. That's why I investigate any fire where local authorities can't find a source. Because, in the jail that night, there was no earthly source. She started that fire with nothing but her own will."

Sarah pulled out her phone and checked the time, angrily blurting, "This is absurd."

"It's the truth," he pleaded with her.

"Are you suggesting a seventy-year-old woman set this asshole on fire with her will?" She sounded out *will* in a ridiculous, contorted fashion to mock the agent.

Mike shrugged, exasperated. "I have no idea how, but I assure you that's what happened here."

"And I assure you, senility is an indication it's time to retire, Mike. I'm sure you've done great service for the bureau over the years, but I think it's time you retired your badge." With that, she turned and started back toward the loading dock.

Mike chased after her. "Ms. Dempsey, you've got to listen to me. I don't hold you or your mother responsible for any of this. I never even intended to approach you about this at all, but when she made this ridiculous display right in your backyard, I couldn't pass up the opportunity to talk to you. I had to see if she'd made some kind of contact with you."

She stopped cold and glared at him. "Contact?! Are you charging me with aiding and abetting now? 'Cause you better come up with some evidence, buster."

"What? No, it's nothing like that. I just want to know. A 'yes' or 'no' would suffice and you have my word I won't pursue it as a legal subject."

She'd gained the upper hand. Taking a moment to look over the now agitated old man in front of her, she made no pretense of evaluating the scars framing his weathered face. Mike felt it was only fair to allow her some time to process all she'd just taken in.

Finally, she spoke. "Look, Mike, I can tell you've been through quite an ordeal, and based on what you've told me, this fire bears many of the same marks as the one you were in. How badly were you burned?"

"Third degree over sixty percent of my body and first or second degree over the rest. I haven't grown hair on top of my head for fifty years," he calmly replied.

"I can only imagine the pain you must have gone through. I've investigated my share of burn victims over the last ten years, and I know there's no injury a person would rather avoid."

He nodded. "I appreciate that, ma'am."

"But you need to understand my position. My childhood wasn't exactly normal. My mother was... affected. Do you understand what it means to me – the person who sends nearly half of her take-home back to Oklahoma for her mother's care – when you say the memories her mother struggles with are not of a loving sister who protected her through all of the terrible things that happened, but are rather of an arsonist and a murderer? And, that that woman is still out there killing people? At seventy?" Sarah threw her hands up and started back toward the loading dock.

"I wasn't the only one who survived that fire," Mike blurted quickly and started after her. "There were two other men who identified her."

She wheeled around, stopping him dead in his tracks. "Oh yeah? Then why wasn't her name in the paper as being linked to the fire?"

Acknowledging Sarah's growing anger, Mike kept his distance. "Because her arrest wasn't related to the fire and no one could figure out how she started it. It would have made the police department look ridiculous. They contacted the FBI and claimed she'd been abducted so they could try to hunt her down and get answers."

Sarah took a step toward him, and he and Brad took a step back. "Okay, so what was she arrested for?"

"What your mother told you about that was true. There was a series of bizarre deaths at the Catholic school they attended. Your aunt was identified at the scene of one of the deaths with blood on her. The coroner's office later declared that the deaths were all self-inflicted and her record was cleared."

Sarah's anger abated slightly and she backed off, saying, "That's right. But I bet you think my aunt killed those teachers, don't you?" He nodded uncomfortably, not wanting to antagonize her again. She shook her head and took another step toward him. "I understand that these cases may be somewhat personal to you, and I'm sorry if I got angry. But I have to tell you, I don't have much to offer. I never met my aunt. My mother would get post-cards from her every couple of years, but they're all in Oklahoma. I would hope that you wouldn't bother my mother about those."

Mike shook his head. "We ruled your mother out as a witness to any of that many years ago. After all, she was only six years old, and even if she did remember it, the testimony wouldn't have held up in front of a grand jury. I can promise you she won't be bothered."

Sarah looked toward the entrance, took a deep breath and said, "Well, what can I do for you, then?"

Mike turned back to Brad and nodded, and Brad went to warm up the car. "How about you let me buy you lunch and just answer some very friendly questions?"

"They haven't been very friendly so far, Mike."

"Fair enough. I promise they'll be friendlier, Ms. Dempsey," Mike assured her.

She sighed. "Oh, shit. You can call me Sarah."

Mike nodded his head, chuckling. "I think for now I'll stay on the safe side and call you Ms. Dempsey." She relented as Mike motioned for her to follow Brad out of the building toward the car.

She called her camera man to let him know he could leave, and then her studio to let them know she wouldn't be back for a while. Sarah and the two men rode together in the bureau cruiser to a local diner, discussing general pleasantries and trying to avoid the subject at hand until they could rest in a more formal setting. After a short drive, they stopped at a greasy spoon lodged in the shadow of the Edsel Ford Freeway. The two men looked around curiously, positive that the peeved journalist would drag them to the most expensive restaurant in town. Sarah's philosophy, however, was to drag them instead to the greasiest restaurant she could think of. Judging by Mike's age and Brad's uptightness, she figured her revenge would hit them about an hour after they dropped her off at the television station. And, she'd get some decent hash browns in the process.

As they entered the restaurant, most of the regular clientele stopped and took note of the strange-looking trio. A few of the patrons identified Sarah from her morning broadcast and whispered to the people sitting next to them. The waitress on duty recognized her from a previous visit and welcomed her by name. "Hi there, Sarah! I've got a table for you over here."

The three interlopers were seated in a booth in the corner of the restaurant that had a view of the freeway overpass, the fenced-in parking lot across the street, and a corner store with heavy iron bars guarding its windows. They ordered their beverages quickly then sat momentarily in silence. Brad spoke first in a loud tone, asserting, "Nice place." Sarah smiled as Brad caught the stares of several other patrons and shrunk into his corner.

Deciding to get down to business, Mike picked up from where they'd left off at the warehouse. "I suppose it would only be fair for me to fill in a few holes here."

"That would be great," Sarah said.

"I fought in Korea back in '52 and '53. Lost my right pinky in the process. After a couple years strugglin' for work, I landed in prison for a year."

Sarah leaned in, intrigued. "Hmm, what for?"

"Sadly, nothing particularly interesting. I got in a bar brawl with a guy who sorely deserved it. He also had better lawyers than I did. After I got out of prison, the fellas on the local police force in Tulsa offered to let me stay in the jail at night instead of having to sleep in the alley…"

Brad interrupted. "You never told me that."

Mike replied, "That's because I don't like you." He smiled as Brad sneered and returned to perusing the menu. Mike continued, "Then your aunt came along. There were four other guys in the drunk tank that night. After she was brought in, they died, and two of the officers and I got burned pretty badly. I spent a few months in the hospital, mostly dealing with pain management. I got bored, though, and started studying up on law enforcement. The force wouldn't take me on account of my right hand, but the FBI was taking all kinds of people back then as long as you bought into their methods."

"And what methods were those?" Sarah asked.

"Shoot first and ask questions later," Mike responded glibly. "At least it most easily breaks down that way. I had no problem with it at the outset, but by the time I did start to question things, the bureau had become more regulated, so any argument I could have made wouldn't have mattered. Anyhow, after a couple years workin' for the local bureau in Tulsa, the Kennedy thing happened.

The local branches were much more free with sharing information with each other after that, and I managed to pull a Telex from an office in Boston that reported a bizarre house fire in Concord, Massachusetts."

Sarah picked her hands up off the table while the waitress delivered their coffees. "Let me guess: there was no source for the fire?"

Mike nodded. "That's right."

Sarah smiled at the waitress. "I'll have the hashbrowns, the breakfast ham, and an orange juice. And can you bring some Tabasco sauce?"

The men both ordered the special, precisely as she'd hoped they would. Only then did she regret she wouldn't be around when they realized their error. Then again, she was also glad she wouldn't be around for it. Once they'd finished ordering, the waitress retreated to the kitchen.

"Tabasco sauce?" Mike questioned.

Sarah grinned and nodded. "I like my breakfast spicy. You should try it."

"Oh, no. I have tried it. It just surprises me that you would."

"I'm full of surprises."

"No doubt. Well, you're right. There was no initial cause for the fire. When I read the memo, I recognized the M.O. and asked my boss if I could go to Boston and check it out. There were a few more similar events in rapid succession on the East Coast, and my familiarity with them got me promoted to the headquarters at Langley. I've been working these types of cases ever since."

"Fascinating," Sarah interjected flatly. "So, do you ever get tired of working unsolvable cases? I mean, your contemporaries get to arrest people and put them in jail, but you just keep on investigating without having anyone to collar."

"I'd be a liar if I said it didn't weigh on me that I don't get too many arrests for these types of things. However, the reason these cases end up with me is because there's no plausible solution for them in the first place. They're low-percentage cases, and this is where they belong." He indicated Brad and himself. Brad flashed a sarcastic grin, then went back to sipping his coffee and drawing doodles in the notebook.

Sarah assessed the two men at that moment as something of a curiosity, but sadly pathetic as well. One was a man about her age who had found a comfortable dead-end job that didn't require results, just paperwork. The other character, however, was a man with great aspirations and an insurmountable goal, one that he was increasingly aware would likely go to the grave with him. She pitied the old man while simultaneously disregarding the young man. She asked them, "Do you ever get crap from other guys in the bureau about not arresting anyone?"

"Sure we do. Although we do get the occasional arrest. Obviously, the infrequency of it is part of what allows a man my age to keep the job. I think if we were chasing folks over chain-link fences every other day, I would have been taken off the task a long time ago."

Now Sarah's appetite was whet. "You have had arrests? Tell me about them."

"Different cases. Maybe some other time. For now, I'd like to focus on this case."

As they consumed their breakfast laced with cholesterol, salt, and Tabasco sauce, Mike explained the myriad events and crimes he'd investigated as a result of Sarah's aunt and the cross-country travels this had precipitated.

Brad excused himself at one point to head to the men's room, leaving Mike and Sarah alone. Mike watched Brad clear the corner and then leaned toward Sarah. "You don't look anything like your aunt, you know."

"I don't?" Indeed, Sarah was blonde and blue-eyed like her mother and deceased uncles had been. Sarah was surprised to learn that her aunt didn't fit the family mold.

"No, you don't. When I first started following your career, I half expected you to look just like her," he added.

"To be truthful, my mother did tell me once that she occasionally thought her sister may have had a different father," Sarah informed him, piquing the old man's interest. "My grandparents had had some trouble conceiving before Aunt Rebekah came along. My mom thought maybe her mother might have tried giving the whole thing a kick-start by... sleeping around, I guess. She didn't know much about my grandmother, but I get the idea she didn't have the best reputation where they were from."

Mike was highly intrigued. "Was that in Massachusetts as well?"

Sarah looked curiously at him, the wheels starting to turn. "You think Rebekah went back there to find him?"

Mike responded, but Sarah couldn't hear him. As soon as the words had escaped her lips, her eyes were drawn to a person standing across the street from the diner. She'd never seen anyone like this woman, particularly in the lower-income neighborhoods around Detroit. The woman seemed fixated on her, a pained look on her face. After a few moments, Mike interrupted himself to ask, "Sarah? You okay?"

Without taking her eyes off the young woman, Sarah responded, "There's a girl on the sidewalk across the street staring at us. She sure looks odd for this neighborhood."

Mike wheeled around in his seat. He didn't know what he expected to see, but it was certainly not what he saw. There, on the sidewalk, a mere sixty feet from where he sat, was the same woman he'd locked eyes with fifty-two years before. The dark hair, shock-green eyes, and pale flesh he remembered so vividly from the night of the fire stood there staring at him, completely unchanged by time. The only thing he could utter was, "My God," his jaw fully agape at the sight before him.

"What is it?" Sarah asked.

Without answering, Mike leapt to his feet, as best as a nearly eighty-year-old man could, and bolted to the entrance. Sarah looked around at the confused patrons in the diner, then rushed after him. The girl ran to the end of the block and turned the corner of the fence, dodging behind a row of bushes. Sarah followed Mike to the corner and crossed the street.

They were now on a wide boulevard, lined on either side by shops or fences, none of which appeared to offer openings or access without entering the buildings directly. Mike fumbled agedly for his sidearm. "You go on that side and look in the fronts of those buildings. See if you can see her."

Sarah allowed herself to get caught up in the moment and crossed to the other side of the street. By this time, Brad had run out of the diner after them and now led chase ahead of Sarah down the east side of the street while Mike checked out the buildings on the west.

When they reached the next street, the chase all but ended. They were now on a bustling, business corridor in which a person could have disappeared into any of one hundred or more locations. Brad and Sarah returned to the west side of the street where Mike was gasping for air and cursing.

"What was that about?" Brad asked.

Mike picked up his head, keeping his hands on his knees. "That was her."

Brad looked up and down the street, putting his hands on his head in frustration as he realized they'd missed out on a potential collar.

"Who? That was her, who?" Sarah asked, bewildered.

Brad shot a warning glance at Mike, who nodded and continued anyway. "Ms. Dempsey, that was your Aunt Rebekah."

As the two men stood on the sidewalk gasping for air in the Michigan winter, Sarah stopped huffing. She'd caught all the oxygen she needed and all of a sudden felt like punching someone. Instead, she stepped into the street and hastily crossed it, nearly getting hit by several unsuspecting motorists. Brad shouted after her to be careful but she didn't hear him. Mike grabbed his arm to let her go and waited for the light to change. They then embarked across the street after Sarah, who by then was making her way toward the city, watching behind her for a cab or bus along the way.

Sarah stomped down the sidewalk somewhat angry, but also quite frustrated with herself. Multiple times she even shook her head and laughed at her own foolishness. What kind of ridiculous nonsense have I been listening to? she thought. For almost an hour she'd been captive audience to two men who had clearly lost their way in the world. While her view of Brad hadn't exactly changed, her concept of Mike had become that of utter delusion. He'd been chasing a ghost for fifty years, steadfast in the belief that the random pictures he must have seen of some mystery woman were of her aunt. Even through the passage of time, all the stories of Rebekah's associations with known criminals and practitioners of dark arts were just hocus pocus spun by a man who couldn't deal with the demons evoked by a very unfortunate incident in his past. Mike managed to make her believe that her aunt was responsible for his injuries, but everything he said after that she simply couldn't trust. All this passed through Sarah's mind as she sped down the sidewalk of one of Detroit's major thoroughfares that late morning, hoping to evade the two strange FBI officials attempting to chase after her.

Despite their best efforts, the men continued to be inconvenienced by various circumstances. The stoplight took an unusually long time to change, and before they were even able to cross the street, Sarah had already walked yet another block. When they finally reached the other sidewalk, two men carrying a couch exited a building, blocking the path in front of them. Just as the couch had almost cleared the sidewalk, the leading man suddenly dropped his end, shattering one of the legs and ripping the couch from his partner's hands, causing him to drop its full weight on his foot. The two men began to shout at each other, continuing to block the sidewalk while Brad and Mike tried to pass. Eventually, the two officers walked out into traffic to go around the movers' rental truck. As Brad and Mike were about to step back onto the sidewalk, the parallel-parked sedan in front of the moving van backed up suddenly, plowing into the van and almost crushing Brad's legs. Brad struck the sedan on its trunk, yelling, "Watch it!" to the driver who apologetically threw up their hands, shifted the car into drive, and caused a tractor-trailer to veer into the next lane as it pulled away. Horn blasts abounded and Brad and Mike lurched onto the sidewalk in order to assess the near-mayhem from relative safety. There had been no crashes, but traffic was now nearly at a standstill. The two men recovered their bearings in time to see Sarah a full two and a half blocks ahead of them, storming down the sidewalk while shouting into her cell phone and gesticulating wildly with her free hand.

Mike was almost completely out of breath but Brad started to run after her. He hit a decent stride and quickly reached the next street. As the stoplight changed to red, a large panel van screamed across the intersection in front of Brad, clearly having anticipated the change to green. He reeled back, slipped on a patch of ice and met the ground with great force, his ass and back taking the brunt of the fall. Mike caught up to Brad as he was getting up and made sure his partner was okay. By this time, Sarah was nearly three blocks ahead of them, but was equally frustrated by her inability to procure transportation. "Go back and grab the car, Brad," Mike ordered, and the younger man darted across the still-green intersection back toward their parked cruiser. Mike waited patiently for the light to change and figured he'd pursue the woman as best he could without forcing the issue.

"No, I have no idea what these guys are hung up on, but they seem to think I'm somehow involved!" Sarah screamed into the phone.

The voice on the other end asked, "Do you think you could do a story about it?"

Sarah cackled into the phone and shook her head in wild amusement. "The bureau would just disregard the story as bullshit and a conflict of interest. But who knows? Maybe for the evening guy, Tony? Why don't you send him an email and ask him if he'll meet me tomorrow for lunch? Or, I guess if he's free before his broadcast today he can…" She shouted down the street behind her at the lack of transportation. "…*come and pick my ass up!* Seriously, I haven't seen a single cab or bus for almost a half mile here. This is ridiculous."

The voice responded, "Do you want me to have Jerry come and get you?"

Sarah replied, "No, by the time he gets here something will eventually come by. Don't worry about me, I'll make it back. Just send that email to Tony, I wanna talk to him about this." She hung up the phone and placed it back into her coat pocket.

Sarah turned to look for transportation again – the formerly wayward semi just now passing her – when she heard a noise. She stopped and looked around for what seemed to be someone whispering at her. From the barely open door to a loft apartment above an abandoned storefront, peeked a bright green pair of eyes. "Over here!" they intoned in a hollow, echoless whisper.

Sarah looked behind her, and when she didn't see the men who had been chasing her, she casually stepped to the door. Upon reaching it, the door swung open and the girl grabbed her by the arm and pulled her in, slamming the door behind them. Rebekah flipped on the light to reveal they were standing in the bottom of a stairwell.

Sarah held her hands up defensively, having never been accosted in this manner before. "What's going on here?!"

Rebekah grabbed her by the shoulders and asked intensely, "Are you her?"

"Am I her?" Sarah responded, confused and frustrated. "Am I who?! What the hell is going on?"

"Please! I need you to answer my questions. I don't have much time!"

"Fine, whatever. But I don't know what you mean. Who are you looking for?"

Rebekah shook her with a surprising ferocity that rattled Sarah to the core, fear finally overtaking confusion as the emotion foremost in her mind. "Are you Samantha Dempsey's daughter?!"

"Yes. What do you want with me?" Sarah asked carefully, not ready for the response.

The young woman in front of her now slackened her grip, beginning to let an expression of joy wash over her. "You are? You're really her?"

"What do you want with me? What do you want with my mother?"

A tear welled up in Rebekah's eye, a firm blink squeezing it down her face and onto her coat. Sarah was completely lost. Her fear and confusion overtook her and all she could utter was, "Who the hell are you, girl?"

"I've dreamed of the day I'd finally meet you," Rebekah continued, barely acknowledging that Sarah had spoken. "You look just like her."

"Like my mother?"

Rebekah nodded, placing her hand on Sarah's cheek, running it down to her shoulder, and pulling her into a hug. Sarah allowed the embrace momentarily, but brought her arms up to break it and pushed Rebekah away. "Okay, I get the idea that there's something going on here with you and those guys out there, but I have no idea who you are, and I'm done being everyone's emotional dumping ground for the day. So, what is this? What's going on here?"

Rebekah nodded, acknowledging the oddity of the situation, and gathered herself. She explained, "I've led such a crazy life, Sarah. I don't always communicate that well. Look, I know this is going to be very difficult to believe, and I completely understand if you don't, but..." She hesitated, then continued, "I'm your mother's sister, Rebekah. I'm your aunt."

Sarah was dead still. She contemplated numerous possible responses to this information. Primarily, she wanted to smack the girl in the jaw for having been in on the ruse with the FBI agents. Then, she surmised that perhaps someone had brainwashed the girl into believing she was some kind of criminal, that maybe it wasn't the girl's fault and that hitting her would likely accomplish nothing. Besides, the girl seemed awfully strong and might hit back. The response Sarah settled on was to nod her head and say, "Sure. Sure you are. That's cool. How ya doin', Auntie Becky?"

Rebekah was dismayed at that response. "No, I'm serious. I don't know what those men have been telling you, but I am your aunt. I know this all sounds ridiculous and crazy, but you have to believe me. Those men think I'm a criminal, but I'm not. Please, listen to me!" Sarah was starting to drift off into incredulity. "That fire... I had to kill that man. He was a horrible, horrible person and no one was doing anything about it. Those men out there want to kill me, or at least lock me up, but I haven't done anything wrong."

Sarah stopped listening to her, assuming what she was hearing was nothing more than the rantings of a brainwashed child, uttering, "Tony is going to love this..."

"*Please!* I only have a few moments before they find us. Here." Rebekah reached into her pocket and pulled out a locket on a chain and handed it to Sarah. "If you won't believe me, at least take this. I'll give you a few weeks and I'll come and find you again."

Rebekah grabbed Sarah by the shoulders, kissed her on the cheek, hugged her, and then ran up the stairs. Sarah opened the locket to view the photo within. To her astonishment, it was a photo of her mother as a child sitting on a swing with another girl who was indistinguishable from the young woman she'd just been talking to. Sarah bolted up the stairs after her, bursting into the studio loft beyond. The space was completely vacant, with no indication that anyone had recently passed through. No curtains fluttering, no door closing... nothing. She darted toward the back door and pulled it open, seeing only a vacant parking lot and the fire escape below. The girl was gone. Sarah exited through the back door and descended the fire escape to the vacant lot, turning down the alleyway leading back to the main road.

Sarah stood on the sidewalk looking up and down the street, then back at the locket. Emotions washed over her: confusion, disbelief, anger. The question interrupting every thought she had was, how would it be possible? How could a seventy-year-old woman appear to be nearly half Sarah's age? Over and over again, she tried to calculate what might have happened. Had this girl become obsessed with her somehow, studied her family's history, and digitally superimposed herself in the photo? And if that were the case, shouldn't Sarah report the obsession to the authorities? The girl had admitted to her that she murdered a man and started a fire in the process.

Sarah was conflicted about how to deal with the information, and when she looked up from the locket again, she realized she only had a few seconds to act. The two men were pulling up in their FBI-issue sedan, and Sarah began to formulate her options. Her next move could put the young woman in prison for the rest of her life. If they could catch her.

Mike climbed wearily out of the passenger side and strode to where Sarah was peering oddly off into space. He looked down at her hand and the locket, then up at her. "Ms. Dempsey, I'm truly sorry for the bizarre nature of this morning's events. I do wish you'd let us give you a ride back to your station."

"What if you find her?" Sarah asked.

"I'm sorry?" Mike replied.

"If you find her, are you going to shoot her? Are you going to arrest her and try her for murder, arson… the whole works?"

Mike sighed and stuffed his hands into his pockets. "To be perfectly honest with you, I don't know. It might be just as difficult for me to prove her guilty of these crimes as it would be for you to report on it. Who would believe it?"

"So you'll shoot her then?"

"Like I said, I don't know. After all these years, she's long since got the drop on me. You saw that. If I'd been able to catch her, I probably would have by now. Shooting her certainly wouldn't accomplish anything either. Maybe I'd just try to get some peace of mind. Why? What are you thinkin'?"

Sarah finished her last moment of consideration and then made up her mind. She knew the man wasn't lying. Whether what he said was fact or not was up for debate, but the truth of it couldn't be denied. "I spoke with her. She pulled me in there and admitted to me that she started that fire, that she killed that man. I can't abide that, family or no." Mike nodded, but made no attempt to persuade her one way or the other. She continued, "But you're right that I can't possibly report this, and I certainly don't want her to be hurt."

"Are you trying to negotiate, Ms. Dempsey? Because I am a law enforcement agent, and that could be seen as withholding evidence. If you have information, you need to share it."

"I don't know where she is, so there's nothing to share. And, withholding or no, you can't prosecute this. You said it yourself. But I'll help you catch her, if for no other reason than I need to speak to her again."

Mike looked off down the road, squinting as the sun began to peak through the clouds. He sighed heavily and looked back to Brad who was sitting in the car picking at his teeth. "You want to help catch a fugitive, eh?"

"I have a vested interest."

"I don't think the bureau would look too kindly on my bringin' a civilian along. They like to avoid the appearance of impropriety whenever possible."

She laughed at this, tossing her hair to one side. "In this circumstance, I don't think impropriety's the issue, Mike. You've got a reporter wanting to tag along on a ghost hunt. Is that something you can live with? 'Cause, I don't particularly care what the bureau's opinion is."

"No, I'd imagine you don't. Still, my ass is on the line, so I do have to care."

"No, it's not. Mike, this case is your career. Does it really matter who you have tagging along if you make the collar? Or if you at least solve it? You won't even have to escort me. I'll drive my own car," Sarah argued.

Mike knew she was right, but he feared appearing desperate. He wasn't sure that he needed Sarah's help, and felt her involvement may actually compromise the investigation. However, Sarah was tenacious and his suspect had reached out to her. Reluctantly, he replied, "There really isn't anything I can offer you. If you come, it's on your own time, your own nickel, everything."

"That's fine."

"So, what is your vested interest in this?" Mike queried.

Sarah held back at this point, answering, "I'm a journalist. I'm curious about everything. And right now, you're going to have to accept that as a response."

Mike shrugged and turned back to the car. He opened the back door for her.

"Thank you kindly, sir," she said, climbing into the back seat.

"Don't thank me yet, Ms. Dempsey. You're going to get more than you bargained for. Once you've seen enough, then decide whether you wanna thank me or not."

She winked at him playfully and Mike rolled his eyes, closing the door after her. He then climbed into the passenger seat and they set off toward downtown.

Chapter Five

May 1961

Frederick's wife, Louise, slept in the passenger seat. In the back seat, also asleep, was his 15-year-old daughter, Calypso. On the radio was a news clip of a recent speech by President Kennedy. Frederick listened with mild disdain, wondering why it was so important to land on the moon when he and his family were still prohibited from drinking out of certain water fountains. Young and idealistic or not, this president had a long way to go to prove to Frederick that his priorities were in the right place. He checked the mirror every few moments to see if his daughter was still sleeping. For the better part of 100 miles, she slumbered, clutching her book, her body drooping lazily toward the window.

Frederick checked off the markers in his head as they passed – the Deleware border, the Pennsylvania border – and they now approached Philadelphia on their way to Boston. The fuel-gauge needle lolled near empty, and he started looking for places to stop. Frederick pulled off the interstate and rolled up to a pump at a Texaco station. He climbed out of the vehicle, but just as he reached the pump, an attendant came out of the station and walked toward him, saying, "I got that, sir. You want me to check the tires while I'm at it?"

The family had driven up Interstate 95 from South Carolina, and Frederick wasn't used to gas station attendants pumping gas for him. With some apprehension, he replied, "Uh, yeah, that'd be fine. If you don't mind."

"Not at all. There are some drinks and snacks inside if you like," the attendant said as he placed the nozzle into the fuel opening.

Frederick sensed there was something off about the young man's behavior. Something told this visitor from the South that the young man was simply going through the motions; that maybe he'd been trained to treat everyone the same even though he wasn't trained to think it. It wasn't just intuition with Frederick either. For more than a year he'd been having strange sensations about people around him, which was a result, he believed, of his near-heart attack the year before. Whatever the initial cause, he'd started breathing more deeply and tried to be more aware of his world as he went along. The odd sensations he received knew no convenient timing and seemed to come from the most unexpected people.

Back in South Carolina, Frederick had begun having uneasy thoughts about a good friend of his. When Frederick confided this thought to Louise, she agreed that she felt the man had been making overtures toward her, and it made her uncomfortable. There were numerous other examples, many that occurred in church. During Sunday services, Frederick would be standing in mass, singing with his family, when an overwhelming sense of discord overtook him. To him, some of the people in the room didn't have the same feelings in their hearts as on their lips. The church had an integrated congregation, something quite advanced for South Carolina at the time, and Frederick seemed to feel what was on the minds of everyone there. He told himself that it was perfectly natural for both white and black parishioners to feel uncomfortable, and that it was no great feat to sense the tension.

Between that and a lead he had from a relative on a job in Boston, he had more than enough incentive to leave. Aside from not wanting to deal with Northern winters, his wife and daughter had no objections either. Louise didn't like the area they lived in, and Calypso's intellectual aptitude was wasting away in the South Carolina school system.

Frederick gave one last look at the man checking the air in his tires and then walked into the station to grab some Cracker Jacks and a Coke. When he returned from the shop, he paid the attendant for the gas, tipped him for the tire pressure check, and set back on the path toward Boston.

They stayed with Frederick's relatives on Boston's south side for two weeks until Frederick settled into a job at the mill and they were able to find a proper apartment. Their relatives also brought the family to service at a local Protestant church.

While Calypso and Louise seemed to quickly take root in the new denomination, Frederick still had a deafening sense of hollowness about his presence in church. Perhaps, he thought, it was time to search for something different entirely. He had no concept of how to look for it, though, and continually prayed during service for an answer. He felt remiss about declining to share his spiritual troubles with his wife and child, though equally sure they wouldn't react well to the news that he didn't feel comfortable in the House of God. So, he kept it to himself.

Through the church, their family, and work, Frederick had been invited to join numerous groups and causes. Civil rights organizations and demonstrations were gaining momentum, and Frederick's poise and personality were highly sought after by local officials. After living in Boston for a few months, he began to exercise these abilities by speaking with several organizations about the family's experiences in South Carolina. What he kept to himself was the feeling he had about the Northerners among whom he lived. While their actions were different, their emotions and thoughts were very similar to the Southern ideals he had tried to escape. Attempting to curtail racist behaviors could eventually change what happened in hearts and minds as well, and he was willing to continue the effort with that hope in mind.

A year went by, and Frederick stalled in his involvement in the cause. He wasn't ready to give up hours and income at work to travel. Though, if he had shared his feelings as well as his experiences, something more useful might have come of his continued involvement, but the thought of being ostracized by others was crippling. Eventually, Frederick withdrew from involvement altogether, much to the dismay of Louise and Calypso. They argued with him furiously, which with he was actually quite comfortable. One of the things he valued most about his family was that there were no mixed signals among them. When his wife or daughter shouted at him, he could sense that their emotions matched what they said. This was a great comfort to him, so he welcomed their disagreements.

The answer, for Frederick, eventually came at church. For the previous few weeks, a tall, middle-aged man had been attending services, hiding in the back pew. Frederick learned through the gossip channels that the strange man was a defector from an Eastern Bloc nation. This information was perplexing to Frederick. Why would a man from a staunchly Orthodox background attend such a Protestant-oriented service? Moreover, why would he do so with no consideration for socializing with the rest of the parishioners? The man had been there for almost a month and hadn't stayed for coffee hour once. Frederick had been assured the man spoke English, so a language barrier was clearly not the cause.

For the first time, Frederick actually tried to use his empathic gift to read someone. Ironically, it was also the first time it didn't work. The man was an enigma in every way, including being the palest individual in the church. The man's presence caused unease in not just Frederick, but Louise, Calypso, and numerous others as well. He was out of place and aloof to boot. Finally, Frederick decided to be the first to make a goodwill gesture.

After service on a particularly warm spring Sunday, Frederick followed the man out of the church and partway down the block. "Sir!" he shouted after the man. No response. He sped up and again called, "Sir!" This time the man stopped and turned around, still saying nothing. Frederick caught up to him and extended his hand, saying, "Sorry for shouting. Just wanted to catch you before you got too far away. I'm Frederick Casperson. My wife and daughter and I attend church here."

The man cautiously removed his hand from his pocket and shook Frederick's. "I've seen you."

Befuddled at the man's non-response, Frederick continued, "Oh. I suppose. Well, I've seen you back there... in the back of the church. I don't know if anyone's welcomed you officially yet, but I just wanted to introduce myself."

"My name is Daniel," the man said, betraying only the slightest accent. "Thanks for welcoming me, Frederick." He grinned mildly at Frederick and turned to walk away.

Frederick could still glean no sense of the man except that he was maybe a bit socially awkward. "Wait!"

"Yes?" Daniel replied, turning curiously back to Frederick.

"Well, why don't you stay for some coffee. We could talk."

"What would you like to talk about, Mr. Casperson?" the man asked.

By this point, Frederick was quite flustered, un-able to crack him at all. "I don't know. Well, where are you from? What do you do?"

Coolly, Daniel asked, "You have questions that need answering, you mean?"

At this, Frederick was taken aback. Daniel didn't seem to be referring to cordiality at all. For the first time, Frederick was able to sense something, but it wasn't anything about man himself. Instead, Frederick got the sense that Daniel was intensely curious about Frederick, and that it had nothing to do with church. Daniel's face hid any discernable expression, but his curiosity was evident, as well as the possibility that he was intentionally allowing this to be seen. Frederick took a leap of faith and responded, "Yes, I do."

Daniel finally smiled at Frederick. It wasn't much, but it validated some of what Frederick had sensed. "Good," the man responded. "We can talk, but unfortunately I have a prior commitment this afternoon. Perhaps next week, Frederick?"

"Yeah, that would be fine. I'll see you next Sunday."

"Next Sunday then," Daniel echoed. He finished his walk to the bus stop at the end of the block, just as the bus pulled up. He took one last glance at Frederick (who hadn't taken his eyes off the man) and climbed on.

Louise had been watching casually and walked up behind Frederick while the man boarded his bus. As it pulled away, she asked, "So, who is he?"

"I have no idea," he replied.

"Well, what did you talk about?"

"We're going to talk after service next week," he answered, turning back to her.

She nodded her head suspiciously. "I see he had to catch his bus."

"That must be it. He seemed..." he stopped as caution overtook him.

"What?" she pried, with no response. "Damn it, Frederick, you always do this. I can ask you what color the sky is all day long and you'll answer me. But whenever you're asked to say what you feel about something, you close up like a trap."

Frederick looked around, embarrassed, to see if anyone was looking. "Quiet, please! Maybe I just don't feel like sharing what I'm feeling sometimes."

"Sometimes?!" she shot back indignantly. "Don't you lie to me, I've known you too long. You haven't told me anything about how you've felt for over a year. Since before we moved up here you've been a ghost, and it's startin' to piss me off." Frederick put his hands on her shoulders to calm her. She responded by shrugging them off and admonishing, "And don't you try to handle me."

"I'm not trying to handle you! I just want you to calm down. Do you really wanna make a scene in front of the whole congregation?!" Frederick pleaded.

"If it gets you to stop avoiding the subject, I might just pull your ass into the street." She folded her arms and awaited his reply.

Frederick quickly guarded her from doing so. "Fine! Just get a hold of yourself."

"Oh, I'm perfectly calm. Now."

"Good!"

"I'm also still waiting, Mr. Casperson," she pointed out acerbically.

Frederick shook his head. "You really... you really have some bad timing, Louise."

"Well, since there doesn't appear to be a *good* time to discuss this, I felt now was as good a time as any."

"You wanna hear the truth?" Frederick asked, exasperated.

Louise pleaded with him. "I'm your wife!"

"You won't believe me."

"Try me. I'd believe just about anything at this point."

Frederick looked down the street in the direction the bus had gone, then back at Louise. He cautiously gazed up toward the church, grabbed her arm and started walking slowly away from the church. "I haven't wanted to tell you anything because I don't know if I believe it myself. Remember when I had those palpitations?"

"Your angina?"

"Well, whatever it was called… the doctor told me I should try to take deeper breaths, so I did. Ever since then I've been gettin'… feelings," he uttered hesitantly.

Alarmed, Louise asked, "Chest pains?! Why didn't you say so, Frederick?!"

"No, no, it's nothin' like that. Up here," he whispered, indicating his head. "When people say something, but they're thinkin' something else, I can feel it. Like… like the hair stands up on the back of my neck."

"You mean like intuition?" Louise asked. Her tone changed quickly to sarcasm. "Honey, all women have that."

Frederick pursed his lips and held out his hands. "Fine! But I didn't! Now, I do. Baby, one of the things I love about you is that you never send me mixed signals. You always mean what you say, and I can tell. But when the preacher's preaching somethin' he doesn't follow himself, I feel that."

"What?" Louise asked.

"When white folks shake my hand, I can feel how they're just not comfortable. And when the boss tells me I can't have overtime because of seniority, I can tell he's lying."

Louise affectionately placed her hand on his face. "You feel this is abnormal?"

Annoyed, Frederick shot back, "You're telling me you actually already have those sorts of feelings? *That* level of intuition?"

She shrugged. "I don't know that I do. I know I can tell when someone's givin' me a line of bullshit."

"Thank you very much. You asked me to tell you what I was feeling…"

"Yes, I did."

"So, I did, and you're makin' fun of me."

She sighed loudly. "Is that really what you've been so uptight about?"

"Louise, you know I've always been a good card player. I could tell when people were feedin' me a line, too. But this is not the same. I'm telling you I can really feel what other people are feeling. Now whatever you may call it… intuition, this is very unnerving for me. I've never had these feelings before and they make me uncomfortable. Scoff all you like, this is what's been wrong with me."

Relenting, she again placed one hand on his face, and circled the other around his waist. "I'm sorry, baby. I shouldn't have said that. I shouldn't have reacted that way. It's just… It's just that I was startin' to worry you were having an affair or something."

"I thought you said you had intuition. Wouldn't you have known that?" he barked at her.

"Very funny," she replied, taking her hands away from him.

Frederick insisted, "No, I'm serious. If you had what's been happening to me, you would have known if that's what was going on."

"Now Frederick, that's just ridiculous. No one can tell what another person is thinking."

"I'm not saying I can… I can't hear people's thoughts, Louise. But, I can tell when they've got something to hide, and I get a pretty good idea what it is they're hiding, too."

"You're serious, aren't you?" she asked.

"Baby, I'm telling you what's happening to me. The doctor said 'breathe,' so I did. And when I breathe, the air around me changes temperature and I can tell what people are feeling."

Silence fell over them. Louise realized Frederick was deadly serious and her first reaction was fear over needing to have him committed. Then, she thought back to the incident with his friend in South Carolina, and how Frederick's feelings toward the man had changed after he had been to the emergency room. She began recounting his behavior over the previous year. Frederick had become more introverted, yet infinitely more empathetic. She never had to ask him to take out the garbage anymore. He knew when Calypso needed help on her homework before she asked. The list stretched out in front of her, and as ridiculous as the answer sounded, it made sense. Perhaps Frederick really was experiencing these things.

Louise very carefully continued, "Frederick, I don't know if I believe you. But," she held her hand up as he started to protest, "...I don't know that I don't believe you either. Baby, you gotta understand that even though I asked you to tell me what you were feeling, no person in their right mind would be prepared to hear this as a response."

"That I understand," Frederick responded.

"So, I want you to be honest with me. We'll start small. For the next seven days, you tell me when you get these feelings. I wanna know what's going on, okay?"

Frederick breathed a sigh of relief. He was pleased that she was willing to make the effort. "Great. I can do that."

"C'mon, baby. Let's go get something to eat," Louise asserted, taking his hand and leading him back toward the church. "Oh, but let's not bring this up around Calypso. She's got tests coming up next week, and this kind of thing might be too much for her."

"Agreed," Frederick said.

For the next week, before and after Frederick's shifts at the mill, he and Louise would take long walks, trying to encounter as many people as possible. She would identify the person whose circumstance she was most curious about and Frederick would tell her what the person was feeling. Most of the people they encountered were just regular folks, not exhibiting extraordinary effort toward duplicity, and so Louise was seldom surprised at Frederick's response. When she was caught off guard, Frederick would shrug, explain that he wasn't a mind reader, and they'd continue down the street to the next subject.

Louise carefully examined both the individual and Frederick each time they assessed someone. After a time, she began to realize that everything he was saying was true. It simply wasn't possible for someone to invent so many accounts of people they didn't know. Eventually, her skepticism began to fade.

On Friday morning, as they walked toward a corner diner she said, "Freddy, I believe you, you know?"

He looked at her for a moment, analyzing both what she said and what she felt. "Yeah. I do."

"I don't know how it's possible, but obviously, you're not lying to me."

"Thank you, Louise." Frederick lovingly put his arm around her and nudged her head with his own.

"I know this must be difficult for you, and I don't want you to feel alone anymore," she told him.

He pulled his head away and looked into her eyes. "I don't. Not anymore." He took her hand and they continued to the diner.

***

When Sunday morning arrived, and Frederick and Louise were preparing for service, Louise asked, "What are you going to talk about? Do you think?"

Frederick was fussing over his tie, tying and retying it to get the right length. "I have no idea. He didn't seem interested in talking to me until I told him I have questions that need answering."

"Questions that need answering?" she clarified sarcastically.

"His words, not mine. And he's right. I do have questions. I couldn't read the guy at all, though," Frederick admitted.

"Really?"

"It normally comes naturally. I don't have to do anything to make it happen, but with him… it was blank. I wonder if I start asking questions – the right questions – if maybe I'll be able to sense something." He stopped fussing with the tie and turned to his wife to discover her looking at him incredulously. "This sounds asinine, doesn't it?"

She threw her hands up. "Yes. But I can't think of how it wouldn't."

Frederick shrugged and resumed tying his tie. Louise put her hands on her hips, sauntered up behind Frederick as he worked in front of the mirror, put her arm around his chest, and in a sultry voice intoned, "Can you tell what I'm feeling now?"

Frederick smiled deviously. "I'm thinkin' you're gonna have to wait 'til after church, baby."

They finished preparing and departed for service. Frederick was nervous the entire time. That Sunday's service seemed to last an eternity. By the time communion came, Frederick was sweating with anticipation of his later meeting, the overwhelming data flowing from the people around him, and the lack of ventilation in the sanctuary. Walking back to his pew, Frederick looked at the man as if to ask, "Are we still on?" Daniel nodded affirmatively and Frederick continued to his seat. It was while they sang the recessional hymn that Frederick again locked eyes with the man, who nodded and walked out the door at the back of the sanctuary. Frederick quickly shook hands with friends and family, then followed.

This time, the man started away from the church in the opposite direction. Frederick caught up with him, asking, "So, you don't have to catch a bus this time?"

"You are my schedule for the day, Mr. Casperson," Daniel replied, as they walked up the road toward an adjacent park.

"Why? And please, it's okay to call me Frederick."

The man shrugged. "Okay, Frederick... 'Why' is because this is what I do. I travel. I find people with questions, and I try to point them in the right direction."

"Well, how do you know what the questions are or whether you can answer them. And how do you know where to find people with questions?"

"Your curiosity is well justified, Frederick. You appear to me to be a man in transition. We all want to know where we're going. Even if the answer is undesirable, most people will choose to know what it is rather than be startled by it later. I regret to inform you that I cannot tell you where you are going. But I do believe that most people can progress toward their goals more effectively if they know where they are. Would you agree?" They were now near the middle of the park and Daniel stopped to face Frederick.

Nodding, Frederick examined their surroundings. It was a well-groomed park consisting primarily of a large grass field bracketed by trees. They were positioned on the edge of the tree line. Through the trees stood the church and the overheated, mingling parishioners. In the field, there were children playing and a number of adults supervising.

"You, sir, know neither where you are nor where you're going, do you?" Daniel asked.

"I'm not comfortable with this… you understand that?" Frederick started. Daniel nodded and Frederick continued. "But I'm at a point where I can't really move on until I get some help. If I share this with you, if I ask you these questions, I'm taking a big risk. What assurance do I have that you won't turn around and report me to the authorities… have me committed?"

Daniel smiled comfortingly. "I assure you, I have no intention of using any of this against you. Indeed, I would gain nothing by doing so. I can see your confusion and frustration and I want to help."

"Well, how do I even know we're talking about the same thing?"

"All right. I'll explain what I think about your situation and you tell me if I'm wrong. If I am, I go away and you don't have to think about me anymore. But if I'm right, then we talk. Yes?"

Frederick nodded in agreement. "That should work."

"You are new to your circumstances. Be them a new city, a new home, new friends… But what's really new to you, is you. You're what, forty?"

"Thirty-nine."

"So close. You're thirty-nine and you feel you should have things pretty well understood, but you're actually just now starting to feel how little you know. Things are changing, they're not constant. There is something important to you that you're now very uncomfortable with, no?" Daniel pried.

"I was working on becoming a spokesman."

"A civil rights activist?" Daniel wasn't needling Frederick, but rather was trying to get as close to the mark as possible to encourage Frederick into participating.

Sourly, Frederick responded, "What made you guess that?"

"You did. But I must remind you of something I believe you are well aware of. Your color does not define you. Man has been isolating himself from his world for thousands of years by trying to conquer it. You and I, we stand here as two men, but we are not so different. We drive cars, ride buses, feed off the benefits of agriculture… all things that separate us from our world by commodifying it. True, my skin affords me comforts and privileges yours does not. But, it's the practice of drawing distinctions between ourselves and the rest of the creatures on this planet that allows us to draw distinctions amongst ourselves. If we believe we're better than everything else, why would we not automatically believe that there is a hierarchy among us as well?"

"You got something better?" Frederick answered defensively.

"No," Daniel answered. "Not better. Maybe different? I believe that you are becoming conscious of an altered perspective. There's nothing wrong with the one you have; all aspects of the good cause must be fought. But whether you're prepared for it or not, I believe that you're becoming aware of something else. Who knows, perhaps you could use it to help your cause?"

"And exactly what am I becoming aware of?"

"This is where I must ask you to share, Frederick. I find lost souls. I help put them on a track, but I cannot read minds. I don't know why you're lost. As it is with a church, trusting a stranger takes a leap of faith."

After a long pause, Frederick admitted, "I've been having these… sensations. When I'm around people, it's like I can sense what they're feeling." Daniel nodded but didn't respond. Aggravated, Frederick blurted, "Damn it, this is stupid. You asked me to tell you this. It doesn't make any damn sense, and now you think I'm crazy!"

Daniel excitedly shook his head. "No, I don't! This is what I was hoping for. You breathe, yes?" Frederick indicated that he did. "You exhale and give part of yourself to the air. When you inhale you get something back. It's the flow of the natural world. This is not crazy."

"It's not?"

"Certainly not. In your country in the seventeenth century, men and women were hanged and crushed because of the fear people had about these sorts of things. The people who were killed were scapegoats for misunderstanding. It is basic human nature to destroy that which we do not understand. But we are above fear now, you and me. What we don't understand, we study. What frightens us, we explore. There is no need for rash reactions and criticisms and hangings." He paused to read Frederick's reaction, which was guarded at best. Daniel continued, "This is a practice that goes back thousands of years. When people did not understand their world, they reached out to it. They didn't ask for a book or for a conversation with the gods that created it. They tried to be a part of it. We cannot understand that which we separate ourselves from, Frederick. We must be immersed in it. You look at me and I can see you are lost; confused. I look at you and I see a man who loves his fellow man. I see a man whose empathy for his fellow man is manifesting in truths even he cannot understand. At some point, mankind became lost and we separated ourselves from our earth. We closed ourselves off and our misunderstanding of the world turned into fear. And that fear turned into anger. Frederick, you may not understand and you may well be afraid, but you are not angry. You seek answers and they are all around you."

Wind rustled through the leaves on the trees. The sound was vibrant and joyous, like music Frederick had heard his whole life but never listened to before. He felt the earth beneath his feet and could smell the warm, spring air pass through his nose, into his lungs and back out, a ceaseless flow of suddenly identifiable particulates. In that moment, he began to feel life around him even though there was only one human soul near.

"It's beautiful, isn't it? People kill for this, Frederick. What you are experiencing is what most people spend a lifetime trying to find. The ebb and flow of existence. No alive, no dead, just a continuum of swiftly moving air, water, and earth. These people in your country, they died because others were afraid of having their faith questioned. Fear is the most powerful of motivators. They felt they had an understanding of something and the practices they punished called that understanding into question."

"You mean, this is witchcraft?" Frederick asked, almost surprised by how natural the question sounded.

Daniel laughed and shook his head. "Witchcraft. I don't know what to call it, Frederick. Yes, witchcraft is what the colonial Americans feared; they thought they were going to be turned into frogs and sacrificed on altars. I don't even know when the last organized religion voluntarily sacrificed humans on altars, and I've never heard of one case of someone being turned into a frog. Those are fairy tales. Stories to tell children so they stay awake at night and sleep late so parents can have a peaceful breakfast without them. Perhaps prana is a more accurate term for what you are experiencing."

"What's... *prana?*" Frederick asked.

"Well, the word is Sanskrit, but the concept is universal. It is the breath of life. Through prana you can communicate with all the world... or none of it. It is a choice. You appear to have made a choice, Frederick."

"I don't recall making that choice."

"And yet here we are. You felt concealed, closed off from the world around you, yes? That's usually when people either die or begin to live."

Frederick recalled when his symptoms started. He had indeed nearly died. Upon his release from the hospital he began to breathe more deeply. As he did, he could feel his anger subside. "It's called prana?"

Daniel again shook his head. "It's a word. An explanation… and not a precise one at that. Perhaps placing a label on what you're feeling is not helpful. It's like the questions people ask to explain their existence. The truth is that you do exist. Take it for what it is. Similarly, you do breathe. This connection exists, no?"

"Yeah," Frederick replied.

"Then the question is unnecessary, unless you want to be a philosopher. And, from my experience, philosophers are boring."

Frederick chuckled, bobbing his head in agreement and thinking back to all the philosophical debates he had engaged in over beer and cards. Neither the philosophy he'd read in books nor the sermons in church ever sounded much more coherent than those conversations. Still, he was curious what the man wanted. "All that makes sense. But, you said you wanted me to ask questions. If those aren't the questions, then what are? I want to know what this is."

"Now we're getting somewhere! What is the question?" Daniel rocked back and forth as if the wind were pushing him from side to side, a sail in the breeze.

Frederick paused for a moment to consider what it was he truly wanted to know, then stumbled on a question. "Who are you?"

"It seems almost elementary, doesn't it? The fact that it hadn't occurred to you earlier to ask?"

"I'm sorry about that," Frederick admitted sheepishly.

"Don't be. This is ebb and flow. Frederick, I am a traveler. I'm from Belarus in the Soviet Union. Well, it wasn't the Soviet Union until later, but I originally came to the United States in 1937. As with many people at that time, I was concerned for my safety. After the war, I went back to Belarus, but the Soviets had turned it into part of their… empire, I guess you'd call it. There were many like me, like you. We feared for our lives. There was no room for people to think differently. Even in this country, freedoms aren't always what they seem. You are afraid to speak about your experiences because what is socially acceptable is bred into you. You know how people will respond before you even tell them." Daniel shook his head, reflecting.

"I have been open to this experience since I was a child. My mother was a very gifted woman. She taught me how to see things. How to ask the air and the earth and the water a question, and then how to listen for the answer. I guess she would be viewed in your country as a witch. And now I watch as humanity evolves. With each passing year, we develop more and more barriers between us and the natural world. We are cut off, and there are fewer and fewer of us who are able to establish this communication. In simplest terms, Frederick, I am a witch. I take after my mother and you likely take after yours. The ability to listen is passed down from generation to generation, through the womb. You just needed something to wake you up. Who am I? I am the person who can guide you now that you've woken up."

"So, it's genetic? Is it not possible for someone to do these things if they aren't related to someone else who is?"

"Genetics. Science is a beautiful thing, but it cannot explain the connection between mother and child. Perhaps it's genetic, but I don't know anything about that. I have heard from other American witches rumors of a man who became a great sorcerer with no training or assistance at all. Maybe it's just a legend, I don't know. In any case, I believe that this communication between us and our world is open to all people. All people who are not ruled by their fear, that is."

"What can I learn? What can I do with this?" Frederick asked, trying to understand what the man was offering.

"I don't know. That depends on you. But I believe that if you assess your life, you'll start to see where this newfound ability could benefit not only you, but those around you. If I am to be honest, though, there may be something that I'll need from you. You might be able to help me, you might not. I can promise I won't withhold my assistance based on what you can do for me, though."

Frederick nodded, knowing that what the man had told him was well worth some personal sacrifice. "Name it."

"I had a pupil about three years ago... three and a half or so. She presented as a very powerful witch, very in tune with her world. But she was not in control of her communication with it. She would reach out in anger. Bad things happened. She has disappeared and I believe that you can help me find her." Daniel appeared serious, and Frederick could attain no notion that he was lying.

"How can I do that?" Frederick asked.

"I don't know yet. I need to know more about who you are, and before that, you need to know more about who you are. Let's meet next week and discuss this some more. In the meantime, try to breathe even more deeply. Do it with real purpose and try to focus on the breath as it flows in and out through your body. If nothing changes, then we know what we're dealing with. But if you become able to see past the feelings of others and see… something else. Well, then we'll know that, too." Daniel smiled at Frederick, clapping one hand on his shoulder.

"Should we meet after service again?" Frederick asked.

Daniel shook his head, reaching into his jacket pocket. "I think you should visit me next Monday night, at this address." He wrote on a small, spiral notepad, tore out the piece of paper, and handed it to Frederick. "There are two other people I would like you to meet."

"Other witches?" Frederick asked hesitantly.

"Kindred spirits, Frederick. Try not to use labels; it only con- jures up images that are not useful in your search for answers. They are friends of mine from Belarus. We have tea and discussion, very low key. Come if you like, but you're not obliged."

Frederick looked at the sheet and back to the strange man in front of him. "Okay. I'll think about it. Thank you for talking with me. I feel much better about where I'm at."

"Good. You should never be ashamed of yourself, Frederick. You are who you are, and that is enough."

They shook hands and the man walked across the park away from the church. Frederick pocketed the piece of paper and walked back to the church where Louise and Calypso were waiting. A few parishioners were conversing in the sanctuary, and his wife and daughter were speaking with the reverend by the door. Feeling a unique sensation of comfort, he approached them. "Sorry it took so long. Guess we got caught up a bit."

The reverend then asked, "And do you know the man now, Frederick?"

Realizing it to be true, Frederick responded, "No, not at all."

***

Grabbing a beer from the refrigerator, Frederick looked around to for Louise and Calypso. Spying them in Calypso's room working on homework, he crept to the living room window, pulled up the screen, and climbed out onto the fire escape. The family lived in a well-loved brownstone overlooking a series of shops. From their third-floor window, he could see down the hill and out over the neighborhood.

Here, he chose to work on his breathing. Frederick carefully placed the screen back in the window frame and sat down, putting his beer on the metal platform next to him. For a moment he only observed, taking in the neighborhood, the diminishing sunlight, the city lights, and the myriad sounds around him. He perceived cars passing by, their brakes creaking at intersections, and the occasional horn; people talking in the other apartments; television sets playing *Andy Griffith* or other various programming – he couldn't tell for sure.

But mostly, he heard the wind. It flowed from the southwest, circling the building and swirling in a current around the corner into the nest where Frederick sat watching the reflection of the sunset in the sky above him. As a breeze picked up, he drew a deep breath, summoning up sensations from air and dust particles that had travelled the earth from lands far removed from his own. Despite sitting alone on the fire escape that night, he felt connected to places and people he'd never met. He felt connected to the earth that yawned under the building to give it rest. Connected to the air that stirred within the planet's atmosphere. Connected to the waters bubbling with fermentation in his bottle, and those that roiled with ancient currents only a few miles away.

Frederick took another deep breath. The swirling currents outside plunged through the bedroom window several feet away and vacated through the living room window behind him, gathering up the perfume dabbed around Louise's neck and saturating his senses with it. He could see her the day they met, one week after V-E day. Her brown eyes glistened with hope, fear, and affection. Her warm skin soft and dewy with anticipation as he took her hand and asked her to dance. History passed swiftly through his senses. He recalled their wedding, a small, outdoor event that had been softly rained upon. Their brief hospital stay after Calypso's birth where they discussed Homer's *Odyssey* and the origin of their daughter's name. The horrified yet willful look on Louise's face when he exclaimed that he was having chest pains, as if she could keep him alive through the sheer force of her love for him.

Exhaling, he gave back to the atmosphere and asked nothing in return. Slowly, he picked up his beer and lifted it to his lips, sucking down as much as he could in one swallow. Frederick questioned if there was a protocol. Should he not drink? But he felt that fermentation was a perfectly natural process and that nature wouldn't hold it against him for imbibing while communing. As he breathed, he could almost feel the world slow down. The sensations that raced through him were numerous yet compact, and his experience of them supplanted his need to feel forward motion. For the first time in his life, he was truly still and open. Frederick wondered if he could focus the sensations he received. Not necessarily control which sensations he received, but the type of information they imparted. He took another deep breath. Nothing. Another breath. Still nothing. Deciding not to be frustrated by the lack of accommodation from his newfound connections, he returned to breathing for the sake of breathing. The information began to flow again, but it still proved to be out of Frederick's control. He felt this was enough of a step for Monday but that he would try a bit more every night. For that moment, he was happy with the connection he'd made.

A noise jostled him, and he realized that Louise had moved from the bedroom to the living room. "So that's where you are," she said, relieved. "I've been wonderin' what you were up to, Mister. Mind if I join you?" She leaned on the window-sill behind him.

"Not at all. Come on out," he entreated, removing the screen again, and helping her onto the fire escape.

Once they were comfortably seated next to each other and Louise had had a moment to take in her surroundings, she turned to Frederick, saying, "It's pretty nice out here, Freddy."

"Yeah, I think so. Want some?" he asked, offering his bottle. She feigned disgust, then snatched the beer from him and downed a large portion of it. "I'll take that as a yes."

She handed the bottle back to him. "So, what are we doing up here?"

"Just listening," Frederick answered and polished off the bottle, placing it on the grating.

"That's it?"

"In a sense," he shrugged, looking out over the landscape.

She followed his gaze. "Ah, I see." There was a long pause in which she tried to get a sense of what he was listening for, looking at him, then back out at the neighborhood, then back at him. "Okay, no I don't."

Frederick smiled and took her hand. "There's nothing in particular we're looking for or listening for. Just listening."

Confused, she tried again. But she knew she couldn't follow. "I'm sorry, I don't get it."

"Okay, try this. Do you feel the breeze?"

"Yeah, it's nice and warm."

"Good, start with that. Now, the breeze isn't just a breeze you feel. There's more to it. You can smell it, taste it, hear it – you can't escape it." He held her hand tight. "Now, when you breathe it in, allow it to touch your lungs, your heart, your hands, your feet. Smell it, taste it."

She tried this for a few moments as Frederick breathed with her, watching her expressions, her eyes sealed shut. While she didn't have any epiphanies, she did manage a slightly elevated sense of well-being. Frustrated, and attributing the sense of well-being to the few swigs of beer, she opened her eyes. "What am I supposed to hear or see or whatever?"

"Nothing. At least I don't think. Or everything. The point is that there doesn't have to be a point. Just breathe for the sake of breathing. It's pretty easy to forget the air is there. I think there's a simplicity in focusing on something so... elemental." She nodded and shut her eyes tightly. Frederick responded to this comfortingly. "Your eyes aren't bottle caps. There's no need to close 'em, but you can. Just try to relax, baby."

Again, she nodded and shut her eyes. This time she took a deep breath and relaxed her shoulders and neck. Frederick joined the exercise, continuing to hold her hand. He let his mind wander, soaking in the atmosphere that enveloped them for a few moments. Then, Louise began to feel the sensations pass from Frederick to her. Ever so faintly, she sensed the stress Calypso was having about her upcoming tests and the end of her school session. And it wasn't simply in the vague, empathetic sense a parent has for their child either. This was a very real sense of experiencing the emotion for herself. She panicked, breaking the bond and opening her eyes. "What the hell just happened?!"

Frederick sensed what she had felt and was surprised at the incident himself. "I don't know."

"Did you do that on purpose?!"

"I don't even know what I'm doing! How could I do it on purpose?"

"Did you feel that?" she asked. He nodded. Her hands were shaking and she felt as if the wind were passing through them, the warmth piercing every crack and pore. She shook her head. "Now I think I understand why you've been so upset. Is it like that for you all the time?"

He shrugged nonchalantly. "Only when I'm breathing correctly."

"Wow," she uttered, shaking her head and looking out at the sky. A smile graced her face as she said, "What a gift. Baby, you are something special. I mean, I thought you were before, but now I know it."

"It's not me!" Frederick insisted. "That man, Daniel. He said it's everywhere. It's not limited to special people."

"Well, he can hold his tongue because I don't want anything to do with that." She folded her arms, keeping her gaze on the neighborhood. Finally, she stated, "I don't know if I could live with that. Can you?"

"I think that's what this man wants to help me with. Maybe if I get some control over it, I'll find a way to live with it."

She looked at him apologetically. "Freddy, I'm sorry I doubted you. I'm here for you, baby, and we're going to get through this together. I'm not going anywhere."

With some difficulty, he smiled at her. They took each other's hands and touched foreheads, taking a collective deep breath. They stayed on the fire escape until the timer in the kitchen sounded and Calypso summoned them into the apartment.

The following Monday, Frederick hurriedly completed the last round of finishing at the mill and punched his timecard. As soon as he had changed out of his coverall he darted out to his car. The address was near Concord, an almost thirty-mile drive, and he had explained to his family that he would not be home until late. Louise had understandable anxiety about the strange meeting, but after the experience on the fire escape, she was confident that Frederick needed some sort of assistance. It was far from her mind to keep him from acquiring it.

The drive was frustrating at first, the traffic grinding to a halt in some locations. But, when Frederick started to feel the collective distress of his fellow motorists, he took a few deep breaths and gained comfort in the fact that they were all in it together. Eventually, he came upon the old colonial-style home in a sparsely populated area north of Concord. The brick façade was untended and weathered, the white paint chipped, and the wood underneath split and permeated with earth and water. The leaded glass windows were heavy with age, the reflections framed within the warped treatments noticeably distorted. Frederick looked around at the nearby homes and determined that they were more well-kept. Considering the conversation he'd had a week earlier with Daniel, the disrepair of the home made him all the more certain he was at the right place.

Frederick knocked on the door, taking a step back to casually peer through the adjacent windows into the foyer. After a moment, the door opened and an elderly white woman with gray hair and spectacles greeted him. A warm smile graced her face and in a thick Belarusian accent she said, "You must be Frederick."

"Yes, I am," he replied.

"I am Ekaterina. Won't you please come in?" She held out her arm, motioning beyond the foyer to the parlor to the right of the stairs.

"Thank you," he answered and stepped into the house. The interior was in a similar state of disrepair to the exterior, but the architecture was far more interesting. The foyer he stepped into flowed openly into a hall containing the main staircase, the first flight rising two thirds of the distance to the second floor. At the top of the flight was a landing beset by large windows overlooking the kitchen roof and the backyard, and from there two smaller flights completed the ascent to the second floor on either side of the landing. The ancient oak stair treads were adorned with a threadbare green carpet runner. The ceiling above the staircase was devoid of the conventional chandelier; rather it housed a subtle dome feature.

From the stairs on either side, the second floor sprawled out in both directions, the walkways bracketed by balusters and railings on one side and liberally-decorated walls and doors on the other. The decor in the house appeared haphazard and uncoordinated. Tools and paintings were hung on the same wall section, while further down the balustrade a small tapestry hung above a ran- domly arranged table and candles. It was clear the objects had meaning, though their placements were unclear.

Downstairs, the house was equally spectacular. Frederick was initially ushered into the front parlor on the right side of the hall through an archway with no doors. While the floor in the hall bragged a stately marble, all other rooms maintained a more modest solid oak flooring. Behind the parlor was a dining room, then the kitchen, each with doorways connecting to each other and the main hall. The kitchen sprawled from behind the dining room to the space underneath the staircase landing.

On the left side of the hall was another large entryway into the lounge, a room with numerous bookcases, couches, chairs and a desk. The back wall of the lounge opened through double doors to the music room beyond. Behind that was another door, this one closed to Frederick's view. He took this all in briefly, moving along to the parlor.

"Would you like some tea, Frederick?"

"That would be fine, Ekaterina," he replied, taking special note of the pleasure she took from having her name pronounced correctly. She passed through the doorway to the dining area and into the kitchen.

Frederick took stock of the room. There was a small loveseat made of a dark hardwood, the many layers of finish obscuring the original material. The loveseat was covered with wool upholstery, as were the two matching chairs in the room. The chairs, loveseat, and center table were a matching set that Frederick estimated at almost 200 years old and quite possibly original residents of the home. Afraid to damage them, he remained standing.

"Beautiful isn't it, Frederick?" Daniel asked, nearly sneaking up on Frederick as he crossed from the far back corner of the hall.

Frederick turned, startled, and caught his breath. "I've never seen anything like this place. Is this yours?"

Daniel padded into the parlor and sat comfortably in one of the chairs, motioning for Frederick to sit as well. "No, it is not mine. It belongs to the lady of the house. She is anxious to meet you."

Sitting in the other chair, Frederick asked, "Is that the woman I met at the door?"

Daniel shook his head. "No, Ekaterina is her sister. Marya only recently defected from the Soviet Union, though she's travelled here before and has owned the home for some time. I regret I didn't inform you earlier, but she doesn't speak English, so when you speak with her, Ekaterina and I will be interpreting. Have you ever worked with an interpreter before?"

Frederick was now self-conscious. "No, I haven't."

"It's nothing, really. Just remember that if you're speaking to Marya, address her, not me or Ekaterina. Understand?"

"Sure, I can do that," Frederick answered, starting to wring his hands.

Daniel smiled reassuringly and Frederick began to feel more comfortable. "Relax, Frederick. You are our guest. It is our honor to have you here, not the other way around."

Ekaterina returned from the kitchen, setting the tea tray on the table and pouring out four cups. "Would you like milk or sugar in your tea, Frederick?"

He shook his head politely. "No, thank you. It'll be fine."

"Here you go," she said, and handed him a cup and saucer.

"Thank you," Frederick bowed slightly, took the cup, and reseated himself.

Ekaterina sat closest to Daniel, leaving an open seat close to Frederick. They sat, sipping tea for a few moments, the mood clear that nothing would be discussed until Marya appeared. Frederick didn't know what to expect, but assumed from the sensations he was getting that she was a few years older than Ekaterina and very much the matriarch of the group.

A door opened upstairs, above where they were sitting. Frederick listened to the footsteps as they padded out of the room, a door closing behind them, then tracked across the balustrade to the stairs. As the footsteps reached the landing and started their way down the main stairs, the woman appeared in Frederick's view from behind the ceiling. To his surprise, she didn't look at all like she could have been Ekaterina's sister. Ekaterina appeared to be in her late seventies or even eighties. As Marya descended the stairs, she appeared no more than 50 or 55 at the oldest. She wore low heels, slacks, a modern blouse, and over the top of it all, a lengthy shawl draped over both shoulders that hung down past her waist. Her hair was exceptionally long and was twisted up in a knot with wisps streaming out on the sides. A contented smile spread from one cheek to the other as her heals clicked across the marble flooring toward Frederick. She was eager to see a kindred spirit, confused though he was. They stood upon her entrance.

In Belarusian she said, "Welcome," while extending her hand to Frederick. Daniel translated, though the meaning was obvious.

"Thank you," Frederick said, his incredulity palpable for all, including himself.

Marya turned to Ekaterina and seemed to ask something about the tea. Ekaterina nodded and waved her hand at the tea dismissively while sitting back in her seat. Marya crossed around behind Frederick to sit on the loveseat. She picked up her cup and sat with her legs folded to one side beneath her, leaning on the arm of the loveseat as she directed her energy toward Frederick. She smiled at him again, and breathed in deeply the sense of community she felt by his presence. "Frederick," she began, then continued in her native tongue.

Daniel translated as she spoke. At first Frederick had to work to keep up, but it became easier as they went on. "I am happy that you are here," Frederick acknowledged, nodding his head in gratitude.

Marya and Daniel continued. "There are so few of us, like a dying breed. You see all of these strange belongings on the wall, and initially, yes, it is odd decoration. But for us, these are the last vestiges of our friends long gone. We…" She took Frederick's hand and continued, "…You are a practicer of an ancient spirituality that connects us to the earth. To the land from which we come." She shook her head. "Daniel brought Ekaterina and me to America from our country because we were persecuted. But we now see that the persecution exists here, too. Life will not be easy for you, Frederick." She nodded as if to seek a response.

Frederick heeded her cue. "I understand. If it has to be, then that's okay. I'm used to it."

She nodded her understanding. "We... none of us will live forever. We may be able to hold off the inevitable for a time, but it is the handing down of this connection that will allow it to survive. If we all die, there will be no connection left, and the earth will forget us." She paused briefly to lean back in her seat, but did not release Frederick's hand. Her tone became noticeably self-aware. "This is my fear. Perhaps I am wrong. Perhaps the only way for us as people to regain our connection is to lose it entirely and to be cut off from the earth. I would be sad, though, to see entire generations of our kind lost to their true origins. You agree, no, Frederick?"

"Yes, actually I do," he said, surprised at himself. With every phrase, the news was more disheartening, but his comfort with the people in the room became greater.

"I see great things in store for you, Frederick," she continued. "People will be lost, and they will come to you. You must help to send them on their way. This is your gift. To share with others is to perpetuate the connection we are losing. Do not be afraid of who you are. Immerse yourself in it and share it with others."

Frederick nodded. After a long silence, he took a deep breath and addressed Marya. "When people come to me, how will I know who they are or what they need?"

Marya was now giddy at the addition of a new ally. "When you meet them, they will identify themselves by the objects they pass along to you. Study them, understand them, and listen to their fears." Marya motioned beyond the walls of the room.

Frederick could feel the fears, doubts, loves, and passions of hundreds of individuals. Perhaps Marya was passing thoughts to him, but Frederick smiled and welcomed the sensation with contentment.

Chapter Six

December 1959

Missouri's Ozark mountains afforded them a gently winding, yet inconsistent ride along Interstate 44 as Rebekah and Al wound their way through southwestern Missouri. The pavement tilted up and down through the landscape with such gradient contrast that Rebekah's ears popped too frequently for her to sleep. She had no idea how many hours would pass before the sun rose, but knew it would be best if she could find time to sleep before they reached St. Louis.

Al had invited her to sleep earlier, informing her that he made the overnight trek on a regular basis and did not require alert company. Still, there was something unsettling about the man and she struggled to wrest her body from consciousness. She took a long, deep breath that eventually stretched into a yawn, and a shudder passed from her fingertips through her body and out her toes. Her muscles began to relax and a wave of exhaustion set in. Her eyelids sagged on the brink of closing. She nestled into the seat, her arms folded in front of her, her head falling back against the headrest and up against the car door. Fatigue finally overtook her and the lingering discomfort with which she regarded the man was pushed to the back of her mind.

Memories mingled with fears, events with feelings. A canvas of blank sleep began to fill with horrifying imagery generated by a mixture of her life and the one she was beginning to carve for herself. Hot coals paved the trail she tread upon, yet her feet didn't burn. Still, the rising heat urged a clear, syrup-like fluid to flow from her pores. Waves of putrescent air obscured her vision, the wilderness before her bending and twisting. Blackened, leafless trees sagged in the oppressive heat. Within the diseased, scorched bark, faces appeared. One of the faces appeared to be that of her father. To her horror, the gaping, pained expression represented in the tree's gnarls transformed into the weathered, stubbly crag of middle-aged flesh she had come to loathe. His arms, strong beyond human capacity anchored her to her bed sheets, still hot with the residue of the coals she'd been treading. Sweat dripped from him onto her skin, releasing plumes of black ash into the sky. Behind him were the man's sons, one holding a jagged bottle, the other clutching a human scalp. Their faces were obscured, covered with blood that seeped down their necks to their chests and beyond.

Rebekah tried to scream, but there was no sound. Instead, muffled wailing and puffs of air replaced the gut-wrenching, blood-curdling sounds she was attempting to produce. She struggled to free herself, to stop the activity that amused their grotesquely animated corpses. The boys then traded places with their father, the background beyond them ever changing. As if in a slideshow, the sky overhead faded from flames, to storm clouds circling with thunder and lightning, and finally to green-brown trailing smoke that reeked of sulfur. From within the sulfur clouds, acrid rain poured down, striking the three men and dissolving their flesh like the witch in a story she'd heard as a child. Hot coals and sheets beneath her were doused in blood, streams of crimson meandering through the piles of earth and bones and disintegrated structures littering the ground.

A reservoir opened in front of her with a cool, blue lake framed on all sides by the death and devastation she'd been conjuring. Mist floated over the lake, transforming into stinging, burning-cold needles of ice as they reached the charred landscape. Slowly, an amorphous figure began to emerge from the glass lake. No ripples formed from the disturbance, but rather the lake protruded from its own stillness to form the figure that stood upon its surface. The form approached the shore slowly, causing the lens through which Rebekah viewed the scene to throb audibly and pulsate in her fragile ears. The figure reached for her, grabbing her around the neck and forcing her to her knees. The burning ground pierced through her legs into her abdomen, two red-hot rods of spiked steel.

With a hate-spewing, near-mechanical demonic voice, the figure pressed its mouth to her already pounding ears and belched in a fiery tone, "Pay!" It grabbed her left knee, locking eyes with her and laughing in her face, a blinding light glaring from its mouth. A white-hot pain shot through her and she looked to see the spiked steel rod turning and twisting through her knee. The demon grabbed her chin and, turned her face to one side, put its mouth to her ear one last time, shaking its head and screeching, "But not yet!" Then it pulled the metal rod out of her leg, the pain so great she awoke.

When she did, she realized she had turned in her sleep and her bent knees were now facing the driver of the vehicle, whose hand was stroking her left knee. Instinctively, she reached out with her hand and a jagged fingernail caught his flesh. As he pulled his hand away the nail tore through his skin, slicing it open. The car swerved and pulled to a stop on the side of the road; Al yelled and writhed in pain along the way. Still groggy and horrified from her dream, she struggled to wake herself to the now very real horror happening in the car.

Al reached out with his right hand and slapped Rebekah across the face, yelling, "You damn fool!"

She brought her hand up to sooth her cheek as he grasped his bleeding hand in agony. She looked at her fingernail, identifying the chunk of flesh that had previously belonged on the back of Al's hand. He shook his head back and forth, breathing heavily, trying to quiet the pain that now seared through his arm.

"What the hell is wrong with you?" he barked.

Not knowing how to respond she muttered the first thing that came to mind. "You were touching me... my knee."

"Just who do you think you are, little girl?"

Frightened, she answered as if she hadn't heard the question. "I'm sorry?"

Al put the car in park. He put his left hand on the steering wheel, smearing blood along its surface. He moved toward her. She recoiled, fumbling for the door handle, but Al grabbed it and forced it down to her side, away from the handle. The same as in her dream, she struggled to call for help. Sounds came out in a series of 'No's and whimpers. She tried to move her arms to attack the man, but he was much stronger than her and pinned both of her hands to the seat underneath her. With his bleeding right hand, he grabbed the waistband of her skirt and pulled her closer to him on the bench seat. He then thrust her torso down onto her arms and grabbed her left leg, pulling it up against the back of the seat, lunging on top of her. Using his weight to stifle her attempts to resist, he reached down between their legs and began unfastening his belt and the button on his slacks.

She couldn't breathe. Al's weight and the heat in the close space was smothering. Struggling for his zipper, he fell on her, his forehead smashing into her nose. Rebekah tilted her head up quickly and bit his face next to his right eye, cutting teeth marks above and below it. He recoiled to grasp his face and yelp in pain.

She then freed her right hand and swatted at his face. She connected, and dragged her serrated fingernails across his cheek and nose.

Mangled, Al paused in his attack to fuss over his wounds. Rebekah used the moment to finally catch her breath. An indignant rush of anger warmed over her and she brought her focus to the blood pouring from the man's body. He cocked his fist to punch her, but a sudden pang of burning overcame him. Shocked, he brought his hand up to his face to inspect it. The blood shone black in the dimly-lit cabin of the vehicle. Smoke began to rise from the blackness and the stinging pain grew. The sensation traveled from his hand to his face, where more blood was oozing out. Rebekah frantically grabbed the door handle, opened the car door, and tumbled out onto the ground. She scrambled to her feet as Al tumbled from the vehicle to chase after her. Thoughts of a chase were fleeting, however. He began to look around for a source of water to cool his wounds.

Rebekah stopped behind the car and watched the helpless man try to douse the scalding flesh with dirt from the roadside. She looked around to see if there were any other cars or homes, but there were none. Realizing they were alone in the wilderness, she brought all of her focus to Al and quietly told herself, "But not yet..." She breathed deeply, focused, and watched as fire burst from the man's bloody wounds.

Al had lost his voice and flailed aimlessly. His burning body bounced off the passenger side of the car and landed on the ground. Trying to seek cooling in the dewy grass, he rolled onto the embankment and began plummeting down the hillside. Rebekah didn't allow the dew to quench the flames, and the fire burned hotter and hotter as he reached the tree line, his body snapping up against a tree. When she heard the crack of his bones, she released the flames and they subsided. Though dark, she could see smoke rising from his charred remains.

Standing at the top of the hill, Rebekah shivered with rage and horror, a stream of blood dripping from her nose. She looked around her, again verifying no one was present. Then, she climbed back into the vehicle, its engine still running. Systematically, she searched the car to take stock of what was present. The glove box contained the lighter, cigarettes, and a few maps. Turning to the back seat, she saw the man's coat. Picking it up and quickly rifling through the pockets she found his wallet. She opened it to count his remaining cash, which totaled $123.00. It was the first piece of good fortune she'd encountered that night. Reluctant to dally at the scene, she sat in the driver's seat, wiped the blood away from her nose with the man's coat, jammed the car into drive, and slammed on the gas.

By the time Rebekah reached Lebanon, the sun had begun to rise, intermittently peeking out from behind hilltops only to hide again as she descended another valley. Eventually, the car crested a hill, and the sun remained exposed. The car's interior was bathed in light, giving new perspective to the extent of the evening's carnage. Her blouse and the front of her skirt were spattered and smeared with blood, as was the vinyl bench seat. Upon inspecting her face in the mirror, she saw a dried smudge of blackish-red material stretching from her nose, down her lips and chin and under the collar of her blouse.

She carefully considered her options. A decision would have to be made shortly as neither fuel nor light of day would permit her to hide for much longer. She focused primarily on staying within the speed limit and out of sight of the police. In addition, Rebekah was keenly aware that as the day wore on, missing person reports might start filtering out from Tulsa and from wherever Al was supposed to arrive. In the meantime, she chose to stop in Rolla to change clothes and wash her face.

Exiting the highway, she began looking for anything that might pass as a clothing store, which resulted in the discovery of a farm supply and clothing store located next to a quaint country diner. After parking the car, she put on the long coat she'd stolen from her foster parents to cover her blood-soaked clothing and walked to the front of the store. It didn't open until 10:00 a.m.

"Damn!" she thought, and pounded her fist on the doorframe. She then recalled she hadn't eaten in nearly a day and resolved to summon the courage to explain her bloody nose and buy breakfast at the diner next door.

Immediately upon her entrance, the locals took notice of the bizarre-looking young woman, but she pretended they didn't bother her. A waitress approached her, smiling at first, then concerned, asking timidly, "Are you okay?!"

Rebekah faked laughter and dismissively tossed her hand from side to side as she responded, "Oh, it's just a nosebleed. Been drivin' all night, so I'd love some breakfast. Do you suppose I could wash up, first?"

"Absolutely, honey. Here, let me take your coat. Your table will be all set up for ya by the time you get back."

Panicked, Rebekah ripped her coat out of the waitress' hands. "No!" she barked. The outburst caught the attention of numerous patrons. Startled, the waitress stepped back from the young woman, who corrected herself. "I'm sorry, I'm oddly cold. Must be the blood loss or something. I'll be right back," Rebekah stated, and she marched off to the restroom. Inside, she slammed and locked the door behind her and raced to the mirror. She was an absolute mess.

Tracks of mascara stained her face like murky finger paintings of distress. Blood was caked onto her lips and chin, painting a ghoulish mask. Rebekah hung the coat on the back of the door, unbuttoned her blouse, and hung it – also coated with blood – on top of the coat. Blood had even managed to soak through her blouse, through her bra, and spread in streaks down her abdomen. She began to realize allowing her nose to bleed freely and not using the man's coat to stop the flow had been an unwise decision. Turning the water on, she filled her hands and rinsed her face over and over again until she could hardly see a tinge of red. Then she picked up the bar of soap and began furiously scrubbing her face and neck to make herself presentable.

Nearly five minutes had passed, and Rebekah began to suspect that her long absence from the diner might seem suspicious. No longer able to spot blood or mascara on her face or neck, she put her blouse and coat back on and walked casually back to her table.

The waitress came by and again asked, "You sure you okay, honey?"

"Yes, much better now," the young woman responded, smiling like she felt a dutiful young girl ought to.

"Well, you let me know if ya need anything. We got a first aid kit in the back, okay?"

"You're very sweet, thank you."

The waitress smiled, sensing the girl was much calmer than she had been previously. "So, what can I get ya? Coffee?"

Rebekah had never been allowed coffee in her father's house and the thought of absolutely anything that had been prohibited sounded delightful to her. "Definitely!"

"Great. You want any cream or sugar with that?" The waitress watched Rebekah decide. Having never had coffee before, her face shifted back and forth, not knowing what she would prefer. "Don't worry, honey. How 'bout I bring both, and you can try it for yourself, okay?"

"Thanks," Rebekah muttered sheepishly.

"Here's a menu," the waitress said, handing the young woman a shabbily folded piece of paper. "You take a few seconds to look that over and I'll get right back with ya." She winked, and shuffled back toward the kitchen.

The remainder of the breakfast was largely uneventful for Rebekah, save the extra trips to the restroom she'd not anticipated due to the coffee. Rather, her time spent after breakfast was surprisingly productive as she tried to pass the time before the shop opened. The caffeine had given her a rush of energy, and after paying for her meal, she took one last trip to the restroom to grab extra paper towels. She doused them in her water glass on the way out the door she labored away cleaning the front seat of the car. Most of the blood came off the vinyl, though it was clear some of the stain, particularly in the seams, would be permanent. The steering wheel, on the other hand, came perfectly clean.

Rebekah threw the paper towels and the coat into the garbage and drove the car down the street to a service station where she had gas pumped. For the most part clean, refueled, and highly energized, she returned to the now open farm supply and clothing store. She bought a skirt and blouse that to her looked the least like she should have been wrangling cattle and departed.

She stopped half way between Rolla and St. Louis to pull onto a side road and incinerate her old clothes. As she headed farther east, Rebekah made up her mind to ditch the car and continue to Boston by train. While this would save further expense on gas, she would eventually run out of money. The young woman had no possessions to sell, and she wasn't planning to stay anywhere along the way long enough to earn money. She came to the conclusion that she would need to pickpocket if she wanted to stay afloat. *Just until I get to Massachusetts*, she told herself. There, she would get a job and be a productive member of society.

Rebekah reached St. Louis just before lunchtime. After parking the car on a side street near Union Station, she worked in front of the mirror for a moment, trying to match her hairdo to her new cowgirl look. Once she was satisfied she'd manufactured a reasonable facsimile, she grabbed her coat, the cigarettes, lighter, registration from the glove box, and the wallet, and exited the vehicle.

Rebekah ducked down an alleyway containing a row of garbage cans. There, she pulled out the vehicle registration, wallet, and other belongings she'd taken from the car. She was about to drop them into the garbage when something moved behind one of the cans. She stepped back to see what it was and discovered a man lying on the other side of the can she had opened. Woken by the sound of her approach, he removed the newspaper covering his head and laid eyes on the young woman. Delighted, he tried to get up, but failed.

"Don't. It's okay, you can stay where you are," she urged the man. "I won't bother you." Pleased, he rested back on the ground.

"Thank ya, little girl. Hey, you ain't throwin' that coat away, are ya?" he asked.

Considering the man's question, she took stock of the objects in her possession, looked back at the man, and handed him the coat and cigarettes. She then considered the lighter. "I'm going to use this for just a second, then you can have it too." The man's eyes lit up. Halting him with her hand, she added, "But, you have to do something for me."

"Sure!" he agreed excitedly.

"You can't tell anyone you saw me or that you saw this happen, okay?"

He waved his arm in a large, sweeping motion. "I never saw

ya!'"

She smiled at the man. Placing the registration on top of the other objects in the can, she emptied the remaining contents of Al's wallet into the garbage and lit it on fire. Rebekah and the old man watched it all burn, the flames reflecting in their eyes. Contentment spread across her face while the old man looked on.

"They say, 'Hell hath no fury'..." he said, forgetting the rest of the phrase.

She turned to him and patted him on the shoulder, handed him the lighter and finished the phrase for him, "...like a Zippo lighter."

He laughed, taking the lighter and walking away from her down the alley, shaking his head as he went. Rebekah finished watching her items burn and walked away before the flames spread to the rest of the garbage.

Reemerging from the alley, she continued on to Union Station. She took in the grandiose arches and vaulted roof above her on the left, and the bizarre figures in the fountain to her right. The noon crowd was heavy and she quickly made her marks. Two businessmen in three-piece suits walked past her on their way into the station. Each passed through the main entrance into the ticketing area with a briefcase and overnight bag.

Casually, Rebekah climbed the stairs to the entrance and followed closely behind the men, listening carefully to their discussion. From what she could tell, they were insurance salesmen of some sort. They were discussing a "visit to headquarters" in Connecticut as part of a sales presentation about fire insurance. The irony struck her as a sign and she stayed with them.

Once the men reached their designated ticketing counter, she sat on a nearby bench and worked out her distraction plot.

She did not have to wait long. The men finished their purchases and headed past her toward the train shed behind the ticketing office. Rebekah quickly got to her feet and started after them. Within a few steps, she kicked off her shoe and yelped as though she had tripped, collapsing to the ground with her naked foot in front of her. Initially, she was annoyed by her own use of the helpless maiden routine, but when both men turned and rushed back to help her, she quickly validated the use of the device. One of the men reached out a hand to her, placing his briefcase and overnight bag on the ground; the other ducked behind the first to pick up her shoe.

Wasting no time, she extended her left hand to the man leaning over her as he asked, "Are you okay, miss?" Simultaneously, her right hand slipped into the breast pocket of his coat and gracefully retrieved his wallet. The second man was blocked from the theft by the first, and the first was so focused on Rebekah's unfortunate accident that he paid no attention to the slight contact she made with his chest as she faltered to her feet. Her pride swelling at the success of such a daring act, she added a final flourish by stumbling forward into the man with her hand on his shoulder. This masked the less elegant motion of placing the wallet into her skirt pocket. She may have hated the fashion, but had to admit to some usefulness in the design.

"Oh, thank ya kindly, mister!" she stated loudly in a perfect Oklahoman accent. "I'm sure sorry 'bout that. I think my shoe must a' broke." When she said this, the first man turned to the second who had been standing behind him inspecting her broken shoe. He had yet to made eye contact with Rebekah.

"Yeah, Bill, this looks broken to me for sure," said the second man who finally raised his gaze to the young woman. With copious amounts of false Southern modesty, she flirtatiously reached out to the man to retrieve her shoe. In doing so, she ran her hand across the back of his before taking her now-maimed Mary Jane gently from his hand.

"Thank ya so much for helpin' me, gentlemen. I been meanin' to get rid of these for a while now, and I guess it just caught up with me, now didn't it?" she said, refusing to take her eyes off the second man.

Bill saw what was happening and coughed deeply to interrupt. "Uh, well, Stu..." Stu did not respond. "Stu!" Bill repeated, and Stu snapped to. "Maybe we should be going now? That is, as long as you're okay, miss."

"Oh, I'm just fine," she reached her hand to Bill, drawing out the *fine*. "Thanks again for your kindness."

Rebekah made eyes one last time at Stu, took her left shoe off, and walked past the men toward another ticketing counter. She knew she didn't have much time before Bill recognized his wallet was missing, so she hurried to the closest counter. Reaching the window, the ticketing agent asked, "What can I do for ya, miss?"

Dropping the fake accent, she answered, "I need to get to Boston, Massachusetts. Is it possible to get there without going through Connecticut?"

"Well, sure you can. You'd have to make a connection to get to Connecticut anyway. The Pennsy will get you as far as New York, and you can connect to Boston with the New York, New Haven and Hartford Railroad. Or, you can just take the New York Central all the way to Boston. The Pennsy leaves at 1:15 PM and the New York leaves at 1:45 PM."

"Do I have to buy a new ticket at the connection?" she asked, mildly frustrated. She didn't want to spend too much money on rail fare, but she also didn't want to linger in St. Louis if Bill started sniffing around for his missing wallet.

"Not as long as you stay with the same company. Tickets don't transfer between rail companies."

She considered the conundrum for a moment. While she didn't want to stay in St. Louis too long, she also knew she needed some sort of luggage case, and that it would also be a good idea to purchase a new outfit and shoes. "I'll take the New York Central. You're sure that goes to Boston, right?"

"You can take my word for it, Miss." He smiled and punched up the ticket. "That'll be $36.75."

The ticket price caused her heart rate to jump. Remembering the money wasn't hers to begin with, she swallowed hard, pulled out the cash, and handed the agent two 20-dollar bills. He completed the transaction, handing her the change and the ticket. "You have a safe trip, now!"

"Thanks," she said, disillusioned, and walked swiftly out of the station. With the remaining 45 minutes until departure and the dwindling cash from Al's wallet, she procured a handsome satchel and a new outfit that she felt was perfectly cosmopolitan: shoes, a skirt, a blouse, and a hat. With the last of the coins, she bought a chocolate bar from a local chocolatier and stuffed it into her satchel with her cowgirl outfit. The final touch to her ensemble was a pair of oversized sunglasses just like those she'd seen in the movies. Amazingly, in just a few minutes, she'd managed to transform from a disheveled Annie Oakley to a modestly-dressed and inconspicuous Sabrina Fairchild. She was pleased with the makeover.

With still 15 minutes before boarding time, Rebekah sat on a park bench to analyze the contents of Bill's wallet. He had a driver license, a Diners Club card, a paper American Express card, and more cash than she had ever laid eyes on. To avoid suspicion, she opted not to count it then and there. She threw the wallet and its contents away, having no clue how the cards worked anyway.

Rebekah reentered the station. Out of the corner of her eye, she saw the two insurance travelers speaking with a police officer. She kept her head down and her hat tilted toward them as she passed through the headhouse into the train shed.

An overwhelming sense of awe overtook her as she entered the facility. The shed's expansive roof stretched out above her as far as she could see in one direction and disappeared behind the train at the first terminal in the other. Giant steel I-beams propped the roof at ascending intervals to the roof's apex, then back down on the other side. In between were the tracks and platforms that carried the massive steel snakes and weary travelers within. Plantings and statuesque decorations adorned the walls and floors, while a cacophony of sound invaded her ears: people talking and shouting, announcements over loud speakers, and the visceral heaving of the locomotives.

Keeping in mind that police officers were in the building, Rebekah made her way to the third platform and approached the first uniformed man she saw. She handed the man her ticket, who verified it and said, "You're in the third car, the first coach car." He smiled at her as she nodded her thanks and walked away.

Breathing a sigh of relief, she moved calmly toward her car. She selected the seat closest to the exit where she could see the entire car and placed her bag in the rack overhead. She plopped down in the seat, and after a few moments, the train started to move. As it pulled away from the station, she relaxed into the upholstery, wrapping the long jacket around her like a blanket. She recognized a dried spot of blood near one of the buttons. Feeling the spot with her fingers, she began to laugh. She breathed deeply for the first time in hours and a flood of emotions overtook her all at once. She laughed, then cried, then laughed again, then rested in a completely numb state as the tears dried on her cheek. Rebekah felt some of the other passengers looking at her, then looking away, but she didn't have the energy to care. "Let them come," she thought, referring to the authorities. But none did. Two days later, she was in Boston.

Upon her arrival at Boston's South Station, Rebekah went to the ticketing office. She purchased bus fare to Wellington Hill and boarded as soon as the bus arrived. The towns and neighborhoods zoomed across her vision, almost indistinguishable from each other. She clutched her bag on her lap, ready to hop off at her stop. The bus eventually stopped at Walk Hill Street. A moment later, she was standing on the corner of the intersection, her bag in hand, staring down the street at her old neighborhood.

There were few good memories from that street. There wasn't anything inherently wrong with the neighborhood, but despite the troubled condition of her family dynamic after she moved to Tulsa, the time prior to her mother's death had been even worse. While her mother still lived, her father had another target for his rage.

On one side of the street were the multifamily homes her schoolmates lived in, and on the other side were the apartments where her family and myriad immigrants and young adults lived. Rebekah had been scorned for her family's lack of funds, even in a low-income neighborhood, but there was nothing she could do about it. As it was in Tulsa, she had been unsafe both at home and at school. She began to question what she expected to get out of coming back to this place. But, her mother had died here, so she believed there must be answers.

She strolled down the sidewalk, observing the children playing in the yards in the afternoon daylight. The youngsters playing here were too young to know who she was, and the ones who were old enough were inside doing homework, away at work, finished with school, visiting family for the holidays, or in prison. Whatever the reason, she knew she wouldn't have to interact with them.

Half a block later, she reached the door of her old apartment building. It was a newer complex than the brick dwellings in the neighborhood, yet the painted wooden siding was cracked and peeling, belying its disrepair. It was undeniably a slum, and it had only become more dilapidated since her family's departure. Rebekah opened the door and walked down the hallway to the second door on the left. There were four units per floor, and her family had resided in the larger, two-bedroom unit in the back.

Initially, she walked past the door, afraid to knock. She then walked past it again, toward the front of the building. *They'll think I'm nuts*, she thought. *Then again, if they come out and find me pacing here, they'll think I'm nuts anyway.*

She found herself rushing to the door and knocking on it before she could convince herself to walk away. *You've come all this way, Rebekah*, she explained to herself. There was no answer. She knocked again – again with no response.

Prior to the family's departure from Boston, Rebekah had made a copy of the apartment key. She wasn't quite sure why, but assumed it was a means of maintaining the link to the last place she'd resided with her mother. She and her mother never spoke much, but they had a bond Rebekah was unable to explain. She dug in her coat pocket, retrieved the worn, rusty apartment key, and slid it into the lock. To her surprise, the lock had not been changed. As quietly as she could manage, she twisted the knob and nudged the door open. Ever so slowly, she moved the door far enough to peer inside. It was empty.

She swung the door open, taking in the image as it revealed itself to her. To her immediate right was the kitchenette her mother had slaved over on a daily basis; it consisted of a shabby metal sink, with no more than ten square feet of salmon-colored laminate countertop, a mismatched set of metal cabinets, and a short, single-chamber refrigerator that had been consistently stocked with beer. Beyond the kitchenette to her left was the dining space they had converted into sleeping quarters for her parents when the second boy was born and they decided to separate Rebekah from her siblings. To her right through a double-door-sized opening was the living room. This space had been filled with a tattered green couch, the dining table, and her father's radio, as they hadn't yet upgraded to a television set. Beyond the living room was the hallway that led to two small bedrooms and the microscopic bathroom the six of them had shared. On one side of the hallway was the larger bedroom and on the other was the smaller bedroom and bathroom. Despite the decidedly negative memories she had of the place, it was almost more daunting to see it empty.

Rebekah set her bag on the counter and allowed herself into the space. Since she had made the trip, she opted to stay for a time and look around. Starting with the bathroom, she looked under the sink, in the cabinets, behind the toilet, in the toilet tank, scoured the shower stall for loose tiles, leaving no surface unturned.

Her parents frequently fought about her mother's late nights. Her father was convinced she was cheating on him, and she continually retorted with the same argument, that she was studying at the library. As it was the one place he wouldn't be caught dead, and there were too many libraries in Boston to check them all every night, he never had proof of an affair. Rebekah, on the other hand, privately hoped that her mother was having an extramarital relationship. She'd never been fond of her father, and at times wondered whether or not he was her biological father at all. In her mind, she had conjured images of the man her birth father might be. Nothing concrete, but likely tall, handsome, educated… a stark contrast to everything her real-life father was: a Neanderthal, simple and vile, devoid of any culture or credibility. If she indeed had a different father, she hoped he was the opposite of the man she had grown up with.

In the bedrooms, Rebekah tore through every possible space she could imagine. She removed the shelves in the closets to inspect the tops and bottoms, looking for any evidence of a life she imagined her mother should have had. Despair began to spread over her. Had she made the trip for nothing? Was there no actual life left behind for her? The sensation became more and more frantic. On the train, she'd imagined a scenario in her mind where the current tenant of the apartment had found some information and kept it in a secret place until the former tenants returned to claim it. Having no idea what that information would be, Rebekah didn't know what to look for. She'd hoped to find anything. A love note, a poem, a picture… anything.

She stormed into the living room, scouring behind the radiator and underneath the shelves. There was a built-in cabinet in the corner, and Rebekah tore the drawers out looking for anything that may have been written underneath them. The fading daylight made it more difficult to see, but the message was consistent. There was nothing to be found.

After half an hour of turning the apartment inside out she came to the kitchen. Every cupboard and drawer was empty. The refrigerator was bare. The only unique element in the entire apartment was the shelf paper in the third drawer on the left side of the sink. It struck her suddenly that it was the only shelf paper in the apartment. Her family had been gone for three years, and it was likely that the dwelling had been rearranged and redecorated numerous times since then. Still, she pulled the drawer back out, and slammed it down on the counter. She turned on the light over the sink and began carefully peeling the shelf paper from the bottom of the drawer. It separated from the wood in one large piece, and just as she'd given up hope that there was anything underneath it, she saw a tiny bit of writing in the back corner of the shelf paper.

Rebekah threw the drawer on the floor and laid the paper out on the counter. The writing was small yet clear. It was a phone number. She tore the corner of the shelf paper off and packed it neatly in her bag, then gathered her belongings, replaced all of the upturned items in the apartment and left, locking the door behind her.

Eagerly, Rebekah made her way to the first available pay phone and picked up the receiver. She immediately replaced it in the cradle. *This is ridiculous*, she thought. The number could have been put there by anyone, though she did have to admit the handwriting looked quite similar to her mother's. She convinced herself to pick the phone back up, dropped a dime in it, dialed, and waited. After four rings, there was an answer. A middle-aged woman with a thick accent responded, saying, "Hello?"

Dumbstruck, Rebekah didn't respond at first. The woman on the other end said "Hello" two more times before Rebekah could speak.

"Yes, I'm Rebekah Boyd. I'm looking to see if anyone there knows someone by the name of Cora Boyd. Does that name sound familiar, ma'am?"

There were some excited whispers in a foreign language on the other end of the phone, finally resulting in a confused utterance from the woman. "Cora Boyd?"

Eagerly, Rebekah repeated, "Yes, does anyone there know her?"

The confusion on the other end continued, and the middle-aged woman eventually put the phone down. Rebekah waited on pins and needles, until a man's voice came on the phone.

"Hello? Who is this?" The man also had an accent, though it was much more diluted, and he had a stronger grasp of English.

Rebekah put the phone back to her ear. "My name is Rebekah Boyd. I'm looking for…"

The man interrupted her. "Cora Boyd? You want to know if I know Cora?" the man asked calmly, almost as if he'd expected her call.

"Yes, I do. Do you know her?"

"Are you her daughter?" the voice responded.

"Yes. Who are you? Do you know her?" Rebekah asked frantically.

There was silence on the other end. She didn't want to break it because she sensed the faint murmurings of conspiracy. Her heart raced with anticipation.

Finally, the voice returned. "We need to meet. Are you in Boston?"

"Yes. I am now," she answered excitedly.

The voice replied, "For your comfort, we could meet somewhere public. Say, tomorrow at noon. I'll be at the corner of Charles and Beacon overlooking the pond. Okay?"

Rebekah took a deep breath, closed her eyes, and replied, "Okay. I'll see you then." She hung up the phone and started back down the street to the next bus stop, waiting for her ride back into town. She spent the night at an hourly hotel in a questionable part of town, sirens, shouting, and general chaos surging all around her. Still, she slept.

Rebekah woke the next morning with excitement and anticipation of her noon engagement. She had eaten very little over the past three days, yet despite the resulting dizziness and enervation she was experiencing, the thought of having to obtain – much less con-sume – some sort of sustenance in light of her pending encounter seemed to be an inconvenience more than anything else. So, she went for a walk to stay active and alert.

She reminisced about the times her mother had taken her on that same walk, along the pathways through the public garden, around the lagoon, and along the adjacent metropolitan streets. The trees were bare in preparation for their winter slumber, and the last of the migrating birds paddled across the lagoon to pluck up final nourishment before their journey. Rebekah wondered what had become of the life she could have had, the contrast between the family she was given and the family she wished she had. Her mother and sister had deserved better, she thought. Whatever power was driving her forward had escaped them, and while she didn't understand it, she was grateful that it had taken her away. Anything, regardless of how foreign, was an improvement.

Christmas Day. An unsettling feeling came over her as she sat on a bench in the garden. Save for her sister, to whom she could never return, Rebekah no longer had a family. In the world all around her, families were opening presents, taking pictures, laugh-ing, and sharing memories they'd keep for a lifetime. She breathed in the crisp air, hoping to capture some of the affection those other families must have been feeling. But there was nothing, just cold air. She flipped the collar up on her jacket and tightened it around her, shuddering against the decreasing temperature.

"Miss Boyd?" a man's voice came from behind her, shaking the young woman out of her trance.

Rebekah stood and turned to see a tall, middle-aged man with a square, firm jaw and pronounced nose protruding from his craggy yet clean-shaven face. She said nothing, only nodding acknowledgment.

"I am the man you spoke to on the phone yesterday. My name is Daniel." He took a step down onto the level of the garden where she sat, twenty feet still between them, and held out his hand for Rebekah to shake. She didn't speak, but rather countered his move, keeping the bench between them. He lowered his hand and nodded. "Don't worry, I'll stay here. It is less busy today than I would have hoped for your comfort. I had forgotten about the holiday; people are inside with family. No?"

"You forgot?" she asked skeptically.

Daniel smiled. The sweetness of her voice matched the innocent yet haunting look of her face. "I don't celebrate. It slips the mind when you're not preparing for it. Did you celebrate this morning?" She shook her head. He continued, "This will be difficult with only one of us talking, but we can proceed in this manner if you please."

She assessed him carefully. The accent was something she'd never heard before, though he seemed to have an excellent grasp of the language. His face, on the other hand, was familiar. She couldn't place how or why, but she felt she'd seen the man before.

He threw his hands up and sat on the bench. In turn, she moved to stay in eye contact with him. Daniel analyzed the young woman carefully, taking special note of her health. Something had been eating away at her. She wasn't physically ill, but her guarded nature indicated a mental state that had become quite fragile.

"Do you still live in Boston?" he asked.

"Who are you?" she insisted, not interested in small talk.

"I was a friend of your mother's," Daniel replied slowly.

"How did you know her? When did you meet?" Rebekah was becoming more agitated.

"I think maybe we should start with something smaller…" He tried to divert the conversation, but she interrupted him.

Her emotional state was deteriorating rapidly. "They're all dead," she exclaimed. Daniel didn't know how to respond. "They're all dead and I think you had something to do with it. You have to tell me how you knew my mother, I don't care how. I won't be angry, but you have to tell me."

Daniel raised his hand to try to calm her. "Please, I think you may be upset…"

"Now!" she shouted, the echoes of her voice reverberating off buildings and causing birds to flutter from their perches. Her face was pained, the toll of travel, death, destruction, and incomprehensible compulsions had finally cracked her last layers of decorum.

Daniel, frightened by the outburst, looked around. There were two couples walking nearby, and he smiled in their direction to assure them. They continued on their paths, shaking their heads in an annoyed fashion.

He returned his gaze to Rebekah and kept his hand up, saying, "Okay. I'll tell you what you need to know, but you need to breathe. You need to relax because if this becomes troublesome, I might not be able to help you. Do you understand?" She nodded but refused to breathe deeply, instead she trembled in place, her hands folded over her stomach protectively.

"I first moved to this country in 1937. I am from Belarus in the Soviet Union, have you heard of it?" She shook her head. "It is due east from Poland. My people were taken over by the Soviets and there was a fear of war, so I came to America. I tried to teach myself English at the library here, and that is where I met your mother. She taught me to speak and read English."

"She didn't work at the library. What was she doing there?" Rebekah asked.

"Rebekah, I get the impression you had a difficult family life, no?" She nodded. "Would it be permissible to speak candidly about your mother and father then?" Again, she permitted him. He took a long, skeptical breath and proceeded cautiously. "Your mother was a very unhappy woman. Your father was abusive, as I'm sure you know, and she would go to the library to read… to escape. She saw me struggling with an English language book and offered to help. I couldn't even read it. She was very kind."

"Did you…" She couldn't bring herself to ask what she was dying to know.

Daniel made no expression. "Your mother and I had an affair. I'm very sorry to tell you this; you were never supposed to know. It went on for a number of years…"

"How long?"

"Rebekah, perhaps you are not ready for…" Daniel was trying to dial down the discussion.

"How goddamn long?!" she shouted.

"What do you want me to tell you? I don't know the truth. She would bring you to the library with her sometimes and we would go for walks together, the three of us… in this park. I didn't care whose child you were, it didn't matter to me. She loved you with her whole heart regardless of where you actually came from. You belong to your mother, Rebekah, not your father. And not to me."

Rebekah finally took a deep breath, exhaling thoroughly and closing her eyes. For some reason she didn't understand, her situation had become simpler. The possibility of having a father who was not the man she had grown up with explained so many of the complex dynamics in her personality and how it related to the rest of the family. She opened her eyes, taking in the sights around her. Memories started to return, awash with images of her mother, the lagoon, the bright green grass and trees, and the man who was sitting in front of her. His hair had been much darker at the time, but his face was unmistakable.

"I do remember you," she admitted. "I just thought you were a friend."

"Please, do not be angry with your mother."

She turned to him with a surprised expression. "Angry? How could I possibly be angry at her for that? Besides, she's dead now, and it wouldn't accomplish anything."

The first sign of emotion crossed Daniel's face. He'd heard her before when she had said, "they were all dead," but didn't know exactly what she'd meant. Now, he was sadly sure. Over the past few years he'd had a notion of the possibility, but nothing had ever confirmed it. "She is dead?" he asked.

"Three years ago. Why did you go away? Did you go back to your country?"

He nodded. "I'm so sorry I left her in that situation. She was such a good soul." He had no concept of what the girl actually knew of her mother, or what she knew of her mother's beliefs. Without thinking too long though, he stated, "The earth spoke to her."

Rebekah locked eyes with the man, all exhaustion and sadness fading instantly. "What?"

"You mother. She could hear things. Did she ever speak to you about it?"

"What kinds of things?"

"She could listen to the wind, to the air, and hear the life around her. Can you hear it, too?" he asked. There was no response, just an incredulous expression. "No, of course not. This is ridiculous talk, no? I'm sorry to be strange…"

Desperate to believe there was anyone on earth who understood something of what she was going through, she blurted out,

"Yes, I can."

Her admission was precisely what Daniel had hoped for. "You can? What do you hear?"

She wasn't sure what to say. "I feel like, when I breathe, I'm swimming… or like the air is thick. I can make it move."

This was not what he expected to hear. Daniel was taken aback, almost frightened. "You mean, it moves around you?"

"Well… yes. That, too. But I can make it move… do things," she struggled to explain.

"What kinds of things?" Daniel pried.

Finally, discretion caught up with Rebekah's curiosity and excitement. "I think I'd rather not say."

A silence fell over them. For the first time in days, Rebekah's mind was entertaining only one thought: "What does this man want?" Daniel's mind, on the other hand, was whirling with excitement and fear. In all his life he'd never met anyone who had passed beyond communicating with the natural world, and had begun to control it. At least not without a particularly gruesome and terrifying process he'd only heard of in stories. Perhaps the girl's experiences had in some way opened her to a larger level of control. But, it left him chilled, facing the possibility that someone as out of control as she seemed to be could have such an ability. She was dangerous not only to herself, but to others.

"I believe you," he said coldly. He stood and was pleased when the action failed to frighten her. She smiled weakly, happy that she'd made a connection with another human being. Her mother had hidden these things about herself from her, and the only person Rebekah had communicated with was her sister, who was in no way capable of contributing to conversations of such notions.

Not knowing what to say, she shrugged. He followed suit. They laughed at the awkwardness.

"So, you have no family at all anymore?" Daniel asked.

"My sister is still in Tulsa, but she's only six years old... I couldn't bring her along."

"Will you be going back?"

"I don't think so. I don't think I would be welcome there."

He bowed his head thoughtfully, then offered, "If you have no family and nowhere to stay, I would like to invite you to spend the day with my family. At least you'll have somewhere warm to rest for a while."

She breathed, and the air between them secured her understanding that the man in front of her was her real father. Without listening further, she chose to trust him in that moment. "I would like that. If it's okay."

"It is my invitation. Please, it's no trouble."

In Rebekah's limited experience, she had lived in a slum of a two-bedroom apartment and a rundown two-level house tantamount to a shack. Accordingly, the hair on the back of her neck stood on end when Daniel pulled the car up in front of the colonial house in Concord. Along the way, Daniel had explained his life on the outskirts of Minsk and his modest Belarusian upbringing. The house she now stood in front of did not match up to the descriptions he'd given of his life before coming to America.

They were greeted at the door by Marya and Ekaterina, who showed Rebekah to the lounge where she placed her coat and luggage. The house was breathtaking. From the marble and hardwood floors, to the ornate crown molding, to the antique furniture, it was everything she'd seen in movies and read about in books. Despite being the voracious reader she was, however, she'd never before been privy to the bizarre assortment of decorations in that house. Marya tried to gauge Rebekah's reactions as she took in the items.

"Hello," she said, sitting across the coffee table from Rebekah. Ekaterina sat in the chair at the end of the arrangement to translate.

"Are you the woman I spoke to on the phone?" Rebekah asked. Marya tried desperately to understand the girl, but eventually turned to Ekaterina, who translated.

Marya replied, "Yes," then continued in Belarusian, "I do not speak English. I am newly arrived from Belarus. Ekaterina and I have been in this country before and she speaks English, but I never bothered to learn." Marya laughed proudly at this.

Rebekah replied excitedly, "Please, I don't mind. It's a beautiful language, I love to hear it."

Pleased, Marya continued more comfortably. "Daniel tells us that you are Cora's daughter. Is this true?"

"Yes!" Rebekah's mind didn't know which direction to go. Everything that did not make sense only days ago now had a profound opportunity to come into focus. "Did you know her?"

"I met her once, briefly, but no, I did not know your mother. Daniel told us about her, though. She was a remarkable woman. Can you tell me more?"

"I wish I could," Rebekah started sadly. "I didn't know her very well... at all. My father..." In all the years she'd lived with her father, she didn't know how to explain him. So much of his behavior was too taboo to discuss. Yet somehow, in that setting, nothing seemed taboo. "My father was abusive. She was afraid to talk. To be herself. I think it's what killed her."

Marya gasped in horror, then whispered back, "He killed her?"

"No," Rebekah corrected herself. "Not directly. The doctors said she died of a heart attack."

Somewhere in the translation – whether through language or subtext – Marya interpreted Cora's cause of death as a broken heart and met Rebekah's grief. "She deserved better than that. She deserved to be loved. We all deserve to be loved, including you, Rebekah."

Rebekah loved the sound of her name in Marya's speech. Her name was pronounced with the care and love Marya was trying to convey. The woman's entire being was invested in what she said, sending the message through every possible method of communication. Rebekah understood Marya's last phrase without translation.

"Love is what we all seek. You have it here. Stay. Rest. We will help set you on your path."

Ekaterina, Marya, and Rebekah sat, content in the knowledge that a lost soul had been found.

Chapter Seven

Hattie and Isaac's wedding was a jubilant, midsummer affair in the park adjacent to the church. Dozens of friends, family, and townsfolk jammed the small hill leading down to the creek, the bank of which played host to the celebrants. Most weddings are joyous affairs, but the circumstances surrounding Hattie and Isaac's nuptials made their wedding particularly satisfying. Isaac was quickly becoming a lonely old man and Hattie was already considered by some to be an old maid. Their union came as a sigh of relief to a great number of people.

Prior to the wedding, Isaac made his trip to Washington, securing a large enough commission to pay for setting up the shop he'd wanted in the town square. While neither Vilas nor Heatheridge himself directly purchased the bowl Isaac had labored so long to create, it did find its way into the hands of Heatheridge's wife, who gave it to her husband for his birthday. With the connections Isaac made through this sale, he was able to secure a number of other commissions that would guarantee him income for the foreseeable future. In short, only a month of work had secured the start of a life for the two lovers, and all this was accomplished with Isaac actually spending less time working on his craft than he had before their engagement. The percentage of his day devoted to other tasks had greatly increased.

Hattie, as wife-to-be, had discovered her own way to help Isaac in his new business endeavors. The success of her initial baking ruse had motivated her to start baking on a regular basis. Isaac's shop door was locked much more frequently as a result, and while Cynthia and Richard had a pretty good idea of what was happening, they did nothing to discourage it. After all, their son had found love, and who were they to question it?

Isaac paid for the wedding out of his savings, not wanting to put a financial strain on Hattie's father. This made for smooth planning between the two families, as neither Hattie nor Isaac seemed to care about the details at all.

On that hot day in early August 1888, the two lovers were the center of the local universe. They exchanged vows, kissed, and celebrated with their friends and family on the bank of the creek, then held a processional to the tavern, where the party lasted long into the night. Hattie's mother and sister took special care to make a number of alterations to the dress. Most notably, they shortened the hem a solid two inches to accommodate Hattie's expressive – and immutable – dancing style. It was a lovely white dress with short, loose sleeves, a slight, ruffled collar, and rather elaborate embroidery lining both sides of the bodice. A lace ribbon weaved through her hair and extended halfway down her back. Isaac's suit consisted of gray, pin-striped trousers, a black jacket with tails, a white vest with embroidery matching Hattie's dress, and a black cravat.

The entire town commented on how beautiful the couple was, and Isaac and Hattie accommodated the attendees by dancing as frequently as possible. The band played standard formal dance music, but, with greater frequency than at most weddings, they also obliged Hattie the faster paced, vibrant music she favored and regularly listened to herself.

After the reception, the newlyweds were escorted by carriage to Isaac's new shop. The second floor was already furnished and they planned to move in within the next week. Their new home was almost directly across the town square from the tavern, which made the carriage ride not only short, but convenient for the rest of the wedding guests, who followed the carriage from the tavern to the front of the shop. Isaac leapt from the carriage to help Hattie down. Her feet had barely hit the ground before he swept her back up and, with the assistance of Hattie's little brother opening the door for them, Isaac carried her into the shop. The door closed behind them and he carried her up the stairs into their new home.

At the top of the stairs, Isaac paused to allow his bride to survey their home. The stairs opened into the kitchen area, which consisted of a counter, sink, and numerous cabinets. Beyond the kitchen was the living space. There were no walls, but rather designated spaces for the bedroom and sitting area. Aside from the bed, the rest of the space was bare, with only some chairs and a table. At the far end, on the other side of the kitchen, was a second staircase that led to the back of the shop and outside. At the front, facing the town square, were three tall windows bordered by a red brick wall and a wide windowsill. In the center of the north wall, to the right of the front windows, was a fireplace.

As Isaac stepped across the threshold, Hattie jumped from his arms and kissed him passionately. They worked in tandem to remove Isaac's hat and coat, then began unwinding Hattie's bindings. After a few heated moments, but before anything critical was disrobed, Hattie heard sounds outside the building. "Wait a minute," she said, holding her finger up to Isaac's lips.

Isaac heard it too, and they slowly crept to the window at the front of the studio. He opened the window. Down on the street, three of the musicians, Hattie's brother and sister, and a number of other singers were performing *Jeannie With the Light Brown Hair*. Hattie and Isaac sat on the windowsill, embracing each other and soaking in the music. It was still hot, but there was a light breeze that passed through the home. They swayed back and forth on the windowsill, breathing in the summer air and singing along. The song ended and the musicians shouted their congratulations up to the couple one last time, then departed across the park to the tavern.

With savage energy, the couple pulled the curtains shut over the windows, ripped the curtain away from the bed, then fervently removed each other's clothes and made love.

After, they lay spent in their bed, in their own home. To each, it felt as natural and comfortable as breathing. They laughed over the freedom of it all.

Hattie turned to Isaac, smiling playfully. "Tell me you love me."

"I *do* love you, with all my heart," Isaac replied instantly. "Tell me you love me?"

"There is none other," she answered officially, taking his hand and studying his fingers, one by one. "Honestly, Isaac, I've never loved anyone else. I remember when I was a girl in school, and you and your father were building stools for the tavern. We'd come over to your shop and I'd watch you work in the back while our fathers talked and smoked and... I wasn't really paying attention to them. Do you remember?"

He shyly averted his eyes, betraying that he held the moments just as fondly she did. "I think a little, yeah."

"I think anyone else would have been annoyed with me. I was so curious about you and what you did. I kept talking to you, interrupting your work, and you were so earnest about it. You'd never get distracted from your work, but you never ignored me either. You'd always just keep working and answer my questions. You were never short with me."

Isaac didn't know how to respond. He knew how he felt, though. Even when Hattie was a child, her energy was always intensely focused on whomever she was talking to. That person became the most important person in the world, and it was supremely comforting.

"I could never have been short with you. I'd never known anyone so well-meaning," he explained.

"Yes, well, the effort was entirely worth it. You're mine now, aren't you?" She glowed childishly with pride and accomplishment.

"Without question. For all my life."

Hattie bit her lip, keeping her eyes on Isaac. "What do you think our life will be like?"

He shrugged. "Anything you want. What do you want, Hattie?"

"I think we should travel. And we should have at least two children. I can just see little Isaac running around the shop, getting in your way, knocking things down…"

"That would be fine, but not Isaac," he insisted.

"Why not?"

"I'm Isaac. He'll have his own personality, I'm sure."

"Good point," she conceded, and went on with the list. "…and a girl, Tabitha. And they'll go to school and be famous, important people."

Isaac laughed. "I don't see why they shouldn't."

Hattie began running her hand through Isaac's hair. "And I want to grow old together, and tease you about your gray hair, and sit out on the porch and watch our grandchildren play."

"There's no reason why not," he assured her.

"But for now? I just want to be here and love you." She put her hand around his head and brought him to her, kissing him softly.

They parted for just a moment, and Isaac said, "Darling, you'll have all of it." And he kissed her back.

Years passed and Isaac and Hattie's business grew. Shortly after their wedding, Isaac had Hattie's name added to the corporate charter. It was highly unorthodox at the time, and Bernard was reticent when helping them file the paperwork, but Isaac was insistent that Hattie own half the business. For her part, she was the saleswoman and business mind of the company. She had a hard nose for it and helped to keep costs down. Selfishly, it also allowed her to make sure they had enough time and profit to travel to all the exotic places she'd imagined when they first were married. They had a sign painted in the front windows that read, "Truesdell Furnishings." Hattie designed it and was very particular with the contractor who painted it.

Many of Isaac's projects the first few years included the furnishings for both the shop and the apartment upstairs. He installed a wall separating part of the bedroom from the rest of the apartment, but which still allowed access to the fireplace. He constructed a series of cabinets in the living room and kitchen, and a window seat configuration allowing them to sit together while looking out the windows at the world outside. Despite Hattie's nearly iron grasp on the business' finances, Isaac managed to slip a number of side jobs under her nose and save up enough money to buy a piano. After a visit to see her family one Saturday, she came home to find Isaac, two movers, and a piano tuner laboring away on the placement of the piano. The couple would reenact their first night together on the piano bench to celebrate their anniversaries as they passed.

Neither of them had any intention of owning a home or property, but instead focused their energies on each other, their business, travelling, and the children they were trying to conceive. Hattie's budgeting took them to New York, San Francisco, Chicago, and as far as London, Rome, and Athens. She was committed to seeing everything she could before she was required to settle down. Still, had she become pregnant, she told Isaac, she would have no regrets about giving up their travels.

Isaac honed his craft with every passing year and had progressed to the point where he could coerce varnishes and stains to saturate deeper into the wood, ensuring his products would last longer. He loved to listen to Hattie play piano upstairs while he worked in the shop. As she played, the ceiling below her would warm and glow with energy. It vibrated in chords and melodies through every object in his shop, creating a symphony of movement concentrating itself on pressing the stain farther and farther into the finish. With every layer, he could see Hattie's love for him resonating outward from the object. Their shop was filled with it. Their home was suffused with it. Their lives were defined by it. Her energy and joy moved through the air like a dancing spirit.

On a cold winter evening in 1895, Isaac returned to the shop with supplies and stoked the fire to warm the room for an evening's work. He heard piano music upstairs and assumed it was Hattie. Not wanting to disturb her, he chose to start working right away and greet her later. He pulled out a chisel and began carving the face in a set of cabinet doors he'd been working on for a client. The task took little to no effort. He laid the chisel gently on the wood, breathed, focused on her piano playing, and began hammering. The room came to a glow almost instantly, and the design began to take shape.

The sun had only just begun setting when he started, and the room was initially light enough to work in without lighting a lamp. Yet by the time the sun disappeared behind the buildings on the other side of the square, Isaac's charms illuminated the room enough that he did not need any further lighting.

"Working in the dark now, Isaac?" Hattie asked, having halfway descended the stairs before he noticed her.

He stopped, frightened, and looked at her. Realizing it was dark outside, he became self-conscious. "No... not intentionally. Who's playing the piano?"

"My sister. She's been practicing. Father says she wants to play at the tavern, so I thought I'd give her a few lessons. But you haven't answered my question. You're carving in the dark? I don't think that's good business, Mr. Truesdell," she joked, finishing her descent and walking over to him.

He was still completely incredulous. He'd been sure his charms were only definable as the way he saw the world and that he hadn't been lying to Hattie by withholding the information. As she approached him with a sly grin on her face, Isaac was presented with a problem. In order to explain what he was doing he needed to either tell her the truth – and run the risk of altering the dynamic of their relationship – or lie to her. The second option was so far outside of Isaac's moral code that doing so would inevitably alter their relationship anyway.

"Are you ignoring me now?" she asked, putting her hand on his stomach and looking up at his conflicted expression. "Are you okay? You seem worried."

"I don't really know how to answer you, I guess."

"What do you mean?" she asked, her concern for him growing.

"I mean. I... I didn't know I was working in the dark."

She looked around, "Isaac... it's dark in here. There's no light.

Well, there's some, but how can you see well enough to work?"

"I don't know, it's just something I do," he answered.

"Really? I've never seen you work in the dark before."

"That's because I wasn't. I mean, I didn't think I was…"

She reached up to check his temperature. "Are you okay? Do you not feel well? Because you're not making any sense, Isaac."

"I wish I could explain it, but when I'm working down here, and I breathe, and particularly when you're playing the piano…" Terror suddenly struck him, feeling he'd crossed a point of no return. "Oh, please don't think I'm crazy, Hattie. I love you so much."

"And I love you, too, Isaac. Why would I ever think you're crazy?"

"…because the room lights up, without light."

Hattie, pursed her lips and considered what he had said for a moment, finally asking, "What was that?"

"I don't know what it is," he answered, taking her hands. "It's just this thing that happens. Ever since we were first together. I see light in objects… furniture, walls, the air. I see light in you."

"In me?!" she squeaked, swiftly examining herself.

"Not an actual light, Hattie. It's… I don't know what it is. It's like I can see light and energy moving."

She stopped searching herself and looked at him skeptically. His eyes were pleading with her to believe him. Placing her hand on his cheek, she sighed and said, "Then I guess that's just how you see things." As she exhaled her phrase and touched Isaac, something glinted out of the corner of her eye. She turned to the front of the store, but there was nothing.

"What is it?" Isaac asked.

"I thought I saw something." Shrugging, she turned back to Isaac, placing her hands on his face and kissing him. As she did, her eyelids warmed as if the room were suddenly alight. While still engaged in the kiss, she opened her eyes and again caught light out of the corner of her eye, this time much brighter than before. She abruptly pulled away from him, breathing deeply as she did, and the room faintly glowed with light. Isaac saw it too, but when she exhaled, the light diminished and died. "Did you see that?!" she exclaimed, frightened.

"What?" he asked cautiously, not knowing if she was playing a joke on him or actually seeing what he had also seen. It wasn't like her to play those kinds of jokes; her genuine nature was playful but not cynically comical.

"Light! I think I saw what you were talking about. Isaac, what is that?"

"I don't know."

Determined to see it again, she kissed Isaac excitedly and opened her eyes. The room glowed for a short time, but when she pulled away and exhaled, it died again.

Frustrated, she asked, "Why does it do that?"

"Go away, you mean?"

"Yes! It was there, then it was gone. I believe you, Isaac. I really do, and I can see it, but then it goes away on me." She folded her arms in frustration.

Isaac considered what she had said, then revealed his own process, "Breathe, Hattie."

"What?"

"Breathe," he insisted.

"I am breathing!" she complained.

"I mean, relax and breathe. Listen to your sister play. Think of when you kissed me just now and breathe," he explained in a calming voice, holding his hand on her back.

Hattie reluctantly dropped her hands to her sides, breathed

deeply, and closed her eyes. Jacques Offenbach's *Barcarole* vibrated through the floor, the notes lilting back and forth, a nearly visual sensation conjured in her head. Embellishments lead to downbeats and the downbeats rolled inexorably from one to the next, coaxing each other to move closer and closer together. Chord changes pleaded with one another for continuation. She breathed and opened her eyes to a sight she never knew possible. The music danced through the room, playing along the air currents and twanging off objects as the delicate notes were struck by hammers on strings. At the crescendo, the room became alight and Hattie's breathing deepened.

Slowly, the music reached its finish. Hattie turned to Isaac, tears streaming down her face. "I saw it. It's so beautiful, Isaac."

From that moment, there was no longer anything they didn't share. It was as if their hearts beat together. When they made love, when they took walks, when they worked together in the shop, they breathed together, and saw the beautiful energy of the world… together.

Summer arrived and the Truesdells entered the busy season. Projects stacked on top of each other, one finished right after the last – metal projects on one side, wood projects on the other. They weren't overwhelmed, but they were certainly profitable, as Hattie noted. In the past few weeks, however, she'd become simultaneously more excited and more concerned.

They had been trying almost since the day they were married to conceive, but with no luck. Seven years had passed, and while their relationship grew stronger every day, they each questioned what they were bringing to the table. Isaac secretly felt that he was the cause of their infertility, while Hattie felt she was. They'd spoken about it, and each continually reassured the other that they were not responsible. Yet it weighed heavily on their minds. Friends and neighbors regularly asked when they would be settling down, to which they would outwardly espouse their love for travelling and spending time with each other.

By the end of May, Hattie was three weeks late. Another morning passed and another night. With significant reluctance, she approached Isaac early one morning while he was applying another coat of varnish to a chessboard.

She admired the work for a moment, then said, "I love how the grain alternates different directions based on the color of the square. What's the space for?" she asked, referring to a one-eighths-inch groove he'd left between the edge of the chess pattern and the edge of the table.

"That's for a brass inlay," Isaac explained. "I have to varnish it first in this heat because the wood may expand and bend the metal, or make it difficult to insert. You can help me if you like."

She shook her head. "No, thank you. Actually, I came down to tell you something."

"Sure," he replied, and returned to applying the varnish.

"Isaac, I'm late," she said, wringing her hands nervously.

"For what? Oh! You are?!" he asked excitedly, putting the varnish down and placing his hand on hers. She nodded cautiously. "Well, that's good news, isn't it?"

"I don't know," she answered, trying to avoid eye contact. "I've been having pains… these pains that I don't think I'm supposed to have."

Isaac finally took note of her distress and wrapped his arms around her. She crushed him to her, burying her face in his chest. He stroked her hair and kissed her cheek. "It's okay. We'll go see the doctor and find out what's going on, okay?"

"Okay," she muttered, muffled by Isaac's shirt.

"We'll get through it. I promise you. I'm sure it's nothing, Hattie. I'll set this all aside for a day or two and we'll go to see a specialist, okay?"

Hattie nodded, then started to cry, holding Isaac tighter. As they stood there in the shop, a strange sensation started to creep into the back of his mind. The feeling that crept into his mind was not in reference to a child – it was focusing specifically on Hattie. He immediately blocked the notion and focused on comforting her.

By noon, they had packed, left a note on the door of the shop with an apology to their clients, and hired a coach to take them to Dover, where they would connect with the railroad to Wilmington. In somewhat better spirits, Hattie climbed in and awaited Isaac, who spoke with his mother outside the shop.

"So you're going to Wilmington, Isaac? Are you going to see a doctor there?" Cynthia asked him impatiently.

"As a matter of fact, mother, we are…" Isaac was interrupted by his mother's exaggerated embrace. "Mother, please, we don't know anything yet. Hattie hasn't been feeling well and we're just going to make sure she's okay."

Concerned, Cynthia asked, "She's not okay?"

"I'm sure she is, we're just going to take a couple days of rest and see a doctor to make sure. Please, mother, we need to go."

"All right, but if you're going to stay much longer, please send word. We're so excited, Isaac."

"I know, mother," he replied flatly.

She then walked to the coach and leaned in, grabbing Hattie's hand lovingly. "Take care, dear. I want you to know we love you very much. Have a safe trip, both of you."

"We will," Hattie responded pragmatically.

They made the trip in almost complete silence. Isaac knew

better than to try to comfort Hattie with words. Instead, he held her hand, put his arm around her, and rested his head on hers, occasionally kissing her hair or forehead. When the train reached Wilmington, it was late evening, and Isaac secured them a room at a nearby hotel, as well as a table at the adjoining restaurant. When Isaac finished carrying their luggage to the room, he found Hattie sitting on the bed, staring into the mirror. She couldn't take her eyes off the image in front of her.

"Are you supposed to lose weight when you get pregnant?" she asked, almost childlike.

Isaac placed the luggage on the floor and closed the door behind him. "I don't know. Do you think it's different depending on the person? I mean, what's supposed to happen when you first… get pregnant?"

"You're supposed to eat a lot and… vomit. At least I think that's what's supposed to happen. My mother went through that with my sister and brother. What about your mother?"

"Now that you mention it, I do seem to recall something of the sort. I think she said it was different with each of us, though. Are you hungry? We have a table waiting downstairs." He motioned to the door.

She turned sideways in the mirror, focusing on how the bodice on her dress was not fitting properly around her corset and pouted at the change in the shape of her body. Ignoring this for the time being, she turned to Isaac. She laughed lovingly at how pitiful he looked and consoled him. "Oh, Isaac. I'm fine, darling. We all go through phases in our lives. I'm no child anymore. Perhaps it's just a sign of getting older."

They embraced and then went to the restaurant. In truth, Hattie wasn't hungry, but she felt she should eat anyway and didn't want to keep Isaac from a meal.

At the hospital the next morning, the doctor introduced himself to both Hattie and Isaac, inviting them into his exam room. They discussed her lack of appetite, the type of work she did, how long it had been since she last ovulated, and anything else that might relate to the early stages of pregnancy.

Based on her lack of fundamental symptoms, the doctor found no indication that Hattie was pregnant. He asked if he could perform an examination. Isaac was welcome to stay in the room, and he held Hattie's hand throughout.

When the examination was completed, the doctor welcomed Hattie to redress, while the two men exited to the hallway. The troublesome sensation in the back of Isaac's mind had been growing throughout.

"How long did you say she's been like this?" the man asked.

"I don't know. I think her appetite's been down for quite a while, though. Three weeks, I think."

"Well, we'll want to take a closer look, but from what I can see, the news isn't good, Mr. Truesdell," the doctor intoned, checking over the things he'd written on Hattie's chart. Isaac struggled not to react as the doctor spoke. "It would seem from her lack of appetite, along with a growth in her lower abdomen and swollen lymph nodes... that your wife may have cancer."

Isaac's calm ceased and the tears that had welled up as the doctor spoke began to stream down his face. "Are you sure?" Isaac pleaded, already knowing the answer.

"Mr. Truesdell, I need you to know that if it is cancer, the swollen lymph nodes likely mean it has spread, and there is very little we can do for her at that point," the man stated, trying to remain as business-like as possible.

An otherworldly pain invaded Isaac's chest. His arteries constricted, and his breathing labored. He tried not to pass out. The sound of his own heart drowned out the doctor's voice, and all he could hear was a dull, deafening thump that reverberated throughout his skull.

The latch clicked open and they fell silent. Hattie appeared in the doorway, fully dressed, a blank expression on her face. She took one look at Isaac, walked calmly to him, and wrapped her arms around him. She knew precisely what the doctor had told Isaac, and that there was nothing she could do about it. The sensation Isaac had been experiencing was present in her mind as well, and after her examination, she was prepared to deal with it.

They remained in Wilmington for several more days and had appointments with numerous experts who specialized in cancer therapy. One specialist recommended a fairly new treatment called the Coley vaccine. This method involved injecting a fluid mixture of bacteria into the tumor, which would induce the symptoms of an illness within the body and thus cause an intense immune response to the illness as well as the tumor. However, even the specialists who were proponents of the Coley vaccine cautioned a low probability of success in this instance considering how Hattie's illness had spread. If they treated all the occurrences of it, she could die from the bacteria before the cancer was cured. Hattie was firmly confident that there was nothing to be done, so both the Coley vaccine and the more standard surgical option were declined. Isaac would not question her judgment and promised to support her decision no matter what. With those matters settled, they returned solemnly home.

Over the next two months, Hattie's condition deteriorated. She ate less, and had begun to have night sweats while feeling cold during the day. She became weak and incapable of helping in the shop. When she first started to weaken, Isaac all too readily took up the tasks she could no longer do. Hattie didn't mind initially, but when he started having to carry her up and down the stairs and help her out of bed, she truly began to resent her condition. It was even more upsetting to her when she could no longer perform simple tasks like cooking or the piano playing she loved so much.

When Hattie could no longer perform even the most basic of daily living activities, Isaac enlisted his mother and eldest sister, as well as Hattie's sister, Margaret, to help Hattie in the apartment upstairs.

As the time closed in, her pain increased dramatically, yet she refused offers of laudanum. She didn't want to miss the few days she had left.

Hattie's brother Henry was brought on to help in the shop. He was young, but highly intelligent and picked up on the small tasks Isaac taught him quickly. The women played cards with Hattie to keep her company, and Hattie's sister played joyful tunes on the piano.

One late August evening as the women prepared to leave for the night, Hattie asked Margaret to stay and play the piano a while longer, promising that Isaac would make sure Henry walked her home.

"What do you want me to play," Margaret asked, putting her shawl down and walking to the set of shelves Isaac had built for Hattie's sheet music.

"Stephen Foster. You know, *Jeannie With the Light Brown Hair*?" Hattie asked, her breathing labored, and her eyes on the brink of sleep.

Margaret grabbed the requested music, thought about the tone of the song, and said, "I can play something happier if you like."

Smiling and shaking her head weakly, Hattie replied, "There is no happier song, Margaret. I'd like it if you played it for me. You don't have to sing though if you don't want to."

Margaret frowned, sat at the piano, and began to play.

Downstairs, Isaac heard the tune and stopped working. He leaned feebly on the workbench in front of him. Henry started toward Isaac and asked, "Are you okay, sir?"

Isaac put a hand up for Henry to stop. The boy did. "Henry, why don't you pull the shades and wait outside. I think we're done for the night. I'll send Margaret down in a minute."

Henry did as he was told. As soon as the door shut, Isaac collapsed on his work bench, sobbing uncontrollably. He choked it back as much as he could, not wanting Hattie to hear his weakness, but he could not stop the flood of sadness that had overwhelmed him. He remembered back to the night of their wedding when the musicians had serenaded him and Hattie at their window upstairs. He remembered the times they'd heard it at the tavern, and the times she'd played it for him on the piano. An overpowering weight pulled him down. He landed on his back on the floor of the shop, feeling as though his insides might convulse and burst forth from his chest. He wanted to scream, to kick, to wail, and to break every object in his shop, in his home, and in his life.

Hattie was the reason Isaac had discovered the world that was hidden to everyone else. They had discovered it again, together, only a few months before in the shop. What had he been doing all this for? A disease beyond even his control had consumed her, eaten her from the inside, and would soon take her from him for good. He wanted to take away her pain, then her weakness, and then the disease, and see her happy and full of life again. Or, he wanted to be able to go with her.

Margaret finished playing, and the music ceased. Isaac crawled to his knees and wiped his face with his shirt. He breathed as hard as he could, but nothing came. No light. No radiance. Just breath.

The breath was helpful though, as his entire body had constricted in remorse and despair. Isaac collected himself as best he could and started up the stairs. When he reached the top, Margaret was leaning over Hattie, telling her she loved her, and kissing her good-bye. He waited for their moment to finish, then moved toward Hattie, propped up in the window seat, her head leaning on the wall behind her.

"Henry's outside, Margaret. He'll walk you home," Isaac assured her.

"He's such a good boy. Thank you, Isaac," Margaret said, and began walking toward the stairs.

Isaac smiled. "You make sure to remind him of that. He's liable to forget it the way he's moping around these days."

"Oh, I will." She descended the stairs and slipped out of the shop.

Isaac turned to his wife, frail and sickly in the corner of the room. Hesitantly, he took a seat next to her, and looked into her eyes, which had become two shadows of their former selves. The bright green had given way to a dull gray, and her flushed cheeks had sunken to hollowed bones. "I'm not going to ask you how you are."

"Nor should you," she replied. "But I am worried about you. Don't think I don't know what you were just doing downstairs, Isaac." For the first time, Isaac broke down and sobbed in front of Hattie. She smiled a weak smile and put her hand on his. "There's nothing wrong with it. I'm worried because it's the first time you've let yourself feel anything for two months."

"I don't want you to go," he said childishly.

"Oh, darling, I have to. I love you so much, but this is my fate. You'll have yours someday, too. But not yet. This is my time." There appeared a curious smile on her lips, a smile born of knowing something Isaac would not for a very long time.

"What am I going to do?" he pleaded.

Her response was swift and simple. "Live."

Isaac was confused at the response, and indeed would not gain full comprehension of its meaning until much later. Long after people no longer traveled by horseback; after antibiotics had been developed; after nuclear weapons ignited the atmosphere, and while man was trying to land on the moon, the answer would come to him, and from a most unlikely place. For the time being, he was destroyed – a puddle of a man grasping for a weak understanding of life and death in the company of someone who grasped it fully.

"I've known what it means to live, Isaac. I had you to teach me about myself, to teach me about the gift you have, and to love me. If there's one thing I could change, it would be to spend more time with you. I wish I could have given you a child, too. We so wanted a child. What would you have named him, Isaac?"

Without hesitation, he replied, "Her. I would have named *her* Tabitha."

"Now, how do you know it would have been a girl?" she asked, her voice fading further and further away.

"Because you're perfect. God wouldn't have created someone like you then taken you away without replacing you."

"I'm dying, Isaac. There is no choice in this. There is no intention. We can't choose how life ends, only how we live it. There will be another woman…"

Isaac interrupted her, "No there won't. I promised you I'd love you all my life."

"But you have so much love, Isaac. It's okay to love me, but you have to let me go. I have to go." When she said this, Isaac nodded and squeezed his eyes shut, tears streaming down his face. "Now breathe, Isaac," she implored, and he did. The room became ablaze with light and sound. The piano twanged in a beautiful melody as if it were a harp played by the air. The walls glowed a cool blue, and the plants reversed their wilting process, the leaves turning brilliant shades of green. He peered around in wonder, then turned to Hattie. She reacted with no amazement at all. "We do this together."

"How will I do it without you?" he asked.

"You'll find a way." She nodded at him and clutched his hand. With one last burst, the room warmed, the piano twanged, and then the room fell silent. "Now, take me to bed and tell me a story."

He wiped his cheeks, stood up, and carried his wife to their bed. He laid next to her and began his story.

"There once was a young couple. They were meant for each other. From the moment they met, he knew she was the most vibrant, loving woman on earth, and he loved her dearly. One summer day, they decided to take a walk along the river. They talked about their lives together, and how they cared for each other. This went on for hours. They would stop and make love in the grass on the banks of the river, then walk for a while, then kiss... and then make love again. Late in the afternoon, a storm came along and soaked the young couple right through. Most people would have run home and changed out of their wet clothes, but these two just kept on walking. Laughing and talking. Eventually, they made it home, and when they walked in the door he picked his bride up off the floor and put her down on the kitchen counter. He looked into her bright, green eyes and fell in love with her all over again. Her brown hair dripped with rain, her clothes hung off her like laundry on a line, but that light shown from within her like a beacon, calling me home..." As he spoke the word "me" he began to choke up, "...and I sang her this song...

'I dream of Hattie with the light brown hair. Floating, like a vapor, on the soft summer air...' ...and she loved me." He lay with his arms around her, willing her to live long enough to hear the song one last time.

She did, and replied, "I love you. Always."

"I love you, too, Hattie. I love you, too. I love you, too..." he repeated over and over, rocking her to sleep. And she slept.

"Dearly beloved," the pastor began, and Isaac didn't hear a thing after that.

What could the man possibly have known about being beloved dearly? The pastor's wife was alive, his daughter was alive, and his heart still beat within his chest. Isaac had none of these. His heart was cold and still, wrapped within the bosom of his newly deceased love, the woman he had intended to spend his life with. But, if there was no longer anything to share, then what was his life? He remembered what Hattie had told him, but without her to reassure him, it made no sense.

After the ceremony, he helped her family place the earth over her grave. It wasn't the cathartic moment he'd hoped it would be. It was just dirt, a shovel, and some hostility toward the disease that had killed her. To make him feel even more helpless, he'd become the object of pity by the local citizenry. At the church, they'd filled out a sign-up sheet for each family to pick a day of the week to bring him meals and check up on him. He tried to be as cordial as possible, but all the spirit Isaac had was broken. He explained at one point to his sister, Jane, "It's not as though I can go back to the way I was before her. I didn't exist before Hattie."

"I can assure you, you did," Jane said as comfortingly as she could manage.

A long silence ensued. Jane knew her brother would never

recover from Hattie's death. The purity and intensity of their relationship was too powerful to ever be forgotten or replaced; everyone agreed on that. But they couldn't help but hope to see him happy again.

"We're worried about you, Isaac." He looked at her with reproach. "*I* am worried about you," she admitted, correcting herself. "Everyone else is worried about you, too, but I'm worried you won't get through this."

"What if I don't?" he asked, revealing a callous exterior.

"You're my brother, Isaac. You practically raised me. If I lost you, it would be like losing a part of myself, and I know I can help you. You just have to tell me how."

After much contemplation, he confided in her. "I sold the shop."

"What?!"

He nodded. "I sold it, and I'm going away. For good."

"For good? You mean you're never coming back?" she asked.

"I don't know. Hattie told me I have to get past this. And she's right. I just can't do it here."

"How long do you think that'll take?" Jane asked innocently.

"As long as it needs to. If you want to know what you can do for me, you could make sure to take care of mom after I leave. It won't set well with her, I'm sure. Make sure she knows I'm safe."

"And how will I know that?"

"You'll know," he said comfortingly.

Jane was the last member of his family whom Isaac ever spoke to. He disappeared the next day. What felt like an end to his family and the town, Isaac knew to be a beginning. He had answers to find, and though it would be painful, he needed to find them.

The next day, when they entered the apartment to look for Isaac, they found sheet music sitting on the piano for Jacques

Offenbach's *Barcarole*. No one else knew for sure what the hand-scrawled writing at the top meant, but Jane did, and she smiled reading it. Underneath the title, Isaac had written, "We do this together."

Chapter Eight

February 2010

Police tape had been wrapped from one tree to another, as well as to the small white picket fences on either side of the property, fluttering in the chilled, late February air. Only the driveway was free of the yellow signal warning, *Police Line Do Not Cross*. The temperature sat right around freezing, and sleet was falling in icy spurts. A haunting brick mansion sat nestled among the evergreens and barren maples in the center of the lot. Crusted, icy snow blanketed the front of the property while gloomy, gray clouds shielded the sky behind it.

The two officers guarding the cordoned-off street in front of the mansion lifted the tape to allow a cab to pass through. Inside the cab was Sarah Dempsey from Channel 3 News in Detroit. The officers had been given explicit orders to allow no press, but were given this one exception. The reporter inside flashed her credentials and was waved through.

"You know why a Michigan reporter's the only one allowed at a murder scene in West Chester, PA?" one officer pestered the other, and shrugged off a gust of sleet.

Shaking his head, the other replied, "No, but I bet it's bullshit."

"I bet it is."

The cab driver ground to a halt when a curmudgeonly-looking detective in a long, black topcoat stepped in front of the vehicle.

Sarah passed her fare to the driver through the slot in the glass and reached for the door handle.

"Right this way, ma'am." Unexpectedly, the detective held the door open and offered his hand.

He led her through the maze of officials and vehicles and up to the front of the house. The mansion's façade loomed over her, a massive embarrassment of a palace, opulent to the point of gaudiness. She peered up at the gargoyles with caution, as if they'd fly down to attack her. Shuddering, she continued through the entrance into the enormous hall that was thick with statues, dark wood décor, marble floor, a grand staircase, and a wrought iron chandelier. Crystal accents illuminated the hall. The smell of avarice and contempt inundated her nostrils.

Sarah knew about the victim before she'd left Detroit. Mike had called to inform her that yet another corrupt, wealthy businessman had been incinerated without any noticeable source or accelerant. This scenario had become Rebekah's calling card over the years. But, even if they caught her, she could never be convicted for it. It appeared she was aware of this, because the M.O. never changed. Mike informed Sarah that he'd gotten some pressure from a senior official at the bureau about why no one had ever been arrested or charged in the case, as it had been ongoing for almost fifty years.

These crimes of incendiarism had increased in frequency over the past year. This was two murders in just over a month, which was a stretch, even for Rebekah. At least forty such events had occurred in the fifty years since Mike's hospital stay, never at a greater frequency than four a year. At times, there would be a matter of years between them. Mike's real concern, however, was the crimes that had gone unreported. With the exception of the incident that had brought him to the East Coast in the first place, all of the crimes he had knowledge of were high profile murders, resulting in the death of someone who many people felt actually deserved it.

The requisite question was whether or not she had another M.O. Sarah Dempsey was a woman, the premier criminal investigative journalist in Detroit, and a blood relation to the perpetrator. By bringing Sarah on board, Mike felt they'd be able to think at least as fast as Rebekah. The next question was whether the motley crew could work in the same direction as the ageless witch.

In previous years, Mike hadn't been able to anticipate Rebekah's next target for a number of reasons: her ability to travel, her complete lack of an address, and the glut of viable targets. It simply wasn't possible to anticipate where she might strike next. But Sarah knew things about the family. She understood — on at least a subconscious level — the dynamics that created the criminal in the first place. Between the two of them and Brad's coffee acquisition skills, they now had a chance.

A mass of gawking, coffee-slurping detectives crowded the door to the mansion's billiard room. At the outskirts of this throng, the officer motioned to the door on the other side, saying, "The FBI guy's through there." He then turned on his heel and exited the building.

"Pardon me, boys," she barked and pushed her way through the throng. The detectives reluctantly stepped aside so she could pass through.

"Over here, Sarah." Mike motioned for her to meet him by the wall next to a set of leather chairs and a table displaying a nickel-plated cigar case. She stopped dead in her tracks, assaulted with the image of the victim, a charcoaled body lying prone on the billiard table in the middle of the room. She relaxed, took a deep breath and clicked across the parquet floor to where Mike and Brad stood near the police department's senior detective.

"This is Officer Perry of the West Chester Police Department. Officer Perry, this is Sarah Dempsey, a reporter from Channel 3 in Detroit."

Perry turned to Mike, refusing to shake Sarah's hand, clearly perturbed. "A reporter? Seriously?"

"Don't worry, officer. I'm not here as a reporter. Your name will stay out of the papers, I promise," Sarah assured him.

"Listen here, Agent Kirkpatrick," the detective started, squaring off with Mike. "I don't want anything to do with this case or my department to have anything to do with it. You get that? This is fucked up, and I'm not stickin' my or anyone else's neck out here. If there's any name in the papers, it better be yours."

Mike glanced at Sarah. She smirked at him as if to say, *You got yourself into this*. He glared back at her, saying to the detective, "Thanks. Look, Perry, you don't have to worry about it. You're right, the case is pretty messed up. My partner and I will take it from here."

"Well, then what the hell's she doing here?" the detective asked.

Brad finally chimed in. "She's seen a number of these cases and is acting in an advisory capacity. She hasn't reported on *any* of them as a matter of fact. She has a familiarity with the M.O., that's all."

"Wait, this is a series?" the detective asked, dumbstruck.

They all looked at Brad. A petrified, hangdog look washed over his face. "No?"

Perry asked irritably, "Have there been any others in the area?"

"No," Mike and Brad answered simultaneously.

"Fine. Fuck it. It's all yours." He threw up his hands and turned to exit the room, shouting, "All right everyone, let's go. The feds got this one. Time to clear out." He waved his subordinates out of the house, leaving only Mike, Brad, and Sarah in the billiard room and a small contingent of agents scattered throughout the house.

"What an asshole," Mike uttered.

Brad walked to the door to make sure they were gone. "I kinda feel like one, too."

"I was talking about you."

"I was trying to diffuse the situation!"

"Well, it worked," Mike chortled. "They're gone. Remind me to buy you coffee later."

Sarah tried her best not to laugh and busied herself by pulling out her phone and initiating the recording app. She stepped toward the table, beginning her dictation. "The body is pretty well charred, though the hands and feet are more or less intact. The face and chest are particularly… crispy."

Mike looked at her skeptically. "Never took those pathology classes, huh?"

She paused the recording software. "Never managed to fit it in, and you know how hard it is to go back after you graduate, right?"

"Never went to college," he answered.

"Well, it's hard to go back. Besides, complicating the language just makes viewers change the channel."

Mike moved toward the table to analyze the body with Sarah. "Maybe you need to move to a different market."

"I'll ignore that comment," Sarah sighed and restarted the recorder. "The flames must have been concentrated there, and the rest of the body burned by proximity. Judging by the state of the billiard table, it would appear the body was burned elsewhere and brought into this room. My guess is that aside from whatever fluids have leached into the felt, this table's still pretty playable." She stopped the recorder and turned to Mike. "Why not the table? Why not the house for that matter?"

"That goes to motive," he answered.

"Well, you said all of her victims are rich assholes. This guy was a rich asshole. Why not burn the house down too? Why not burn it all and pour salt on it?" she asked, mostly to herself.

Mike shook his head. "I've been asking myself the same question. She torched the toy factory, but this palace goes free. Somethin' about that's... kooky."

Sarah laughed. "Now there's the slang I've been waiting for, Mike. Why do you hide it from me?"

"Maybe I'm trying to impress you?" he joked.

"Oh sure, trying to sound smart in front of a woman who refuses to use the word *incendiary* in a newscast..." She trailed off, suddenly very deep in thought.

Mike noticed the change and moved closer to get a better view of her face. "You okay?"

"I don't know. I just got a cold feeling up my spine, that's all."

"By saying 'incendiary'? That's a bit ironic, isn't it?" he asked sarcastically.

She turned to him with her hand on her hip and stated, "Now you're showing off."

"You got me." Mike smiled, putting his hands up in surrender. "Incendiary. You're talking about the device used for starting a fire."

She spoke into her recorder. "But the word also applies to a person. Depending on the definition, a person can be an incendiary. An arsonist is technically an incendiary. So, the word has more to do with the function of starting a fire than what it is that started the fire. Right?"

"I guess. What's on your mind, Sarah?" Mike asked.

"Now, I am in no way condoning murder, and I have this recording to verify that. But, I have to admit that most of these guys pretty much had it coming. She picks people who make their living from the suffering of others. While I can kind of see the point in that, I can't understand why she would do it in this fashion. So, let's just suppose that she felt she was serving a purpose. If she views herself as a device of... I don't know, fire, destruction, justice... It just seems odd that a seventy-year-old woman would still be heavy into vigilantism."

Mike frowned at her. "While I resent the comment about age, I see your point."

"But why commit yourself to something like this? She's been doing it for fifty years and knows that the motive never hits the papers, so there's nothing to be learned publicly from her crimes. Why do it then? There're so many of these types of guys out there. She could be torching one a day and probably make some money at it, too."

Mike nodded emphatically. "That much is definitely true."

"So why these men? Why with this frequency?" Sarah asked, becoming increasingly frustrated.

"Her frequency has been picking up lately. Maybe she thinks she's hitting the end of her rope," Brad added.

"I saw her! She looks half my age!" Sarah replied.

"Yeah, but maybe it's not an age-related rope. Maybe she's got a goal in mind." Brad clarified.

"Fine, what is it?" Sarah asked. "What else do these guys have in common? Are they part of some secret society and she's cleaning them out one by one? What association might she know about that they'd be members of?"

"No. No secret societies. Normally, they'd have something around the house to indicate that. A couple of them were Skull &

Bones, one was in The 21 Club, a couple were members of a men's club in Manhattan, but not statistically significant. Most of 'em weren't members of anything except a local gym," Brad stated.

Sarah pondered for a moment, thinking back to the events that had occurred a month earlier. "Well, she starts fires by looking at people and can disappear from right in front of your face... Is she a witch?"

"You probably want to be careful about using that word when and if this ever goes to air. Over the years we've combed through local Wiccan organizations in the areas that these men lived, and the truth is those people want nothing to do with it," Mike explained.

"What do you mean?" Sarah asked.

Brad added, "Wiccans are pretty much tree huggers. Radical Christians like to paint 'em as Satanists and occultists, but that isn't really how they operate. If your aunt is a witch, it's not in the sense that any organized or even unorganized form of Earth-worshipping recognizes."

"Tree huggers?" Sarah laughed.

"It's true. We even got spat at once for suggesting an association between your aunt and witchcraft. These people believe in a connection to nature, not killing people and taking justice into their own hands."

Sarah started chewing a fingernail. "Well, what is witchcraft then?"

Brad began explaining while Mike countered to the other side of the chairs to analyze the deceased owner's book collection. "The details are pretty varied, actually. In the loosest terms, a witch is just someone who practices Earth worship. Be it how they bury their dead, or daily devotionals, or praying to trees, or whatever. It's kind of a loose association of pagan practices. Wicca itself wasn't even formed into an identifiable religion until about 100 years or so ago. A combination of the non-Christian, spell-casting, antiestablishment types you read about with the Salem thing, and a series of Eastern philosophies like karma, prana, and balance... kind of the yin-yang thing."

"We talk about prana in my yoga class, Brad. That doesn't make me look a third my age. Trust me on this," Sarah joked.

"Hey, you asked. The point is, it's not the demon culture the zealots make it out to be. They're hippies for the most part. Besides, if you believe in karma, why wouldn't you allow karma to take care of it?" Brad asked.

She nodded. "That's a good point. What she's doing is forcing bad karma on herself instead of just allowing them to meet theirs." After a moment, a thought occurred to her. "But, what if she believes she's an agent of karma. A deus ex machina, so to speak?"

"An incendiary," Mike chimed in.

"The incendiary is the device in this case. The device just happens to be a person, or so she thinks she is," Sarah added. "That still doesn't narrow down the list. What else do these guys have in common, other than wealth and abuse of power?"

Brad replied, "Domestic violence. Sometimes toward a wife, other times a child. In all of the cases there wasn't enough evidence to convict, or the police botched the case, or, nobody seemed to care. But not one of these guys was an angel, especially at home."

"An activist then?" she asked.

Mike interjected, looking up from his perusal of the man's library. "Like you? Continuing to report the hard stories in a dying city?"

"I'm trying to be serious here. You guys have a pretty big head start on me here, so I'm bound to ask a few basic questions," she defended.

"I'm not completely teasing. Maybe it's a family trait. One of the reasons I was so interested in bringing you into this case was to see if there was a family resemblance in more than just looks. I've seen your news stories. You regularly report on things the mainstream media avoids. Maybe it's why you work in Detroit. In any case, you've chosen to put that ahead of personal advancement. If you've got the slightest bit of shared intentions with your aunt, I'd like to know what they are." Mike picked up a book and started thumbing through it.

Sarah turned to the remains of the man on the billiard table and tried to put herself in her aunt's shoes. She imagined how she might feel if she were a victim of domestic violence or assault, and how it would feel to have the power to do something about it when the system failed. The lure of vigilante justice had struck her many times in her tenure as a reporter, but she just couldn't psychologically take that next step.

"There's something else missing," Sarah said, shaking her head and tapping her foot impatiently.

"What's that?" Brad asked.

"Okay, she was abused. These guys abuse people. That's one motivation, but there's a giant leap between being a victim and convincing oneself to murder forty-some people. What could she think she was accomplishing that wouldn't have extreme ramifications for her? Plus, abuse is a rampant problem. How did she come to the conclusion that sacrificing her own soul, karma, what-have-you was worth knocking off a few guys who happened to get away with it?"

"Well, that's the big question, isn't it?" Mike replied, shrugging.

Sarah asked, "So, do you guys have a process for how you look for potential future victims?"

"We have a list compiled at the local office we can check out.

Maybe you can help us pick where to look next?" Mike asked.

"Sure, I'm stuck here until tomorrow anyway."

"Great," Brad interrupted. "Can we stop for coffee on the way then? You said you were going to buy me one, right?" Mike shook his head and exited, with Brad and Sarah following close behind.

The coffee shop was a shabby local establishment with a brick interior that offered baked goods, soups, and the kind of random seating acquired through the highly scientific process of grabbing furniture off curbs. Sarah looked around at the offbeat paintings and decor and decided this was her type of coffee joint. After paying for their coffee and baked goods, the trio retreated to a small table surrounded by duct-tape-clad 1950s kitchen chairs.

"So... Mike and Brad, I want you guys to tell me, and you don't have to if you're not allowed to or whatever, but I want you to tell me more about my aunt. I would imagine that over the years you've investigated more than just her crimes, right?" Sarah asked, and then slurped the foam off the top of her latte.

"Why wouldn't you be entitled to that information? You're family," Mike said, wiping his chin with a napkin, a bit of scone crumbling onto his suit pants.

"Tell me about her childhood. How does someone grow into a serial killer that burns people from the inside? When she and I talked, she seemed perfectly cogent and not at all unhinged. Desperate and upset, but not unhinged."

"That's a good question, and the answer wasn't easy to come by. It took the better part of the summer in 1983, but I managed to find a couple neighbors of Rebekah's family from when they lived in Boston and Tulsa. The general consensus was that your grandfather had a bit of a temper..."

Sarah interrupted him. "I always got the impression that she and my mom were abused children. But what do you mean by a bit of a temper?"

Correcting himself, Mike added, "Okay, not a bit. He beat his wife and kids. Particularly in Boston. After your grandmother died, he kept it up in Tulsa until the night their house burned down. By the time I questioned the Boston neighbors, they'd long since forgotten most of the specifics about the arguments they overheard. But apparently, a running theme had something to do with the local library."

"And there were no cases of an assault on library property?" Sarah asked.

"None involving your grandparents or aunt at least. Even if there were, police departments purge the files of non-arrest-related complaints after a period of time. If there had been an assault, it wasn't serious enough to warrant an arrest. And, there were no library personnel left to question. Besides, we never managed to get a discernable picture of your grandmother anyway. That being said, it would be reasonable to assume that the library was her alibi for any affair that may have been going on at the time. If they argued about the library frequently enough that the neighbors remembered it as a bone of contention thirty years later, I'd say it was a useful hiding spot that he never checked out personally."

Sarah nodded in agreement. "That's sound reasoning."

"The neighbors in Tulsa had a bit more information, though nothing including your grandmother, since she had passed before they moved…"

"Sorry to interrupt," she interjected. "…but do you know my grandmother's cause of death? My mother never knew her and like you said, the people in Tulsa never did either."

Mike finished chewing a bite of his scone. "Heart attack. She had a medical chart at the hospital in Boston, but there was nothing to it except for the day she was brought in with chest pains. No prior medical history, family medical history... just her death."

"Well, who the hell was this woman? She had no family, no background, just a marriage to an abusive asshole, an affair, and a heart attack. And you know nothing else about her?" Sarah asked.

Mike shook his head, choking down another bite of scone. "We really don't. She was married in 1933 to your grandfather, Jack Boyd. He was a steelworker in Pennsylvania at the time and they relocated to Boston in 1935 when he got a job as a welder."

"What about before that? Where's her family?" Sarah asked.

"Gone. She didn't exist in this country before that wedding certificate," Mike stated ominously.

"I wonder what makes someone stay with a man like that for so long."

Mike raised his eyebrows. "Times were different back then. There was a lot of fear and no money. Leaving meant losing food and shelter. Hell, even today a lot of women go through the same thought process and never leave abusive partners, you know that."

Sarah agreed. "The more I think about the family dynamic Samantha and Rebekah survived, the more I think how amazing it is that *I* was born at all. So, did you ever talk to my mom? I mean, I know you said you wouldn't question her now, and I appreciate that. But back then?"

Mike nodded hesitantly, peering up at Sarah over his coffee cup. "We did. Well, I did. *He* wasn't born yet. I'd imagine if a guy that looks like me now came up to a little girl she wouldn't have said word one. Although, she was pretty fascinated by the scars. I went to see her after the fire in Concord. It was on my own time and nickel since I wasn't officially heading the investigation at the time. The two incidents just sounded too similar and I wanted to know more about the girl. That would have been some time in '64."

"What did she say?"

Mike took a deep breath and tried to recall the conversation. "I told her I was a friend and made sure the Dempseys stayed in the room so she was more comfortable. She must have been 11 or 12 by then, so there wasn't as much reticence as there might have been had I asked her back when the fire happened, but she was still understandably... aloof. Anyway, I asked her to tell me about her parents, but she didn't say much. She said her dad was angry. She didn't say that he'd hit her, but it was clear the Dempseys had instructed her to keep quiet about it. I wasn't about to push anything. Aside from that, she didn't have much to say about your grandparents. She said her brothers were 'mean.' The person she had the most to say about was Rebekah. The way she talked, you'd think she was her mom. I guess it would make sense in a house-hold like that for the older daughter to want to take care of the younger one. Apparently, Rebekah protected your mother quite regularly. Maybe she kept her from getting hit. I don't know, and she wouldn't go into any great detail. It was just very clear that she saw her sister as an angel of some sort. That didn't sit too well with me at the time, but I got over it. Then I asked her about the night their house burned down and she clammed up... started crying. The Dempseys explained to me that it was a sore spot with your mother, that she didn't like talking about it. I told 'em 'of course it was' and that I had no intention of hurting the girl... just needed some information that might help save other lives."

"And did you get it?" Sarah pried.

Mike sighed. "Yes and no. It helped us know something about Rebekah, but nothing that's helped us track her down or anticipate who her next victims would be."

"What did she say?"

"Samantha said she was ultimately responsible for the fire. She said Rebekah started the fire because of her, because she had talked about some book or other. After that, she was pretty cracked up and I wasn't about to question her again. I'm sorry about that, Sarah," he admitted.

"Don't be," she reassured him, sipping her latte.

"We searched the property. It was a long shot, but we wanted to know if there was a book Rebekah had hidden somewhere. We found all kinds of stuff that had been buried, though we don't know by who. Personally, I think it was her. The night of the jail fire, I noticed your aunt's clothes were worn and her nails were yellow and ratty. When I was searching the property, I thought back to that night. I think she'd been digging with her bare hands."

"What kinds of things were buried?" Sarah asked, leaning in.

Mike put his coffee down and sat up straight. "It was bizarre. There were animals, objects, a couple human skeletons…"

"Wait, so she was killing people *before* she left home?"

"No, there was no indication she'd killed any of the animals or people back there. The forensics fellas said the bodies had been dead for quite some time, since before your aunt even moved to Tulsa. She put the bodies in graves, like she was trying to give them a proper burial. Each of the sites was marked with a stick of some sort. No stone, no collection of stones or anything, just a stick jammed into the ground." Mike demonstrated with his hands. "The most interesting thing we found, as well as most disappointing, was the corner of a book."

Eagerly, Sarah asked, "What book?"

"That's what was disappointing about it. Your mother gave us that nugget about the book and we were really pleased to find it in one of the graves out there. It sounded like the book was some source of tension, but we couldn't identify what book it was to know why. Frankly, it could have been anything. *Catcher In the Rye* for all we know."

"Damn," she uttered. "You ever read *Catcher*?"

"No, when your momma tells you not to read something, you listen," Mike admitted.

Sarah waved her finger. "Wait a minute, that book came out in what, 1950? '51? How old were you then?"

"Sixteen or seventeen. But you need to understand, a good Southern boy always listens to his momma." He toasted with his coffee. "Maybe we should head back to the office. Got some searchin' to do."

They grabbed their belongings and adjourned to the local FBI office to review the case information. Mike, Brad, and Sarah pulled the blinds and plugged Mike's laptop into the projector. After some cursory finagling of the projector connection to the laptop, they managed to get Mike's mini-dossier spreadsheet up on the screen. He started a new line for the latest victim, then clicked over to another tab titled 'potential targets.'

Seeing the title of the tab, Sarah asked, "So, if you have a list that you update regularly, why don't you warn these guys? Why not stake out their houses and wait for her to show up?"

"For starters, the list is longer than you'd think," he said as he started scrolling through. "Realistically, she's never killed more than four people in a year. Let's say there are a hundred guys on the list. That means a minimum of three months sitting outside their house waiting for her to show up. Two agents times a hundred guys... it's not in the budget. Don't get me wrong, I wish it were, but even if we could afford it, she'd undoubtedly see the car sitting out front and either go somewhere else or wait us out."

"How many rich guys who abuse their wives and/or children can there be?" Sarah asked.

Mike directed her attention to the list on the projector screen.

"See for yourself. In my experience, abuse knows no social class. If anything, it follows two primary types of people: people who feel they have no power and people who feel they don't have enough."

"Which fits these guys," Brad interjected. "From what we've seen, these guys are statistically more likely to abuse the people around them. They're only invested in the parts of their relationships that benefit them, and the parts that don't…"

Pointing at the list with her pen, Sarah asked, "How often do you update this?"

Mike scrolled to the bottom and highlighted the date. "Once every other week or so. There isn't always someone new to add. Some of these guys have been on a paper version of this list for 20 years. I really wish I knew all of her criteria so we could narrow it down."

Sarah looked at the last three entries. The first of the three names was a meatpacking executive in Chicago. According to the notes, the man had been under investigation for tax evasion, racketeering, attempting to bribe and intimidate federal officials, and much more. As she read, she began to remember hearing about him while working on a story about a local racketeering case in Detroit. Largely ignored by the mainstream media, however, were the additional charges of child abuse lodged against him by his then 32-year-old daughter. Since her claims didn't affect the public at large, it didn't make the news.

The next entry identified a crooked New Orleans politician who had not only profited from Hurricane Katrina relief funds, but had also been accused of assaulting his son as a child. The charges stemmed from an interest piece published months earlier in the *Times-Picayune* that included an interview with the man's ex-wife. The boy, in his early 20s at the time of the article, denied the claims – as did the father – but speculation lingered nonetheless. One of the notes referenced a local psychologist who appeared in court and suggested the boy might be suffering from repressed memories. Another note added that the ex-wife had been attacked in the media and by the man's attorneys for possibly fabricating information.

The final entry referred to an entire series of news stories related to the owner of a gentlemen's club in Toronto. On top of numerous allegations of making untoward advances on his employees, the club owner had also been officially charged with criminal sexual assault by a family who'd been his neighbors years before. After their daughter had been through considerable therapy and the family had moved to another province, the district attorney agreed to file the charges.

"Have all the people she's killed been on your list before she killed them?" Sarah asked.

"Five of them have," Mike answered.

"Do you warn them in advance or question them beforehand?"

Brad sighed deeply. "I tried that a while ago. The bureau thought it would blow their investigations if we started nosing around asking unrelated questions. Personally, I thought if we went to these people and said, 'Hey, you might be killed soon if you don't confess to these other charges,' that it might help the bureau's case. Mike's tried that before, too. One point the chief made was that these guys we tip off would think we were nuts and wouldn't take us seriously anyway, so why bother. That I can understand."

"So, what do we do? Just sit around and wait for her to kill someone else?" Sarah asked, exasperated.

"We wait for a better clue," Mike insisted. "Besides, this isn't the only case we have to investigate. We do our best, but in the end, we're doing everything we can. Trust me on this, Sarah. No one would like to see Rebekah brought in more than me." He held up his hand, showing his scars. "If for no other reason than I need to know why she does it. Fifty years of this, though, and you have to cut your losses."

Sarah exhaled, suddenly realizing why she was there. "I see why you brought me on. Fresh eyes, maybe someone who can take over the bulk of the work…"

"Someone who's personally invested, Sarah. That's what you are. Now, I don't want to take advantage of you. Truly, I don't. But I have looked at every lead and every piece of evidence a thousand times. So has Brad. Unless she starts leaving new bits of evidence at the crime scene, we're stuck until she gives herself up." Mike felt bad for using Sarah, but he also felt sure she'd agree to help.

Sarah looked at the two men and considered her options. "I'll tell you what. I'll give this a few months. I'll stew on it, check out a couple of the crime scenes, and I'll let you know what I think."

"That's all I ask," Mike said.

"I have a conference in New Orleans next week, so maybe I'll look into this politician guy. If I get anything, I'll let you know first, okay?"

Mike smiled hesitantly, then mentioned, "Just don't talk to him, okay? That could go badly for everyone."

"Of course not. Why would I do that?" she replied. The two men looked at each other cautiously before sending her on her way.

Sarah stopped in Detroit briefly to repack and spend time with her cat, Saint Francis, then boarded a flight to New Orleans.

* * *

One of the benefits of the nonstop flight from Detroit to New Orleans was extended drink service. "My kind of flight!" she stated cheerfully as she raised her glass to a bewildered flight attendant. Prior to her departure, Sarah attempted to schedule a meeting with Bobby J. Rutherford, the crooked politician from Mike's list. She'd been informed, however, that she would have to settle for an appointment with the man's attorney, Tim Jackson, instead. Jackson's name had come up in years past. He was something of a notorious defense attorney who had managed to secure the freedom of a number of prominent Southern politicians, businessmen, and other shady scions of fortune. She wasn't excited about interviewing an attorney, but she had done it frequently enough to know what to expect.

She checked into her hotel the weekend before the conference began. While she had every intention of attending some of the events, she was more concerned with seeing Jackson and taking in some of the local color. She walked past many of the standard attractions: The House of Blues, Café du Mond, and numerous other sites she recognized from magazines, television, and film. On the return trip, she ventured down a side street to admire the balconies and architecture. Halfway down the block, she walked past an unassuming antique shop. As she did so, she felt a chill run up her spine. She looked up at the sky overhead, a clear, warm air flowing through her hair.

Sarah hesitantly assessed the exterior before entering. A print in the window said, "Sonja's Antique Shoppe" in a frilly green font with a gold shadow outline. The posted hours indicated she had five more minutes to sate her curiosity.

Once inside, an odd sensation overtook her. Glass top shelves and tables were jammed into the tiny shop, each packed with some of the most bizarre and random items she'd ever seen. Objects dangled from the coffered ceiling overhead, and the floor was a patchwork of every era and style of architecture she'd ever observed. Inside the glass cases, each object had its own hand-written description of time period and location.

All at once, she got the notion that she was being watched. She tried not to let it overwhelm her; she would have heard the bell ring on the door if anyone had come in from the front, and she could see the back of the shop from where she was, so it wasn't possible for anyone to actually be watching her. But the feeling persisted. And it wasn't just one set of eyes. She felt an indeterminate number of gazes fixed on her.

After five minutes or so of milling around the shop, the owner emerged from the basement and took her place at the counter at the back of the shop. "Hello," she stated warmly.

"Hi," Sarah replied. She felt she should initiate some form of conversation to ask about the trinkets, but wasn't quite sure how. "Are you Sonja?" she asked, pronouncing the name with a 'y' sound.

The woman smiled, but shook her head. "Sonja," she corrected, making the hard 'j' sound as well as a long 'o'.

Sarah winced. "I'm sorry. I probably should have asked." She walked toward the woman with her hand outstretched.

"Don't worry. I get it all the time," Sonja said, and smiled reassuringly.

"My name is Sarah," she replied, and took close stock of the woman. She was a black woman in her early to mid-40s with a snappy fashion sense, clad in on untucked purple button-up, black slacks, and polished green heels. Her hair was swept up in back with thin braided sections framing her face. Sarah thought, *This woman's got style*. Sonja responded by smiling and nodding.

"So Sonja, this is your shop?"

"It is. I've been running it for about ten years now, I inherited it from another woman. She was the one who laid the floor and started the business back in the seventies," Sonja explained, rising from her stool.

Sarah shook her head in amazement. "It's a wonderful shop." As she talked with the woman, she became more and more at ease, sometimes catching herself being a bit too comfortable. "It's a little out of the way, isn't it?"

"I cater to people who are looking for something other than the mainstream."

"I can see that. Some of these items are incredibly... unique. Oh, that reminds me, I want to ask you something," Sarah walked to the nearest glass case. "What does this mean, when it says 'donation' on the bottom of the tag?"

Sonja took a breath and cocked her head, sizing Sarah up. After some deliberation, she replied, "When a... wayward traveler visits the shop, sometimes they'll leave something behind. In thanks."

Her reporter sense kicking in, Sarah asked, "For what?"

Instead of directly answering Sarah's question, Sonja asked, "Why are *you* here?"

"Am I a wayward traveler?" Sarah asked. "I'm here for a conference of television reporters."

"I hope the conference isn't being held in my shop," Sonja joked, smiling broadly at Sarah.

"Oh, I'm sorry, I'm a little tired, I guess. Maybe too much scotch on the plane..." Embarrassed by her admission, Sarah changed the subject. "Why am I in the shop? I get it now. Well, I'm not quite sure. I've been getting a lot of cold drafts lately. You ever get those? Maybe it's because it's winter in Detroit or something, I don't know. I got a chill outside your shop and I thought

I'd take a peek."

"Most people turn the other way at such sensations. Is that the journalist in you?"

"Journalist? No, I won't be doing a story on you, I'm a criminal reporter. Might turn the guy who does human interest pieces on to you, though. This place is amazing."

"But why are you here? I get the idea you're not looking for any object in particular. Were you just browsing?" Sonja prodded playfully. "Perhaps there is an object that called you in here?"

Sarah smiled, embarrassed. "I don't believe in that. I mean, that would be… fascinating if there was, but I don't think I believe in that sort of thing."

"You don't? But what was the cold feeling then?" Sonja waited for Sarah's response, which came in the form of a baffled, soundless headshake. "Have you had a thorough look around?"

They began strolling around the store, seeking objects that might fit the unnamed bill. "I don't know. Like I said, it's been happening more and more lately. Some old FBI guy got me involved in this really bizarre investigation about an old woman who starts fires," Sarah started. When she said this, Sonja stopped in her tracks and turned to Sarah, who was looking through a set of dishes in a glass case, her back to Sonja. "I guess I probably shouldn't be telling you this, but it's just so damn weird. Anyway, she's starting these fires and causing minor havoc at the bureau because no one can figure out how she does it…"

"What did he look like?" Sonja asked, very seriously.

Sarah turned back to her to describe Mike. "He's in his seventies – should probably be retired by now – and he's covered almost head to toe in burn scarring. Got kind of a claw for a right hand. Wears a hat indoors even, because he can't grow hair on his head. He says he was one of her first victims. I told him she failed on that one…" Finally noticing Sonja's intense interest, Sarah asked, "Do you know him?"

Sonja shook her head. "No, not him. At first I thought you were referring to someone else."

"Wait a minute," Sarah began, baffled. "Do you know about the case? The burnings?"

Sonja retreated a bit, suddenly guarded. "I've heard about a similar case."

"No, not a similar case – there's only one. What man were you thinking of? Was he a young guy, pretty plain and doofy-looking?" she asked, referring to Brad.

"You work for the FBI?"

"No, I'm a crime reporter from Detroit. I swear, if you know something about it, I promise not to tell the FBI if you don't want me to." Sarah begged.

"Wouldn't the FBI find out when they read your story?" Sonja asked.

"I'm not reporting on this one. You can take my word on it."

"But you're a crime reporter. These are crimes, yes? Why wouldn't you report it?"

Sarah gulped and blurted, "Because the killer's my aunt."

When Sonja first looked at Sarah, she had had the feeling that the two were meant to meet. Relation to a killer or not, Sarah seemed trustworthy, and Sonja opened up.

"I've never met either of those men; it was another man… older, though not scarred. He had white hair, he was tall and had a bit of a European accent. He came into my shop, oh… five years ago? Told me he was looking for a young woman and offered me *this* in exchange for my help." She reached behind the counter and pulled out a rolled-up paper bag, slowly unraveling it and crossing the floor to Sarah. "He told me she'd been doing horrible things, and that he was trying to stop her. I didn't trust him. He said 'thank you' and left, leaving this with me anyway." She finished opening the paper bag and pulled out a hairpin, handing it to Sarah.

The hairpin was silver, with an ornately looped cincturing design and three jade stones mounted in the center. The pin was topped with matching jade and was sharp enough to prick.

"He told me this had belonged to her, but at the time, it felt like maybe he was trying to pawn something off on me. He said there were all these rich men she'd been killing by burning them to death."

"That's the one. That's my aunt." Sarah paused, then went on to reassure the woman. "Don't worry. I'm way more adjusted than she is."

"It's okay. You don't worry me. He did, though. So does she."

"Look, I know this is all really strange, but do you know anything about the man? His name? Where he's from? 'Cause right now just about anything would be useful," Sarah pleaded.

Sonja contemplated for a moment. "He said his name was Daniel. Wouldn't say where he was from, but... can I confide in you?"

"Absolutely."

"Because you said you don't believe that an object called you in here. This pin belonged to your aunt. I believe it was calling you in here. I also believe things about this man. But if you don't believe in the supernatural, then I don't know how useful the information would be to you," Sonja offered.

"I want to believe. Trust me, I really do. I can't explain how these things have been happening and I'm in a profession where I need three sources for something if it's at all in question. Otherwise my producer and director won't go to air with it. And these crimes don't make sense with what I've got so far, so I'm willing to take whatever you've got."

Sonja asked, "What does your heart tell you?"

"My heart?"

"Yes, your heart. When you walked in here, you felt compelled to do so, right? You said you felt a shiver. You weren't even supposed to be walking down this street, but you were. I think there's something inside of you that's sending out a distress signal and the winds picked it up."

Sarah rolled her eyes at herself. "That's as good an explanation as any."

"You're skeptical. It's a start," Sonja said, pleased. "I believe the man is related to the woman who owned that pin. His words indicated that he was worried for her safety and that she was committing horrible crimes, but his heart said the opposite. To me, he appeared to be more afraid for his own safety, and that he had something to hide. Perhaps you are the key to it. Maybe you can find who is telling the truth and who isn't."

Sarah looked cynically at the pin. "I can't even find Rebekah. I don't know how I'd be able to find him. Daniel, you said?"

"That's what he said."

"No last name I assume?" Sarah asked. Sonja shook her head regretfully and smiled at Sarah to comfort her. Sarah breathed deeply and a small shimmer of light shot across the outside of the pin. She barely noticed it, assuming it was a reflection from a ceiling light and looked back at Sonja. "Thank you for telling me this. I know you don't know me, so I really do appreciate it. I promise none of this will ever end up in the papers. You're safe."

"Thank you. It's a frightening circumstance and I had begun to worry I was alone in it. It's nice to know someone's out there looking for them."

"*Them*. Yeah, now I have two targets instead of one," Sarah acknowledged reluctantly.

"I'm sure you'll figure it out."

"Thank you for letting me see this," Sarah said and held out the pin for Sonja to take back.

Sonja refused. "No, keep it. If that really was your aunt's, then I want you to have it. No charge."

"But I have nothing to give you."

"The gifts come from those who are lost, not those who are found. It is yours to keep," Sonja explained.

"But I'm the one who's lost."

"And I am now found. For five years, I've had the presence of that object in my shop, and that man's face has haunted me. Knowing you're out there, finding him, and her… You've put my mind at ease, Sarah. If it makes you feel any better, if you ever come back to New Orleans, you can stop by my shop and donate something. I just hope that won't happen until you find what you're looking for. I can only trust that this will help you somehow."

Sarah again assessed the object, feeling its weight in her fingers. "I know this doesn't get me much closer, but I can't help but feel like you've helped me immensely."

"Trust your feelings. And remember to breathe," Sonja added.

Laughing, Sarah said, "You and my yoga instructor. He always thinks I'm too wound up. Maybe he's right." She put the pin back in the bag and stowed it in her purse. "Thank you for this. For everything. Can I call you if I need to?"

Sonja went back to the counter and grabbed a card. "I don't think you will, but if you do, don't hesitate." She handed the card to Sarah. "You've come this far, haven't you?"

Sarah nodded, took the card, bowed her head and turned to

exit. Sonja watched her go, closing and locking the door behind her. She took a deep breath of thanks, turned out the lights, and went home.

Sarah traversed back to her hotel room and cracked open the minibar. She opened the window that looked north over the business district and French Quarter, put the little paper bag on the table, and turned on the TV. A few drinks and three channel-flipping trips past the room service menu later, she had passed out.

Sarah arrived at the bottom of a large hill. The valley below was lush and green, an oak savannah with a creek running through the tall grass, the breeze warm and invigorating. The wondrous sound of wind through leaves and grass surrounded her. The hill was dark, lifeless, and cold, but at the top was a lone tree. She started to climb, sticking her feet deep into the hill's surface and discovering that it wasn't solid, but rather like mud. Sarah kept climbing, inching ever so slowly closer to the tree. The sky overhead began to roil with clouds and thunder, rain pummeling her as she climbed, her clothes drenched and her feet and hands almost worn to the bone. Still, she kept climbing.

Immediately ahead of her, the hill suddenly separated top from bottom. Sarah leapt to catch the fringe of the bifurcated hill, clinging to the edge with her fingernails. As the hill rose slowly into the sky, increasing its distance from the earth, the tree began to wither and sag, and from a gaping knot within the tree, a young woman emerged effortlessly toward her, completely unaffected by the otherwise impassable surface. Her hair was dark and her eyes bright green, but she was otherwise a mirror image of Sarah. In her hair was the jade hairpin. The woman removed it and bent down to offer it to Sarah. As she did, a werewolf-like creature erupted from the cave and grabbed the woman from behind, carrying her up the hill screaming. The pin dropped on the ground inches from Sarah's reach. She let go with one hand to reach for a higher handhold, but her grip slipped and she began to fall. BANG BANG BANG!

Waking from her dream just as she fell off the bed, Sarah smacked the back of her head on the nightstand and landed in a heap on the floor next to the bed. There was a solid rapping at the door and the sound of hotel management saying, "Miss Dempsey, are you okay?" She discovered that she was fully dressed and soaked through with sweat. Humiliated, she climbed warily to her feet, plodded to the door, and unlatched and opened it, saying, "I'm fine. I'm going to go back to sleep now."

"Are you sure you're okay? We were told there was some shouting. Is anyone in there with you? Are they okay?" the young manager pried, his voice whiny and scrutinizing.

"Anyone... else? What? No. Just me and the scotch. Thank you for checking on me; I need to wring out my hair now." She closed the door and locked it again, listening behind it to make sure the manager had gone. Sarah walked back into her room and flopped down on the bed, face first.

As she lay there, trying to catch her breath and feeling her heart pound uncontrollably, a soft light began to warm the side of her face. When she opened her eyes, she froze. The paper bag on the table in the corner of her room was glowing.

"Lord," Sarah pleaded, inching toward the object cautiously. "I don't know if you're out there, but if you can keep this thing from killing or... maiming me, I'll give up scotch for a solid... I don't know, week..." It seemed the heavier she breathed, the brighter the object became. She grabbed the bag off the table and let the pin fall onto the bedspread. Light pulsated from within and produced a ringing in her ears she couldn't silence. "Okay, maybe more like a month," she added, and slowly reached for the object, afraid it might burn her.

It was just as cool as it had been before, but now seemed to be singing to her. She put the pin up to her ear. She tried to breathe calmly and deeply, as Sonja and her yoga instructor reminded her to do, but the more she did, the louder the singing became and the brighter the pin resonated. "What the hell do they know?" she thought and held her breath instead. Instantly, the light dissipated and the sound stopped.

"Great. All I have to do is hold my breath all night long and I'm golden."

Sarah managed to make it 30 seconds before she relented, drawing in a huge breath and letting it out. As she did, the object glowed brighter than it ever had and the air in the room became as visible as dust, waves of light dancing along the particles. The sound expanded exponentially from a single, strange melody to an entire chorus of dissonance twanging in her ears. In the background, she swore she could hear a voice – a connected series of whispers that all seemed to be saying the same thing over and over again, albeit in an accent and overlapping pace that made it nearly indiscernible: "Boston." She asked, "Where?" but no answer came. Just "Boston."

All at once, she passed out, dropping the pin on the bed. The next moment the alarm was screaming in her ears, and her head was throbbing from drink and dehydration. Instinctively, she turned to shut off the alarm, then instantly laid eyes on the pin lying on the bedspread.

"Holy shit," she muttered. "That was real…"

Her morning regimen highly abbreviated after sleeping through 20 minutes of her alarm, Sarah brushed her teeth, showered, did her best with hair and light makeup, hung last night's clothes up to dry, and dressed herself for the day's conference and interview. She grabbed her laptop, phone, and hotel key and darted out the door to the conference room.

The initial session had already begun, although there were still some people milling about. Out of the corner of her eye, she spotted a friendly face — a woman she'd attended college with named Debra Olson, who was now a special events reporter for the NBC affiliate in Minneapolis. She waved Sarah over to avoid having to sit next to a rather obnoxious man, the usual specimen who plagued them both at these sorts of events. Sarah spotted the man moving toward the seat next to Debra with coffee and breakfast roll in hand and rushed to beat him there.

"Thank you!" Debra emitted in a whispered yell. "I don't think I could sit next to that guy all day."

"Don't mention it," Sarah muttered as she put her laptop down and silenced her phone, noting several unread and unheard messages.

"Were you out partying last night?" Debra asked. "That's not your usual M.O."

Sarah rolled her eyes at Debra. "No. I still don't party. Why, were you?"

She smiled. "There's this guy from UPN in Baltimore. He got a room at the wrong Marriott…"

"Rookie."

"Well yeah, but he was really nice and bought me a couple drinks…"

"So, where is he?" Sarah asked.

"Oh, he's a producer. He's at the thing next door. Some presentation for a bunch of college kids." A number of convention staff handed out packets while the speaker prepped the crowd for the presentation. Debra continued, "Hey, are you coming with us this afternoon to the session on live setups?"

Sarah grinned sheepishly. "Uh... yes? No, I can't. I have an interview."

"During the conference?"

"It was a spur of the moment thing. Some crooked politician's attorney..." Sarah said, booting up her laptop.

Taken aback, Debra asked, "You mean Rutherford's attorney?" Sarah nodded. "I hope you're going through the local affiliate. If you spoil their source, they'll hang you."

"I'm not doing that either. Look, it's really weird and it's not even for a story, so can you keep it under your hat? It's strictly off the books." Sarah pleaded.

Debra nodded, but was concerned. "No problem. You okay?"

"Girl, you wouldn't believe it if I told you."

Sarah managed to stay awake through the two morning sessions with some help from Debra's elbow and several strong cups of coffee. After the second session, she packed her belongings and took a cab to an old boy's club in Metairie.

The cab pulled up in front of a moss-covered, plantation-style mansion with a circle drive. The valet opened the door and Sarah paid the cabbie, climbed out, and stood between the massive Romanesque columns in front of the building. He closed the door to the cab and ushered her in through the front door to the desk. Sarah looked around, telling herself how typical the décor was. Dark green carpet, Cherrywood moldings and furnishings, plush leather chairs, gold-framed mirrors and paintings... The works.

"And who are you here to see, ma'am?" the young man at the desk asked her.

"I'm here to speak with Mr. Jackson," she answered, trying not to laugh at the excess of it all.

The desk clerk looked through the log, found the name, and said, "I'll go get him. Feel free to have a seat." He motioned to the grouping of leather chairs to the left of the front door and walked off in the opposite direction, down a long hall with dark green walls and plush carpeting.

After several moments, the desk clerk returned from the hallway with the attorney in tow. Tim Jackson was a short, pudgy, balding middle-aged man with confidence enough to wear suspenders with slacks and a tie, as well as a pink striped shirt. Sarah confirmed to herself that the interview would definitely be short.

"Thank ya for comin', Miss Dempsey," he said with a smooth Southern drawl and a wide, plastic smile. He shook her hand and motioned to the chairs. "Why don't you have a seat and we'll get started."

"I'm a vegetarian," she explained, referring to the leather chairs.

He chuckled, adding, "Don't worry, I won't be asking you to eat the chair." Sarah smiled politely. After an uncomfortable silence, Jackson turned and gestured toward the back door. "I suppose we could take a walk around the garden. Would that suit you?"

"I would like that very much, Mr. Jackson."

"Please, call me Tim."

The garden boasted a number of live oaks, hanging greenery, and sculptured bushes that bordered the clay walking trail. Once they started along the path, Tim spoke. "Now Miss Dempsey, I'd like to start by saying that right now we're a little dry on the information I can provide to you. I realize you're from Detroit, so perhaps you haven't had the opportunity to stay involved in the case, but we did have a fairly lengthy press conference last week.

So, I must admit I am a bit curious as to the nature of your inquiry."

Sarah nodded. "I understand. Actually, I'm not planning on asking any questions about the hurricane funds."

"Well, and I hate to be a negative Nelly, but I'm afraid we won't be discussing the other this afternoon either," he added, referring to the incest charges lodged against his client.

"Mmm, not that either. Not really. My questions do, however, come as a result of those charges."

Tim intoned sternly, "I can assure you the questions had better be unique."

"And I can assure you they are."

He made a gesture of deference and shook his head. "Shoot."

"I understand that your client is facing some rather unfortunate charges in relation to his son…"

"See, now that's precisely what I didn't want to talk about, Miss Dempsey."

"It's Sarah, Tim. The reason I bring it up is because it's the basis for my line of questioning. I believe it's in the best interest of your client to hear what I have to say and in your best interest to protect your client. To be perfectly honest, your participation in this conversation is purely voluntary. Do you gamble, Tim?" she asked, as smoothly as she could given she was desperately wishing she'd brought her sunglasses.

He nodded, suddenly eager. "Those are good odds. By all means, proceed."

"I've been working with the FBI on a case involving the deaths of a number of wealthy businessmen. Now, these weren't heart attacks or suicides or professional hits involving corporate competition. These men were the victims of a serial killer who targets such individuals who also happen to be defending themselves against charges of domestic abuse in some form or another…"

He stopped and turned to her, putting up his hand to stop her. "Now wait just a minute, miss. If you've been working with the FBI, you might want to remind them they have a responsibility to protect the public. If they have evidence that someone is targeting my client, then they sure as hell better inform him and not send some reporter to do it."

"I understand the responsibilities. As it happens, I'm not the person you should speak to about that. That being said, the people working the case are hamstringed by certain procedural limitations you are also likely aware of." Sarah chose her words carefully.

"And what's that? That trying my client is less expensive if he's dead?"

"Considering your client has more funds allocated for this case than the federal government does, it shouldn't surprise you that cost is a factor. However, it's not a matter of will, but rather a matter of means. The information is only useful if they know who the next target is going to be."

He sized Sarah up, thumbing his suspenders thoughtfully. "I'll hand it to ya, Sarah. You're smarter than any fed I've talked to. Most journalists, too. Where did you go to school?"

"Columbia."

"That's a good school. They teach 'em right there." He paused for another moment to let her speak. She said nothing. "I tell you what. I'll call. You show me your hand, and I'll tell you what we're willing to share."

Sarah took a deep breath. "Okay. This is a woman who was abused as a child. For whatever reason, she seems to have taken it upon herself to make examples of those who would do the same to their families. As I'm sure you're aware, domestic violence is rather common, so her pool of potential victims is sizeable. However, one thing all her victims share is newspaper ink. We might be able to help you, but without knowing how your client plans to plead, we've got nothing." She winced internally, knowing she'd over-played her hand.

"Ah, a plea bargain. That's pretty ballsy of you, little lady. Those must be some influential friends at the bureau indeed. Or some real idiots…"

Backpedaling, she blurted, "Hang on. I want to make it clear that I am in no position to offer a plea bargain…"

"You damn well better not be. Now, you've warned me about a possible threat to my client, and for that I am appreciative. I intend to speak with the bureau about it in the morning, so is there someone I should ask for?" he uttered in a greasy, superior tone.

Sarah's bluff had been called. Knowing it would shortly get back to him anyway, she replied, "Agent Mike Kirkpatrick. He's at Langley. Send him my regards if you do speak to him." Tim chuckled as he entered the information into his phone. "I have his phone number if you like," she offered.

"That would save me some trouble indeed," he added.

They parted and Sarah was escorted back to the entrance to wait for a cab. "Dammit," she muttered, chastising herself for the whole encounter. "That was stupid." Assessing her options, her mind wandered to the hairpin and the conversation she'd had with Mike about interviewing her family's old neighbors. Moments later, she was scheduling further care for her cat and a flight to Boston.

Chapter Nine

April 1959

Marya sat on a bench in the backyard, wearing soft shoes, a long dress, thick shawl, and the trademark hairdo Rebekah had come to envy – a delicately pinned up coiffure with lengthy wisps dangling over her ears to her shoulders. She held a half a loaf of bread in one hand, and with the other, she tore off small pieces and flung them into the pond, enjoying the company of a raft of feathered friends swimming close to the water's edge. Spring had finally emerged, and Marya's shoes were covered in mud. She worshipped the outdoors, and couldn't be kept inside when temperatures were remotely sufferable.

Marya and Rebekah would go for long walks around the pond feeding the waterfowl, observing squirrels and rabbits, and talking. Not verbally, as Marya had made little progress and even less effort at learning English. They were able to communicate without speaking at all. Over the past three months, Marya had taught Rebekah how to pay attention to the air around her and translate emotions and sensations into language. She was still learning, but her progress was faster than any pupil with which Marya had ever worked.

Rebekah grabbed her tea off the kitchen counter and put on her boots and jacket to join Marya in the backyard. After a rather athletic feat to dodge the puddles in the yard, she reached the bench and sat down next to the woman, cradling her tea carefully in her hands. They smiled at each other.

"Hi," Rebekah said.

"Hello," Marya answered in her thick accent and tossed a handful of bread crumbs. She had a childlike disposition in these sorts of settings. The smile never left her face, and she continually regarded the animals and plants as though she was seeing them for the first time, perpetually caught up in the wonder of it all. Rebekah admired the woman's verve and did her best to achieve some of the same clarity of thought.

This was something they had been discussing since shortly after her arrival at the house. Rebekah's experiences and the resultant anger she suffered caused her to have a very specific relationship with her environment. There was more to achieve from the world around her, and with each passing day, she would learn the histories behind the objects in the house and the people who had brought them.

"What do the objects mean?" she had asked at one point. Between Ekaterina and Marya's methods of communication, the message came out slowly. "The objects are representations of the people who bring them. If the object has meaning for the person, then it will be endowed with a part of their essence. We all have our purposes in the world. At some times, we're travelers. At others, we're sentries who help to point lost souls in the right direction. At other times, we are the lost souls. The world speaks in a very structured format of give and take. If a lost soul is willing to give up a part of themselves, what they can receive often outweighs the gift. It's the willingness to share oneself and to be a part of the larger picture that determines the value of the gift, and therefore the value of the receipt.

"For example, a million-dollar house that is given, with all the gold and fineries within it, can be a thoroughly hollow gesture if the house means nothing to the donor. But a simple spoon, forged with the love and care of the blacksmith who created it, can mean the world to the donor. The receipt for their gift might be immeasurable. The more meaning there is to the gift, the more energy that passes between donor and recipient. It fosters good will and charges the air. We are all able to see this, but most people cannot open their minds past the material worth of objects to see there is a soul behind them."

Marya and Rebekah sat in silence watching the birds and squirrels vie for bread crumbs. Marya loved to watch their tiffs as they scrounged for the only worry in their worlds. The vitality of it all rejuvenated her spirit. Winter was a difficult time for Marya, as the air was harder to breathe and there was less life to share it with. People did not delight her half so much as nature did, though Rebekah had given her hope. They never spoke of the events that brought Rebekah to Boston, but Marya had an inkling the young woman had done some dreadful things. Being able to look past nurtured character traits to the young woman's soul, Marya had no fear of what those things were and was more interested in what Rebekah would become.

She took the hairpin from her own head and applied it to Rebekah's, shaping her hair flatteringly as she went. "It suits you," Marya intoned, smiling.

Rebekah chuckled, noting Marya's fallen hairstyle. "It's just hair."

They laughed and rose to walk around the pond. Along the way they said very little, but Marya began to sense Rebekah was hiding something from herself. Marya didn't quite understand what it was, but it continually manifested itself in relation to Daniel. She wondered if Daniel had been telling Rebekah something that the young woman knew to be false but was willingly interpreting as true anyway. Had he told her something that was in contrast to what Ekaterina or Marya were imparting? The overarching impression Marya received was that Rebekah was getting divergent information, but Marya couldn't tell what it was about or how it was actually affecting her. Rebekah had so many layers of conflicting emotions and socialization that pinpointing the specific proclivity presenting itself at that moment was quite difficult. In fact, Marya believed it was beyond her abilities. Doing her best to hide her discontent from Rebekah, Marya resolved to speak to Daniel about it directly.

She was aware that it could be possible for Daniel to hide something from her, but it was not very likely. The execution of such a feat would have required a great deal of effort on his part, and Marya was confident her powers of intuition were evolved enough to sense such an attempt. Still, when she approached Daniel later that evening she was nervous nonetheless.

Rebekah was watching television accompanied by Ekaterina. Rebekah had never had a television before and it was something she'd now taken to doing in the evenings, desperate to catch up with the rest of the world. When Daniel entered through the front door, Marya immediately sidetracked him. Rebekah caught the exchange out of the corner of her eye and fixed the image in her mind. She didn't know if anything was wrong, but perpetually worried that her three generous landlords would evict her if they discovered her violent past. The image stowed, she sat back and continued to watch television.

Marya was able to pull Daniel into the far back corner of the first floor, a seldom-used anteroom decorated as a library and a study. In the floorboards, a pull-up hatch under which a staircase descended into a basement had been dug separately from the rest of the house. This had been used as an upper-class speakeasy during Prohibition. The owners were eventually arrested and thrown in jail. During the war, Daniel picked the house up cheaply off tax liens.

Marya closed the door behind them. Daniel was concerned by her tone and asked, "What's the matter? Did something happen today?"

Without sounding accusatory, Marya replied, "Should something be the matter? The girl seems troubled, do you know anything about that?"

"Troubled? Her family is dead, shouldn't she be troubled?" Daniel retorted, his glib reply not at all a surprise. He and Marya had butted heads in the past, and over the years, Daniel had become increasingly defensive of being questioned by her.

"She is confused, conflicted. Whenever I try to find out why, I feel something about you. Have you been telling her something?"

Daniel walked to the liquor cabinet and poured himself a drink. "Like what? What is she conflicted about? You spend more time with her than I do."

Irritably, Marya barked, "Why do you play at questions? This world is new to her and she doesn't need to be confused about it."

"I understand that. What I don't understand is why you're upset. What is the girl confused about?"

"She has barriers."

"We *all* have barriers, Marya. Consider her circumstances. She should have more than the rest of us."

"Ekaterina and I work with her to break them down but after she spends an evening out of this house with you she builds them back up again. Do you even know what she's capable of?" Marya asked, her eyes pleading for him to take the subject seriously.

Daniel nodded soberly, grasping his drink in his hand and sitting on the corner of the desk. "Actually, I think I do. She isn't safe, Marya."

Shocked, Marya lurched forward, pointing her finger at his chest. "Is that what you've been doing? Trying to make her question her abilities? She's a goddess, Daniel! She doesn't belong to us, and it's not up to us to control her. She is a medium between us and the natural world, and she'll never understand her purpose in it if she doesn't at least know that. I thought we were in agreement about this!"

Daniel stood from the desk and slowly halved the distance to Marya. "Do you know what she's done?"

"I don't know and I don't care. Think of her soul, Daniel. You can see as well as I can that she is a force of nature, not a peasant like the rest of us. You should be celebrating that fact more than anyone – she's your daughter!"

Daniel stood in furious silence for a moment, then replied slowly, "I thought we wouldn't discuss that."

"I know, but…"

"I thought we had all agreed that my relationship with her mother was unimportant and that the girl came first. Was I mistaken?"

"I know, but you can't deny who she is. Forget that I said anything about her parentage, but she is so much more than a child. She can save us all!"

He thundered back at her. "She'll be the death of us all!"

Disturbed and confused, Marya asked meekly, "Why do you say this? There is good and hope and life in her. She will outlive us all. She will love for us all, and you want to stifle that?"

"I didn't want to tell you this, but you're pushing me. Have you looked into her past? Have you tested to see what she's done?"

Folding her arms, Marya replied, "No. I told you, I don't need to know."

"Oh, she hides it well. You're right, she is gifted, Marya. But she's killed people."

"No."

"Yes, she has. She's confused to be sure. I don't know how, or why, and I'm not sure I want to know either. It's grisly and frightening but she has killed people," Daniel insisted.

Partly through emotion and partly through drink Daniel started to let his guard down. Marya saw something she hadn't noticed before, and she did her best to conceal her discovery of it. It was apparent that Daniel was telling the truth about the girl, but his stifling of her abilities had a personal motivation behind it as well.

Daniel leveled his gaze at Marya. "I can't say for certain that she's harmless, and neither should you. Don't be blind to the fact that she has a violent past. Everything she touches now is colored with that."

"Including you?" she asked pointedly.

He started to respond but thought better of it. The young woman's abilities had caused a crack in his façade. Before she had come along, he was a rock. A man people could rely on. Since she'd appeared in his life, however, her energy had begun to work on him in ways he couldn't explain. In response, he'd started to hide, masking the energy that was building up in him and portraying a calm that wasn't there. Marya on the other hand had become more open. Her lack of faith in mankind had been breached by the existence of this person. While Daniel saw her gift as a thing to fear and a source of jealousy, Marya found it a source of strength and faith.

Marya sighed, her hand on her head. "I'm sorry, perhaps that wasn't fair. But you have to understand that if we push her away or make her afraid of who she is, then she may as well become precisely what you're afraid of. If we show her how she can help people and how she can grow within herself, then she'll be a source for good. Why would you take that opportunity away from her? From us? I've been afraid for my life all my life. For the first time, I see someone who can bridge the gap of understanding in this world."

Daniel shook his head. "She's a child. She has no control over her powers and has already caused irreparable harm. What good can she do, if any? I don't know, but the harm is real. We know precisely what she's capable of and if she's not managed properly, it will end badly. Is that something you want to risk?"

"Absolutely!" she responded without hesitation. "That girl is our future. If I die tomorrow, I'll have lived knowing that she's out there. That's living. Being constantly afraid of death and annihilation isn't living, Daniel! She is the difference between the two."

"And what about the other?"

"He's a legend," she responded quickly, dismissing the thought. "She is *real*. She's here… now, and no one is beyond forgiveness. Whatever she's done, the good she can accomplish will outweigh it, I promise you. You're right. She's young. But that means she has the time and ability to do great things. Do you really want to remember yourself as the person who stifled that potential?"

Daniel snapped, "I don't want to be the person who's responsible for all that she destroys. If I know this girl is dangerous and I do nothing, then all the good intentions in the world won't save me. Some things cannot be undone or forgiven."

"She has a soul. Would you crush that and all she represents to save your own?"

Marya's ultimatum landed heavily on Daniel. He sat back on the corner of the desk, took a drink, breathed deeply, and closed himself off again. Marya felt his breath mingle with the liquor and burn hot and red in the back of her skull. She had felt the jealousy well up in him throughout the argument, but then it stopped, replaced by a wall of anger, and she became uncomfortably aware of what he was doing. She took several deep breaths to calm herself, careful not to let him feel her trust diminishing.

Daniel took another drink and turned away from Marya to look out the window at the setting sun. She straightened up and shook the last few remaining pins out of her hair. "We must agree on a course of action," she stated soberly. "Perhaps we should be more honest with her about the powers she possesses. We'll take turns. You take her for a drive tomorrow into town. Bring her in contact with other people. See how she fares… but be honest with her. In whatever way you feel is appropriate. She and I will discuss how she felt about it the next day. Does this sound reasonable?"

He nodded reluctantly. "That does sound reasonable. If you believe it's best, then perhaps that's what we should do."

"Good. She's watching television now. Go. Join her and spend some time with the girl as a person. Try to get to know her soul. It is a good soul. Don't ask questions and don't judge. Just be in her presence for a time," Marya suggested.

Ekaterina and Rebekah watched as she ascended the stairs to her room. Once the woman's door was closed, the two looked at each other, then back to the television with a curious set of glances. "Oh, to be a fly on the wall…" Ekaterina said in her thick Belarusian accent, staring down at her knitting.

Rebekah exhaled and refocused her attention on the television.

The next day, Rebekah and Daniel headed into Boston for lunch and a walk through the park. Rebekah felt Daniel might have an ulterior motive, but she was happy to get out of the house and see some of the sights. Stopping first for coffee, they continued to

Boston Common, where they had met months earlier. Rebekah was excited to see all the people out walking, playing, and sharing the space together. She felt their energy and it strengthened her spirits.

Daniel saw the appreciation Rebekah showed for her surroundings, and asked, "Are you happy to be here, Rebekah?"

"Sure, I love the park," she responded in a youthful, joyous manner.

"That's good. Actually, I was asking if you were happy to be in Boston. And in Concord with Marya and Ekaterina and me."

She thought about this for only a second, then replied, "Absolutely. You understand me. All of you do. I've never been around people who understood me before. It's comforting."

"I'm happy about that. I do have something we need to discuss, though," he started gloomily.

She shrugged and sipped her coffee. "Okay."

"It's about who you are. About what you're here to do."

"You mean like religion?"

"No, I mean like purpose. Like a river has purpose. Like a tree has purpose... humans have purpose, too. Ours is more complex and we often forget to look for it because all of our fears and troubles get in the way. And, humans have the ability to reason, and it's that reason that makes us responsible. Do you understand?"

Rebekah stared blankly into space, objects around her blurring in confusion. "No, I don't."

"Purpose is not meant to be complex. But sometimes, explaining something cosmically simple in words is profoundly complicated." Daniel regrouped his thoughts. "Life is balance. Does that make sense?" She nodded enthusiastically. "Okay. Newton said that for every action, there is an equal and opposite reaction. When he said that he was talking about physics. About objects and molecules bouncing off of each other in nearly invisible encounters. But what he might not have known at the time is that the law applies to everything, not just physics. All things have balance. Where there is negative energy, there is positive energy. Make sense?"

She nodded hesitantly. "Sure."

"Good. I may not be that good at explaining this, but I'll try. The energy out in the world is generated by all people, all things, all creatures. This may sound incredible or unbelievable, but when an excess of one energy or another builds up, the opposite energy will pool itself somewhere until it is ready to act."

"Like a blister?" she asked.

He considered the comparison for a moment then responded, "I suppose. Maybe that's quite accurate. Well, we each exist to one degree or another to serve a purpose in this balance."

"But, if we have reason like you said, shouldn't we have a choice in that?" Rebekah asked, starting to catch on to the concept.

Daniel smiled. "Actually, we do. Most people choose to ignore it and go about their lives sending whatever energy they have out into the world. What they get back, they term *luck* or *karma*. And to an extent, it is, but it's really balance. It's science. It's quantifiable and mathematical. Some people are more in tune with their surroundings than others. You are one of those people, Rebekah. And as a result of that, you have the ability to balance the scales of nature on a voluntary basis. Instead of your surroundings controlling you, you can control your surroundings. This is a very rare ability. So rare that it is almost mythical."

As Daniel spoke, Rebekah realized his meaning was something she already knew, yet she had no perception beyond how her ability made her different from everyone else – until now. Using the term "control" made it sound more real. It was a term that defined precisely what she'd been lacking all her life.

"You have control over balance, Rebekah. This is a dangerous and powerful thing to possess. Do you understand why it is dangerous?" he asked.

"Because I could misuse it?"

"Because you don't understand it. You don't even know how you came to have this power, do you?" She shook her head, troubled. Daniel continued. "I don't know the truth behind how everything works, but it is believed that there are two ways to gain this kind of ability. To be born with it, a person must be born half into the world that we see and half into the world that is beyond our view. It's a world where air becomes visible and the connections between all things are tangible and accessible without a second thought. There have been legends of these types of people, but I've never known someone who possessed this gift."

"Am I one?" she asked.

Daniel shook his head. "I don't know. Marya believes you are, though. She believes your soul is only half in the world we see. The other half connects you to the earth."

"What do you believe?"

"Legend talks of another way for this connection to be made. It requires the death of another human being. Rebekah, I have listened to your fears since I met you and believe that this may be how you do the things you do. I believe you've killed someone. Tell me how you came to be here." He stopped in the trail as he said this.

She took a couple extra steps, then stopped and turned back to him, trying to manufacture a truth that sounded like anything other than what actually happened. She fumbled, mouth open for a moment, then with great difficulty said, "The house burned down. I tried to go back in and save them…"

"How did the house burn down?" Daniel interrupted.

She shook her head, trying to rattle something loose. "I don't... I don't know. I ran upstairs to grab Samantha and took her outside, but they were already on fire."

Daniel pried harder, leaning toward her. "How did the fire start, Rebekah? You say they burned but you don't say how."

"I don't know how!" she barked back at him, the noise startling several other patrons in the park.

He looked around cautiously. "What do you mean you don't know? A fire doesn't just start from thin air."

At that moment, something in Rebekah's mind snapped and she shut down. She knew what happened couldn't be explained or allowed to pass from her lips, but there was no convenient lie to cover what happened either. As a result of the clanging thoughts in her head, she hardly noticed the soft, swirling breeze developing around her. Daniel, on the other hand, was acutely aware of it; he was also aware that the winds could be a result of Rebekah's fragile emotional state.

It started small at first. Daniel felt the hairs on the back of his neck and hands stand up with the coolness of the breeze. Looking down, he saw the bottom of his coat flapping gently. As Rebekah retreated further within herself, the breeze picked up force.

"Rebekah," he started, putting a hand on her.

She pulled away from him, grimacing as though he'd dug claws into her shoulder. The breeze accelerated into a small, swirling wind, and others in the park started to notice the increasing gusts. A man's hat flew from his head and he ran to chase it; skirts, coats, scarves, and other loose articles of clothing began reacting as well. Daniel's hat also flew off, passing by a couple farther down the path, but he stayed with Rebekah, trying to call her back. Yet despite his efforts, the wind continued its acceleration with every passing moment. Her hair wrapped around her face and whipped viciously into a funnel above her.

Daniel continued to shout at Rebekah, but the wind was becoming so great that little could be heard over it. Patrons scattered, searching for any kind of cover, as the funnel expanded out to the surrounding streets, now carrying enough strength to pick up small, yet weightier objects. Rocks and various personal belongings collided with cars and buildings, shattering glass and sending innocent civilians to the ground with their hands over their heads. Daniel himself would have been knocked over by the force of the wind if he weren't at the epicenter with Rebekah. He held tightly to her shoulders as much to try to break her out of her trance as to secure himself to the ground. Moment by moment, his tenuous connection to terra firma weakened. Newspapers, loose fabrics, and tree branches flew through the air, and calls of "tornado!" were heard as people ducked behind cars and buildings.

What Daniel experienced next was a bizarre state of calm. He saw Rebekah swaying back and forth as if nudged by a gentle breeze. The tears on her face had dried, and her closed eyelids gently pulsed with the movement of REM sleep. Nearby, a tree cracked, split, and a limb snapped off and launched through the air away from them. Upon perceiving the sound, Rebekah's eyes snapped open. She drew a deep breath, and the winds began to subside. Daniel let go of Rebekah and fell, exhausted, to the ground as the winds slowed to gentle gusts. Policemen walked from person to person throughout the park, checking for injured.

Rebekah had yet to move. She still stood on the trail, her coat tattered, her coffee missing, and her hair tossing gently in the breeze. She barely seemed to blink, her gaze piercing through the trees, people, cars, and buildings into the ether beyond. A strange, contented smile spread across her face, and she laughed at the simplicity of it all. Daniel's attempt to explain how she was different from other people had helped her to break through a barrier. The violence and danger inherent in the experience didn't occur to her at all, only the powerful visceral nature of it.

Daniel stumbled wearily to his feet. There was a tear in the knee of his slacks and blood oozed down his lower leg. Despite the injury and the profound soreness in his body, he was happy that she'd been able to calm the winds. He walked over to her just as a police officer reached her.

"Are you all right, miss? You're not hurt, are you?" the man asked, hurried in his effort to move along.

Rebekah looked at the man, barely hearing what he had said. Instead, she listened to the waves passing through the air, ricocheting off air currents moving in divergent directions. Eventually, the waves met her fragile eardrums. The sensation of the waves coming in contact with her tickled, and she laughed. Saying nothing, she only giggled at the officer's questions.

Daniel watched the moment with curiosity, understanding completely that Rebekah was not emotionally or psychologically inhabiting the same space as he and the officer were. Daniel touched the police officer on the shoulder and breathed deeply to calm him, replying, "I think she's a little shaken, but she isn't injured. She'll be fine."

"Okay," the officer said, moving on to the next closest civilians.

Officers all across the park were quick to allay people's fears over the incident by explaining that it had been a short-lived tornado, though none could explain how it had formed or where it had come from. Daniel himself couldn't find words or thoughts to define what happened. His best conclusion was that a synapse had fired in Rebekah's mind, and the winds instantly responded to her command. She was lethal.

"Are you here?" he asked. "I'm sorry I yelled at you. I shouldn't have done that. Are you going to be all right if we leave?"

She turned to him, the bemused smile still on her face, and said, "I burned them. I saw the particles in their blood and split them into pieces. They burned so easily." The smile never left her face as she spoke, yet it wasn't malevolent. It was understanding. "They brought it on themselves. It wasn't blood. It was hate and drink seeping from their skin. It was a weight that came out of them, pressing on me and Samantha, and the furniture... everything. All I did was push back. It was as easy as breathing."

"We have to get rid of her," Daniel announced, hobbling through the back door, blood soaking through his sock and into his shoe.

"You're hurt!" Marya exclaimed, rushing to him and grabbing his shoulder. She observed Rebekah standing in the backyard staring in her catatonic state at the pond below her. "What happened?" Marya asked.

"She's out of control. I think I made it worse. I tried to explain how it all works. I tried to get her to understand her weaknesses and her powers and how she had a responsibility! She almost killed people in the park," he explained.

Marya took a step back, horrified by what he was saying. In a state of disbelief she asked, "How did she do that?"

Daniel ripped the lower half of his pant leg off and sat down on a chair by the kitchen table as Ekaterina brought a rag and some warm water to nurse his wounds. "I don't know, but she started with a little breeze, and before I could get through to her, she was sending people and things flying through windows and into cars and trees. She almost killed me, too."

Ekaterina and Marya looked at each other. The radio had been on in the house, and they had heard on the news about a bizarre weather event that occurred in the town center, the effects rippling out to the surrounding suburbs. Ekaterina addressed Marya. "That was her. I knew she would learn about it eventually. She's too intelligent not to."

"What do you mean, 'that was her'?" Daniel asked, annoyed.

Ekaterina explained, "We heard on the news about what happened in the park. That is where you took her, no?" He nodded his reply. "We need to protect her."

"You and Marya both! Who's going to protect the people she kills?" The women refused to answer and stared at him as he ranted. "She told me about how she killed her family. Not her mother, but her brothers and father. She killed them. She made their blood boil and burst into flames, and she *laughed* about it as she told me. She was fascinated not with the life she'd destroyed but the simplicity of making fire out of nothing. This is a game to her."

"Do you know what they did to her?" Ekaterina asked gently.

Daniel nearly shouted, only limiting his volume to keep the conversation from the girl outside. "I don't care! Violence begets violence, and she doesn't understand that she has control over where it stops."

"Daniel, you must see past the fact that this power is in someone else's hands," Marya indicted.

He glared at her and gestured to his bleeding leg. "You think this is jealousy?"

"I know it's jealousy! You thought you were incredibly powerful until she arrived, and now you cannot stand the thought of this kind of power existing in someone so young and unrefined. It haunts you and you're trying to get rid of it instead of celebrate it."

He breathed hard, closing his eyes and reopening them. "You

weren't there. You don't know how her family felt as she split their blood, lighting it on fire from inside their bodies. You don't know what the people in that park felt when the winds turned and tried to throw them through walls. For you, this is some fun new toy. For me this is a matter of trying to control a monster before it destroys everyone and everything around it."

"Life is balance, Daniel. You've said so yourself, many times. Don't you think life is using her to balance the scales of what happened to her, her sister, and her mother?" Marya asked.

"I'm not concerned about her settling debts. That's her own business. What I'm worried about is who's going to keep her from killing innocents."

Marya crouched down in front of him, putting her hand on his uninjured knee in an attempt to calm him. "Surely, if you believe in balance, you must believe that it applies to all people. She will find balance."

He shook his head angrily. "No. We all have choices to make. Protect her if you insist, but I'm choosing to act as her balance. She leaves tonight."

The two women looked at each other. Ekaterina refused to take a side, though it was clear that in principal she agreed the young woman should be cared for. Marya frowned, but understood why her sister wouldn't commit. She looked at Daniel, heartbroken. "Okay. Tonight she leaves."

Daniel finished bandaging up his leg and went out to pick up supplies. His experience told him the girl could react badly if she were asked to leave and left to her own devices, so he'd convinced the women to drug her in order to keep her unconscious until they were able to find a safe place to drop her. What he didn't want the women to know was that he was making an additional stop to the hardware store for supplies. While the women believed she could do good somewhere, Daniel was convinced she was a danger to everyone, including herself. At the pharmacy, he purchased chloroform and sleeping pills. At the hardware store, he bought a shovel, duct tape, lighter fluid and matches. He could conceive of no positive way out of the situation they'd created and believed the only safe end was for Rebekah to die. In addition to planning her demise, Daniel's brain whirred with the thought of utilizing the young woman's soul to give him her powers. He wondered how the process worked? Were there other souls she was using for the same purpose? If he killed her, would he become possessed by those souls as well? The questions kept popping up and he could only imagine answers to them. Whatever the case may be, he was determined to find out.

Once Marya was confident the car had cleared the corner and out of sight, she hurried into the lounge where Rebekah was watching television. She knelt down beside her and took the young woman's hands in hers. "Rebekah," she started, Ekaterina standing by to translate. "Rebekah, you have to leave now."

Rebekah had been sitting in a contented state, appreciating the myriad technologies involved in how a television works, scarcely aware of what programming was playing. Marya's statement jolted her out of her trance. "What?" she asked, the fog slowly lifting.

"Daniel thinks you're dangerous. He's going to drug you and take you out into the middle of the forest to leave you for dead. You have to go now so that he cannot do that."

"I don't understand. Doesn't he want me here?" Rebekah asked, adding a nonverbal inquiry of whether he'd been concealing feelings of animosity, as she clearly hadn't felt them.

"He's been hiding many things from us and particularly from you. He thinks you're dangerous, but I won't believe him."

"But he's right. I am dangerous," Rebekah stated matter-of-factly.

Marya shook her head. "No. Not to me. Not to the people who truly love you. You can control this. You can be so much more than Daniel is willing to believe. You can be so much more than *you* are willing to believe."

Rebekah looked at the woman with sadness, but also pity as a realization came to her. She didn't need Marya or Daniel anymore. Instantly, the fear subsided and a calm warmed over her.

"I don't know what my purpose is, but you're right. It isn't here. And that's not Daniel's fault." Tears tumbled down Marya's cheeks. She knew Rebekah was right but couldn't bring herself to say it. She wanted to have a hand in this girl's life and to help her grow, but she realized that it couldn't happen that way. Rebekah saw the struggle in Marya's face and put her hand up to the woman's cheek. "Thank you for being kind to me. I need to go now."

Rebekah stood and walked upstairs to begin packing her few belongings. Ekaterina looked at Marya as if to say, "That was easier than expected," and left the room to call for a taxi.

As she packed, Rebekah thought about all that had been said over the past few months, and particularly the previous few days. She knew that she hadn't killed her family and the others for the purpose of gaining the abilities she had. What she experienced now had begun to appear before the deaths, and was in fact, the cause of them. Deep down she knew she would have to answer for all the pain she had caused, but in the meantime, something was happening to her that was still beyond her grasp.

When she killed her father and brothers, a wave had come over her before the fire even started. It was as if she could see ripples of blood and rage trickle out from them before she had done anything, and she started to wonder if it wasn't related in some way to what Daniel was referring to when he spoke about balance. No one pushed her. There was no voice or order she received prior to doing it. It was a compulsion, like breathing.

She finished packing the last of her clothes, the hairpin, and a number of other small belongings into the bag she'd purchased in St. Louis. Ekaterina hurried through her door. "The taxi has arrived. You must go now."

Rebekah nodded, zipped the bag shut and threw it over her shoulder. Marya met her at the bottom of the stairs. "I'm so sorry it turned out this way. I don't know how to repay you for all the faith you've given me," she sobbed, holding Rebekah tightly. Ekaterina barely needed to translate, as the impression was perfectly clear. "I hope I'll see you again."

Rebekah returned Marya's embrace. "You will."

Not five minutes after the taxi took Rebekah away, Daniel returned from his trip to town, quietly walking through the back door with the chloroform and sleeping pills. The two women were sitting at the kitchen table, drinking tea in abject solemnity. He stopped to assess their demeanor and asked, "Is she upstairs?"

They looked at each other, then at Daniel. Marya couldn't speak and refused to answer. Ekaterina replied calmly, "She's gone."

"What?!" he shouted, nearly dropping the glass containers on the floor. "What do you mean she's gone?!"

"She must have heard you shouting before and run off. We've been here drinking our tea. Marya went upstairs to check on her, but she had taken her things and was gone."

The lie was so perfectly crafted and skillfully delivered that Daniel didn't even consider he was being misled. The two women had agreed to keep their involvement in the young woman's disappearance from Daniel as long as they could. They thought they would tell him about the ruse eventually, but that for the time being, it was critical to keep their deception a secret.

Enraged, Daniel placed the jars on the counter and returned to the car to try to follow the girl. Marya and Ekaterina stayed in the kitchen, drinking their tea and trying to send Rebekah on her way.

Rebekah informed the driver to head toward the train station but hadn't given much thought to the destination. For the first few minutes of the ride, she was simply trying to wrap her thoughts around the fact that she was on her own again with little money and no home. Knowing that feeling sorry for herself wouldn't accomplish much, she started to think about where she could go. Most importantly, where Daniel would not find her. Marya and Ekaterina told her he planned to take her out to the middle of nowhere, yet the impression she got was that there was a much more sinister purpose for getting Rebekah out of the house. She had no idea what it was, but she knew she'd be safer where he couldn't find her. Without warning, she yelled to the driver, "Stop here!"

"Here?" He asked, indicating that they were on a highway.

"Pull off the highway and drop me off at the first intersection," she clarified. The man tossed his hands in the air, pulled off the freeway, and stopped the vehicle. Rebekah reached for the clutch in her bag, but the man motioned to her to stop.

"Your fare's already been paid."

"For how long?"

"Another twenty minutes if you need it," he explained.

She considered that it might be best to get farther away before resorting to walking again. "Take me as far south as you can," she agreed.

They continued down the road. Rebekah didn't care where.

1964

Frederick's new occupation kept him both busy and satisfied. Nicky McKay, a friend of his from the mill, had long been wanting to open a shop for antique goods, and Frederick was trying to find ways to execute the order Marya had given him two years earlier. This sideline started out somewhat awkwardly for Frederick. The message he sent into the ether was partly generic, simply inviting people who received the transmission to show up at his door. But it was also partly specific. From the bits of information Daniel had provided about his "former pupil," Frederick tried to send the message directly to her as well. No young woman fitting Daniel's description arrived, but many other individuals did, occasionally in pairs.

Louise understood what Frederick was up to and welcomed the guests. Calypso did not, however. She'd asked her father numerous times what these people were doing in their home, why they brought junk into the apartment, and what he talked to them about. He explained to her that it was all for a new company he was trying to get off the ground and left it at that.

Calypso found it easy enough to get out of the house and away from the strangeness around her. She'd begun dating a well-respected young man from the neighborhood, and the two of them spent evenings together for the summer before she was set to go to college. Frederick and Louise approved of the young man but not of the intensity of the relationship. Their courtship began young enough that they weren't interested in becoming grandparents just yet. Still, Calypso assured her parents that she was able to take care of herself, and that there was nothing more to the relationship than casual dating.

As for the shop, Nicky was a fiend for antique goods. He

loved studying the histories of the companies that made the items, the people who owned them. Most of the time, information was scant at best, but he gave himself professional license to fill in the missing pieces. Frederick, on the other hand, could hear the objects speaking to him and knew their history without error. For safety's sake, he never offered this information, but rather helped nudge Nicky in the right direction. The two men saved for an antique shop for two years before finding a rundown old bookstore they could renovate. It was in a less than perfect neighborhood, but one that needed local businesses. They agreed as partners to purchase it, with Nicky spending the larger share and moving into the upstairs while the two remodeled and did business downstairs.

As soon as the shop opened, Frederick began spending upwards of 15 minutes a night meditating and sending his messages. In the mornings, he'd bus to the shop, allowing his wife to use the car, and greet the customers who were waiting. Recipients of the message didn't appear every day, but frequently enough that Frederick needed to make sure he didn't miss work. The customers brought everything from lockets to furniture. The more the sentimental value, and the more they appeared to need Frederick's guidance, the more likely the customers were to part with the objects at no charge to the store owners. Nicky was baffled by the incongruity of the arrangements Frederick set up, and told him so. Frederick always smiled and replied, "I just have a way with people." The shop gained notoriety as having some of the most rare and valuable gifts around, and various other stores began to open up nearby as a result of the increased consumer traffic.

Had Frederick not been bringing in so much business, Nicky might have been put out by the fact that Frederick frequently went on walks with his customers. It never took more than an hour out of his week, and Frederick never did it at a time that compromised

Nicky, so he accepted it as part of the partnership.

When Frederick first received Marya's direction as to what he should be doing, he didn't understand what the intention was. He began by trying to send messages instead of receiving them. Marya and Daniel had assured him that only people like Frederick would be able to pick them up anyway, so he was in no danger of summoning those who weren't ready to contribute to the resultant conversation. The pair further informed him that the guidance he would provide would be of his own ilk, not something they could prescribe. Considering his success with the civil rights movement, he started by reaching out to those who were likewise disadvantaged. Within a couple weeks of the first message, he'd met with a number of prominent civil rights activists in the Boston area who also practiced a form of Earth worship. Mostly, he just listened to their concerns and let them know that they were not alone in their uniqueness. This in itself was empowering information.

One of Frederick's visitors brought him the very personal and serious conundrum he faced as deacon at a local Christian church. The ties between the African-American Christian community and civil rights activism was quite strong, and it was frowned upon when the church was shunned in favor of Earth worship. Frederick invited him to breathe and to join him on the fire escape for a moment of peace. The man agreed, and they discussed the basics of what they were going through.

"Christianity," Frederick explained, "...isn't defined by how it excludes all else but rather by how it includes the life and times of Christ. It's up to you what you include on top of that."

The deacon was skeptical at first, but when Frederick showed him all that could be seen, heard, and felt by listening to one's surroundings, the man came to the conclusion that neither God, Jesus, nor the Holy Ghost would begrudge him an experience so profound. The man was comforted and gave Frederick an engraved lighter in return. While the actual monetary value of the gift may have been low, it had been given to the deacon as a wedding present from his deceased father-in-law. The emotional value attached to the gift was sufficient to balance the sense of comfort and belonging the man had found in Frederick's few words.

And this is what he became known for. Frederick didn't guide people by explaining volumes of philosophy to them. He didn't have a classical education and was a better listener than a speaker anyway, so it suited him. He would listen to the concerns that people had, then ask questions about how the powers of the world helped them to grow and become stronger individuals within the context of those concerns. Marya met with Frederick every few months to check on his progress and was pleased with how he represented the mysticism they practiced. He was pragmatic but caring.

Occasionally, Marya and Ekaterina trekked in from Concord to visit the shop, bringing numerous objects they'd kept in the house from previous visitors. Marya would never ask when Daniel was present, nor Daniel when Marya was present, but they each inquired after the missing pupil, and both continually omitted who Rebekah truly was or anything about the things she'd done. Frederick dutifully kept reaching out to her.

He'd considered numerous times asking Marya about her youthfulness. Being the considerate man he was, he couldn't find a proper way to word it, however, since asking a woman about her age was taboo in general and could only be downright rude when directed toward someone who should have looked much older. Instead, he chose to sidetrack Daniel one day and ask him. "I don't mean to be rude, but there's one thing that confuses me."

"What's that?" Daniel asked, as they walked casually down the street.

"I've been wondering since the day you brought me to the house in Concord. I guess it doesn't matter too much, but it just kind of gets jumbled up in my head on occasion. You told me that Marya is Ekaterina's older sister, right?"

"That's right," Daniel smiled, knowing where the question was leading.

"Well, she doesn't look old at all. I don't mean to say that Ekaterina looks old. I mean, she looks her age, I guess. But she looks like she could be Marya's mother... I don't really know what I'm asking."

Daniel patted him on the shoulder. "You know exactly what you're asking. Don't be so hard on yourself. You're just trying not to be vulgar. To be honest, I don't know. I can tell you about Marya in general, though I'm not sure even she knows how she came to be this way."

"Well, what about her? If it's none of my business, then that's okay. It's just a curiosity, that's all."

"You said it clouds your thoughts. Then it should be asked. Any question is worth asking, but certainly one that presents itself more than once. Marya's mother was friends with my grandmother. When my parents died, my grandmother and Marya's mother raised me along with Marya's children."

"How many children does she have?"

"Had. Three. Two of them died during the second war. Her daughter is living in Minsk now. She has a husband and children and didn't want to move the family when we defected, so she stayed there."

The turmoil clearly present in Marya's life was to be expected, considering her background, but it still took Frederick somewhat by surprise. "Wow," he muttered.

"She was one of four children in her family. She had a brother who died during the Bolshevik Revolution in 1917. You know Ekaterina, of course. Her other sibling was her twin, a boy who died at birth."

"Now, you said Marya's parents raised her children. Marya didn't raise her own children?" Frederick asked, perplexed.

Daniel shook his head. "I apologize for the confusion. In that part of the world, at that time, there wasn't much of a concept of a single-family home. Marya was there. She was a free spirit, as the Americans would call it today, and so were her parents. Families were raised by the community rather than by individual parenting. I was absorbed into their family early on.

"In 1918, Belarus became its own nation. A few years after, we were part of the Soviet Union. Then we were divided between the Poles and the Soviets." Daniel relayed the information with an underscored sense of annoyance. "The constant political and ideological changes made our way of life dangerous, and people like us retreated. We hid. Marya was one of the ones who refused to hide. She spent time in prison, protested, travelled back and forth to the States... By the time the Second World War came along, she was nothing but a curiosity to the local officials.

"After that, the clamps were screwed down by Stalin and the Soviet hierarchy. Everyone hid, even Marya. Since her first daughter and only son died in the war, most of us felt she was closing herself off out of depression as well. We never really knew what made her tick, but by that time, her distinction from the rest of us was becoming quite acute. When I went back to Belarus after the war, I expected a sad, white-haired old woman like Ekaterina had become – her children were dead from the war as well – but that wasn't the case. Marya appeared only a few years older than me. It was a great sense of pride for her, her youthfulness. Maybe it's why she didn't retreat as far into depression as she might have, I don't know. Her daughter and grandchildren gave her a great sense of purpose as well. As Stalin cracked down on gypsies and Jews and dissidents, we all began to keep much lower profiles. When I came back to America to stay in 1957, I brought Marya and Ekaterina with me. Ekaterina said there was nothing left for her in Belarus, and Marya wanted to 'find purpose' in something new, she said. Who was I to question it?"

Frederick shook his head. At first it seemed like a lot to take in, but then he thought back on his own life in the South and his parent's and grandparent's generations in the United States, and decided it was completely plausible. "So, she left her own child in Belarus?"

"Marya may look young, but you have to remember, her daughter is older than me. Her grandchildren are Calypso's age or older. Her daughter is grown and can take care of herself. It wasn't as if the girl was being ripped from her arms like you see in the news."

"I guess not. So Marya had a twin?" Frederick asked.

"Yes. I would like to have met him, had he grown up. She was lying right next to him when he died…" Daniel's mind rattled with the conflagration of two previously unrelated thoughts. "My god…" he uttered, and started back toward his car.

"You okay?" Frederick asked, starting after him.

"Uh, yes, I'm fine. I just remembered something I have to do." Daniel reached his car and drove off before Frederick could inquire further.

Frederick sauntered back to the shop, kicked a pebble regretfully, and returned to the process of cataloging the intake.

Daniel sped down the highway, exited at the city limits toward home, made several speedy, ill-advised turns, and eventually pulled into the carport next to the kitchen. Seeing Marya and Ekaterina sitting on the bench by the pond, he hurried out to meet them, angrily asking, "Why did Rebekah leave?!"

"What?" Marya asked, confused and still half-laughing from her discussion with Ekaterina. Her sister rolled her eyes and turned her attention to the birds and squirrels.

Out of breath, Daniel continued, "You said she must have overheard me, but I don't think that's it. I think you lied to me. Both of you. Tell me why she left."

"Daniel, sit down. You're being rash. I've told you what I thought. If there was another reason, I don't know what it is."

"And you?" he asked, directing the question to Ekaterina.

She turned her attention to him only momentarily and sardonically replied, "You don't think this attitude is enough to make someone want to leave?"

"Daniel, it was five years ago. Why would I remember all the details?" Marya questioned.

"Because I know you do. I understand now. I never used to understand, but I do now. We can argue until we're blue in the face as to whether the girl got her powers from birth or from death, but *you*... I know what's behind your mind now. I can't believe I never saw it before, but I understand it for the first time. Your brother."

Marya's demeanor changed instantly as she sharply stood up, her finger pointing at Daniel's face. "Now, you be careful."

"This visage, this power, your abilities to see things no one else can see. You have these things, but you deny to me and to everyone else that you do. And you deny where they come from. You have the soul of an infant buried in your chest..."

She rapped him across the face, the crack reverberating off the house, the tree, and the pond. Ekaterina lurched to her feet as quickly as she could, the aging trio at a standoff in their backyard. Daniel put his hand to his face to sooth the sting. Marya shook her hand, having injured herself as well.

As she massaged her wrist, she seethed at him. "I am not all powerful. I see what I see, but I don't try to stifle others to get it. Who have you been these past five years? A human being. You were a coward and a wastrel when Rebekah was here. Jealous and childish. Since she's been gone you've come to your senses. Who do you think you'd be if I'd allowed you to get rid of her? Who do you think you'd be if I'd allowed you to kill her?" Daniel looked askance at her, not wanting to admit the weakness. She picked up on it and dug in further. "Yes, don't think I didn't see that. Once I realized you'd been hiding things from me, I looked harder to find them. And now you think I've done something awful by saving a life? Oh, I know, you'll tell me how many other lives I've destroyed by letting her go, and then you'll tell me how I'm weak and afraid to die. This is my lot! I never played games with someone's life and death to prove it. You want the truth? I let her go."

Daniel turned to Ekaterina, the admission not coming as much of a surprise. "And you?"

"I couldn't let her die, Daniel. I never meant to hurt you or dictate how you should live your life. I just wanted to protect the girl."

He was furious. "Five years you've kept this from me?!"

Marya matched his intensity. "It worked, didn't it?! How would you have lived with yourself knowing you'd killed your own daughter? How would I have lived with myself knowing I'd allowed it to happen?"

"We could have talked about it!"

"Don't lie to me. There was no talking about it. You had decided on your own what the outcome would be. No amount of talking was going to change that. I did the only thing I thought was right."

"Who can I trust? You don't believe me and you don't tell me things. What am I doing protecting you?" he asked cruelly. Marya moved toward him, and Daniel backed up slowly, Ekaterina trying calmly to part them.

"Fine," Marya barked. "Tell the authorities you're protecting witches. Tell them you're one yourself for that matter. What will it get you? Learn to live with the fact that Rebekah is alive and a good person. Learn to understand that there are things in this world bigger and greater than yourself. Once you let go of this fear of what you don't understand then you'll be free of the anger and jealousy." She lowered her hand, and her brow unfurrowed.

Exhausted from anger, Daniel exhaled and walked away. Marya took a deep breath and touched Ekaterina on the shoulder.

Frederick had become attached to Marya. She was the first stranger who looked him in the eye and saw something. He knew his gift was there, but he'd never had the experience of understanding what it was before he met her. A few hours after Daniel so strangely ran away from Frederick and his shop, he received a very strange sensation about the woman. An ache travelled down his spine to the pit of his gut and he spontaneously decided to drive out to Concord. Louise was annoyed that she had to spend the night at home alone, since Calypso was out again, but she had grown accustomed to Frederick's strange endeavors.

He drove as fast as he thought he could get away with and pulled up to the front of the house while the sunlight still peeked over the horizon. He walked to the door, trying not to look worried, and knocked. No answer. Again he knocked, and again there was no answer. Frederick cautiously started around the side of the house toward the back door. He walked through the carport and was about to reach the kitchen door when Daniel stepped out, a panicked look on his face. "Frederick! What are you doing here?"

Knowing it was a bit unorthodox to show up unannounced, Frederick rationalized that his relationship with the three was close enough to warrant an occasional dropping in. "I'm sorry to bother you. I got the feeling that something was wrong. Is everything okay?"

He watched Daniel's face change emotions from shock to anger, to perturbation, and finally to concern. "Yes, there is something wrong. Come in, will you?" Daniel held the door open and led Frederick through the kitchen, around the stairs, and into the study. "I don't quite know what to do. I came home and no one was here. I called and called, but nothing. I checked all the rooms and the backyard. Around the pond, in the basement... no one answered. So, I thought I'd check in here."

Once in the study, Daniel rolled up the carpet to reveal the trap door to the second basement and started to pull up the door. Frederick helped him as he continued with his story. "We keep some of our valuables down here, some of the contraband liquors, things of that nature. I didn't know if maybe Marya and Ekaterina were working on a project and had gotten locked in."

They climbed down the stairs and started through the space, which had a dirt floor, low ceilings, dozens of shelves built to house liquor, and then a few steps down to a lower level with higher ceilings. This was where the speakeasy had been. There was a make-shift bar, timbers for ceiling supports, and shabbily mortared stone walls. "And when I came down here, I saw them." He covered his mouth and started to shake uncontrollably as he said it.

In the far corner of the room, Marya and Ekaterina were lying on the floor, dead. The air left Frederick's lungs and he struggled to breathe. Tears welled up in his eyes, and he brought his hand to his mouth. "Daniel, what happened?" Without thinking, Frederick crossed the space to the two women and knelt down by their heads to examine them. There was no breathing, no transmission of any kind. They were gone.

He turned to Daniel, who still hadn't answered his question. "Daniel, how did this happen? You came down here and they were already dead?" It didn't occur to Frederick to try to read Daniel at that moment, but the signals he was feeling were so mixed that he couldn't hear himself think much less make sense of them. Blood was rushing so quickly through his body that he was starting to feel faint.

Daniel nodded in response, then breathed and finally spoke. "The door was closed when I came here, so whoever did it must have closed it and replaced the carpet when they left. Frederick, what do I do? What can I do?"

When he left his apartment, Frederick never considered he'd have to be making decisions of this kind. He tried to breathe and think, but the dank air and mortifying scene were making it difficult. "Don't touch anything, first off. Let's go upstairs and call the police." He rose to his feet, walking toward Daniel and the exit.

"The police?" Daniel asked. "Do you think that's a good idea?"

Frederick's own experience with police had not been positive. He'd been in jail three times already in his life: once for eating in the wrong restaurant in South Carolina, and twice for protesting. As the wheels turned in his head, Frederick began to realize that being at the scene would likely make him a suspect. Taking a deep breath, he looked at Daniel and said, "Let's go upstairs and get some air at least, okay? Then we can try to work it out."

Frederick went up the stairs first and into the kitchen, opening a window to ventilate the room. While his back was still turned, he suddenly heard two sets of hurried footsteps, someone screaming, "NO!" and then felt a crack on the back of his head. All went dark.

Frederick dreamed of nothing specific, but light and sound roared around him as though he were engulfed in flames. Then there was silence, and he began to gain a semblance of consciousness with the lilting motion of the backseat of a moving car. He lifted himself up long enough to realize he was lying in a pool of his own blood and to see a long lock of nearly black hair hanging down from the head rest in front of him. The next thing he remembered was a nurse saying, "He's coming to…"

1965-1971

As it turned out, Calypso's late evening dates were not so innocent. Frederick was still in the hospital when she and her boyfriend, Jonathan, approached Louise with the news they would be having a child. Louise berated them as best she could but in the end, couldn't bring herself to be too angry. Once Frederick was released from the hospital, he used his contacts at the mill to secure Jonathan a job that would help support his new family.

Frederick found it was fairly easy to return to work. He'd been questioned by police on a number of occasions, but his wounding and subsequent short-term kidnapping all but eliminated him as a suspect in the bizarre fire that engulfed the home and the two women inside. His memory loss also allowed him to focus on his daughter and son-in-law as well. Not interested in paying for a large wedding, Frederick was grateful the couple opted to marry at the courthouse. Frederick funded the small party for friends and family that followed.

Calypso and Jonathan were devout Christians and named their son Ezekiel. It was the first Biblical name that popped into Calypso's head. The couple moved in across the hall and made sure to knock loud and clear on Louise and Frederick's door every Sunday morning to ensure their attendance at church.

"Am I getting that old?" Frederick asked once. "That my own child is waking me up to go to church?"

Louise laughed at him saying, "You better not be, because I know I'm not. She's just excitable, Frederick."

He chuckled heartily and replied, "And we've got the grand-child to prove that." Louise smacked him in the face with a pillow and got up to get ready.

Their lives settled into the strictest normality they would observe until December of 1970, when Jonathan was drafted into the war in Vietnam. He spent Christmas with his family but was then required to ship out immediately following. The family was distraught over the event, particularly Ezekiel. He would be perfectly calm one moment, then impossible to control the next. As time went by, he relaxed some, but letters from his father were not the same as his actual father, as Calypso knew all too well. Frederick provided some comfort and used his empathy to its fullest to calm the boy.

In an effort to bring Ezekiel closer to his father, Calypso began volunteering for the USO. Louise wasn't driving as much and Frederick had become accustomed to busing, so they lent the car to Calypso. It was an amusement to Frederick that he would watch his daughter and grandson pass by as he waited for his bus, which headed the other direction, and looked forward to seeing them on the days she volunteered.

On a rainy day in August, Frederick stood under his umbrella, a good ten minutes from the next bus, when his daughter pulled to a stop across the street from him. "You want a lift?" she asked.

"No thanks, girl, you keep right on," he answered, smiling and waving at them.

Ezekiel waved from the passenger seat and smiled. Calypso blew him a kiss and said, "All right then. You stay safe."

"I love you both!" Frederick replied, shouting across the street. Calypso closed the window and pulled away.

As she pulled the car up to the stop light at the intersection, Frederick heard the sound of a racing engine and turned to his right. Barreling down the street was an out-of-control pickup truck, the driver honking and flashing his lights in an attempt to alert vehicles and pedestrians in front of him. Tragically, the man somehow didn't see the car Calypso and Ezekiel were sitting in stopped at the intersection. Frederick watched in horror as Calypso let off the breaks and tried to hit the accelerator to drive out of the way. She had no time to react, though, and the pickup truck slammed headlong into the back of their car, pushing it into cross traffic where it collided with another car.

Frederick dropped his umbrella and ran to the intersection. When he reached the car, it had been crushed on three sides and the doors wouldn't open. Calypso was unconscious and had hit her head on the steering wheel. Ezekiel was lying in a heap on the floor on the passenger side of the car. He looked around and shouted to the bystanders, "Is anyone calling the medics?!"

A number of people responded, running into nearby shops to use the phone. Out of the corner of his eye, Frederick saw movement in the car. When he turned, he saw Calypso's head bobbing up and down and heard her crying.

"Baby? Baby, can you hear me?" he asked, rubbing his hand on her back.

"Daddy?" she said, unable to look at him. "Daddy?"

"It's me, baby. Are you okay?" He tried to move her head but she screamed in pain and he stopped.

"Daddy, it hurts," she responded, then noticed her son on the floor. "Oh my God, Daddy, what's wrong with Zeke?"

Frederick allowed his tears to flow, the rain drowning them on his salty cheeks. "I don't know. They're calling the medics." He pulled her hat off and brushed her crimson-colored hair out of her face. Blood was streaming down the side of her face.

"Zeke!" she called to him, but no answer came. The boy's head bobbed up and down but there was no sound.

A burning smell began to rise from under the hood of the car. Frederick turned and saw smoke escaping the mangled heap of metal at the front of the vehicle. He looked toward the heavens, thinking the rain would help, but the twisted hood provided shelter for the flames, and they increased in intensity. "Baby, we gotta get you out of here. The car's on fire," he said and reached in for her.

"I can't move!" she shouted, her sobbing becoming more and more desperate with each passing moment. "Why can't I move?!"

Another motorist had gotten out of his vehicle and rushed to help Frederick. When he heard Calypso say she couldn't move, he explained, "Hey, man. She might o' broken her neck. They say you're not supposed to move people when they got spinal injuries."

"She and her son are gonna to burn to death if we don't!" Frederick shouted back.

The man looked around and noticed several other people standing by wondering what they could do. "Maybe if we get this hood up the rain will put it out," he suggested.

Frederick assented, and they all hurried to the front of the car; one person retrieved a tire iron from the trunk of their car and began trying to pry the hood up. The metal was hot, burning hands and arms, but the group kept working. Try though they might, the fuel spilled and the flames quickly spread. The crowd jumped back as the blaze took hold, two sets of high-pitched screams emanating from within.

Frederick bolted toward the car. At that moment, a large burst of flames shot from within, lighting his clothes on fire. He was restrained by the crowd, who helped extinguish his clothing. Several bystanders held Frederick on the ground once his clothes had been extinguished, refusing to let him put himself in harm's way again. The shrieks had stopped, except for Frederick, who wailed and cried, "My baby! My baby!"

The fire department and a police unit pulled up. Firefighters instructed the civilians to move away and began dousing the flames. Two paramedics wrested Frederick from under the good Samaritans and began tending to his wounds. Once the flames were under control, one of the firefighters made his way to the paramedics and explained that the two in the car could not be saved. Frederick flew into hysterics and once again had to be restrained, with the backdrop of the afternoon deluge, twisted metal, and rising smoke.

Frederick spent a short stay in the hospital with first-degree burns and was released in time for his daughter and grandson's funeral. After that, he took to working in the shop and locking himself in the apartment at night. Louise went through a similar depression, but did her best to get them both out of the apartment as much as possible. Frederick was unwilling for the most part, however, and so they sat, watching television and resting. He'd all but forgotten his ability for empathy and his breath shortened considerably, causing his circulation to slow. They both knew he'd need to get exercise at some point or he might have a relapse of his heart troubles, but he refused to discuss it.

One evening in September while watching the news, there was a knock on their door. Knowing Jonathan had been released from his tour due to psychological strain brought about by the death of his wife and child, their hearts hit bottom when they heard it. They looked at each other, acknowledging they'd have to see him and help him move back into his apartment. Frederick choked up and a tear streamed down his cheek. Louise patted him on the hand, kissed his forehead and made the difficult walk to the apartment door. Upon opening it, however, a most unexpected face appeared.

"What are you…" she started. "We hadn't heard from you for years. We thought you were dead."

The aging, lanky Belarusian man took his hat off and bowed his head gently to Louise. "I'm very sorry not to call first. I heard about your child and felt it was time I made a visit. I am so terribly sorry for your loss."

Louise embraced Daniel and kissed his cheek, welcoming him in. When Frederick heard the man's voice, he stood up from his chair and turned around to look. It had been seven years since the mysterious fire that nearly killed him, and he'd assumed Daniel had perished altogether. It was as if a ghost had returned to visit. Frederick greeted him. "You're alive?"

Daniel bowed his head, somewhat ashamed, and replied, "Frederick, I am so sorry for your loss. I'm sorry I didn't come sooner."

Frederick ran his hand over his mouth, unable to breathe and not believing what he saw. He touched the man on his shoulders, confirming he was really standing in their kitchen. "I don't know what to say. It's been so long, I thought you'd been…" but he couldn't finish the sentence.

"It's history now, Frederick. Under the circumstances, and having been injured as I was, I thought it best to disappear. But I couldn't stay away now. I knew you might need someone."

Frederick and Louise looked at each other. She smiled at him as if to let him know it was okay to invite the man in, so he did. They sat and talked for hours, Daniel regaling them with stories of his past seven years traveling into Canada, back to Poland and the border with Belarus to visit friends. One particular story would be the central part of Frederick's life for the next few months, though, and he and his wife listened intently to it as it unfolded.

"I was in Toronto for two months in 1969 when I heard about a man. Now, I had heard rumors of him before from various sources, but I never believed he existed. A friend of mine works for a security company that was transporting some sort of historical artifact to New York, and they hired a security specialist to guard it the night before it was moved. As it so happened, this man of legend was the man they hired. He told me about it in passing, not thinking his troubles as a security guard would interest me, but I asked him to tell me more and he gave me this."

Daniel reached into his pocket, brought out a frayed, stained business card, and handed it to Frederick. The information was the absolute minimum. No address or vital information at all, just a name: Truesdell Protection Services – Isaac Truesdell, and a New York phone number.

"He didn't understand why I found it so interesting and I explained the legend," Daniel continued, as Frederick and Louise listened. "In 1905, just a few years before I was born, a special security firm was hired to protect a valuable piece of artwork that was being transferred from a wealthy West Virginian businessman to a museum on the East Coast. Only one man showed up for the job. He provided references and they hired him. The building was enormous: dozens of entrances, windows, doors, and there was a known warning that a group of thieves had tried to steal it before and would likely try again before it was transferred to the museum. The job was ridiculous for one man to take, but he did. That night, men showed up with climbing equipment and ropes and tried to break into the building – five of them. Supposedly, they also carried firearms, but it's a legend, so who knows. The men couldn't even break through a window. Two of them saw the man through the window, smiling at them, as they tried to get past him. He just stood there, not moving. The doors didn't budge, the windows didn't break. When morning came and the truck arrived to pick up the piece of art, five men were sitting unconscious in a circle in the driveway, their own rope tied around them. The police took them away and rewarded the man for his efforts. The painting is now permanently installed in a museum in Washington, or Baltimore, or wherever it was intended. In any case, no one could explain how it happened. The man never left the building, and the burglars never got in."

Frederick looked back down at the business card, taking in the name. "Isaac Truesdell."

"So, my friend the security guard and I sat outside the building where the artifact was being kept. All night. We occasionally saw the man inside, just walking around…"

"Wait," Louise interrupted. "You said this *legend* happened almost 70 years ago?"

Daniel nodded, smiling. "That's right."

"Which would make him, at the least, 90 years old? And they gave a security job to an old man? A really old man?" Louise asked.

Daniel's eyes blazed with fascination. "That's just the thing, though. He looks younger than all of us! Thirty, maybe a year or two more but no older."

"Could it be his kid, or his grandkid?" Frederick asked.

Shrugging, Daniel replied, "Why not? It's only a legend any-way, but just think about the possibility. Frederick, remember the day of the fire, you asked me about Marya's age. How it was she looked so young despite her years?" Frederick nodded that he did. "I think this man may know how, but I think I do, too. Marya's brother died next to her when they were infants. I believe his soul was locked inside her, connecting her to nature in ways we can't possibly understand. If this is true, there's no telling how old the man is, or what the limits of his power are."

Louise had been willing to go along with the bits of the craft Frederick practiced and the breathing, but she was not able to swallow what Daniel was saying. "Hang on. You're telling me that when people die, other people can absorb their souls?"

"It is a possibility," Daniel acknowledged. Frederick looked down at the card again and brought his hand to his chest.

"I appreciate your coming here and expressing your condo-lences, Daniel, but what I don't appreciate is you playing on the grief of me and my husband," Louise explained, agitated, and stood from her chair. "And I think I would like you to leave."

Daniel stood up and gathered his hat to his stomach. "I'm terribly sorry to have disturbed you. I just thought that maybe this man could give you some peace of mind in your time of grief."

Frederick was still holding his chest as Louise ushered Daniel out the door. She stated firmly, "Our time of grief needs to not include you at the moment."

"I understand completely," Daniel replied, and started to move through the doorway when Frederick stopped them.

"He's right, Louise."

"What?" Louise and Daniel both responded.

"I should have died. I should have had a heart attack after the crash but she's in there. She's keeping my heart strong. He's right, baby," Frederick explained.

Louise didn't know how to respond. Part of her was furious with Daniel for getting Frederick's hopes up, but another part saw the gravity in Frederick's face and knew it was true. Daniel looked to her for permission before stepping back in. She shut the door behind him.

"Is this what you believe, Frederick?" Daniel asked.

Frederick looked up at him, an expression of joy on his face, "Yeah. It is. She's here. So is Zeke." Louise finally exhaled on the mention of her grandson and sat next to Frederick, taking his hand. He breathed in and out fully for the first time since their deaths, and the room glowed with their presence. Daniel and Louise could see it as well and looked around them to behold the beauty of the sight. Solid objects glowed from within and glasses and windows hummed in harmony. Frederick held the card out in front of him and saw it pulse with warmth and light. Frightened, he let it go. To all of their surprise, it didn't fall. It hovered in midair, suspended as if by string from Frederick's fingers.

After his breathing calmed down, the room returned to normal, and the card fell on the floor. Frederick picked it up again and set it on the table, looking at Daniel with gratitude. "How can I ever thank you for telling me about this?"

Daniel sighed. "Frederick, you owe me nothing. I believe you would have discovered this at some point in the future anyway."

"Please. You don't know what this means to me."

"I have still been looking for the girl who started the fire. Who kidnapped you. If you are so inclined and wish to call to her, I would be grateful, but it is not necessary that you help." Daniel said this with great hesitation.

Frederick nodded gratefully and replied, "Absolutely. I'll do everything I can."

Knowing he did not wish to trap his daughter and grandson's souls perpetually in his body, Frederick began to consider ways to remove them. Daniel had no insight and there had obviously never been medical precedent, so Frederick was left to surmise on his own. While in his shop, he began to focus on the objects therein to see if anything popped out at him. As he'd begun carrying Isaac's business card with him, he would occasionally receive sensations that tied the card to objects in his shop. After a few more months, he began to seek out objects specifically based on whether or not they were connected to Isaac. When he'd collected enough of them, he began fashioning a box out of parts of the objects. There was no road map or instruction manual that told him to do this, but just a feeling that guided him to trust the impact Isaac would have had on the materials.

On an evening in early December, his call was answered just as he was putting the finishing touches on the box that would become the home for his daughter and grand-son. Nicky had left for the evening to have dinner with his wife, leaving Frederick to close up shop, when the door opened, ringing the bell overhead. It seemed to ring slower and lower than it ever had before and it caught Frederick's ear, sending a shudder through his head and chest. He exhaled, trying to warn Daniel about what he was seeing. A young, white woman with long, dark hair, pale skin, and bright green eyes was casually moving through the tables, looking at objects as she passed, a quaint smile pressed between her lips.

"This is a lovely shop you have, Mr. Casperson," she said, still not making direct eye contact with him.

Frederick was frozen with fear yet couldn't take his eyes off the girl. "Uh, thank you. Do you... do you need help finding anything?"

"Most definitely. I understand that you buy antique goods as well as sell them, yes?" she asked.

"Uh, yeah. We do. We can buy items from you if you have things you'd like to sell."

"Actually, I was thinking I might just give you something. See, I don't need the money and I've been told that you provide a form of… shall we call it, guidance? In return for the item." Frederick labored not to give anything away, and while he was successful to a point, he couldn't conceal the fact that he was hiding something. Rebekah continued, "I've been out of town for a few years and have been… struggling a little with what the next phase in my life should be."

"I don't know if I'm able to help you."

"Oh, I don't know about that. You've helped many other people before."

"I just think your path is quite a bit more… clouded than I'm used to dealing with. It's much harder to tell."

Rebekah acknowledged the difficulty, reached up into her hair, and removed the hair pin. "Okay. I see your point, there's no such thing as a free supper. Take this." She handed the object to him. "I'm not asking you for a horoscope or anything like that. Just dig like you do with everyone else. Ask me questions." He was silent as he examined the hairpin. "Is there a problem, Mr. Casperson?"

He considered what he knew of the girl. He knew she'd been a student of Daniel's and that she'd left under suspicious circumstances, only to return years later to murder Marya and Ekaterina, assault Frederick, and burn down the house in Concord. This was what Daniel had been able to provide. The waves coming from her at the moment felt no less sinister. He could tell she wanted something but it had nothing to do with her path, as she suggested.

"No, no problem. I just really think this is more complex than in other cases. I'm sorry, I can't accept this." He held the object out and his palpable fear out for her.

She did not take the hairpin, however, and paused to let him simmer before she replied, "Interesting." She turned and started through the space, analyzing the contents as she spoke. "You called me. Numerous times, actually. You've been looking for me for quite some time. So, here I am. The truth is that you need something from me, and while I'm not sure what it is, I know I could probably get some assistance from you as well. We can help each other, I'm sure. And yet, now that I'm here, you're not interested. Why is that?" When Frederick didn't answer, she turned to him, standing in front of the back door, and looked at the object on the counter. "What's in the box, Frederick?"

The instant the words left her mouth, Daniel burst through the back door with a length of pipe in his hand and cracked Rebekah across the head. Frederick's heart jumped when the door opened and was still racing at full speed when the young woman lay unconscious and bleeding on his floor.

"How did you get here so fast?" Frederick asked.

Daniel was breathing heavily as well and had to gather himself prior to responding. "I've been staying at the motel on the next block. I didn't have far to go." He could see Frederick was conflicted about the outcome of the encounter. "She'll be okay. But you need to understand, she's a murderer. She's been collecting the souls of the people she kills and using them for her own purposes. She would have taken yours and your daughter and grandson's if she had the chance. She had to be stopped." Frederick nodded.

Daniel opened the door to the basement, threw the pipe down the stairs, closed the door, and started maneuvering Rebekah's body to pick it up. "Help me take her out to the car." Frederick didn't move. Daniel stood up straight and stepped to him. "I promise you I won't kill her. I'm going to attempt to rehabilitate her, but I need your help to get her to the car."

Reluctantly, Frederick agreed, and they took her out the back door, placing her in the trunk. He shook his head as the trunk lid closed. "I feel like this is wrong, Daniel. I truly do."

"And you should. We shouldn't have to resort to this, but she has forced us." Frederick nodded reluctantly. "That box. Is that for Calypso and Zeke?" Again, the man nodded. "You have to keep that hidden. Protected. Rebekah has seen it now, and you must do whatever you have to do in case she returns. Don't let her get hold of it. Do you understand?"

"Yes," he answered and walked back toward the shop.

Daniel called after him. "Thank you, Frederick. I know this hasn't been easy, but I appreciate everything you've done to help."

Frederick became silent, walked back into the shop, and closed the door.

Daniel pulled the car up to a grove of dead trees along an abandoned country road. He took the shovel from the backseat and started digging a shallow, circular trench approximately ten feet in diameter. He gathered leaves and sticks into a kindling pile in the center of the circle and placed lighter fluid and a book of matches on the outside of the trench. Once the clearing was properly prepared, he cautiously opened the trunk of the car. Confident that Rebekah was still unconscious, he opened it fully and picked her up. Nearly collapsing twice, his aged form carried her to the center of the clearing and set her down. He took a few moments to catch his breath, then picked up the lighter fluid and began spreading it over her body and the kindling. Once finished, he put the container down and picked up the matchbook. Taking one final deep breath, he struck the match.

With the sound of the match lighting, Rebekah's eyes snapped open. She smelled the lighter fluid on her and sensed the heat from the match only a few yards away. She scrambled to her feet and met Daniel's eyes. Horror swept over him. He blew the match out, terrified of the fire she was capable of producing.

"This is it? This is what you've come to? Using a pawn like Frederick to get rid of me? You're pathetic. You're weak and jealous, and I should put you out of your misery." She assessed him coolly before continuing. "But I won't. I know the men who protect you. I know how you blackmail them into giving you safe haven. As long as that's how you operate, then you can have it. That's no life I'd want to keep you from. And it is, as it happens, useful to me."

Rebekah raised the wind, swirling leaves into Daniel's face to obscure his view and casually walked past him to the car. She started it and drove off, leaving the man in the middle of the dark forest. She headed west until the car died, then started walking, and never stopped.

Chapter Ten

February 1965

Seventy years from the last time he saw his sister Jane, Isaac found himself parking in a lot adjacent to the hospital in Wilmington. He retrieved a bouquet of flowers from the back seat of the car and made his way toward the hospital entrance. Both the lot and the hospital overlooked the Christina River, a stark view as snow fluttered harmlessly to the ground. He shrugged off the February cold, walked through the geriatric ward entrance, and made his way to the counter. Isaac asked, "Am I too early for visiting hours? I'm here to see Jane Truesdell."

The young woman at the desk looked up at the dashing gentleman, the glint in his eye softening her usually gruff hospital desk demeanor. "Well, technically you are, but I think we can let it slide this time. Are you her grandson?"

The question struck Isaac as amusing, so he smiled and played along. "Yes, I am."

She blushed and pointed down the hall to her right, explaining, "She's in room 153 to your left."

"Thank you," he replied and tapped the counter lightly as he started down the hall.

He began recounting all the moments in his family's life he should have been present for. Alice's marriage (he and Hattie had been present for Jane's), their children's births, their parents deaths... the list went on, and he worried that if Jane would remember him at all she'd be angry with him for having disappeared. The reality of the situation hit him as he got closer to the door. It was a thought he'd been coming back to ever since he found out she was terminally ill. She was 94 and would have a great deal of trouble believing he was the man visiting her, if she remembered what he looked like at all. He stopped outside the door, struggling to decide how to identify himself. Then he debated over whether to go in at all.

What he'd done was horrible and selfish. He'd abandoned his family because of his own personal loss. The wound was so deep that he couldn't bear facing anything with which he'd previously been familiar. He had needed to begin an entirely new life, devoid of all the people who had populated the first, regardless of the positive or negative influence they'd had. Selfish or not, it had happened seventy years in the past and couldn't be changed. Though she might have no idea who he was, it was important for him to have a connection to his family again. He opened the door.

Jane was in the final stages of her illness. As he entered the room, he saw her lying with her head elevated toward the television. She shared the room with two other elderly patients, and as Isaac closed the door behind him, all three turned to see if the visitor was for them. All three satisfied that it wasn't, they turned back to the television. Jane occupied the bed closest to the window. As Isaac approached her bedside, she turned to him again, confused, and asked, "Thank you for the flowers, young man. Do I know you?"

He put the flowers on the small cart filled with empty dishes and sat down in the chair beside her bed. "In a way, I guess. You don't remember me?"

"Young man, my body may not work anymore, but I never forget a..." her voice trailed off as she took in his form, paying special attention to his eyes and hair. "Well, I'll be damned," she started. For a moment, the hair on the back of Isaac's neck stood up as he thought she might remember him. "I must have done somethin' right. You're one of those Kennedy boys, aren't you! Did I win a medal?"

The hope Isaac had felt was quickly exchanged for mild amusement. "No, I'm sorry to disappoint you."

"Damn, I was excited for a second there."

"Do you remember you had a brother? An Isaac Truesdell? Do you remember him?" he asked.

She turned to him with a reflective look on her face. "Isaac. Now that's a name I haven't heard since the depression. When that damn fool Alice let her husband convince her to move to London. I kept telling her, 'What if Isaac comes back? You'll miss him.' I guess we all missed him; he's probably dead by now. Poor Alice, bless her soul, died in the blitz. If only she'd stayed."

Without thinking, he responded, "I heard."

Excitedly, Jane pushed herself up a bit and her eyes widened. "Oh! Are you his grandson? I can see the family resemblance. You are so very handsome."

He was strongly tempted to tell her that he was his own grandson, but considering how long he'd been away, couldn't bring himself to lie to her. "No. I'm not."

A knowing look washed over her face and she nodded toward him, "No? Well, who are you then?"

With great difficulty, he tried to recall any of the thousand different versions of this conversation he'd rehearsed in his mind on the trip from New York. None of them had sounded good. He pressed on clumsily. "I don't really know the best way to tell you this, or how to explain it, but I'm not a relative of Isaac's at all. I, uh… see, I've been travelling for quite some time, and I felt it was time to visit some family, and—"

"Isaac, I don't have all day," she interrupted.

"I know, I'm sorry, I'm just..." he began without comprehending what she'd said to him. Only after he'd started did the phrase sink in. "What did you just say?"

She nodded toward the curtain divider next to her and muttered, "Why don't you close that and we'll talk." Confounded, Isaac quickly rose to his feet and crossed to the curtain. She watched him as he closed it. "My lord, young man, you haven't changed a bit. You look just like the day you left."

He sat back down and asked, "How did you..."

"What, did you think you could come in here and pull one over on your little sister? I knew it was you the second you walked in that door."

"You did?"

"You have all your life to ask questions, Isaac. I don't have much time left, so if you don't mind, I'll ask a few, all right?" She raised her eyebrows at him, then patted the back of his hand affecttionately.

Respectfully, he agreed. "Certainly."

She breathed deeply, closing and reopening her eyes. "You found it, didn't you?"

"Found what?"

"Your craft. How you stay so young. Judging by the look of you, I'd say you found it around the time you left."

"How do you know about that?" he asked, shocked.

She smiled. "Mother told me you were special, Isaac. She said there was something different about you, about the powers you have. I want you to tell me about them."

In all his years practicing his craft, Isaac had rarely made the effort to interact with people, and thus his abilities in that realm were somewhat stilted. Knowing that he could be honest with Jane made him smile with relief. At least she wasn't angry with him. "It was the night I got engaged to Hattie. I'll never forget. It disappeared for a few years after she died, but eventually it came back. How did mother know about it?"

"She said you used to do all sorts of fascinating things when you were a child. Before Thomas died, you could move things with your mind and the like. Loved you to pieces, but she said how afraid she was the neighbors would find out. They never did, of course, and I thought the old lady was off her rocker. I never stopped thinking about it, though. Looking at you, I can see she was right. It's such an extraordinary strength you have, Isaac," she added.

"Strength?" he asked. "What do you mean by that?"

She shook her head. "All this time and you're still so hung up on the past. Why do you think you have this gift, Isaac? Look at me," she insisted. "I am dying. Just like Mother did. Just like Father did. Alice, Thomas… and Hattie. Just because you have longer to learn the lesson doesn't mean you should take longer to learn it. We all serve our purpose. You may not know what yours is yet, but there's no way for you to find out if you keep living with your head back over your shoulder. That's why you never came back. That's why you fear the things you know, and that's why you've never given up hoping for something that can never be. I would have thought after all this time you'd have figured that out." Isaac felt ashamed that he'd let his sister down, and she sensed his frustration. She relented, "Well, enough of that. Tell me what you've done for the past seven decades."

He took a deep breath, his eyes popping at the thought. "Wow, that's not asking much."

"I think you owe me," she said, smirking.

"You're probably right," he replied. "Well, when I left home I took a train out to the Northwest. I'd intended to try some gold mining myself but couldn't get up the nerve. It all seemed so self-serving. Then one day, I met a fella who was a security guard for an eastern firm who bought gold from the miners. He told me how security guards weren't paid well, and that there was a high risk of robbery, so they had trouble hiring. I have to admit some foolishness on my part, because the danger sounded rather desirable to me. I guess I was a bit self-destructive at the time. So, I joined up…"

Jane interjected, "That *is* foolish."

Sheepishly smiling, he replied, "I know. I'm sorry about that." She shrugged that it didn't matter anymore, and he continued. "Anyway, we were guarding a shipment one night in – must have been 1898 – when a gang tried to rob us. It was bizarre, like you see in the movies nowadays. They came right up in our faces with guns and knives, telling us we'd better find somewhere to hide out if we didn't want to get shot." As Isaac told his story, the patient on the other side of the curtain slowly pulled it aside with her cane so she could listen better. Isaac considered closing it again at one point, but didn't see the harm in continuing.

"My friend grabbed my arm and told me we should hide under the train car until they'd gone and promise not to squeal. But I was young and foolish and said I'd do no such thing. He started to shake and told me I was going to get us killed, so I told him he could go and he did. The robbers came closer to me and one of the men said, 'This is your last chance' in what I'm sure he considered to be a threatening voice. I felt this great sense of indignation and raised my hands to grab his gun from him." At that moment, Isaac stopped and laughed to himself.

"What happened?" Jane asked, wildly curious.

"I didn't grab the gun at all. When I raised my hand, he moved without me even touching him. He flew back against the wall and hit the ground. The other fellas just got scared and ran away. He wasn't unconscious, but he was pretty shaken. I picked up his gun and said in a very official manner, 'The Pennsylvania Gold-Trading Company politely requests that you leave their property, sir.' He ran out of the yard and I never saw him again." Isaac was laughing at the ridiculousness of the story, having never heard it out loud before.

"Remarkable," she uttered, her mouth agape.

"It was a damn silly thing to do. An even stupider thing to say, but I figured I'd done my job. Then I went looking for my partner who was still hiding under a nearby train car. When he saw me with the gun, he was just as flabbergasted as you might imagine. We were partners for years before I went solo. I made sure he retired as comfortably as possible so he never had to do it again. Had a few good scares along the way. Even got shot once."

"You seem to have healed well," she admonished. "My brother, making money protecting rich men's goods."

"*People's* goods. They weren't all men or rich," he corrected.

"Oh, no?"

He crossed his legs, finally gaining comfort with the strange conversation. "I have a graduated pricing structure. The less a person can afford, the less I charge. Sometimes I work for free if the cause warrants it."

"You ever protect people? Politicians and such? I would think the Kennedy's could have used you a couple years ago."

"Sometimes, but never politicians. True, the Secret Service got hold of my resume once and tried to convince me to come work for them, but I declined."

"Why on Earth would you do that?"

"They do background checks, Jane. Can you imagine how that conversation would go? I haven't had legal papers since the '20s. Think how it would look to hire a hundred-year-old man to protect the president. Besides, there's another thought that's been bothering me lately." Isaac drew a deep breath and stifled his mirth. "When I was younger, I took a much more active approach to my life. But, the older I get the more it feels like I don't belong. Like my presence is interfering with what's happening in the world. Like you, Jane, I've travelled on horseback, train, automobile, planes... and now there's this mission to land on the moon. It all sounds like something out of a Jules Verne novel. Don't you feel like you're an observer to all of this?" he asked, indicating the television across the room.

She laughed, resulting in a minor coughing fit. Isaac quickly grabbed a tissue and handed it to her. Wiping her mouth, she replied, "That's precisely how I feel, Isaac, but you need to understand something. You wouldn't be who you are if you were done participating. I am done participating. That's why I'm lying in this bed looking up at you. You're not done, and that's why you're up there looking down at me. Life is meant for the living. To just observe and refuse to participate means you're done. Death is for the dead. You? You must have an awful lot left to do if you're so far from death. You have the power to protect people. To protect things that have meaning for people. Your power must extend much further if you're meant to actually participate in life. I see good things in you, Isaac. You are and can be all that's good in the world. What you've done, what you will do cannot be underestimated or forgotten. Not even in death." She was so firm and resolute in her delivery that Isaac couldn't help but consider it. It was her next instruction that finally convinced him, though. "Tell me a story, Isaac."

Her request rattled from one corner of his mind to the next, twanging off memories and experiences as it went, striking nearly every synapse between him and 1895. "A story?" he asked.

"Remember, I'm the observer. Not you. Tell me a story so I may observe."

He began slowly. "Okay. This is the story of a man who lived a hundred years and finally learned what it meant to actually live." She looked at him lovingly and placed her hand on his, closing her eyes to listen.

Isaac talked throughout visiting hours for the next three days, telling her the story of his life from 1895 to 1965. His travels through the United States and the world. All the people he'd met, the places he'd seen. The wars, the revolutions, the victories, the losses of humanity. All of these things he shared through an unchanging, unfiltered lens. Near the end of visiting hours that Friday, Jane turned to him and told him to stop.

"I can keep talking if you like," he said.

"Don't. You're about to get to the time where you see me again, and I don't want to hear that part. It's time for me to go now, Isaac."

His first instinct was to plead with her for a few more hours, but he restrained himself, thinking back to all he'd learned from the recitation of his story. "I understand."

"Do you?" she asked.

"Yes. I think I do."

"Good. Now, before I make you leave, there's one more thing I want you to tell me," she stated gravely.

He nodded, leaning in and taking her hand. "Name it."

Jane closed her eyes and resumed with labored breath. "You said you lost your powers when she died." He acknowledged. "But you got them back. How did you get them back?"

Isaac sighed, having hoped to avoid the subject. Through non-verbal exchange he tried to explain that it wasn't really necessary, but she insisted it was. Deep down, he knew she was right and that her point was to drag the humanity out of him.

After much consideration, he began. "There wasn't room. Or I thought there wasn't room in my heart for anyone else. Not even for me." He paused, finding it difficult to continue. "There was a girl. She had a somewhat overbearing father, but like Hattie, she didn't have much use for structure or authority. I wasn't of the mindset to allow myself to be attracted to her, but that didn't stop her from... trying to take care of me. I think she felt sorry for me. In any case, I let her visit, and it had some negative repercussions. Some of the local boys followed her to the room I was renting – she'd brought me a cornbread or some such thing – and before either of us could do anything about it, they followed her in. It was surreal and horrifying. I was scared for my life."

"And her?" Jane asked.

"She wasn't scared at all. She was mad. Besides, I think I was scared enough for the both of us. I also think the... fright was a manifestation of..." He couldn't bring himself to say it.

"Love?" she finished for him.

"Not like before. Nothing like that, but I know I cared for the girl. She was practically a child... It felt inappropriate, but I felt it nonetheless."

Jane shook her head. "Worried about what other people feel and not what you feel."

"It was a first, I guess. Or at least hadn't happened for quite some time. I cared for her and I saw her in trouble."

"What did you do to stop it?" Jane asked. She could tell he was wracked with shame. "Tell me, Isaac. I won't be angry. Did you hurt those men?"

He bowed his head and nodded, unable to make eye contact. "I'm still not sure how it happened, and I've never done anything like it since, but... I burned them. From the inside out. They died."

Jane looked at him, emotionless. "Did you ever think that maybe they brought it on themselves?"

"Death?" he asked, somewhat shocked as he returned his gaze to her. "How does anyone deserve death?"

"You say that like it's a bad thing," she replied quickly, knowing it would catch him off guard. He fell silent. "Death is a part of life. Well, maybe not for you, but it is for the rest of us. Perhaps it was their time." She looked for a response, but got none. Redirecting the conversation, she asked, "What happened to the girl?"

He chuckled to himself. "She ran away. Actually, we both did at first, the building was on fire. But after that, she told me she never wanted to see me again. She said I was a witch, or a demon, or something. She never turned me in at least. Then again, I doubt anyone would have believed the story anyway."

"Where is she now?"

"I never had the nerve to check up on her. I think about her on occasion and try to think well of her. I like to imagine that I could wish her well and it would come true. That I could somehow, by shear will of positive thought, ensure good things would happen to her. It's ridiculous, I know, but..."

"No, it's not. People get back what they put out into the world, Isaac. I'm sure she's been getting back from you all the good thoughts she tried to give you back then. It balances out," she assured him.

He clutched her hand to his chest, and asked, "How does death balance out?"

"It never will if you think of it as judgment. Think of it as an end, or even a beginning, but it will always be negative if you think of it as judgment. However you think of it, it's necessary."

Her words were comforting and definitive to Isaac. He struggled with how to apply them in his own life, particularly to the varying sets of circumstances under which he'd encountered death. Yet he knew her words to be true.

"I am so glad I got the chance to see you one last time before I go. You are loved, Isaac, and you should know that," she said, beaming at him.

"Thank you, Jane, for everything you've done for me these past few days. And I'm sorry I never came back. I don't know if you'll believe me, but I love you, too. I guess I just never knew how to show it."

"But I know it now, and that's all that matters."

They sat in silence for quite some time, breathing in the last remnants of the brief relationship they had had as brother and sister. When Jane noticed her breathing beginning to shorten, she patted his hand and said, "It's time for you to go now, Isaac."

He kissed her forehead, rubbed her hand, and left the room, tears streaming down his cheeks but a smile on his face. Her words melded with Hattie's and a refrain began forming in his mind: "Life isn't what we do to stave off death. Life isn't a collection of things we can leave to our families or take with us. There is no magic number of accomplishments that defines a successful life. After all, once we're gone, all that's left is what others know of us. Not the things, or achievements. Just the energy we pass to them as we breathe…"

The words rang like church bells in his mind as he walked toward the exit, not noticing the nurses rushing past him into his sister's room. Then a doctor, then another nurse. Death didn't frighten him anymore. Isaac finished buttoning his jacket and stepped out into the cold. The door closed behind him.

Chapter Eleven

May 2010

In a decidedly nonplussed tone, Mike relayed, "I've been instructed not to allow you at any more crime scenes, Sarah. On top of that, I've been threatened with disciplinary action if you pull anymore of your stunts, so no, you cannot come to Seattle."

Sarah paced in her apartment on the other end of the line, getting dangerously close to lighting one of the cigarettes she'd been saving for the past three years. "I can't very well just sit around here for three days, Mike. You gotta throw me a bone."

He sighed audibly on the other end. "Give me a break, Sarah. I'd be the first 74-year-old to be fired from the bureau. Thank you, but no thank you. I promise if we ever get a lead on one of these things before it happens, I'll strongly consider bringing you along. Until then, you have to stay away. You got that?"

"Peachy," she replied and hung up the phone.

After her trip to Boston, Sarah had been reenergized to look into the case. She'd had encounters with a couple of men who claimed to know Rebekah, but who stopped short of admitting they knew where she was or how she operated. Unfortunately, the case went cold after that, and there was nothing to follow for three months until she saw a story come over the wire about a Seattle millionaire who met his end in a peculiar house fire.

It was only May but Sarah's air conditioner was looking like it might spend the summer on the fritz. She'd tried to give up drinking with reasonable success, and had also managed to stave off her recurring smoking habit. In short, she was cranky. The three days off she was observing for Memorial Day interested her little if she was going to use them as vacation. Spending it cracking an important case, on the other hand, was precisely what she had in mind, and Mike had stifled that.

She stopped pacing momentarily to allow the outside air into her lungs. She walked up to the screen and breathed deeply. Mostly, it smelled like Detroit, but there was a part of it that smelled like water, fresh air, and life. It occurred to her that perhaps she should visit her mother and broach the subject of her aunt for the first time since she was a child. The overwhelming answer she got back from the ether was 'yes.'

"Shit," she muttered, and pulled out her phone to start making plane reservations. The one thing she'd learned from the craft she'd recently begun practicing was that there were no easy answers. Whenever a question arose and she laid out the multiple choices that might result in a solution, the answer frequently came back as the one she was least interested in pursuing. Sometimes, the answer would be that she didn't have the right set of options at all. Talking to herself as she booked her flight, she muttered, "If that's what I have to do, I'm drinking on the damn plane."

Ten hours and two scotch and sodas later, she was renting a car at the airport in Tulsa. Sarah hadn't visited her mother for almost three years. She called her on occasion and her mother always said she understood that Sarah was busy, but the truth was that a phone call was as much as she could commit to. Her mother had been stable for most of her childhood, but as Sarah got into her teens, she began to withdraw. The psychiatrist explained that it might have been troubles from earlier in her life surfacing and causing her to have difficulty adjusting. Sarah's father called it all hoodoo and bullshit and forced his wife to stop seeing the psychiatrist. Her mother's condition deteriorated over the next two to three years and Sarah's father eventually left altogether, leaving Sarah to take care of her mother and go to school all at the same time. She was grateful in the sense that her father and his negativity were no longer around, and that he at least paid child support and alimony.

Sarah had decided to stay close to home and started college in Tulsa. However, two years and an astronomical grade point average later, her professors convinced her to transfer to Columbia for journalism, which took her away from her mother on a permanent basis. Sarah had never seen herself as a country or small-town girl, and going to New York proved that. As expected, her father couldn't be bothered to travel to New York to see her graduate. After a brief internship in Washington, she took a job in San Francisco to help pay off her school loans, although thanks to scholarships and grants, she had few. But it was around that time that she chose to move her mother to a full-time treatment center, and it would fall on Sarah's shoulders to pay for it.

Sarah had stopped in to visit sporadically over the ensuing years, but never on a regular basis. She paid the bills when they came up and kept her nose firmly in her job. The times she did go to the treatment center, her mother was increasingly withdrawn and it became more difficult to make the trip. Sarah hadn't visited her father since high school, but she did speak about him often. It was normally in the "lazy-ass bastard" muttering-to-herself sense, but he was never far from her thoughts. It was a constant consideration that he was fully responsible for her mother's condition, but she knew that wasn't accurate. The demons her mother faced went much further back than that.

Sarah pulled the car to a stop outside the rest home and sat in the driver's seat for several minutes before convincing herself to enter. At the counter, she asked in a tired, raspy voice, "Am I too late for visiting hours? I'm here to see Samantha Dempsey."

An official young man jockeying a computer responded, "Actually, you are. Visiting hours end at 7:00 P.M."

She checked her phone. 7:15. "Are you fucking kidding me?" she blurted, realizing only after she said it that it would probably not elicit the desired result. "Look, I pay her bills. Can you give me ten minutes with the old lady?"

He sighed a deep, self-pitying sigh and stood up. Buzzing Sarah through the door that led into the home, he asked, "Sign in, please. Do you know where she's at?"

"I do," she answered, scrawling her name in the visitor log. "And I appreciate you going to all this trouble for me."

In a passive-aggressive tone, he replied, "We just ask that you not disturb any of the other residents."

"You got it," Sarah assured him and passed through the doors. She tried to breathe as she walked up the stairs and down the hall to her mother's room, but only seemed to muster shallow breaths. She had no sense of what it was she needed to do there, no idea what version of her mother she'd meet, what the room might look like… nothing.

She reached the door of her mother's room and stood outside for a moment, trying to collect her thoughts. Nothing about her relationship with her mother had been simple. Everything had to have some sort of medicated coating on it. Her mother was either on antidepressants or abusing alcohol or stimulants. Looking back on her life, Sarah could barely remember the last time one or both hadn't been under the influence of *something*. *At least we're on a level playing field*, she thought and knocked on the door.

"Wait a minute! Wait a minute!" Samantha's voice rang from inside, "Don't go away, just a minute!"

"We're manic today... I can deal with that," Sarah acknowledged, bolstering her confidence.

There was a great fuss within the apartment, the sound of dishes clanking, then water running then stopping. She heard Samantha say, "Go away!" to her cat, who then meowed and scurried across the linoleum floor. Finally, her mother came to the door, unlocked the deadbolt, and opened it. Upon seeing her daughter, she froze, a variety of thoughts rushing through her head.

"Hi," Sarah blurted, trying desperately not to shy away from eye contact.

Samantha, on the other hand, wasn't afraid of eye contact at all. Her anger got the better of her and she replied, "Oh, it's you," and she slammed the door in Sarah's face.

"Mom! Dammit, let me in, I have to talk to you!" Sarah demanded, pounding on the door. After doing so, she looked around, worried someone might overhear and tell her to leave.

"Sorry, I'm washing my hair," Samantha shouted back from within.

"No, you're not! I just saw you!"

A smattering of vulgar utterances came next, followed by stomping across the floor and the door unlocking again. It opened and Samantha asked, "What do you want?"

"I just need to talk."

"Oh really? What about?" There was a pause during which Sarah tried to make it clear she didn't want to talk about it in the hallway. "You don't even know what you want to talk about? You came all this way for nothing?"

Sarah looked around. "I don't think we should just jump into it, mom."

Samantha assessed her daughter, barely caring what the actual purpose of the visit was. Sarah tried to think of how to convince her mother to let her in, but before she came up with anything convincing, Samantha let out a dramatic sigh and moved aside. "Fine, come in."

Sarah entered the apartment, looking around her mother's quarters. She was in the same room she'd been in for the past three years, but had managed to decorate it some. There was a living room attached to a kitchenette and dining area, and then a cubby with two doors, one leading to the bedroom and the other to the bathroom. The walls had paintings on them, though not like the ones Sarah had grown up with. Her mother had spurned the Norman Rockwell-style paintings they'd displayed when she was a child and instead put up what appeared to be a grouping of original works. Sarah didn't pay particularly close attention to them at first but knew she'd never seen them. There was a new TV and a glass coffee table in between the couch and the lounge chair. Sarah put her bag down and sat on the couch.

Samantha locked the front door and walked to the refrigerator. Retrieving a generic soda, she asked, "What type of small talk did you want to pass the time with before you get to the point?"

"The place looks nice, mom. What have you been up to?"

"I've been working. I've got a job at a craft store now," she replied, sitting on the lounge chair and slurping her soda.

"So they told me."

"Oh, right, the progress reports. You know, I'm curious. What happens when I fail? Do they ask you if you want them to kick me out?"

Sarah considered getting into this debate with her mother, but knew it wouldn't solve anything. "I'm happy you're getting out and working. How do you like the job?"

"It's nice to not feel pathetically non-self-sufficient. I'm saving the money and I'm going to pay you back, Sarah."

"Christ, mom, it's not about the money. I don't want it back." Sarah's aggravation was growing quickly.

"No, you'll get it back. I don't want your money, and I don't want your father's money."

"Wait, you've been taking money from him?!"

Slowly, Samantha sipped her soda, then guiltily replied, "No. Besides, what does it matter to you? You're not the one who has to deal with him."

"You shouldn't have to deal with him either."

"Sarah, it's getting late and my program's coming on soon," Samantha said glibly, trying to change the subject.

"Great, what show is it?"

Samantha took another sip, contemplating. "I'm sure I can find something. What do you want? No, hang on. Let me guess. I've embarrassed you for the last time."

"Mom."

"Or, you're going to New York and not coming back?"

"Mom!"

"No, I've got it. You've fallen in love and you're visiting to make sure I stay here and don't make a scene at the wedding!"

"Well, that doesn't make any sense. That never even happened," Sarah responded, confused.

"Didn't I tell you? I'm psychic – I can see into the future."

"Mom!"

"Too much?"

"It's about your sister!" Sarah nearly shouted.

Samantha paused momentarily, then put her soda down on the table in front of her. "Now, that's a new one," she muttered with great curiosity.

"What do you mean?"

"You haven't asked me about Rebekah since you were a kid. What brings her up now?"

Sarah paused thoughtfully before speaking. "A few months ago, I got pulled into a criminal investigation involving the FBI. I'm not exactly sure how everything happened, or when it started, but Aunt Rebekah is one of the suspects in the case."

Samantha cackled wildly, reaching again for her generic soda. "That old bat?! Christ, that's too much."

"Old? Have you seen her recently?" Sarah asked.

"Are you kidding? I haven't seen her since I was a kid. She calls me every few years to make sure I'm alive, or to tell me she's alive. Whichever. I guess the FBI must be in cahoots with the Tulsa police then."

"Why's that?"

"Oh, every ten years or so they send some new asshole or other to come ask me questions. Want to know if I've seen her, or know her whereabouts. I tell 'em to go fly a kite and they leave me alone for another decade, then come back. She's a suspect for somethin' that's for sure. How she manages to accomplish anything criminal at her age is beyond me. Personally, I think it's all ridiculous."

"Well, ridiculous or not, the FBI wants to find her."

Samantha laughed and shook her head. "What have you got to do with it?"

Sarah paused before asking, "Have you ever seen this before?" She reached into her pocket and pulled out the hair pin.

Samantha leaned in to look at it, retrieving her reading glasses and taking it momentarily before handing it back and saying quickly, "Never seen it before."

"Damn," Sarah uttered and put it away. "I picked this up from a woman who runs a trinket shop in New Orleans. Based on the information she gave me, I traced it back to another trinket shop in Boston. There was an old, African-American man who told me he hadn't seen it for almost forty years, but that it belonged to Aunt Rebekah. Some other guy picked it up years later and said he was looking for Rebekah, but he wasn't the police or the FBI..." Sarah sighed, frustrated. "Quite frankly, I can't get a straight story out of anyone. The FBI won't talk to me anymore, that guy wouldn't tell me anything useful, and I can't find this other old, white guy and it's getting pretty aggravating."

Samantha shifted in her chair. "Let me get this straight. You're performing a criminal investigation into your aunt, and you're not getting anywhere, so you ask her sister – your crazy mother – to fill in the holes? Sister, we should change places because you're more nuts than I am."

"Mom, I don't need sarcasm here." Sarah exhaled broadly, stood, and began pacing. "This has been monopolizing my life for months now, and I can't get anything done!"

"You know what's been monopolizing my life?" Samantha asked, leaning in.

"Fine, mom! Move out! There aren't any damn bars on this place."

Silence fell over them. Samantha chuckled, then hid behind her soda again. "You want one?"

"There's too much sugar in those things."

"Ahh, that's right, you're a health nut. How is your liver these days?"

Sarah waved her arms in front of her defensively. "Okay, okay. We both have our vices. I get it. Can we move on, please?"

"Sure." There was a long silence.

Sarah looked around more carefully at the apartment. The walls had been freshly painted. New carpeting had been installed, she presumed in part because of her mother's endeavors into painting gone awry. Finally, she began to look more carefully at the paintings. A theme emerged that troubled her greatly. All of the paintings seemed to be related to fire or destruction in some way. Oddly, few of them were painted in red or orange, but the impression was there nonetheless.

"What are these paintings about, Mom?"

Samantha shrugged. "I don't know."

"Well, where did you get them? Do you know the artist?" she asked rather pointedly, looking at one image that appeared to be a man in the middle of a scene of carnage with flames shooting from his chest. "Some of it's a little… graphic."

"Of course I know the artist. So do you."

"Who is it?"

"It's me! What, you don't think I'm capable of work of this quality?"

Sarah stopped cold. In truth, the art wasn't particularly good, but Sarah reserved that judgment. In an alarmed tone, she asked, "You painted these?"

"Sure, why not?"

"Then how could you not know what these are about? Have you been having nightmares again?"

"Again? They never stopped, sweetheart. I just paint what I see."

Sarah leaned in to her mother and in a low voice explained, "Mom, this is what Aunt Rebekah does. She burns people… from the inside out."

"That's absurd."

"Why do you think I've been working so long on this case?!

Only one of these incidents ever happened in Detroit, so I wouldn't have followed it had it not been someone I'm related to. That *you're* related to! Mom, you're painting what your sister does to people." Sarah waited for her mother to reply, but instead only received a blank stare. "Do you get these ideas from your nightmares or while you're awake?"

Samantha shook her head, amused. "I can't believe the morons that run this place haven't told you all about it. They complain all the time, but as long as I don't have matches or lighter fluid, they don't do anything to me."

"No, they never told me, but I'm glad they didn't. Up until a couple months ago I would have thought there was something wrong with you because of these. Quite frankly, I'm glad I'm only finding out now because I know it's not you. Tell me where you got these ideas."

"I don't know. While I'm walking around the garden, or to work and back. When I get fresh air, I paint these things. Otherwise I paint you," she explained, climbing to her feet and reaching behind the television to retrieve a questionable portrait of her daughter. "See?"

Unimpressed, Sarah continued. "Tell me, Mom. How's your breathing?"

"Better, why?"

"So, when you go on these walks, you close your eyes, breathe in the air, let your mind wander… you feel calm, more at peace. Is that right?"

Suddenly interested, Samantha asked, "How did you know that?"

"I think your sister is telling you to paint these things. She's sending signals and when you go outside and breathe… however it is you do it, you pick it up."

"My god," Samantha exclaimed. "That's amazing!"

"Isn't it?!" Sarah asked excitedly.

"You really do belong in here. I'll call the manager first thing in the morning and see if they can get you the place across the hall. It picks up the sunrise nicely."

Sarah sat back on the couch, wanting to scream. "Something's been happening to me, mom."

Samantha nodded emphatically, taking another sip from her soda. "Yes it is. You're going nuts like your dear old mother."

Sarah crushed her hands to her face in frustration until a thought occurred to her. Not intending for her mother to hear it, she blurted, "I bet we can find her…"

"What's that?"

She turned quickly to her mother. "Nothing. I tell you what. We should call the manager first thing tomorrow. You're cured. I'm getting you out of this place and putting you in a real apartment." She got up from the couch, grabbed her bag, and started toward the door.

"What?!"

"Sorry, I have to run. I just realized I need to do something back in Boston… Detroit! That's it, Detroit."

Samantha rose as well, following Sarah to the door. "What are you babbling about? I was just kidding about you belonging in here; you don't have to act like it."

"Yes, but I'm not kidding about getting you out. I'll tell the manager that until we find you that apartment they shouldn't withhold things from you anymore. Paint! Paint as much as you can. Have one of the shmucks who works here help you take pictures and email them to me, okay?"

"You're nuts, Sarah! Don't do that. Don't end up like me," Samantha half pleaded, half joked.

Sarah grabbed her mother's shoulders affectionately. "I'm not nuts. And neither are you. Promise me you'll email me the paintings. Please?" Samantha nodded, utterly lost. Sarah kissed her forehead and said, "I love you, mom. I have to run!"

Samantha stood in the doorway and watched her daughter run down the hallway toward the exit. "I love you, too…" She closed the door behind her and sat down, staring at the paintings. "You want me to paint more of that stuff, huh? Okay, if that's what you want…"

Sarah waited in Tulsa for the red eye and made it back to Detroit by morning. As soon as she was off the plane and in her car, she plugged in her headset and called Mike. "Pick up the phone, damn it."

Eventually, a haggard voice responded, "Hello?"

"Mike!" she replied quickly. "Don't hang up!"

"All right, I won't hang up, but it's 6:00 in the morning, Sarah," he answered, annoyed.

"I think I can follow her!"

"What? Who? How?" he asked, disoriented and confused.

"Aunt Rebekah telegraphs her crimes to my mother after she commits them. There has to be some sort of message she telegraphs beforehand. Something about where she's going."

Mike sighed angrily. "Yes, that's what we're looking for. Have you found it?"

"No, but I think I can," she replied, trying to keep him on the phone.

"Great, call me when you do," he said and started to put the phone down.

"Wait, don't hang up! I mean, I think I can now."

A short silence ensued, followed by Mike's skeptical response:

"I'm listening."

Walking swiftly alongside Sarah as they darted out to her car after she finished recording a news segment for another story, Mike asked, "Is there any chance she sends these messages before she commits the crimes?"

"I checked the dates on the paintings. They're always a month or two after the crime. My point is that I think she has a signature. I think all people have a signature. When you're planning, when you're thinking about something, you send an intention..." she began.

"You learned about this in yoga class?" he implied sardonically.

She cocked her head. "Actually, yes, but the theory is sound. She has to have an intention. There has to be a purpose to what she's doing or the victims wouldn't be so similar."

"And you're heading to Boston to check up on that theory? What for?"

"I'm going back to the shopkeeper. He knows her, at least better than anyone else I've talked to. When she visited him she had to have sent an intention in advance, and he or something in his shop has to have a record of that. If I can read him well enough to get a better picture of her, then maybe I can pick up on the signals my mother's been picking up and I can trace Rebekah," she explained.

"You know what the problem with that is, don't you?"

"What's that?"

"What if no one knows her well enough for you to get a good read?"

"Then we're fucked," she replied, reaching her car and opening the door.

"Hey, if this works out, then you could become quite a useful asset in our department. We could use a bona fide tracker on our team," he winked at her.

"No chance, Mike. The bureau doesn't pay enough for the risk involved."

Mike held the door open for her while she placed her bag in the passenger seat. "That being said, I want you to stay safe, okay? This woman's dangerous and the people she kills arc frequently armed or have armed guards. You don't want to put yourself in harm's way if you don't have to. Y'understand?"

"Yes, sir. By the way, what are you doing in Detroit? Not another local burning victim?"

"Sadly, nothing that interesting. Drug cartel committing burglaries over state lines and one in Canada. Local and international agencies fighting over jurisdiction… the usual stuff," he stated, tossing it off.

"Drug cartels committing burglaries? That's the kind of thing I would normally be reporting on. Why haven't I heard about it yet?"

"Because you burned your source?" He glared at her reproachfully, then added, "Also, it's very hush-hush at the moment. Trying not to scare away the witnesses. Should have it figured out by the time you get back from Boston, though."

"Will I be the first to know?"

"It depends on what you bring me, but that shouldn't be too tall of an order," he answered, smiling.

She extended her hand to shake. "You got a deal."

They parted ways, and Sarah left for Boston.

Sarah parked her rental car on the side street so it wouldn't be noticed and strode casually down the sidewalk. She stopped before she reached Frederick's shop and straightened up, making sure to even out her breathing prior to entering.

Before she could even say 'hello,' Frederick was leaving his stool behind the counter and crossing to her. "You again. What can I do for you this time, young Sarah?"

"Young? That's cute. Thank you."

"I don't say anything I don't mean," he responded. She looked him over and breathed in and out twice to assess his meaning. He noticed immediately what she was doing and continued, "You're getting better at that."

"At what?" she asked, suddenly on guard.

"Reading people. You've improved since you were here last."

Surprised, she looked around to see if anyone was watching. "You know about that?!"

"Okay, you're not that good at it yet. Sarah, I've been doing this since before you were born. It doesn't just run in the family," he explained and started back toward the counter.

"How did you know Rebekah and I were... Oh, I get it. You know, you could have told me that last time and it would have saved me a lot of trouble," she snapped, following him back to the counter. On it were a number of new trinkets he was busy cataloging as well as an ancient business card that looked as if it could disintegrate to dust at any moment. Not wanting to destroy it, she tilted her head awkwardly to read it. "What's that?"

"None of your business," he replied hastily and stuffed it in his pocket.

"That's the oldest damn business card I've ever seen. Who's Truesdell?" she asked.

"What did I just tell you?"

"You've got something to hide, don't you?"

"Don't we all?" he countered.

"Maybe, but something tells me the number on that card is

part of what you're hiding. C'mon, you can let me in on the secret. I won't tell anyone." Sarah smiled and rested her elbows on the counter with her head in her hands.

He met her gaze and replied sternly, "You're a journalist. You wouldn't be a very good one if you didn't tell anyone."

"Ohhhh, come on, Frederick! You watch the news these days. Journalism is a subjective craft. I can tell any version of the truth I please. Your name doesn't have to be involved in it at all. Besides, what kind of objective story would it be if I admitted my own relationship to it? Certainly, I can leave a few other details out of it, can't I?" she asked.

He bent down to meet her nose to nose. "But that's not what you're known for, Ms. Dempsey. You are known for being an objective journalist in an otherwise subjective culture of… oh, what are the kids calling it these days?"

"Infotainment. And what's with 'the kids'? Am I not one of them anymore?"

"I said *young*, Sarah. That was in contrast to me, not your viewers."

She straightened up, ran her hands across her abdomen self-consciously, and rested her hands on her hips. "Thank you very little, Mr. Casperson. I'll just pretend I didn't hear that and move on to my point."

"I thought journalists had to work up to the tough questions."

"You ever seen Mike Wallace do an interview? Starts right in there with the tough questions. If he can do it, I can. Plus, I'm better looking."

"Well, I can't disagree with any of that." Frederick smiled and attached his magnifying lenses to his spectacles, bending back over his trinkets. "So, what's your momentous question?"

"Who's that on the business card? Do you know them personally?" she asked. Frederick shook his head. "Now, that's the first time I've asked you anything and gotten the sense you were lying. I mean, I know you've brushed me off before, but this is the first time I've felt any kind of falsehood. Am I getting close?" He turned to her momentarily to glare at her over his spectacles then looked back to the object in his hands. "Okay... you're trying to hide something. Are you trying to hide it from Rebekah?"

"Really, what is the point of this?"

"Because I think I can help you."

"How? By smearing my name and hers all over the evening news?"

"In Detroit? Hardly. Besides, you know I'm not here to do a news story anyway. You're trying to hide something from Rebekah, possibly having to do with this Truesdell person, and I'm trying to find her. I have friends at the FBI who can help me. If they can help me, they can help you. What'd'ya say?"

Frederick took off his spectacles, placed them on the counter, and straightened up. "Do you remember when you first came to Boston and stumbled into my shop?" She nodded. "You were clueless and lost and didn't know your right from your left in this case. Now, admittedly, you're starting to know the right questions to ask but I'm not sure I want you that close. So, let me ask you a question."

"Anything," she replied enthusiastically.

"If I tell you who this man is..." he started.

"It's a man, good!"

"If I tell you who this man is, will you leave me alone?"

"Not a chance. I'm gonna need more than that," she answered instantly, without even a second's consideration.

"If I tell you why I have his business card, will you leave me alone?" he bargained.

She clucked twice then said, "It would depend on what that information is, but I can tell you I'll do my best to make that happen."

"It's you or the FBI, isn't it?" he said in a defeated tone.

"I don't want to twist your arm, Frederick, but I'd much rather play a card that looks something like aiding and abetting than have her kill again. Get my drift?"

"That's an awfully heavy-handed card to play on an old man," he argued defensively.

She shrugged. "Maybe. But something tells me that you're tired of hiding, and that it may even be Rebekah you're hiding from. If there's any chance I can help keep you from having to do that, you need to take the opportunity."

Sighing, he put his hand on the counter and leaned against it. "His name is Isaac Truesdell." Frederick pulled out the card and handed it to her, adding, "He's a private security contractor. I've been thinking about hiring him to protect my shop from your aunt. I was given that card by a man who'd seen his work in Canada in the '60s. The curious thing is that his resume and website say he's only been doing it for ten years."

"Did he take over his father's business?" she asked casually, jotting down the info from the card.

"That wasn't within the scope of our agreement. I'd say I've given you enough to go on. If you're really interested you should be able to track him down."

"I reckon I will. Thank you, Frederick. I really appreciate it." She extended her hand.

Frederick shook it reluctantly and asked, "Will you leave me alone now?"

Sarah winced and hiked her purse over her shoulder. "Can't promise that, but I'll try. Besides, you like me. You don't want to admit it, but you like me, Frederick."

"Goodbye, Sarah," he said, smirking, and put his glasses back on to return to work.

Something felt mournful about this parting. She wasn't sure what it was, but as she left the shop, Sarah felt a slight tug, as though her business there was unfinished. Pausing to look at the flustered old man, she tried to think of what to say next. Instead, she turned on her heel and exited the shop.

"This has to be out of a Bogart movie," Sarah muttered to herself as she stepped onto the landing at the top of the staircase. Truesdell Protection Services' headquarters were located in an old brick office building in Manhattan. The hardwood interior had been meticulously kept up and each of the offices had frosted, glass-panel doors with stenciled names. She felt like she was in an old film noir, hunting down the *I-rescue-the-damsel-in-distress* gumshoe who would help her find her recently murdered father's killer. She beamed as she strolled down the hallway, checking doors to see which was Isaac's. Nearing the end of the hall, she saw two luxury-sized suites, each taking up about half the floor on either side of the hallway. The one on the right read simply "Truesdell." She knocked eagerly. The frosted glass rattled in the door, the door rattled in the frame. She only heard one set of mechanisms clanking and noticed the handle didn't have a lock. The deadbolt was unlocked as well. She reached for the knob and turned.

On the ride from Boston to New York, she'd spent a great deal of time imagining what Isaac Truesdell might be like. Part of her brain suggested a middle-aged man with a dashing foreign accent who could cast spells with a flick of his wrist. She admitted to herself that this was the romantic side of her. Another part imagined him as an old, daffy wizard-type with a cane and an office that resembled a laboratory for the fictionally insane. Then there was a third version she couldn't quite make out. This was the version that popped into her head every time she took a deep breath. In preparation for her possible meeting with the man, she hadn't even attempted to drink on the plane and consequently spent much more time breathing. There was no image to this third version, just a feeling. Comfort, sadness, strength… all rolled into one. What she didn't expect was for the office to be completely empty.

As the door swung open, she stopped in her tracks and leaned against the doorjamb, letting out a frustrated huff. "Shit," she spat, and began traipsing through the space. It was an entire luxury suite filled with nothing but stale, dusty air. There was a separate ante-room in the back and next to it was the restroom. She hurried in to check them both. Both were empty. She returned to the main office and peered out the window at the giant steel creatures that had sprung up around the building over the years. Out of the corner of her eye, she noticed an item on the windowsill – something that had eluded her eyes earlier – a business card holder. She reached down and picked one up. It was identical to the business card Frederick had showed her back in Boston, except his was supposedly 40 years older. But as with that one, there was no address. While web searches had resulted in no address hits, Sarah managed to call in a favor. This was the only known address for Truesdell Protection Services, and the only address ever registered to the bill for the phone number on the card. There was no hardline phone, no furniture, nothing. Just business cards.

She heard a noise behind her and wheeled around. Standing in the doorway wearing a button-up shirt, jeans, and casual shoes, was a man about her age. His hair was dark and his eyes deep and sharp. He was sporting a five-o-clock shadow and a curious smirk on his face. Sarah surmised this might be the living embodiment of the third version she carried in her head of Isaac Truesdell, but she couldn't believe the handsome creature in front of her was anyone but the grandson of the individual she'd heard about.

"I'm sorry, I was just looking for someone," she blurted, failing to sound casual.

"Ah," he replied.

"Uh, do you know the former tenant?"

"Former?" he asked, his casual visage unmoved by her questions.

"Yes. Well, it appears he's only left behind some of these." She grabbed the business card holder and held it up. "Business cards. I'm assuming he's recently moved out."

His smirk grew slightly larger. "It would seem."

"So?"

"Oh, yes. That," he began and started into the room, angling away from her so she wouldn't feel threatened. "Actually, I do. I'm the former tenant."

Her breathing staggered, and her thoughts faltered. Something inside her told her she was never closer to her aunt than right now, but this sensation was clouded by the myriad other emotions she was having directly related to the man himself. "You are? What's with the business cards?"

"I'm paid up through the end of the month, so I figured I'd leave them behind for anyone who happened to drop by."

"And do they?" she asked.

"Clearly," he responded quickly, motioning harmlessly to her.

"Huh? Oh!" she laughed, realizing his meaning. "You mean me… I'm an idiot."

They stood in silence for a moment while Sarah tried to collect her thoughts and start a line of questioning. Isaac beat her to it.

"Were you looking to hire me?"

"Uh, no. Not really. I mean, I'd like to learn more about your business."

"Certainly. What would you like to know?" he asked.

A strange, one-sided sense came over her. According to Frederick's emotions regarding the man, Isaac was some kind of wizard or sorcerer. However, when Sarah tried to read him, she got the impression that she was the only one participating in the activity. He came off as a singularly harmless man. If he was what Frederick perceived him to be, he was far better at the craft than either of them were, but she had trouble believing he was part of the bizarre history at all. Sarah set her mind to practicing her craft and trusting her instincts. She breathed, then asked, "How long have you been in business?"

"I've been doing this for ten years," he answered.

Absolute truth, her mind told her. "What type of things do you protect? Do you protect people?"

"Anything, really."

Also true. "What methods do you use?" she asked, and tried to dig into his shallow, protective breathing to pull it out.

"Well, my references will have to suffice on that front. My methods are proprietary to Truesdell Protection Services. I'd be happy to provide you with a list of references, however," he replied and started toward her. Something was happening but she couldn't tell what. He'd submarined her attempt to get inside his head and gone right through to controlling her emotions, it seemed. *But how?* she thought. Despite her confusion, she was fully comforted with his response as he touched her hand to bring the business card to her eyes. "Why don't you think it over and give me a call. My office is moving to California, but I work all over the country, so don't hesitate when you need me, okay?"

"Sure, that sounds great," she replied, mindlessly.

He ushered her out of the office and onto the elevator where she gladly bid farewell and headed on her way. Only when she was in a cab on the way back to the airport did she realize what had happened. She muttered to herself, "That son of a bitch." Sarah grinned, in awe of what had just occurred. She even considered returning to confront him, but knew he wouldn't be there. Then she thought, *But why was he there to begin with?*

Sarah got off the plane and headed straight to the news station. She called Mike the minute she entered the building. "Isaac Truesdell, Mike! We have to follow him somehow. Is there any way we can get hold of this guy's phone or scan his email accounts?"

"Sarah, you've got to be kidding me. That would take a grand jury, a warrant, and who the hell knows what else," he replied, exasperated.

"Fine, let's get it! Look, this guy's loaded. He's been renting a swanky office suite in Manhattan, for Christ's sake. You don't make that kind of money unless you've got seriously high-end clients. I'm telling you, this guy protects the kind of people she kills. Wouldn't it make sense to tap his contacts and see who he's working for next? Then we can cross-reference it with your target list!"

"And what makes you think that qualifies as probable cause? We could subpoena Blackwater for the same purposes. It still wouldn't hold water with a grand jury," Mike explained. Sarah groaned in frustration. "What ties this guy to Rebekah more than my twenty-year-old niece?"

A long pause ensued. Sarah knew her answer wouldn't suffice for legal purposes. "My intuition, Mike. You wanted to hear it. There it is. My intuition. That doesn't make me wrong, though.

You've got to get a tap on this guy's phone for me. I know you and your NSA pals have been doing all sorts of illegal wire taps since 9/11. Can't you get a freebie on this one? She's killing your highest-earning taxpayers."

"Very funny. I need probable cause for a tap, Sarah."

"No, you need probable cause for an *arrest*, Mike. You can use a suspicious gym bag to justify a phone tap," she countered, unlocking her office door and turning on the lights.

"I'm not going to tap the guy's phone. That ain't happening."

"Mike, I'm telling you, this will have big payoff for you. You're looking at cracking the longest running open case in your department."

There was an irritated sigh on the other end of the phone before Mike replied, "I'll look into putting a car on the guy, but no promises. Okay?"

She raised her fist in the air in celebration. "You won't regret it, pal!"

In typical form, it took more than two months to dredge up the funds to place a tail on Isaac, but it eventually happened. In late August, Isaac worked an overnight job at the home of a wealthy businessman in Arkansas. Two days later, the man was burned to death by circumstances similar to the cases Mike and Brad had been working. By bureau standards, Sarah's hunch had developed into an acceptable level of correlation, and they tapped Isaac's phone. Less than a month later, Mike called Sarah with a curious development.

"Sarah, you won't believe this," he relayed, seemingly incapable of believing it himself.

"Gimme whatcha got," she responded, twirling her pen with one hand and holding the phone with the other.

"This Truesdell guy is booked to work your friend Casperson's shop on September 21."

Sarah sat propped by pillows in her backseat with binoculars, a bottle of water, and a bag of salty chips. Through the bureau, Mike and Brad had negotiated with a couple of nearby businesses to stake out Frederick's shop from their front windows. Two plain-clothes officers watched the back of the shop from a vehicle parked behind a dumpster. They were all set up on radios, prepped to call each other at the slightest sign of abnormality. The shop was nestled in an offbeat, town-square-like corner in Brookline, almost as if it were its own little village. There was a fountain in the middle of the square, and Frederick's shop was at the middle of the block, directly facing the fountain. This made the stakeout particularly difficult because no one could get a direct view of the front of the shop without being spotted.

Late in the evening, Isaac finally arrived at the shop. The radios crackled with excitement at the development, but silenced after a quick admonishment from Mike to stay off the air. A similar event occurred when Frederick left a short while later. Hours went by with nothing to report. Occasionally, Isaac appeared to be talking to someone, but no one else could be seen in the shop, regardless of the angle. Just as they were beginning to give up hope, however, a figure appeared walking near the shop.

"Who the hell is that and where did they come from?" Brad whispered into the radio. "Sarah, they came from your direction, did you see them?"

"No!" she responded irritably. "I would have said something." As the figure got closer to the shop and the dim lighting coming from within, they realized it was a young woman. "Holy shit," Sarah exclaimed. "Is that *her?!*"

Mike cautioned, "All right, everybody. Relax. Sarah, do you have a good view?"

She peered anxiously through her binoculars. "No, I can only see the back of her head. Is she stopping in front of the shop?"

One of the officers stationed at the back of the shop added, "Guys, we got nothing back here. Mike or Brad, can you see her face? We need a positive ID before we can move in."

"I can't see shit," Brad admitted.

"I can't either," Mike replied. "Just stay put everyone. I'll let you know when we gotta jump and how high, but for now we need a positive ID and an inciting action before I'm going to be comfortable running in there. Besides, if this guy's all he's cracked up to be, he may not need help from us."

The young woman they'd been watching had been perched on the ground by the front door for a few moments when she stood up. They watched carefully as she raised her hands to the sky. Above them, clouds began to swirl and the wind picked up from a dead calm to gale-force winds in seconds.

"What the hell is going on here?" the officer from the alley shouted into the radio.

Mike, Brad, and Sarah failed to muster an answer, their jaws stretched wide in awe at the sight before them. Lightning began flashing in the clouds and thunder roared all around. Then, as quickly as the tempest had begun, the wind died and the young woman was thrown from the front of the building back toward the fountain.

"Uh, yeah, that's her," Brad said, dumbstruck.

The two behind the store radioed, "Then let's go get her!"

Mike knew it was the lawful thing to do, but under the circumstances, certainly not the wise thing to do. He barked, "You two stay where you're at so she doesn't get around the building…" but he stopped halfway through his sentence, again dumbstruck by the goings-on before them. This time, their mark disappeared from view altogether. "What the hell?" he uttered.

"I'll be damned," Sarah chuckled with wonder. "That ex-plains how she gets in and out of places without being seen."

"What?" the two men complained. "We can't see what's hap-pening."

"Gentlemen," Mike explained, "I'll call your CO in the morn-ing and uh, enlighten him, but you're relieved for the night."

"Are you kidding me? We've been here for hours."

"I'm sorry about that guys. I really am, but I think this is out of our, uh… jurisdiction, I guess." Mike argued with them briefly, but eventually convinced them to leave. After forty-five years of chas-ing Rebekah, it was somewhat comforting to know that he never would have been able to catch her to begin with. It was also considerably disconcerting, however, since it meant there was nothing he could do about it. At least, nothing he or the bureau could do about it.

Chapter Twelve

September 2010

Frederick's hands were growing rigid with arthritis. After Nicky died in 1992, he'd taken over the shop and moved into the living quarters upstairs with Louise. They kept the box on the mantle over the upstairs fireplace so they were never far from Calypso and Ezekiel. Then, Louise passed away in 2004 and Frederick's health had deteriorated steadily ever since. On a morning in early September 2010, he was working with a small screwdriver and dropped it a number of times before dropping both the trinket and the screwdriver on the counter in frustration.

While he drew strength from the nearby presence of his daughter and grandson's souls, as well as some remarkably in-human abilities, the dialogue was one-way. They could speak to him and help him when he needed, but he could never com-municate back. At least not in a way that allowed for any acknowl-edgment from them. It was lonely and exasperating, but he accept-ed it as punishment for trapping them in the first place and for having agreed to help Daniel. Life is balance, he told himself.

As he stood behind his counter, resting his weakened hands before having another go at the cuckoo clock he'd recently acquired, he heard Calypso whispering in his ear. "Call him. It's time, Daddy. You're getting so old. So tired. You can't protect us anymore. You need to let us go." The refrain had been on an almost constant loop since the quirky journalist from Detroit had shown up months earlier. Clearly, Calypso was in agreement with the woman about finally bringing an end to the decades-long cat-and-mouse game that plagued him. Every few years, Rebekah would try to break into the shop, and Frederick would repel her, strengthened by the charms his daughter and grandson provided. Every time, however, it became more difficult and more draining. Another encounter might kill him, they thought. It was time to stop.

He reached into his pocket and retrieved the weathered old card and dialed. A man picked up on the other end and the voice spoke. "Truesdell Protection Services."

"Is this Isaac?" Frederick asked.

"Yes, it is," the man answered in a soothing voice.

"I have a job for you."

The conversation was quick and to the point. Isaac assured Frederick that he need not provide details, and they discussed a reasonable fee. However, even with Isaac on board to help him transport the souls of his children, he had no idea where to take them. He'd heard from a number of travelers that there was an ancient burial ground near the ocean north of Boston. Unfortunately, those directions were not specific enough for Frederick. Also, he had no idea what kind of man Isaac was. Who knew what he might do once he discovered what Frederick was transporting? Ideally, it would be best to know precisely where he needed to go before Isaac arrived and keep the man in the dark about what he would be protecting. With all that in mind, he scheduled the event two weeks out to give himself enough time to find the site. On that same afternoon, a visitor he'd never seen before entered his shop. She was youthful and strong with a light Cajun accent.

"My name is Sonja," she greeted.

"I'm Frederick. This is my store," he replied cordially, sensing she wasn't there to shop.

"It is lovely. I have a similar shop in New Orleans. How long have you been running yours?"

He stood from the stool and started toward her as she fixated on a clock on the wall. "Well, I've solely owned it for about 18 years now, but my partner Nicky and I bought the place back in '63."

"Wow, that's a long time, Frederick. You enjoy your work, I suppose."

"You said you run a similar shop?"

"I'm sorry for being indirect," she responded, turning to him and shaking his hand. "I'm a sentry, like you. I help people find their paths. That is what you do, right?"

Stunned, Frederick proceeded with caution. "I guess. How do you know me? I mean, how do you know about my shop."

She sighed, thinking of a way to sum up the story. "About seven months ago, I was visited by a reporter from Detroit…"

"Say no more," Frederick interrupted, a slight chuckle escaping his lips. He started back toward his counter. "I know the woman. She's… tenacious."

"To say the least. However, I must continue. I don't want to have made the trip in vain, so if you don't mind…" Sonja insisted. Frederick sat on his stool and raised his hand for her to proceed. "When I first met her, I gave her an object. A hairpin that had belonged to her aunt. A woman I gather you're familiar with?"

"That's right."

"Beyond that, there wasn't much of a discussion. An elderly man from this area had brought it to me years earlier and told me he was looking for the woman as well. Do you know how he came upon it?"

Frederick tried to think back to the night in 1971 when Rebekah was taken from his shop in the back of Daniel's car. She'd given him the pin as payment for a service he refused to provide. For some reason, though, he couldn't recall what happened to it after that. The act of helping to assault and kidnap the girl had been so consuming that he'd forgotten about the pin until later, when he failed to find it. "I don't know," he admitted.

"I spoke with our mutual reporter friend a few days ago and she asked some more questions about it that I couldn't answer. I asked her what the object was telling her and she couldn't say for sure. Something about a small clearing in the woods but no idea where. I thought that maybe it was time for me to be of use."

"Of use?" Frederick asked.

Sonja sat down on a stool next to the counter to rest. "I've known about that man and the pin for over five years. Admittedly, I've also had some inkling of a terrible series of events that has followed him. I'd like to be a part of the events that bring this to a close."

"She tell you to say all that?" Frederick charged.

Sonja smiled. "Not so much. I'm here of my own volition. I know my knowledge is limited and that there's little for me to contribute. I just want to follow the hairpin back to the man who gave it to me."

"You don't want to talk to him."

"Why not?"

"He's a senile old man now. He'd just confuse the situation," he said.

They studied each other for a tense few moments. Finally, Frederick made his decision. "I haven't left this neighborhood in forty years. I never go more than... a quarter mile from this building. I've heard from some of my regulars that there's a place along the coast, either far north in Massachusetts or in New

Hampshire. A few of them bury their family there. Daniel kidnapped Rebekah in 1971 and said he was taking her up north." He lowered his head ashamedly as he spoke. Sonja adjusted uncomfortably in her seat but said nothing. "I shouldn't have let it happen, but I didn't know what else to do at the time."

"Go on," she urged.

"I wonder if he took the pin when I wasn't looking." Frederick shrugged.

Sonja shook her head warmly. "Don't beat yourself up over it, Frederick."

"I would have gone up there to check but I was afraid to leave."

"Because of family?"

"You could say that," he replied.

"That's okay. I'll head on up there and see if anything jumps out at me," she assured him and swiftly exited the shop.

After she left, he made his way wearily upstairs to the living room and sat on the ottoman in front of the fireplace. He looked sadly up at the box he'd made and tried not to cry. "I'm so sorry for what I've done. I did what I did because... Because I thought it was the right thing to do. The safe thing to do. But all that can change now. I can't do it myself, but I think that man Isaac can help us. And if this woman I met downstairs can find what we're looking for, then it can all end. Just a few more weeks. Just two more weeks," he repeated, clutching his head in his hands. "And it'll all be over."

* * *

Sonja loaded some water, snacks, a note pad, a map, and a flash-light into her rental car and set out from Boston to search for the mysterious coastal burial ground that Frederick spoke of. She realized Sarah might be upset if she knew Sonja had gone out on her own, so she sent Sarah an intention that she would duck and run if anything seemed amiss. It just felt like the thing to do, if for no other reason than to clear her conscience. She drove along the coast until the landscape started to appear much less developed, and indeed it was much closer to New Hampshire than Boston. As she drove, she breathed in a highly-focused manner, trying to pick up any sense of the place they were looking for.

The sun was starting to set behind her, and Sonja considered finding a place to stay for the night when she picked up just the signal she was looking for. Approaching a side road, she slowed and took the turn. There was a good distance between her and the ocean with a veritable forest between them. Tall, ominous trees loomed over her on either side, and she drove carefully to avoid potholes and felled branches. To her surprise, there were neither. The sunset's golden ambience illuminated the forest from the bottom up, making tree trunks, leaves, and pine needles radiate organic luminescence. Her eyes were wide with awe at the view and anticipation of what she might find.

The sun ducked out of sight behind her and the ambience turned bright and gray. The live trees gave way to dead ones and the underbrush all but disappeared. Sky opened overhead and a strange, omnidirectional radiance replaced the brilliant sunlight she'd been driving through. The opening in the tree canopy was clearly lit, yet dead and sterile in comparison to the trees around it. *Had a disease passed through all these trees but not the others?* she thought.

Unexpectedly, a wave came over her and she stopped the car. Almost against her will, she shifted it into park and stepped out. To her right was a strange clearing demarcated by a shallow trench. In the middle was a pile of dead leaves and twigs, as if someone had been trying to start a fire. A fleeting thought rushed through her head. *Nothing changes here...* She reached out for a nearby tree and touched it. It had been dead for far longer than it appeared. There wasn't a clear number, but she understood that those trees had been in that spot, dead, for centuries and more.

She returned to her car and kept driving until the trees ended, resolving in a sprawling, grassy plain. It stretched all the way to the ocean with the road encompassing it. She stopped the car when she saw a tidy pile of smooth gray sticks. Kneeling down next to the pile, she picked up one of the sticks and examined it carefully. There appeared to have been meticulous effort put into the cleaning of the sticks, as no knife had been used to rid them of their bark. Left haphazardly next to the neat pile of bare sticks were two others that still had their bark on them. Curiously, Sonja picked one up and held it carefully in her hands. Without much planning or thought, she pulled out her keys and began cutting the bark off the stick, careful not to scrape the bare wood underneath. By this time, the sun had all but set and she was working in near dark to remove the material. She finished the first one and moved on to the second, breathing hard and working intently all the way. Finally, she finished clearing the bark off the second stick and placed it next to the other on the pile, then stood and admired her work. They were indiscernible from the others. It seemed simple, foolish, and silly, but she somehow felt like she had contributed to a centuries-old process and smiled, holding her hand up to her face.

Sonja looked around at the landscape, the strange light that illuminated it, and the crashing waves behind her at the shore, and breathed it all in. It was an overwhelming sense of calm and completeness. Her instinct was to stay, but she knew it was time to leave. She smiled, took another deep breath, and climbed into her car, turning back the way she came.

By the time she reached Boston, it was after midnight. She checked out of the hotel early the next morning and met Frederick just as he was unlocking the front door to the shop.

"Didn't expect to see you so early," he said, delighted, and opened the door to let her in.

She retrieved a folded sheet of paper and a map from her pocket. "I can't stay long. I have a flight. But these are the directions to get there. Just take 95 North. The rest is on the directions," she explained proudly.

"You really did this for me?" he asked. She nodded, grinning. "I don't know what to say."

"Don't say anything. I wanted to help. I needed to help."

"Thank you," he said, struggling to be heard over his emotions.

"Call me if you need anything, Frederick. I know I'll be in touch with Sarah too, so don't be afraid to call either of us. Okay?"

Frederick quietly stared at the map and directions and nodded. She stepped out of the shop and left.

The night Isaac came to the shop, Frederick hired a driver to take him to the site on the map. His eyes weren't what they used to be, and he thought it would be safest to have someone else do the driving. They reached their destination around 2:00 A.M. The burial site was nothing like Frederick had worked up in his mind, but was everything he needed it to be. He'd imagined small headstones with ancient runes on them, ornate rock formations with eternal flames, or even a monument with a list of names and contributions. Instead, the field of modest antennae protruding from the earth seemed a fit testament to the witches and wizards they represented: a unique joining of the earth and the sky.

The driver stopped once they reached the cliff overlooking the shore and handed Frederick a flashlight when he got out to walk a bit. "You just let me know if you need anything, Mr. Casperson."

Frederick nodded and had walked a short way from the car when he saw the pile of sticks. He inhaled swiftly, choking up as he imputed their meaning. Kneeling down on the ground, he looked closely at them, picking one up and analyzing it. A short distance from the pile was a lone stick, still with its bark. Picking it up, he knew at once what it was for and tears began to roll down his cheeks. He laid it on top of the pile, climbed to his feet and walked back to the car.

Frederick asked the driver, "Do you have a jack knife or some other kind of knife?"

"Sure, let me check," the man answered and looked in his center console. He retrieved a large pocket knife kept in the car for its myriad bottle-opening devices, including a good-sized cork-screw. The blade on the knife was formidable and he opened it for Frederick. "Will this do for ya?"

Frederick dried his cheeks. "Yeah." He held out his hand as the driver closed the blade and handed it over. The man then stuck his head out the window as inconspicuously as he could to watch what Frederick was doing.

Frederick trudged back to the site, knelt painfully down by the sticks again, and began to work on the one he'd found nearby. He wept inwardly as he worked, sad but relieved that his journey was almost done. Once the stick was clear, he took it and the flashlight out into the grassy area until he was satisfied he was a safe distance from the car. There, he bent down and stuck the object into the earth at an angle similar to the others around him. In doing so, he inadvertently cut the palm of his left hand. A small trickle flowed gently from the opening, which he allowed to drip onto the stick. The droplet landed on the top edge and flowed around the side, down to the bottom and into the earth. He nodded his acknowledgment of the event and turned back to the car.

The driver was confused, but had been given instructions by his dispatcher not to ask questions unless he felt his safety was in some way compromised. Good to his word, he asked nothing. When Frederick returned and reseated himself, the driver passed a bottle of water back to him. "You all right, Mr. Casperson?"

"Thank you. Let's, uh… let's be on our way now," Frederick replied.

They returned to Boston in silence. The driver dropped Frederick off at the end of the block, granting him a refreshing short walk before returning to the shop, where he found Isaac seated in meditation in the middle of the floor.

Chapter Thirteen

September 2010

Rebekah trudged angrily along the sidewalk, the rain from her un-forecasted downpour still drizzling its last remnants as she walked. Her hair was soaked and plastered to the sides of her face and neck. A shooting pain in her leg from being thrown across the street slowed her to a grinding limp. But she was most indignant that Isaac had disintegrated her temporarily into bits of light even after she promised she would amend for her error. She was incensed.

Despite the early hour, a drunk unluckily crossed her path a few blocks from Frederick's shop and accosted her. "Hey, baby! You look like you've had a rough night, huh?"

"Piss off, man," she snarled angrily.

"Whoa!" he responded, holding his hands up and defending himself from her verbal onslaught. "I'm just tryin' to be friendly, you know?"

"No, you're not," she shot back. "You're drunk and disgusting and I'm not interested, so don't make me hurt you."

"Tough girl, eh? How about you show me something!" he answered and stopped in her path. "Come on, baby."

She glared at him, water dripping down her face and hair. "Trust me. You don't want to do this." Rebekah tried to maneuver around him, but he mirrored her limp sidestep and again blocked her way.

"Sure I do." He stepped up to her, reaching out to grab her hand. In response, she rounded on him, pushing all the nearby air into him and tossing him through the glass of an adjacent store-front. She looked at her hands in surprise, not expecting that result.

Almost with a sense of glee, she realized she could isolate her power. She no longer needed to create an entire tempest to control the air, but could instead use smaller, more concentrated move-ments. More importantly, she realized she no longer had anything to be afraid of. Rebekah had moved objects before: cars, furniture, doors… yet she'd never been able to concentrate air in such a compact effect. This was the distinction that kept her from de-feating Isaac or even Frederick before him. They had had control over the objects, so attempting to move them was futile. But this ability changed the entire landscape of her powers. Whether her adversary controlled the object she wanted or not was irrelevant.

"Adversary," she mumbled out loud to herself. Suddenly, the truth about the souls in the box led her to another startling discov-ery. They weren't the souls she thought would be in the box. She'd been misled – whether intentionally or unintentionally – about the box's contents for nearly forty years. And now, she believed it was time to catch up to the man who'd been taunting her with that vile supposition.

"I know where he is," Rebekah stated triumphantly, only just realizing a number of early morning pedestrian commuters were beginning to take interest in the storefront she'd just demolished. She glared at the drunk, then took off down the street, limp and all, with a renewed sense of purpose and direction.

A few hours, a train, and two buses later, she found herself standing in front of an old brownstone in Philadelphia. She looked up at the concrete and brick façade with an accomplished grin on her face. This was where she would finally have her revenge, she thought. She took the pack of cigarettes she'd been saving out of her trench coat pocket and lit up, waiting a tenant to exit.

The street was damp and gritty with rundown apartment buildings on either side and a bedraggled, unused streetcar rail in the middle of the lane. Daniel couldn't have afforded better, she thought, as she looked up at a broken window. Halfway through her cigarette, a twenty-something student came bursting out on his way to the bus and she thanked him for holding the door for her. He shrugged and went on his way.

Rebekah smiled at the young man and entered the building, tossing the cigarette into the ash can near the door. On the buzzer panel outside the door, she noted the name and the apartment number and made her way down the first-floor hallway. When she came to the apartment she was looking for, she held her hand up to the door and listened for sounds on the other side. Nothing. She turned the doorknob and discovered it to be unlocked. She pushed the door open and brazenly strolled into the room. What she found was a dingy studio furnished with a refrigerator, microwave, television, and a recliner designed to assist its elderly owner in standing. There wasn't even a bed in the room. The television was still warm. She shook her head and laughed to herself. *He's still in the building.*

She left the door open behind her and made her way back down the hall to the basement. The door at the bottom of the stairs was locked. Undeterred, she pulled out her pocket knife and jimmied the lock on the handle, then kicked the door to complete the action. The door opened into a dark storage area. She closed it behind her and began breathing systematically to illuminate the space to her satisfaction. Within moments, the wretched space began to glow, revealing its aged features.

"I know you're in here, old man," she stated ominously. "Why don't you show yourself and be done with it?" But she knew she'd get no answer. After a few more moments, she could see every object in the room. There were bicycles, couches, chairs, a chalk-board, and through the door to her right, washing and drying machines. However, there was one item in the room that didn't match the storage motif. It was the heaving, frightened creature in the corner, hiding behind two piled-up couches and an old refrigerator.

"There you are," Rebekah uttered.

"Please!" the old man whimpered. "Don't hurt me, please…"

"We're long since past that," she sneered, readying her hand to ignite him. "I just need to hear you say it, you son of a bitch."

No longer courageous enough to maintain his position behind the refrigerator, Daniel limped out into the open space. Rebekah paused, somewhat saddened by what she saw. The man was wrinkled, bald, frail, and clad in a pair of spectacles heavy enough to crush his nose. He spoke. "Wait. I'll say whatever you want me to say."

"You don't even remember what happened, do you?" she asked, lowering her hand to her side and pitying the creature.

"I remember a little."

"What did you do with them?" she asked angrily.

"Please! Give me a minute to try and remember…"

Rebekah folded her arms. "Fine. Take your time."

He felt around behind the refrigerator for his cane, using it to help him sit on a couch. Once seated, he began. "They lied to me."

"I can make this as quick as you like, Daniel," she said, freeing her arms and raising a slight breeze in the basement.

"Please! I can only tell you what I know. After that, you can do what you like," he answered.

Irritated, she sighed and nodded her permission for him to continue.

"I was never going to kill you, but she told you to run away anyway. I just wanted to scare you a little, that's all. I wanted you to understand your power before anyone else got hurt. They lied to me about what happened for five years before I knew what it was. They drove me to it."

"So, you let Frederick think that I was responsible for the fire and for attacking him?" she asked, traveling back to the night in Concord when fire destroyed the house they both used to call home with Marya and Ekaterina.

Rebekah had intended to visit for some time and was staying in Boston for a few days prior to heading out to Concord. On her third day in Boston, she'd picked up the troubling sensation that Marya was calling to her. Knowing she had no other pressing business to attend to, she took a cab out to the house. Using the key she'd taken years earlier, she let herself in. The first thing she saw was Daniel coming up from the basement. Staying out of sight, she followed him into the kitchen, saw the wrench in his hand and watched him raise it to another man's head. She didn't recognize the man or what was happening in the house, but instinctively tried to warn him, shouting "No" and ran to stop Daniel, but it was too late. He brought the object down on Frederick's skull, knocking him unconscious.

"What did you do that for?!" she shouted.

"You!" he roared back, turning on her and defending himself with the wrench.

She retreated a few steps, afraid for her life. "What are you doing? Are you insane?"

"You killed them, didn't you?!"

"Killed who?" she asked, perplexed and frightened.

He pointed through the door to the basement. "Marya and Ekaterina! They're dead, lying in their own blood in the cellar. You did that!"

"They're dead?" she asked, instantly affected by the news.

"Oh, you act so surprised. I'm not stupid, Rebekah. You came for their souls, like a vampire sucking your power from the living."

"My god, you're insane! I'm your daughter, Daniel! How can you think these things of me?"

"Because you're evil. Ever since you came here you've corrupted and manipulated every person you've met. You turned Marya into a child with no consideration for her fellow person, Ekaterina into your own personal champion, and me…" he trailed off.

"Yes? What about you?" she asked, shocked almost to the point of speechlessness.

"You've made me see what you are. You're dangerous. You… you must be stopped." As he said it, he moved shakily toward her with the wrench held high.

Defensively, Rebekah took a step back and reached out, causing several nearby objects, including a tapestry and a wooden carving to start on fire. She looked mournfully at the crackling flames, then turned a focused gaze to Daniel and responded, "I am dangerous. I know that, but killing Marya and Ekaterina won't get you anywhere!"

"I didn't kill them," Daniel lied, looking thoroughly convinced of it.

"And you believe your own lie?"

"I'm not lying. You're going to kill me. I know that now, just like you did with Marya and Ekaterina. That's true isn't it?" he asked, still approaching with the wrench.

Losing her concentration and composure, Rebekah inadvertently called a breeze in the house, fanning the flames. She shook her head. "I'll do no such thing." From behind Daniel, the wind picked up a bowl from the counter and smashed him over the head, knocking him unconscious. She grabbed his arms and dragged him out the front door onto the lawn. Assured that he was a safe distance from the burning house, she rushed back into the kitchen where Frederick lay, and pulled him out to the carport. She rooted through his pockets for his keys and opened the back door to the car. With great effort, she hoisted him onto the bench seat and hopped into the front, starting the car and pulling it out of the drive.

She sat at the entrance to the driveway for a time, watching the house burn. It was a sacred house, full of hope, dreams, love, and friendship. As it burned, she could almost see those things turning to ash and falling to the ground. Out of the corner of her eye, she noticed Daniel beginning to stir and shifted the car into gear, taking it away from the grim scene. She raced back to Boston knowing Frederick needed medical attention, and pulled the car up to the emergency room entrance of the first hospital she found. There, she shouted to the nurses within that a doctor was needed, tossed the keys into the front seat and ran away as fast as she could.

Rebekah's mind made its way back to the Philadelphia basement as she stood in front of the old man. She repeated her question. "Frederick thought I attacked him. Why didn't you tell him the truth?"

Sighing, Daniel answered, "Because I was trying to protect myself. You were already a liability, so it wasn't much of a risk to have Frederick think it was you."

"I see. And letting me think that the souls in Frederick's shop were Marya and Ekaterina's. Did you think it was funny to let me think Frederick was in on your plot? To attack an innocent man like that?" she asked.

"That wasn't my intention. I just couldn't…"

"Couldn't what?"

"I refused to take responsibility for their deaths. If I took responsibility, then you would have come after me for their souls. Frederick was a disinterested third party, and any attack you made on him would only strengthen his resolve to help me."

"Oh, I knew you were responsible from the beginning. But trying to involve an innocent man to the point of his own ruin is what makes you truly despicable," she snarled, leaning in and allowing her spit to fly at him as she said it.

"I won't be made to feel like a criminal for doing what I thought was right."

"Say it. Say you killed Marya and Ekaterina," she demanded. He didn't respond, his breaths shallow, tears staining his ashen, wrinkled cheeks. Pushing him further, she added, "I'm going to kill you, Daniel. But you have the power to make it quick and painless. Just tell me what you did." She grabbed the back of his head and pulled him off the floor so that he hovered over the couch.

The energy extracted from his mind began to paint a story, one she'd been longing to hear for forty-six years. Daniel had been hiding the truth all this time, but his advanced years diminished his abilities and he could resist no longer. The story was told in an instant.

After Marya indicted him for his jealousy and fear, he went into the house. With barely a second's hesitation, the rage welling up inside him, he yanked the carpet away from the cellar entrance and angrily hoisted it from the floor. In the past, he'd used the cellar as a place to think and to get away from his troubles, but this time it felt like a trap. He paced back and forth, trying to think of what to do. There was no staying in a house with people he couldn't trust, but if he left, Marya and Ekaterina could ostracize him from their entire community. Myriad scenarios shuttled back and forth through his mind for over an hour before he finally came to his conclusion.

He started up the stairs to the study, to find Marya already at the top waiting for him. She looked down at him accusingly. "We need to talk, Daniel."

"No, there's nothing left to discuss," he responded coldly.

"You can't go on like this," she said, hardly expecting what was in his mind.

Without answering her, he reached for the lead paperweight on the desk and smashed her in the head with it. It didn't kill her instantly, but she fell on the floor, seizing from the blow. He lifted her twitching body and hurled it down the stairs into the cellar. Ekaterina ran from the other room screaming and wielding a large plate. She flung it at him with all her might, nearly tumbling to the floor in the process. It missed badly and smashed on the wall behind him. Daniel deftly sidestepped her charging form, allowing her to fall into the desk, her ribs collapsing along the edge.

She moaned and struggled to turn back to him, but as she did, she looked painfully up at him, sobbing. "Why did you do this?"

"Because there needs to be control," he answered, almost ashamedly.

"There is control." Ekaterina gasped as she spoke. "It's balance. Just because you can't see it doesn't mean it's not there."

"What have we seen in our lives, Ekaterina? Wars, famine, violence... annihilation? The balance is gone. I have the opportunity to help restore it, so I'm taking it." He cocked his arm with the weight and crossed the floor to hit Ekaterina. She put her arms up in defense, but it was too late.

Daniel moved the bodies into the cellar and went upstairs to retrieve his tools from the car, only to find Frederick at the door.

Rebekah exhaled, disgusted by the old man. She looked at his eyes, but they would not meet hers. "And you still won't admit this to me, will you?" He said nothing. She could tell that over all those years he had managed to convince himself that his actions were right and necessary.

Releasing her grip on him, she stood straight and huffed, "You are a pathetic, insignificant old man who has lived his life through fear and ignorance. Don't worry," she added, "I won't kill you. You're too committed to dying alone, full of jealousy and regret, for me to kill you. It's what you've always expected and prayed would make you a martyr, but I won't give you the satisfaction. Die when you will. But not by my hand."

She turned and walked out of the room, leaving Daniel crippled with fear on the couch in the basement. Closing the door behind her, she walked out onto the street and breathed in the fresh, early fall air. Two more targets remained, and from her experiences of the past 12 hours, she had discovered that — by some random form of cosmic chance — they would be in the same place within the next 36 hours.

One complication had arisen, however. At Frederick's shop, she'd felt the presence of her niece. It was faint, but she was clearly there, as well as two men she'd known for quite some time. They were closing in, and she only had one chance to finish the task. If they caught her, she knew she would refuse to harm them and resign to be taken into custody. It would mean her end. How they knew about Frederick's shop or Isaac's purpose there was a mystery to her, and she had no idea how much they knew about her purpose.

Rebekah prepared for the worst and made her way via bus and taxi to the closest forest preserve in Philadelphia. She wandered for almost an hour to arrive at the least disturbed area of underbrush she could find. There, she bent down to the ground and picked up a stick, fashioned it to her specifications, and stuck it into the ground at an angle. As she had done so many years earlier, she inspected it, feeling something was missing. She then sifted through her pockets and retrieved her pocketknife, pricked the tip of her finger, and let the blood run onto the stick. It appeared dark and thick in the muted daylight. She licked her finger to quell the flow and then walked swiftly away from the spot. There were only two tasks left to accomplish.

Chapter Fourteen

October 2010

After several hours of communing with thousands of years of history in the private museum he'd agreed to guard, Isaac heard a gentle knock at one of the windows. As he approached it, he saw Rebekah with her back to the window, apparently crying. As she turned, he recognized her, and a knowing glint shown in her eyes.

Isaac smiled confidently and said, "So, it's going to be one of *those* nights, eh?"

Rebekah shrugged innocently, holding her arms around her knees and replied, "Might as well be. I kinda got a thing for ya, fella."

Suspicious, he asked, "Yeah?"

"Yeah," she answered, and then abruptly stood up.

Rebekah wheeled around with her arms spinning and directed all the fury and power she could muster into the giant pane of glass between them. The window shattered into a thousand pieces and Isaac was thrown back. His body smashed through a priceless painting, then over the top of a wooden bench behind it, landing on the hard, tile floor at the opening to a special exhibit alcove. Somewhere in the building an alarm could be heard, an occurrence that did not particularly concern either of them at the moment.

Isaac's contract with the owner of the facility had been to act as the only security detail that night. However, and this was no news to Isaac, the wealthy man had double-crossed him and allowed his regular security detail to work the cameras. The guard watching the video screens sat upright from his crossword puzzle and knocked over his coffee when he saw the glass break and Isaac fly through the air.

"Holy shit!" the man exclaimed, and picked up the radio to alert the other guards on the property.

With a great sense of satisfaction, Rebekah brushed little bits of glass off her trench coat and stepped through the opening onto the grandiose tile floor of the private museum. She admired the art only momentarily, and called the winds once again when she saw Isaac struggling to his feet, knocking the objects between them out of the way. Her arms parted and a pale glow illuminated her from below. She stepped toward Isaac, flexing her arms briefly, then released the firestorm, hands outstretched. Flames extended dozens of feet in either direction, igniting paintings, furniture, and even the insulated walls. All the while, a quiet grin of success stretched across Rebekah's face.

Isaac looked in horror at the fire and destruction around him. He reached up to push her back, but before he could, she aimed a hand at him and tossed him through the alcove into the wall beyond. He collapsed on the floor, the wind knocked out of him. His vision blurred; he saw only a bright, flaming haze.

Rebekah stopped a few yards from him and dropped her hands to her sides. Glaring directly at the wounded, defenseless man, she shouted over the roar of the flames, "What did you think would happen to you, Isaac? Protecting men like this?" He reached for the wall to give him balance as he fumbled to his feet. He could make no sound. She continued, taking two more steps to-ward him. "The man will die in this fire. I've made sure of that. But what about you?"

Breath slowly sputtering back to his lungs, Isaac bgan to sense something about the woman. He wasn't sure what it was, but it allowed some of his strength to return. He stood wearily and locked eyes with her. When he did, he saw her face. The look of satisfaction was still there, but something honest and sad appeared underneath. Most of all, her eyes entreated genuine trust, not the look he'd seen two nights before.

"Do you know what you did to me?" she asked, closing the distance between them and clutching both sides of his face. Before Isaac could respond, he caught a moving object behind them out of the corner of his eye. It crashed through the burning ceiling above and smashed into Rebekah's back, trapping them both underneath.

In the moment of unconsciousness that followed, Isaac's life flashed swiftly through his mind: from the early part of his life as a craftsman and a husband, to his years as a security guard, to his decades as a traveler, and finally to his eventual return to security as a guardian. What had it all meant? How could a life encompass so much time and struggle, only to end in the process of failing at his craft? Unwilling to endure self-doubt, he forced his eyes open and his body into consciousness.

The sight was grim. Rebekah's lifeless body was pinned underneath the object that had fallen on them. His right arm was trapped with her. With his left arm he pushed on the object, which appeared to be an oddly-shaped piece of modern art, and tried to force it off of them, but it wouldn't budge. Isaac struggled over and over to breathe deeply, but the oxygen in the room had been diminished by the raging inferno around them. The heat began to singe their hair and clothes. With great difficulty, he turned his body from under Rebekah, making more space between her and the object, and giving his lungs more room to breathe. Still unable to get a full breath, the object remained fixed, but he managed to pull himself from under the wreckage. With the little strength he had left, he removed Rebekah from beneath it as well. Gasping more successfully, he hoisted her up from the floor and carried her out the shattered window.

When he was clear of the building, he looked back to see the mansion attached to the museum on fire as well. Knowing the life within had been extinguished, he lowered his eyes and headed toward his car. He gently laid Rebekah in the passenger seat and belted her in. She remained unconscious, though her head was slowly nodding from side to side and a trail of blood trickled from her temple to the lapel of her trench coat. Isaac limped to the driver's seat and started the car.

A distance away and out of view, Sarah, Brad, and Mike pulled up in their four-door sedan. Sarah and Mike leapt out to view the scene while Brad remained at the wheel. The spectacular fire consuming the museum and adjoining mansion entranced them all.

"You think they got out?" Mike asked.

"Christ, I hope so," Sarah muttered, unable to take her eyes off the blazing wreckage.

At that moment, Mike's attention was diverted by a car pulling away fifty yards down the street. "Hey, what's that?" he asked.

Sarah turned her gaze to follow Mike's. She cleared her mind and breathed in the cool night air. "It's them. Let's go!" she shouted, and they jumped back into the vehicle.

"Don't get too close, but don't lose 'em either, Brad," Mike instructed.

"You don't ask for much, do you?" he replied.

The three had driven for much of the night only to arrive on the scene after the damage had been done. Sarah and Mike were equal parts frustrated and elated. Sarah had managed to track down her aunt and knew where she was going to be, but the sensations hadn't come in time to stop another death. Unless Isaac could out-run them or disappear in some way, however, this would be the last time Rebekah ever killed. They'd caught up to her and that was the important thing.

The two cars drove on through the remainder of the early morning and into the waxing daybreak. By then, they'd traversed across the state of New Jersey, Isaac's car rolling up to a desolate spot of shoreline near Atlantic City.

At the time Isaac stopped the car, he'd long since known about the three strangers following him. He had no intention of trying to outrun or mislead them. As long as no sirens sounded or lights flashed, he had stayed his course. He rolled the car to a stop with only a sandy beach between it and the ocean and shut it off. He looked over at Rebekah. The compress he'd placed on her fore-head to collect blood remained, and she was sleeping comfortably with her hands pressed against the glass to support her head. Leaving her in the car, he stepped out and locked it behind him.

Pulling up shortly after, the sedan parked a few spaces away, and the three passengers climbed slowly out. Sarah stayed behind the vehicle and the two agents stepped in front of it, guns drawn. Mike spoke first. "Okay, Isaac. We don't want anyone to get hurt."

Isaac raised his hands over his head, and calmly replied, "Nor do I."

"Good," Mike acknowledged, his heart pounding such that it had become audible. The last arrest he'd made was of a fit, dan-gerous man and Mike had been injured in the process. Still, that man had been mortal, something Isaac didn't appear to be, and so he approached the situation with much trepidation. His gun rattling in his grasp, he continued, "There are a couple ways we can do this." Mike took a step forward.

"Stop there. Let's keep talking first," Isaac responded, lowering his hands halfway, staying planted in his spot.

"Are you armed?" Mike asked, knowing the question was useless.

"No," Isaac answered and lowered his hands to his hips.

Mike holstered his gun but motioned to Brad to keep his weapon trained on its target. Brad acknowledged and refocused his aim. "That's good, Isaac," Mike said, and took another step forward. "We're only here for Rebekah."

"Is that her name?" Isaac asked, his expression changeless.

"She's killed a lot of people. She needs to come with us. If she does, I can promise nothing will happen to you."

Isaac focused on the three individuals in front of him. The two men were precisely what they appeared to be, but the woman behind the car was of particular interest. He examined her emotions and intentions. She gave off a layered set of thoughts, some of them pushing very close to his own. "Who's she?" he asked.

Mike turned to Sarah. "You okay to come over here?"

"I think so," she answered, and walked around to the near side of the car.

"You know this woman?" Isaac asked, boring deeper into her mind. Sarah nodded, but didn't answer. He assured her, "You came to my office." Again, she nodded. "Don't worry, I'm not going to hurt you. You can talk to me."

Sarah swallowed hard, not wanting to give away her relationship to Rebekah for fear any resentment he had toward Rebekah might find its target in her instead. "Vaguely. I met her once about nine months ago."

"And you know what she's done?" he asked.

"I do."

"And you think she's a murderer?"

After a short silence, Mike and Brad looked eagerly at Sarah.

"I don't know," she replied with great difficulty.

"But people are dead," Isaac explained. "And by her hand. You don't think that's murder?"

Emotion began to well up within Sarah. The weight of the moment finally settled on her heart with a gravity she had not anticipated. Rebekah deserved to be arrested and locked behind bars. At the same time, here was a man who could kill them all with the flick of a wrist, not to mention that his livelihood had been destroyed by Rebekah in an instant. Whether desired or not, he had fallen into the position of judge, jury, and executioner for her. Sarah knew she couldn't hide the truth from Isaac no matter what she said; she'd sensed him prying from the moment the car stopped. Her lack of control in the situation frightened her, and she suddenly came to realize that a woman's life – her *aunt's* life – was in her hands.

"What she did..." Sarah began, working to find the words.

Mike was uncontrollably curious by this point and encouraged her, saying, "Go on."

Sarah's downward gaze turned up to Isaac, meeting his steely eyes and their penetrating expression. "...was necessary."

Brad turned to Sarah in disbelief. His frustration was palpable, almost to the point that he let his aim slip, but he turned back to Isaac quickly. Mike stepped carefully to Sarah, addressing her directly. "Say what you really mean, Sarah. No one'll blame you for it, you have my word on that."

Struggling to understand the forces that had overtaken her during the past nine months, she spoke in fits and starts. "It's balance... isn't it? I mean, did she actually murder someone? I don't know... I know that killing is wrong, and that what she did was wrong, but I just don't... feel that..." She brought her hand to her head, frustrated with herself. Finally, she blurted out the best metaphor she could think of. "We use fire to cleanse, don't we? When a forest is overgrown, lightning strikes it and it burns down. Nature has balance. Fire is what forces dust to return to dust when the brush has grown too wild. What if… what if we all just serve a purpose? What if her purpose was to get rid of the people she killed?"

Mike uttered a refrain that had grown on him over the years. "…'tis an unweeded garden that grows to seed; things rank and gross in nature possess it merely."

Isaac's granite expression yielded a wry smile at the reference. Sarah turned to Mike, a desperate look still painting her visage. "Yes. But I'm not saying she's a tool of good and virtue or anything like that. Maybe sometimes we trudge around in the… unweeded garden or muck so much that it rubs off on us." Even as she said it, the realization came to her. "And that's what you're here to do, Isaac. It's time to pull her out. We're not capable of that, but you are."

Brad took a step sideways toward Sarah, keeping his eye trained on Isaac. "Uh, actually, we need to take her with us, Sarah."

"Do you? Imagine the courtroom. She'll never be convicted unless you choose to forget about any of the crimes that give away how old she is. And you can't possibly reveal how she committed them. And then why bother?" Sarah argued.

"How old is she?" Isaac asked, his curiosity piqued.

Sarah turned back to him. "She's seventy."

Isaac rotated slowly to look at the woman in the passenger seat. She appeared no more than twenty, her pale skin, unwrinkled lips, and stark, thin eyebrows piecing together a consistent image of youth. He then brought his attention to his own hands and their youthful nature. They were cut from the same cloth.

"You believe me?" Sarah asked. Isaac nodded, his attention still centered on his own condition. "Look, I know what happens to her isn't up to me. But I know you can do something about it."

Mike looked to the man for his response. In truth, Mike hadn't made up his mind about the case either. Brad was far too focused on making the collar to think about the logistics of charging and prosecuting the woman. The case file was ridiculous and to piecemeal a version of it together for prosecutorial purposes would be a nightmare and, in the long run, illegal. Mike had long been aware that he might have to lose Rebekah altogether in the pursuit of solving the case. Now, in essence, the case was solved. The woman was right in front of them. However, she was beyond the reach of the modern legal system. There was little left to do but shoot her or let her leave with Isaac. The only question would be what Isaac was willing to do.

"How old are you, Isaac?" Sarah asked, noting how he seemed perplexed.

He looked to her and smiled thoughtfully. "One-hundred-fifty," he answered.

Brad lowered his gun in shock. Mike huffed a surprised breath. Sarah nodded and smiled back at him. "Then you know what she has to look forward to. Life's hard enough for the rest of us, I can only imagine what it must have been like for you. Losing family, friends, your entire life having to start over all the time." As she spoke she became aware of his interest in her words. "You lost someone very close to you, didn't you?" He nodded. She went on. "I can only imagine what it must be like, never being able to be close to anyone. The isolation, the mistrust. You understand her better than anyone."

Finally, Brad understood what Sarah was driving at, and why Mike wouldn't argue with her. He still wasn't comfortable putting his gun back in the holster, but he managed to let it drop to his side.

"She's a force of nature, Isaac. She doesn't belong to us. She doesn't belong to anyone, but I'm willing to leave her in your hands. If these two men are," Sarah offered hesitantly.

Mike nodded his approval of the agreement. Brad did not, but instead motioned as if to say '*doesn't matter anyway*.' Sarah witnessed their responses, then turned to Isaac with great anticipation.

Isaac looked back into the car, then back at his hands, then at the three new acquaintances before him. Never in his life had he been presented with such a quandary. He'd always known he had the power to have a hand in the shape of the world, but never felt it was appropriate to use it. Now, the opportunity was not only available to him, but he was required to take it. He locked eyes with Sarah, knowing that was where his answer lie.

Finally, he answered, "I'll take care of her."

The door on the car behind him opened and closed, and Rebekah slowly walked around it to stand next to Isaac. Mike, Brad, Sarah, and Isaac were all on guard as she walked, not knowing what to expect. Mike motioned for Brad to keep his gun at his side and he did so. Rebekah removed the compress from her forehead and stuffed it into her coat pocket. She stopped next to Isaac and looked at him, analyzing his features in the daylight for the first time. She placed her hand on his shoulder and ran it down his arm, establishing that he was who she believed him to be, and took his hand in hers. Saying nothing, she locked eyes with him.

He breathed deeply, squeezing her hand to let her know she was safe. Rebekah blinked her acknowledgment, breathed in return, and looked to Mike. "It's up to you."

Fifty-two years ago, Rebekah had nearly killed Mike. Her actions colored the rest of his life, burning indelible images of her corrupted youth into his flesh. Now, she was turning herself over to him. Everything he'd worked for in that time rested on this woman across from him. He looked to the ground, then to Sarah, expecting some guidance from her, but there was none. She calmly entreated him to do whatever he thought was right. Brad gave a more begrudging version of the same. Boldly, Mike closed the distance between them and moved up to Rebekah. Isaac stepped aside to allow them to speak.

"I know you never meant to hurt me. And I want you to know I never wanted you dead. I just needed to know..." But he couldn't finish the sentence.

With a pained expression, Rebekah replied, "I don't know. I wish I could answer you, but I can't. It was a mistake, that night..."

"And since then?" he asked.

She shook her head unapologetically. "No." Mike nodded, already knowing how she would answer. In his mind, her honesty only made it harder to bring her in. "But none of that can be changed now. Now you have to decide."

"Will you hurt this man?" he asked, indicating Isaac.

She shook her head. "Never again."

"Then I guess there's nothing left for me to say, is there?" They all looked at each other with relieved expressions.

Brad drove into town to pick up breakfast for the group, and they sat near the beach to eat and take in some of the last warm air before fall set in. Isaac and Rebekah sat together on a park bench. Brad and Mike sat on the front of their cruiser, discussing how they would file the report to the bureau. Sarah sat on the beach, playing mindlessly with the sand, soaking up the atmosphere, and enjoying a fruit cup and hot coffee. Eventually, Rebekah broke away from her discussion with Isaac and sat on the sand next to her niece.

They watched the sunrise in front of them. Rebekah eventually spoke. "Thank you for coming after me."

Sarah shrugged. "What kind of niece would I be if I hadn't?"

"You don't know me. I was never around. You had no reason to invest this much in finding me. So, whether you think it's a great feat or not, I appreciate it more than you could know." Rebekah took Sarah's hand and held it in hers. "It's up to you now."

Confused, Sarah asked, "What do you mean?"

Rebekah looked at Isaac who nodded, then back at Sarah. "We need to leave. Maybe not for good, but at least for a while. Now it's up to you to find your purpose."

"My purpose? I'm a reporter. That's what I do."

"There's more to it than that. You haven't become aware of your abilities just to be a better reporter. Everyone is more than what they do, Sarah."

She looked at Rebekah, then at Isaac. Her aunt's words solidified a realization she'd been coming to since the day in January she met Mike and Brad. Before this case, she'd been content to work as a journalist who was an advocate of victim's rights and the pursuit of violent crime prevention. But that wasn't enough anymore. She'd come to the conclusion that she had to be part of the solution instead of just an advocate for it. Exactly what the solution was remained a mystery, but knowing she was working toward it helped to give her direction.

"I think I understand," she said. "What about you two? What are you going to do?"

Isaac joined them in the sand, sitting and wrapping his arms around his knees. "We need to disappear for a while. If you need us, though, we'll be there for you."

"This is for real. You're leaving?" Sarah asked, somewhat perturbed. She'd only just gained a family in Rebekah and was losing her as quickly.

"There's no choice, Sarah. There are some things we have to do. Some loose ends to tie up before we can move on. They've been left unresolved for far too long, and it's time we took care of them."

Sarah wasn't happy with the answer, but was willing to accept it for the time being.

After another hour of catching up and discussion, Isaac and Rebekah decided it was time to go. Isaac thanked Mike for his compassion and shook his hand. Rebekah hugged her niece and then they climbed into Isaac's car.

As he shifted the car into gear, he asked her, "Is there anything you need to stop and pick up?"

She looked at her coat, her sole worldly possession and laughed. "No." After a few moments of silence, she added, "Where are we headed?"

"Deleware first, if that's okay," he answered.

"Sure. I've been to Deleware. It's all right."

Silence fell over them.

After a time, Rebekah said, "I'm sorry I tried to kill you, Isaac."

"You didn't."

"I know I didn't. I'm sorry I *tried*," she insisted.

"But you didn't *try*," he added. "There's no need to apologize for something you didn't do. I know you weren't trying to kill me, so I'm not upset."

"How did you know that?" she asked.

"The eyes. It wasn't in your eyes."

They drove in silence a while longer until a thought occurred to her, and she asked, "What are we going to do? After the loose ends, I mean."

Isaac replied, "I don't know. But whatever it is, we'll do it together."

The answer was satisfactory for Rebekah. She leaned back in the seat, took Isaac's hand in hers, and held it the rest of the way to Deleware.

Since Isaac left, he'd never returned to his home town. As expected, it had changed considerably. The town square was still there, but it now consisted of a number of coffee shops and diners, bars, and boutiques of varying types. It had been paved with modern roads, parking spots, meters, and a grassy park in the center with hedges and trees. A clock tower inhabited the center of the park, with walkways extending from the clock to all four intersections at the corners.

Rebekah watched his reactions carefully to see how he felt about his experience. He regularly huffed at the commonality of change that had taken place, as if he believed the town should have been spared the pedestrian changes that had gripped the rest of the world. Shaking his head, he looked around at the buildings and streets, familiar only with the layout of the town but nothing within it. On the far side of the square from where they entered was the original location of Isaac's shop. It had long since been demolished or burned down and a two-level department store was erected in its place. He stopped momentarily to look at the space that had once belonged to him.

"What used to be here?" Rebekah asked, only able to read his agitation at the building.

"My shop. My home, actually. I guess they paved it along with a couple other buildings in favor of... this. I don't know what I expected. Just, something different, I suppose," he replied sadly.

Rebekah nodded her understanding of his frustration. A car behind them honked and Isaac put the car back in gear, pulling down the road to the traffic light. He made a right turn and drove to where the old church used to be.

When they arrived at the site, he saw the church had been razed in favor of more property for the cemetery, and a small columbarium had been installed on the lot. A large, wrought iron fence now enclosed the cemetery from the surrounding neighborhood. The gate was open and the small guardhouse next to it empty. They turned into the drive and passed through the newer, more sparsely populated plots to the older section of the cemetery. The headstones here had weathered and corroded over the years, some of them leaning in their foundations, the ancient names of families long since departed crumbling and stained by time and the elements.

The car stopped near an open plain bordering the river. Rebekah asked, "Do you want me to stay here?"

Isaac stepped out and closed the door, circling around to her side. She leaned out the window in anticipation of his response. "Actually, I think I'd prefer you come along if that's okay."

"Sure," she answered, and released her seatbelt to join him.

They hadn't walked for long before Isaac stopped at a simple, dual-panel headstone. Rebekah looked at his face, then the headstone. On one side, it read "Hattie Truesdell, 1866-1895" and on the other "Isaac Truesdell, 1860-".

"I feel like I'm supposed to say something. Or do something. It's been so long, though, nothing seems right," he said, perplexed.

Rebekah knew precisely the thing to do and scanned the cemetery for the nearest tree. She stepped back from the stone, and Isaac looked up to watch her walk toward a grove of trees a short distance away, curious to see what she was doing. Looking under and around the trees, she eventually discovered what she was looking for: a stick about a foot in length that had weathered and been stripped of its bark. She picked it up and returned to Isaac, handing it to him. "For Hattie to find her way," she explained.

Isaac's heart warmed at the simplicity of the action, and he nodded in appreciation of Rebekah's gesture. He knelt down and traced Hattie's name with the stick, then gently pushed it into the earth in front of the headstone. There was no momentous event as there had been days earlier with Frederick's family, but the sense of closure this personally provided Isaac was enough to make it valuable. He remembered how unfulfilled he had been when Hattie was buried, and how the week of rain that followed stripped him of the light and love they had shared. The weather and earth were barriers in that time, and he resented them. Now, they acted as the connection between the two of them, and he was able to let her go.

Rebekah stood back from Isaac to give him time at the grave, but she stepped up as he acknowledged the deed was complete, kneeling beside him. "And for you?" she queried.

"Don't know," he answered. "This isn't the place for me any-more, though. Maybe I'll find somewhere more fitting. What about you?"

She shrugged, a curious look on her face. "I had a place picked out. Things didn't turn out like I'd thought, though, so I guess I'll have to rethink it." They stood up and started back to the car. "I'm sorry about your wife."

"I used to be, too. Against her wishes, I might add. She was one of us, you know?"

"Really?" she asked.

"Well, not like you and me. But, maybe like Frederick or Sarah. She had a good sense of the world. She was a good soul. Innocent." They both spent a moment considering how long ago they'd each lost any sense of innocence in how the world worked. Despite their chosen paths in life, however, it couldn't be denied that at the most basic level both Isaac and Rebekah were still very innocent creatures.

Finally, after a few more moments in the cemetery, Isaac said, "I'm done here. Let's go."

They spoke rarely, and for the most part empathically. Given recent events and experiences past, neither was particularly chatty, and each respected the other's guarded demeanor. Conversation was necessary only when imparting specific instructions.

"Do you need to stop somewhere before we get to California?" Isaac asked after several hours on the road.

Rebekah smiled to herself. "Tulsa. If that's okay."

Isaac nodded and the silence was restored. Before leaving the beachfront, Sarah had provided Rebekah with the new address of her sister. Now, after a day and a half of traveling, they exited the Muskogee Turnpike and she guided Isaac to the address on the ragged slip of paper.

What they found was a somewhat upscale apartment complex across the street from a grocery store and a movie theatre. Sarah had chosen the location specifically to reduce the amount of traveling her mother would have to do in her daily tasks. Samantha complained initially that Sarah was treating her like a child, but upon utilizing the convenience of the movie theatre, retracted her complaints.

Rebekah and Isaac parked on the boulevard in front of the building. "Do you want me to come in with you?"

"I would like if you could. You don't have to, though," she replied gently. She touched his hand then climbed out of the car. Isaac followed closely behind.

They reached the door, looked up the code in the directory, and dialed Samantha's extension. Initially, there was no answer, so Rebekah tried again. The second time, Samantha picked up. "Who is it?" the voice shouted through the intercom.

"A friend of Sarah's," Rebekah answered.

After a brief pause Samantha asked, "Sarah's got a friend?"

Rebekah was perplexed and unsure of how to respond. She shrugged to Isaac who shrugged in return. "I'm a friend of hers from up north. She said you could help me with something."

"Help? Why would I wanna help you?" Samantha barked back.

"Please, just let me in and I can explain everything," she pleaded. There was silence on the other end. Isaac folded his arms and leaned against the brick exterior of the apartment building.

After an all-too-pregnant pause, Samantha replied, "Fine. You can come in, but you have to stay in the hall. No tricks, little missy. I've got a knife and I'm pretty sure how to use it."

"No tricks!" Rebekah answered gleefully.

The door buzzed and they entered. The lobby was thickly carpeted and furnished with chairs and a table for visitors to occupy while waiting for residents. There was a dual staircase that wrapped around the lobby. They passed down the hallway to Samantha's new apartment and knocked on the door. Slowly, the lock turned and the door opened partially to reveal the chain still attached. Samantha's wary eye popped into the opening and she took in the two visitors.

"Now, you didn't say anything about this fella," she snapped. "Why should I trust you?"

"Because you must, Samantha. I have something to tell you that is going to be much more difficult to trust than this man," Rebekah answered, plying every bit of calming influence she had.

Samantha would have none of it. "And what's he, some kind

of saint? What's your names?"

Isaac could sense Rebekah was emotional and unable to focus and responded before she could. "My name is Isaac. I'm also a friend of your daughter's. I met her in New York."

"Oh yeah? And you?"

Rebekah looked back to Isaac for assurance. He nodded and she turned back to her sister. "My name is Rebekah." Samantha's eyes widened and the door slammed shut. Rebekah pounded on it. "Wait! I need to talk to you!"

Rebekah lowered her voice and spoke calmly to Samantha through the door. After a time, the chain was removed and the door opened completely. Samantha stood there in jeans and a flannel shirt, paint stains on her clothes, and horrified and confused look on her face. She gripped a large knife in her hand. "Who the hell are you?"

Rebekah put up her hand to indicate she had no intention of entering the apartment and breathed slowly. "Samantha, I'm your sister…"

"Bullshit! That bitch is seventy years old! What are you, her grandkid or something?" The knife shook in her hand.

"I don't know how to explain it…"

"Christ, you look exactly like her," Samantha muttered, her wheels turning.

"That's because I am her! Our mother's name was Cora. Cora Boyd. Our father was Jack, and our brothers were Jesse and Leo. They died in a fire in 1958…"

Samantha raised the knife, still shaking and angry. "Anyone could know that! Tell me something only my sister could know."

Rebekah winced trying to come up with anything that might be convincing, until suddenly it hit her. "The book!"

"What?" Samantha asked, sharing a quizzical look with Isaac.

"The book on witchcraft. I bought it from an old man at a bookstore downtown. I used to read it at nights and practice it during the days, out in the woods," Rebekah explained excitedly. As she spoke, Samantha started to lower the knife. "I loved that book. I worshiped that book. I used to skip classes to go read it and stay in the woods. I used to bury dead animals and give them proper graves. Then I'd come home and tell you the witch's mantra. Do you remember?" Samantha stared in stone-faced silence. "'Do you believe that a moment can last a lifetime? Do you believe that a lifetime can last for centuries? Do you believe in the energy that passes through all things, living and not living? Do you believe that love can be a powerful force of nature?'" Samantha began faintly mouthing along with Rebekah. "'Do you believe that nature is an ever-changing, all-knowing, all-encompassing goddess to which we alone hold the key? As mortals, our eyes are shut, our hearts closed, and our senses dulled. In our quest for wisdom and love, we call to the energies and spirits that bind us to let them be opened.'"

A stunned silence fell over them. Samantha dropped the knife and stepped out of the apartment to stand face to face with her sister. "It really is you, isn't it?" Rebekah nodded excitedly. Samantha wrapped her arms around Rebekah and held her tightly.

When the embrace ended, Samantha held Rebekah's head in her hands. "My god. Come on in." She turned and walked into her living room, Rebekah close in tow. Isaac retrieved the knife from the floor and closed the door behind them.

Samantha's new apartment was similar in layout to her quarters at the home. The major variation, however, was that the new apartment had an extra room for her paintings and supplies. The living room walls were covered with paintings and an old sheet doubled as a drop cloth. Samantha quickly folded it up to allow for foot space and they took their places on the couch and chairs.

"I have to say, I can't believe what I'm seeing," Samantha said, wringing her hands.

"I truly wish I knew how to explain it. I think that mantra had something to do with it, but I don't know," Rebekah responded.

"Sure as hell didn't work for me," Samantha added. They sat silently for a moment, then she asked, "Where have you been?"

"They took me to jail after that teacher died... those teachers, rather. While I was there, things just got out of hand. I didn't mean for anything terrible to happen, but..."

Samantha shook her head. "But it did anyway."

"There was a period of years when I had no control over it. I met a witch in Boston who tried to take me in and help me. But, she and her sister were killed by a man I tracked for... well, the rest of my life up until now."

As Rebekah spoke, Isaac could tell she was conveniently leaving things out, but considering how much Samantha was having to take in already, he understood the omissions. She spoke with a great deal of gravity and sorrow. "I found him a few days ago. He was a pathetic old man. He barely remembered even the most basic and important events in his life. Over the years, I managed to gain control of my abilities."

Samantha interjected. "When you say 'abilities,' what do you mean? You mean other than..." she indicated Rebekah's youthful face. "This?"

"Oh, so much more. Samantha, the fire in the jail... the night I left... I started that fire."

"Well, we all kind of assumed that."

"No," she asserted, "you don't understand." She then picked up a candle from the counter and placed it on the vacant floor in the middle of the living room. Sitting back on her chair, away from the candle, she breathed deeply one time and lit the candle.

Isaac and Rebekah looked to Samantha for a response, but were surprised when there was barely any. Samantha nearly grinned at the event and couldn't take her eyes off it, quietly uttering, "I knew it. I always thought it was a fantasy, always thought I was crazy, but it's true."

"What is, Samantha?"

Samantha looked up at her sister, the flicker of the flame glinting in her watery eyes. "I always knew you saved me. I always knew that. But after you left, I started to imagine you as a sorcerer, or a witch, or something. Like you'd somehow gone beyond human to become something more. Like you were talking to me…" Tears rushed to Rebekah's eyes as she covered her mouth and nodded her head, admitting she had been doing just that. "I always knew you were watching out for me. And for Sarah. And you?" she asked, indicating Isaac. "Who are you?"

Isaac didn't know how to respond. Rebekah answered for him. "He's like me. The things I've done. The places I've been. I couldn't fit in, or work, or…"

"We're going to work together now. My name is Isaac Truesdell. I'm from Deleware," he added, extending his hand.

Samantha shook it and said, "You're going to take care of her?"

"To the best of my abilities," he answered.

"Thank you. It's time someone watched out for her, not the other way around."

Rebekah put her hand on Isaac's, indicating it was time to go. She then turned to her sister. "I'm sorry to do this and then leave, but we can't stay here."

"Why not?" Samantha asked, saddened.

"Actually, Sarah's going to help with that. We can't really talk about it now. We have to disappear for a little while, but I promise to come back. Soon."

As they rose to their feet, Samantha jumped up. "Rebekah Boyd!"

"Yes?"

"Do you still go by that name?"

Smiling, Rebekah responded, "I will now."

Samantha returned her sister's smile and watched them leave the apartment.

Isaac and Rebekah climbed into the car and departed, heading west to Isaac's office. When they reached California, they rested fully for the first time in either of their memories. Two journeys ended and one began.

Epilogue

January 2011

Y ou're on in five," the wiry, hyperactive, college-graduate producer announced as Sarah was prepping her hair.

"Thank you," she replied, furiously readying herself. It wasn't just any news segment. It was her first national segment in almost two years and the biggest one she'd ever done. And it wasn't just a taped national segment where there was no inter-action. This would be a live spot in which the anchor would be asking questions of her for a national audience. She'd been honing her correspondent skills for quite some time and was vying for a bigger piece of the pie.

The story was huge. An international drug cartel was making inroads in Michigan and Ohio, and a major bust had occurred outside Detroit – right in Sarah's market. She broke the story before anyone else by almost a day, and her coverage was far more comprehensive. Witnesses who would speak to no one else con-fided in her. Agents gave her information no one else could get. She nailed the story every way it could be covered. Management was talking about a promotion and she knew her performance needed to be spotless.

She asked Jerry, her cameraman, "How do I look?" He simply smiled and finished checking the connection on the camera, giving her a thumbs-up as he did. "Thanks." Finally, the lights went on, and the producer gave her the countdown. Shortly after, her ear piece picked up the national broadcast, and she waited for her cue. Another few moments, and the producer pointed to her.

The segment couldn't have gone better. Every possible point that needed to be covered was hit, and in a quick, concise manner that left nothing to be desired.

Toward the end of the segment, the anchor asked her a question she had prepared a response to, but didn't know whether or not they'd have the time for. "Now, you had some news on another case the FBI has been working on, isn't that correct, Sarah?"

"That's correct, Ty. Special Agent Mike Kirkpatrick of the FBI recently announced that a forty-year-old arson case has finally been closed. The case involved a confounding series of murders, supposedly committed by the same person. This announcement comes on the heels of the Philadelphia fire that took the life of oil tycoon Malcolm Hargrove as well as destroyed his home and museum. When I asked Special Agent Kirkpatrick if he had a suspect in custody, he indicated that the suspect as well as another man hired as a private security contractor were also killed in the blaze." As she said it, a tiny, imperceptible smirk appeared on her face that only three people on the planet could have recognized.

When the segment ended, her producer, cameraman, and numerous others in the room applauded her effort, and she took an enormous sigh of relief.

Jerry walked to her and whispered in her ear, "Sarah, you've got a delivery in the dressing room."

"Oh, great! Thanks, Jerry," she responded, and walked back to the dressing room. When she entered, there was a large arrangement of flowers on the counter and a business card underneath. At first, she wondered who the flowers could be from, then picked up the card. It read, "Boyd Protection Services" with a phone number and no address. Sarah laughed and stored the phone number in her mobile.

There was a knock at the door. She answered, "Come on in, Jerry," and turned to take off her jacket.

A woman's voice responded as the door opened. "Sorry, but I'm not Jerry."

Sarah wheeled around to see Sonja standing in the dressing room doorway. Surprised, but not completely shocked, she replied, "Come on in, Sonja."

"Nice flowers. Should I venture a guess who they're from?"

"Oh, I think you know who they're from."

Sonja picked up the business card and inspected both sides carefully. "Watermark and all. They've done well for themselves."

"I'm pretty sure the money's Isaac's. After all, the guy has over a hundred years of savings to fall back on."

"I should hope so," Sonja replied, placing the business card down on the counter and entering the phone number in her cell as well. "You did great on your segment just now."

Blushing, Sarah said, "Thanks. Admittedly, I feel a bit guilty about using this... perception, I guess you'd call it, to forward my own career. That's a little selfish, don't you think?"

"If it can help serve the greater good? No."

"I know, I know. You're not the first person to try to convince me of that, by the way."

Sonja closed her phone, turning to Sarah, "Good! 'Cause we've got plans, don't we?"

Sarah finished dressing, "I guess we do."

"Are you ready to go?"

Sarah grabbed her bag and threw on her coat. "You bet I am."

End of Book 1

Acknowledgments

Incendiary was written entirely while laid off due to the market collapse of 2008-2009. I didn't know it at first, but that layoff ended up being a major creative turning point in my life. I resumed writing after a hiatus of almost ten years and discovered a love I'd long forgotten.

The following people supported me in ways I cannot thank enough, all of whom helped to influence this work:

Mary Weber-Moore
Bethany Ford
Joseph Galante
Scott Pakudaitis
Heidi Arneson
John Dittrich

Additionally, the following people took precious time out of their lives to read this ditty and give me the feedback I so desperately needed:

Kelly Joseph
Mickaylee Shaughnessy
Rev. Mark Moore
Kate Elise
Joyce Moore-Gilbert
Benjamin Roesler
Sheree Froelich

Most importantly, absolute thanks and gratitude goes to my proofreader/editor Megan Murphy. I owe you a PBR. Possibly several.

www.ingramcontent.com/pod-product-compliance
Lightning Source LLC
Chambersburg PA
CBHW030552260626
47157CB00006B/2288